Heroes of Princeton

Heroes of Princeton

Christopher Bell

Copyright © 2010 by Christopher Bell.

Library of Congress Control Number:		2010911985
ISBN:	Hardcover	978-1-4535-5830-0
	Softcover	978-1-4535-5829-4
	Ebook	978-1-4535-5831-7

This book was printed in the United States of America.

To order additional copies of this book, contact:
Xlibris Corporation
0-800-644-6988
www.xlibrispublishing.co.uk
Orders@xlibrispublishing.co.uk
300829

Contents

Tommy Atkins,
no finer gentleman could you ever meet.

Acknowledgements

I am indebted to many people who have inspired and encouraged me to complete this book, I would like to pay particular thanks to my wife Leslie and my parents who have supported me throughout this project, Will Tatum who was my inspiration to write this book initially, Warrant Officer First Class Andrew Flint who as my draft reader advised of any continuity errors and finally Jonah Bond and Simone Rodriguez of Xlibris, without their professionalism this book would never have been completed.

Chapter One

The Soar

June 1771

The early evening rain started with earnest, the dark clouds pouring heavy rains onto the shire towns tall slate roofs, the crude cast iron pipe works failed to contain such a heavy downpour and the gutters were soon over flowing with filth and sewage from that day's market, the sellers from the countryside farms quickly abandoned their wares and scrambled for what cover they could find.

This was the wettest June that William James Snow, native born of Leicester town could remember and despite having grown used to the squalor and filth over his short years this constant rain made his bones ache and ache they did, sleeping at best upon a loose straw bale on a cold damp brick floor that had once been the basement of some ancient dwelling.

For Will's life knew little comfort or luxury with barely enough food to feed himself or his siblings Will 'liberated' whatever the market left behind, his father had been without regular work for as long as he could remember although as Will saw things there was always enough coin for strong ale at one of the towns numerous drinking houses. His own mother had perished shortly after his birth and his father had remarried soon afterwards bearing him a further two children, but upon a third pregnancy both step mother and child had succumbed during childbirth leaving Will duly responsible for the welfare of his half siblings.

As the downpour continued Will sheltered under a canopied doorway and waited for opportunity as the scraps of the day would be snapped up by his kind, one thing Will had learned young was to be sharp and not to stand upon ceremony, If it looks like it has been left behind then it probably has, living by the rule that if you didn't take it then be sure someone else would giving them a full belly that night whilst you would kick yourself at the lost opportunity. As quickly as the rains came, the dark skies broke over the towns tall spires leaving silver sun drenched edges to the passing darkness, as the last remnants of the cloud burst trickled through the gullies along the earthen streets and back alleys leaving swathes of large mud filled puddles on the slushy street surfaces.

Life soon sprang back into the market place as Will waited for an opportunity to present itself amongst the fleet footed types that hovered by the markets edge and observing these rural lads looking skyward in anticipation of the next downpour oblivious they hastily loaded their wares onto waiting farm carts as Will helped himself to some apples by tucking them inside the deep pockets of his long brown tattered frock coat and spied around for his next quarry. In the panic of the cloud burst one of the towns bakers had dropped several loaves from his basket and Will, as quick as lightening was upon them, the baker cursed towards him, 'You damn scoundrel! tuppence that'll cost you, you thieving beggar' the Baker shouted as without thought for the remainder of this batch chased Will along the cobbled street towards the corn exchange buildings and beyond, caring not as he splashed through the deep mud puddles young Will quickly out ran this portly baker who clearly spent too much of his time eating his wares rather than selling them.

Though these alleyways and passages lay a maze to some but to those that passed amongst them daily a sharp turn here and there would lose even the best of pursuers. Will caught his breath and leaned backwards onto a crumbling red bricked wall towards the north side of the market place, smiled and quietly chuckled to his self with the thought that by the time the baker got back to his bread the basket would be long gone, in pursuing the chase a two penny loaf had cost him twelve fold.

There was once a time when might have felt some moral guilt of procuring food in such a manner but as the growing industrial town increasingly drew labour from the countryside good employment and fair wages came in short supply. For those that had given their lot for a new life in the expanding towns soon found it to be a matter of cut throat survival, for Will, a native of this old town found his experience gave him the edge over the rural folk who would often stand in awe at the situations the town offered by comparison to a simpler life in the county villages.

Tonight the family supper would consist of four apples and two hard crusts of bread, they'd eaten better but Will knew only too well there were many times they'd eaten far far worse as he strolled leisurely back to the family lodgings on Black Friars Lane. His lodgings, a dilapidated row of deprivation and squalor that professed his family home, consisted of one upper room and one lower one, a small cracked window pane to the rear failed to light this hovel of a home and permanent damp stain on the interior where the rain water pipes leaked inwardly through the crumbling masonry.

The ground floor was of rough sawn timber planking covering the loose rubble that filled a large basement cellar from the buildings better days, the upper floor was connected by a short ladder tied by frayed rope to the warped and twisted rafters that supported the upper flooring, Will had often watched his father stumble and fall from it in a drunken stupor and lay in an unconscious heap twisted around its base until the effects of strong alcohol wore off and once again he attempted to haul his bulking frame towards his bed only to repeat the process over and over.

The room on the ground floor was dominated by his father's framework knitting machine, although Will had rarely seen it used he knew his father could provide at least some small income if he so wished, he'd seen the high quality of his father's work but since his step mother's death Will's father these days seldom left the company of some beer house or another.

Towards the rear of the dwelling Will slept alone, he'd chosen from an early age to sleep upon the cold hard floor in the company of pest and vermin that on many occasions stared blatantly at him as he wrapped himself in a cast off moth eaten blanket for warmth and security. Of his family two half siblings, Rebecca aged thirteen worked at one of the towns new hosiery factories, scrambling amongst the heavy machinery for scraps of cotton to be salvaged for rags, Joseph aged fifteen was bonded to a rope maker on the south eastern side of the town, he'd leave for his employment well before Will arose to the days adventures and rarely returning much before sundown, all this for no pay as the benefits of his indentured apprenticeship would take a few more years yet to reap, had Will the opportunity of an apprenticed trade something could have been made of his life but being the eldest child his responsibility lay with providing food for the family in any way he could manage. This was, it seemed his lot, scavenging for food on the fringe of lawlessness, a pitiful life and he knew it, each day a struggle to exist, this lad's expectations of life stood small. The town of Leicester stood upon the slopes east of the River Soar, once a thriving Roman provincial town it now maintained a population upwards of twelve thousand inhabitants. The fortunes of any town can vary greatly, almost abandoned by the 9th century the town steadily increased its population towards five thousand at the time of Richard Plantagenet's arrival on the eve of Bosworth Field, afterwards the population steadied for two hundred years despite pestilence and plague that decimated the inhabitants of nearby villages, towns and cities.

Now upon on the eve of a swelling industrial age Leicester town poised on the verge of an explosive expansion, soon to be littered with huge red brick mills that would dominate the once spire ridden skyline. The river brought life and commerce into the town but with commercial expansion comes people, the rural poor of the surrounding villages eager to embrace the need for labour in an expanding industrial centre, scarcely a day would go by without new faces to compete for the few well paid employments around.

The Snow family had dwelled in the town as long as anyone could remember, the family had moved to Leicester over a hundred years previous after the short prosperity that came with England's brief commonwealth, from where they came neither Will nor his father knew but with the past now lost to the passage of time the Snow family struck as townsfolk, while some would continue to beg or steal for a living Will knew he could and would strive for a greater lot in this life. By reckoning that he was around sixteen or seventeen years of age, he had been told his mother had died soon after giving birth to him and his father had re-married shortly afterwards, he'd known this poverty all his life and now accepted the fact and as for his future? At best he'd find work as a casual day labourer, at worst a beggar or on the end of a gallows if his luck that he enjoyed today should ever run out. Of education, Will had briefly attended the Free school near the towns high cross, the poor peasant classes teachings were subsidised by wealthy wool and coal merchants of the expanding town until his father deemed it fit for him to seek a wage as a casual labourer with one of the towns many aspiring industrialists, Will had learned to read some simple words but never to write, the mark of his name was the best he could manage.

This family knew its place in their society and mostly knew their prospects miserable, daily scratching out a meagre living as best any opportunity could provide and a very realistic likelihood of days without food or warmth, William Snow had little knowledge or understanding of the world outside the Shire of Leicester let alone the shores of England.

With his exposure to strong drink limited, the few times he would enter a tavern was to guide his father home in the small hours of the mornings, although the family drank small beers regularly especially when the towns water supply became spoiled he'd seen little sense in intoxicating himself to the levels he'd seen his father stoop to, his harsh upbringing had learnt him the need to keep one's wits about themselves as the poverty and squalor had given birth to desperate acts, for it was well known that a hungry man would easily cut one's throat should it provided some ease to his sufferings.

The rains in June had proved fruitful for the countryside, by August the harvest brought daily into the towns markets had been the best in living memory with bushels of wheat, corn and barely crammed into every corner of the marketplace whilst merchants bartered for a good price, the abundance of the harvest meant the price of arable crops had fallen so even the poorest could provide themselves a decent vegetable meal. Will and his family together had eaten sufficiently for several days and frequently the surplus they had left would be exchanged for some cheap mutton cuts or offal, occasionally he'd find a few coins left over in his pocket after the rent arrears were settled, at last with a prosperous economy Will hoped his prospects where improving. The expanding commerce within the town brought an increase in labour demands and Will spent most of July and August employed as a casual labourer unloading coal and timbers from the barges daily arriving at the wharf for the towns new industry constructions, the work was hard and long but the daily wage was good, although a filthy job he would end his day by washing the grime and coal dust off his sun tanned skin in the river where he worked and bask on the baked mud flats that sloped down towards the winding rivers edge.

The sun shone bright and hot long into the evening as Will walked towards his home and family, his damp clothing clung to his back as he passed the dominating walls of St Martin's church by the old towns medieval walls. The corner of Loseby Lane met Silver Street where stood the Globe Inn, a notorious house for drunkenness that in better days had found itself a meeting place for penny labourers to be hired by tradesmen, industrialists and local land owners, however as the town began to constantly draw cheaper labour from the countryside those without employment usually spent the day in the ale house gossiping and drinking themselves into a state of uselessness, Wills father was no exception and often found amongst his kind there in and this hot late summer evening was no different. The children of the Snow family sat around a cheap wooden table to their evening meal of sour bread and salted pork, like most of that month they'd eaten well, like most occasions their father was absent. Joseph had arrived home from work earlier than expected, Will felt a rare warmth and tranquillity as he and his siblings ate well and enjoyed the happiness and relative prosperity of the late summer. The brief moment of family harmony was soon dispersed, 'Will!' came an anonymous shout through the doors weather bleached timbers, 'fetch your father, the old man's drunk again', Will sighed as his moments peace collided with reality, he slid his bench away from the table knowing the routine of carrying his father home and to his bedding would again be repeated.

The Globe inn was just a few hundred yards from the Snow's lodgings, Will gave thanks for small mercies that his father had not chosen one of the more distant public houses to drink in, he entered the pubic house and scanned the room for his troublesome father, the tavern keeper knowing him since he was a boy gestured over his left shoulder that his kin towards the dingy back rooms of the house as he gingerly made his way through the crowded house, nervously watching the movements of the taverns patrons being more than aware of the type of character that would frequent this drinking den and the fun they would have with such an edgy youth.

Although Will thought himself streetwise, these characters that spent their lives in houses such as this were not to be messed with, the din, the smoke, the stench, all sickly uncomfortable to him as he walked towards the rear of the tavern, he quickly spied his father with his back towards him swaying uneasily on his feet and arguing fiercely with another drunkard, he knew his priority would be to get himself and this embarrassment father away from this dangerous situation quickly. On most occasions Will would in some fashion carry his father home and strange logic figured the more drunk equalled the less fuss his parent would be, but this time he detected an uneasiness with the atmosphere, approaching his father he grew nervous of his father's threats towards the other man, before he could intervene his father's adversary clenched his fist and threw it towards his father, too drunk to see it coming his father took the full force of this man's anger and dropped like a stone onto the fixed wooden bench behind scattering drink and drinkers alike as his legs flailed wildly upwards, a cheer went up from the crowd of the house in anticipation of the blood bath that would ensue.

Will's first instinct was to run but as much contempt he felt for his father his duty towards him over ruled. He tried in vain to push the man away, but his size was far greater than his and he could do nothing to stop this drunken thug pummel blow after blow into his prone father's body now barely conscious and bewildered by the attack, Will became desperate as he saw the straw covered floor turn red with his father's blood, almost hysterical with panic he looked for a means to stop the man and instinctively grabbed an earthenware jug of ale from a nearby table, 'Get off him' Will screamed with frustration but the man took little notice and continued to rain violence upon his father's vulnerable body, feeling an anger like never before, the helplessness consumed him and like a cornered beast defending its young he swung his fist in the man's face, the moment seemed to last for an age as the jar shattered into a thousand pieces and patrons became showered in cheap watery ale and fragments of earthenware pot, his adversary stood quietly still, in a daze, dripping with blood and beer he staggered, then slumped backwards falling onto the cold fire hearth.

The tavern befell a deathly silence as the gravity of the situation hit home, patrons turned their backs on the incident in fear of implication in the event Will helped his father to his feet who even with his son's help stood uneasy. Ignoring the downed adversary both father and son made their way to the exit as Wills father draped his arms around his neck for support, with blood soaked onto his shoulders the pair exited the tavern eager to leave the area quickly before somebody alerted the authorities. Will struggled with his father's weight towards the direction of their lodgings his heart pounding as fit to burst, the shouts and jeers from the Inn still ringing in his ears.

Joseph met the two at the door to their house, helping the pair inside Will felt something inside him break, he thought to himself, how much longer could he take this life?, as much as he would struggle to keep his family secure his father undid his work almost nightly. The two brothers lay their inebriate father on the floor knowing it would be impossible to lift him to the upper level, Will sat in silence watching his father lay unconscious and snoring heavily and assessed his lot, becoming desperate to leave the poverty behind him he was wise enough to know the influx of labour from the countryside would drive wages down and it was hard enough to exist already without having to compete for work with a rapidly increasing population, staring at this fathers snorting hulk in a moment Will contemplated leaving his home town to better his luck elsewhere.

His life thus far had fallen short of most expectations, although work was available during the towns more prosperous times periods of unemployment were always threatening convincing himself there must be a better life than what he'd lived so far. Will's employment at the Soars wharfs started at daybreak but due to the fracas at the Globe Inn the morning was spent nursing his father's injuries confounded by his complaints of the self inflicted alcohol abuse, leaving their lodgings around mid-morning Will arrived at the enclosed yard ready to start unloading the row of barges of their wares, the foreman of the jetty made his way towards him, 'sorry lad' he spoke and wiped away sweat from his brow with a filthy rag 'I've hired my men today, I'll not be needing you any longer'. Will turned away and sighed, dropping his shoulders in despair knowing with the harvest coming to an end he would face lengthy unemployment yet again, he could not help but feel the blame for this misfortune lay yet again with his father's irresponsibility. He had sought employment where he could, often working a day unwaged to prove himself to any prospective employer but these days with an abundance of labour this often led to nothing, sometimes stealing food when he had no coin in the pocket was the only alternative to starvation knowing these desperate times were upon him again he vowed not to return to that unlawful existence. Walking around the back streets and gutter alleys of Leicester he paused a moment and watched with curious interest as two men pasted notices on the wooden shutters of an ironmonger's out building. The illiterate Will enquired to the men about the words meaning, the older of the two glanced at his bills and read the words aloud, 'For the King, adventure and the glorious 17th . . . brave fellows answer the call to the colours and do battle with old England's enemies . . . Upon enlistment each recruit shall receive a bounty of three Guineas, eight shillings and be genteelly clothed fit for his majesty's army . . . '. Will picked through the words he understood asking himself could this be the answer to his misery, he pondered to himself scratching his lank dark hair scanning further down the pasted bill, politely he asked the man to read the remainder of the poster to him, the man duly obliged and squinted his eyes to the words whilst running his fingers along the lines, he read them out loud 'for suitable young men to meet Sergeant Lucas at the Saracens Head tavern at eight bells' the man spoke disinterested to the significance of the meaning.

Scratching his head he tried to imagine himself a soldier having on occasion seen recruiting sergeants and drummers pass through the town displaying their fine uniforms and passing stories of adventure and romance, in that moment he decided to see what the crown had to offer, that night he would meet this Sergeant Lucas and if his luck was with him the crown may at least pay for his meal that night.

Wandering the streets counting the bells the many town churches struck every hour, his meal that day had consisted of a little black bread and half rotten beans left behind by the days traders, as the sun began to drop to the horizon Will made for the upper market district and towards the tavern that would host the representative of the 17th Regiment. Arriving at the steps of the inn the faint glow of tallow candles lit the inside of the drinking house, the taverns double doors lay wide open airing the sounds and smells it held within, pausing a moment to gather and tie his hair he entered the house nervous of being in a very similar establishment the previous night.

The tavern was busier than usual and the majority of its patrons gathered around the smart red-coated Soldier, his hair perfectly plated and tied into a neat ribbon behind his head, the landlord passed two large jugs of liquor onto the long wooden bench squeezing his portly frame through the masses that congregated around the gentleman soldier. Will positioned himself into space at the rear of the party as the Sergeant began to pour the strong drink liberally into the tankards of his audience, he eyed over a dozen men gathered around the table from all walks of life, some he recognised from the town but most he did not, he smirked to himself as most were clearly taking chance of the free drink liberally offered by the sergeant, perhaps a few not unlike himself saw this as an opportunity to better themselves from the dirge of a poverty life. Once the tavern filled sufficiently the Sergeant began his well rehearsed speech outlining an easy life of the soldier, these words amused Will as Lucas spoke comically 'If any gentlemen soldiers or others, have a mind to serve His Majesty and pull down the enemies of old England, if any prentices have severe masters, any children have unnatural parents, if any servants have too little wages or any husband too much wife let them resort to the noble Sergeant Lucas in this good and honest town and they shall receive present relief and entertainment'.

The opportunity for adventure and the chance of fame and riches looked good to Will as they did by the expressions of others around the room. Sergeant Lucas observed Wills empty hands and called his accompanying drummer boy to pass him a dented pewter tankard of drink, Will took the offer reluctantly and in sensing this Lucas urged him to sit along the benches around the table ushering the others to make room for the 'fine and upstanding lad' as the Sergeant addressed him. As he sat humbly along the bench Sergeant Lucas opened a pouch containing a dark rich tobacco and stuffed a generous wad into his long white clay pipe, although such luxuries were well beyond his means Will drew long breaths as the Recruiting Sergeant held a long slow match into the fireplace behind and lit the bowl, heartily sucking its tobacco stained end filling the proximity with fragrant tobacco smoke and noticing Will's pleasure Lucas offered him his tobacco pouch raising his eye brows encouragingly, humbly Will declined citing 'I have no means for which to smoke it'. 'Then fear naught' laughed Lucas heartily, 'for what poor lad cannot enjoy the fruits of the colonies?' he continued, reaching inside his smart red tunic, he produced a smaller clay pipe, its thin stem shorter than the one the recruiting sergeant held between his stained teeth, Will took the pipe from him and slid the pouch towards across and opened it to reveal it crammed full of rich shredded tobacco, ''Tis finest Virginian' commented Lucas as Will thumbed the tobacco into the pipes bowl and lit it with the slow burning match left beside the pewter candle stick holder, coughing as he drew breath and filled his lungs with the dry yet sweet tobacco smoke.

For Will, this moment became a mile stone in his life and he knew it, in the company of men and brave men at that, he left behind his boyhood and fledged his first moments into adulthood. Upon insistence of Lucas and encouragement of the other potential recruits Will drank heavily from his tankard as Lucas continued his words exciting his audience with tales of heroics and adventure from the span of the four corners of the world and with dogged interest the crowd listened on.

As the evening passed Sergeant Lucas explained the bounty of enlistment to each man who would swear allegiance to the crown, each man would be clothed in a manner fit for the finest soldier, receive a shilling a day in pay and the generous daily ration allocated to each man. The thought of a full belly each day was enough for Will, long gone would be the days of hunger, poverty and boredom, a soldiers daily pay would be enough for him to survive upon and the surplus provide money to his family. Whether the plentiful drink persuaded him to take the King's shilling offered by Lucas he cared not, the Sergeant produced a tidy purse from his red coat and removed a handful of coins firmly placing them into the open palms of the eager recruits, of the Sergeant's audience, seven men took the King's shilling which in turn was quickly spent by the recipients on more ale. As the night drew to a close, the candles molten tallow pooled onto the scored wooden table, Lucas announced cleverly it would be pointless for the fellows to leave such good company and the party should sleep within the upper rooms of the inn, engulfed by his company Will, in his merry condition had no objection to this as the sergeant led his band upstairs complete with a tanned leather jug of sweet rum. Will Snow passed out from excessive alcohol almost as soon as he lay on the prepared beds on the wooden floorboards of the attic room, Lucas covered him with a blanket and continued his joyful banter to the remaining party.

The morning started at day break for the group, Lucas walked the length of the attic steady sober as though no drink had passed his lips, the drummer boy began to slowly beat the taut skin of his drum to awaken the new recruits from their slumber, 'Come lads' hailed Lucas, 'let us make you into heroes today', still as buoyant as the previous night, the recruits however, nursed sore heads and playfully Lucas passed around remnants of the nights liquor amongst the party, Will refused but to his dismay was taken by all of the others despite their moans and complaints of illness. Sergeant Lucas had arranged for a local baker to deliver loaves of bread to the Inn along with two gallons of fresh milk, cheese and two dozen goose eggs, the mistress of the tavern brought the food to the men who all enjoyed such a hearty breakfast. To most of Will's type this was a feast of Kings, rarely in his life had he eaten so well nor so early. With sustenance such as this Will would gladly follow his Majesty's army wherever it took him. Sergeant Lucas, his drummer and the party of recruits spent the day pipe smoking, drinking small beer and watching the towns barges unload goods from the bridges along the River Soar, day labourers toiled in the summer heat on the opposite side of the river to reduce the flood plane soon to be used to accommodate the much needed housing and commercial requirements of the growing town, to all men the life of a recruited soldier seemed good. As the ale ran dry and the party began to sober Will wondered after his family and coyly he asked Lucas if he could explain his whereabouts to his kin. Sergeant Lucas initially refused with no explanation but Will knew Lucas's fears lay on account of losing the youngster to his families sensibilities, the oldest recruit in the party on hearing of Will's predicament quietly spoke reason to sergeant Lucas.

After a minute of talk between the two Lucas approached him and spoke in a stern but soft voice 'You've an hour to tidy your affairs lad, and woe be tied upon ye should you fail to return', Will thanked Lucas and not wishing to waste his precious hour made his way along the rivers towpath.

The long sun dried grasses brushing against his legs as he ran towards the old town centre, turning into the back alleyways and side streets of the town Will made his arrival a the end of the lane. Knowing he owed his father nothing, years of neglect and drunkenness had taken its toll on his loyalty to him, his siblings on the other hand deserved much better and conscious of the time Lucas had given him Will turned into the lane and walked towards the family's lodgings. Making the most of the hot weather the door to the house was ajar to ventilate the damp rooms, straw still lay on the floor where his father had slept on that fateful night but to his relief the lower floor was empty of life, hearing movement of the wooden boards overhead Will cried after his brother. 'Joseph, Rebecca, it's me, Will' he shouted as he leant towards the roof space, Joseph's feet appeared on the top of the ladder much to the relief of Will for any confrontation with his father would spoil this farewell, 'Where have you been brother?' Joseph asked as he stepped down the ladder rungs, 'I've taken the Kings shilling, I've enlisted' Will replied excitedly, Joseph stood motionless for a second as his feet reached the hard floor of the ladder and slowly turning round to face his older brother Joseph queried his brothers statement, 'The Kings shilling?' he paused a moment 'you've enlisted?'. Will nodded in response, 'Did he recover?' keen to change the topic to his father's welfare 'Aye, soon enough he was back in the taverns again, slightly bruised and cut but no worse than that', Joseph replied. With his conscience eased Will humbly apologised to his brother and asked him to pass his love to Rebecca when she returned, Joseph stood wide eyed, 'When do you leave?' he asked. That Will did not know but explained to Joseph the benefits of his majesty's service almost verbatim Sergeant Lucas's words, 'so you think it's a better life than here then?' his brother spoke soberly 'but I understand your reasons only well enough' he added, 'With Rebecca in full employment and myself apprenticed well there's no reason for you to stay here wasting your life away, brother, it's time to live your life'. The two brothers spent a few final minutes together, Will promising to return as and when he could but both brothers knew this was a promise he could not keep for although the 17th Regiment had recruited well from Leicestershire it had no firm ties with the county or town, once the Regiment had enlisted it's quota they would move on to some remote town or another hoping to swell its rank further. Will shook Joseph's hand firmly and bore him farewell placing what coin he had left tightly into his brother's palm and made his way to the door not looking back, keen to avoid any display of emotion he preferred to make his departure as brief as possible. Joseph called after Will as he turned the streets towards Lucas and the party's direction 'be sure to come back and come back a hero'. Will smiled and waved farewell to his brother, his past and his old life.

Making his way back to Lucas and the party, Will found them sitting on the bank swigging generously from earthenware jugs fetched by the young drummer boy. The older recruit who had earlier persuaded Lucas to allow the boy to visit his family tipped his head and raised his smouldering pipe at Will as he passed and sat on the high banks edge, 'Good lad' he spoke softly 'I knew you'd come back'. This man had somehow persuaded Lucas to allow him a brief absence of leave against the Sergeant's better judgments, his return had proved a safe bet.

By late afternoon Lucas announced to his party that they should eat at the militia barracks at the town magazine gateway and the party of seven led by the drummer boy walked the wide rivers towpath with the drum beating time and soon the dominating battlements of the old city wall came back into view. Outside the militia's stone walled barracks two sentries stood on guard duty each man standing firm as the recruiting party entered the barracks enclosure. The Sergeant marched the party inside the walled perimeter alongside the medieval battlements that stood adjacent to a newly built red brick barrack room block, three stories high with a steep slate roof and wide sash windows, the entire area was immaculate with not a thing out of place, neither Will or his associates stood unimpressed at the sight before them. Lucas led the men to a doorway on the far side of the courtyard and through a archway to a long dark dormitory, 'this lads, will be your quarters for now' spoke the Sergeant, 'rest yourselves a while lads, you've a feast ahead of yourselves'.

The burley sergeant and his drummer returned outside to the parade ground as each of the recruits lay on one of the numerous double bunks that occupied the room, on each bed lay a woollen blanket and a straw filled thin canvas mattress covering the bare wooden slats that made up the bunk, the floor was strewn with hay and straw and a large carved stone trough presented itself at the far side of the billet. A small cast iron hand pump took its place above the trough, whilst the others inspected their lodgings Will operated the hand pump, squeaking into life it began to yield cool water from the natural spring below, dipping his head into the flow of refreshing water the effects of the previous quantities of alcohol and the days heat made him feel dizzy, closing his eyes he rested his hands on the stone sink to be abruptly pushed aside by his fellow recruits eager to refresh themselves as he had done. Lucas stepped back into the room along with three fully equipped regular soldiers, 'Come now lads' he spoke warmly, 'let us show you what you'll become'. The party of seven ushered their way to the outside courtyard and there faced thirty perfectly presented red-coated soldiers each identical in every way, Will was impressed at the high standard each man achieved in his presentation. With this company of professional soldiers, each man wore high polished black ankle boots finished with a bright silver buckle, bleached white duck canvas long breeches, a bright scarlet long wing backed tail coat adorned with intricate lace and high polished pewter buttons, underneath a white cotton undershirt graced with a black cotton neck stock bow tied at the nape of the neck, a white cotton waistcoat and a black tri-cornered felt hat sporting a black with white trimmed lace cockade. Their equipment held its place by intricate whitened leather straps and perched high on each mans back a pack made from goats skin with a lower knapsack supported underneath from which hung a circular wooden water canteen. To their left side hung a seventeen inch bayonet sheathed inside a black leather scabbard frog and below that a fifteen inch short sword tucked inside the folds of the woollen red-coat, with typical uniformity the soldiers hair was tied perfectly with a length of fine black ribbon behind each man's head. The line of smartly presented soldiers stared at an invisible enemy forty or so yards to their front when suddenly the Corporal of the file barked the order 'Company, present your firelocks!'.

The platoon snapped into action instantly raising their long land pattern muskets in unison to the upright position waist high,

'Shoulder your firelocks!' bellowed the Corporal and again the company to a man exercised the movement with split second timing. 'Right turn' came the order with the company acting as one, faced to the right as the seven fresh recruits stood in awe at the lines of smart red coated soldiers.

The Corporal led the company marching in unison towards the barrack gates, 'Left, right, left, right' he barked as a young drummer fell in behind the company and kept time with the steady beat on the drum. The spectacle of drill, presentation and manoeuvre Will was to learn was a company of infantry, the thirty men consisted of three independent files of up to ten men responsible to a nominated Corporal, in addition to the private ranks would be a company sergeant and two company drummers, typically ten companies made up a battalion which in turn became a Regiment.

Will and his fellow recruits would in time merge with other files to form their own company, a Regiment and the life blood of the British line infantry. 'Very well lads' spoke Lucas as the exhibition of trained soldiers marched out beyond the garrison's view, 'let us refresh ourselves after such a fine exhibition, come, to the cookhouse for a feast of heroes awaits us'. Lucas and his party of recruits entered the mess where huge smoked and cured meats hung from the ceiling from barbarous hooks suspended from the rooms exposed beams and wicker baskets of bread alongside sacks of corn cobs and rice lay around the immaculately polished floor. The room was worked as demand saw fit by five people, employed by the Regiment to feed the garrison, 'Now sit boys' spoke Lucas, 'We shall be soon fed'. The seven recruits sat either side of the bench that ran the length of the dark oaken table on which stood pewter tankards and tin plates set at each mans interval, the younger of the women brought a wooden bowl of freshly baked bread rolls, 'Tuck in lads and make haste for your feast is just starting' added Lucas as each man helped himself to the soft bread, as a large iron cauldron was placed on the end of the table near Sergeant Lucas when he began to serve the contents of the pot onto each mans metal plate, the stew consisted of several meats, pheasant, duck, beef, pork and others that Will did not immediately recognise mixed with vegetables of good fresh quality unlike the half rotten types that Will would usually resort to beg or pilfer from the towns market, 'Eat up fine fellows' Lucas continued to speak, 'fill your stomachs, there's plenty more should you wish it'. The serving girl returned and brought with her a large pewter tankard of strong apple cider placing it within the middle of the group and the Sergeant quickly proceeded to pour the liquid into each mans tankard not caring that the liquid spilled liberally over the table, Will and surely most of his fellow recruits had rarely eaten this well, and all this at his majesties expense was surely good living.

Billeted in dry warm quarters, well clothed and fed regularly was more than each man could hope for living on the streets of the towns or in the hamlets and villages of the countryside and although the shire was currently enjoying a degree of prosperity each man present was aware of the uncertainty of his future, work today was no guarantee of work tomorrow and Sergeant Lucas promised them good living with regular payment and lodgings for their term of enlistment, for most experiencing this welcome they should have no reason to leave Lucas or his company. Having been in a semi permanent state of intoxication since the evening before at the Saracens Head inn, as the party finished their meal, Lucas suggested they rest a while back at their barrack rooms, the seven made there way across the square and into their billets.

The seven lads found themselves each a bunk amongst the many that lined the room, as he lay on his bedding Will reflected how the last twenty four hours had been good and easy living and until now had taken little interest in his fellow recruits preferring to concentrate on the tales of Lucas's adventures. In breaking the silence one of the recruits sat upon the edge of his bed and addressed the group, 'So mates, pray tell by what circumstances have brought us together?'. The seven in turn told their tale of how they found their way into Sergeant Lucas's company and as each man's story unfolded Will noted he was the only town dweller amongst the seven with all but himself travelling some fair distance to enlist into soldiering.

As his comrades spoke Will thought to himself how such opportunities come rarely and perhaps these promised adventures would be the escape he sought from the drudgery he'd accepted as his life.

Of the seven new recruits the first to speak was one of two brothers by the names of Allen, Thomas the older of the pair but only by minutes and Daniel had spent most of their working lives as farm labourers, both illiterate they grew tired of the monotony of village life and seeking adventure had followed Lucas as he'd passed through their village on the Leicestershire and Nottinghamshire border and hearing his talk of excitement and heroism in the ranks. Thom was clearly the more dominant of the two brothers, while Dan would often start a sentence only for it to be finished by his brother much to his sibling's annoyance.

John White from Hinckley, a strikingly handsome lad, with shoulder length jet black hair and deep set piercing eyes, the carpenter's mate had found himself dismissed from his employ as economic decline hit hard on the shires provincial town, he too it seemed had been taken by the chance of fame and fortune.

James Walsh, the son of a cooper and visibly the youngest of the party had run away from his responsibilities once a farm girl had announced he was the father of her child. Anonymity suited Walsh and the army would certainly offer him that, he'd claimed to be seventeen years of age but his freckled pale skin and cropped bright red hair gave him an obvious boyish look that clearly betrayed his youth. Will compared Walsh to his own brother Joseph in appearance and not much similar in age but whatever Walsh's true age, he had enlisted as a man and a man he would be treated there as.

Samuel Coles was the next to speak, taken by Sergeant Lucas talk of dashing adventure and romance, the well educated son of a silk merchant Coles by far took the longest time in explaining his personal situation with elaborate and colourful language that often confused his peers. He had been born into a privileged upbringing, his father's influences could have paved the way for a comfortable life but Coles wanted excitement and adventure in life rather than be held hostage to his father's desires.

Will studied Samuel Coles words carefully thinking to himself how foolish a man was to mix with these types when privilege and wealth could pave the way for a comfortable life but Coles pre-empted his audience's doubts on his reasons finishing his monologue with the thought of spending his days behind a desk as his father would wish him to had filled him with dread. As Coles' father fiercely objected to a wasted life in the army it was left to him and him alone to make his way in this life. The lad clearly had the look of intelligence about him, his personal belongings consist of several books meaningless to his new peers but to Coles they were precious and treasured and a calf skin journal soon filled with loose sketches of the men, lastly Coles carried a fine musicians violin, wrapped in an oiled cloth he would treat it as it were a small infant before eagerly entertaining the file with his musical skills.

The Eldest of the seven, Ezekiel Turner was at least twenty years above the others in age, his thin shoulder length hair showed signs of grey and his hardened leather like skin clear signs of hardship. He spoke briefly of his past, born the son of a Dorset smuggler he would spend hours as a small child keeping watch along the southern coasts many inlets and coves for the arrival of customs officers before maturing enough to accompany his father to sea running contraband from the European main land.

Whilst still a child Zeke's father had been caught by the excise officers and hanged for his crimes leaving the child orphaned and alone. Purchased from a work house as a drummer boy to the 6th Regiment in which he'd spent twelve years in their company travelling far and wide during his time with his Regiment, Zeke had served several years garrisoned in the West Indies twice contracting tropical diseases that had decimated the ranks but as peacetime brought little need for large Regiments, Zeke Turner having served the colours for over thirty years found himself without pay after his company was disbanded.

Born in Bournemouth, Zeke's enlistment had ended far from his native home, he'd found himself in Warwick and without profession Zeke elected to re-enlist into another Regiment rather than drifting from casual work to casual work. Zeke explained that it was unusual for a man of his age to be re-enlisted into the ranks, but Lucas had pitied him and recognised the plight of a fellow soldier facing hard times.

Will neglected to speak much on his own life, 'I have no family to speak of and employment is hard to come by these days' he explained, 'so I fare to chance my luck a soldierin'' he added. These seven men now bonded together into the ranks of the army, from different backgrounds and different lives the British redcoat would now unite them commonly as one.

The sun shone hard through the small glass paned windows of the barrack room highlighting the dust in the air, the door to the room was ajar allowing a warm breeze to flow through an otherwise cramped and stuffy room. Eventually Lucas reappeared along with two other ranks and announced 'come lads, let us settle your bounties', the seven stood from their bunks and casually followed Lucas out once again onto the courtyard. Each man silently thought of ways to spend the three guineas Lucas had offered upon enlistment, in his own mind Will had allocated the majority to his siblings, Joseph and Rebecca, his father who had been sickened by the wasteful life he'd led subsequently Will allocated him none knowing it would soon disappear into one of the towns many taverns. Lucas led the seven across the square, exiting the garrison and towards a modest merchant house opposite, the house before them stood tall and proud, of magnificent construction it belonged to the local Magistrate whom the seven would soon stand before him and swear allegiance to the King. The Sergeant led the party through the old town battlements and under the archway that had once offered protection from the towns enemies, a studded wooden door on the right hand side lay opened as the file passed through it, 'Wait here' Lucas raised his hand and spoke before departing around the path to the back of the lime washed house. The seven stood quietly when Zeke spoke up 'No turning back now lads, for now you're the Kings men'. The two red-coated rankers stood silently behind the line making their presence clearly known to the recruits, only Zeke knew it was their duty to stop any nerves getting the better of any of the recruits for now Lucas had almost completed his role, he would be well paid in delivering seven fir and able men to the Regiment and unbeknown to the recruits he would have raised his bounty much higher had it been necessary although this would cut deep into the profits of the Regiments recruiting party. Sergeant Lucas soon returned accompanied by a clerk of the courts, a tall wiry man sporting wire framed spectacles perched on the end of his long bony nose. The man was dressed head to toe in black save a fancy white silken laced collar, Mr Murray briefly addressed the recruits in his thick Scots accent and peered over his long nose, 'Come this way, the magistrate is ready for you now' he spoke adding an afterthought 'and speak only when you are spoken to'. As he led the group into the stone building the line of seven walked singularly in file to the magistrate's office where presently behind a desk sat a portly middle aged magistrate. This was a wealthy gentleman of good standing who wasted no time in attesting each man, asking his name the clerk noted in it the ledger and that the recruit was of free spirit and gave voluntarily enlistment to the crown. The recruits spoke no words other than to acknowledge when each man's name was called and if their length of enlistment was of either twelve or twenty years, to a man the file of recruits opted for the longer period much to the delight of Sergeant Lucas who would be recognised for doing his work well. The duration of attestation lasted no longer than a strike of the quarter hour and as the clerk received his fee coyly from Lucas the newly enlisted soldiers were marched out back into the militia's barracks. Lucas and his two aides escorted the file to the barracks and their billet room 'Tomorrow' grinned Lucas, 'you'll start your careers a soldiering' he turned to exit the billet room he paused and commented over his shoulder, 'get a good night's sleep my boys for you've a long day ahead'.

As he lay on his bunk Will heard the eight bells from the Church behind the barracks, the last of the daylight was fast disappearing as Zeke and Dan Allen together lit the stubs of candles to illuminate the dingy room. The summer months had lasted longer than usual this year and the heat from the day had adequately warmed the room as to make each man comfortable with just the grey woollen blanket provided to his bunk by the militia garrison. The men talked well into the night of their life experiences although most dwelled on Zeke Turners experiences within the ranks of the 6th Regiment pressing his tales of adventures across the oceans into distant lands few had heard of before. As the candle stubs dissolved into a waxen pool and the tallow wicks burned their last flickering light Zeke told the youngsters of his times overseas, although careful not to make glamour of his times the six youths viewed him as a fatherly figure, a figure it would turn out that would teach the lads how best to survive in King George's armies.

The night previous, Sergeant Lucas had promised a long day ahead and the billet room was awoken early as the Regimental drummers beat a fast rhythm on the parade ground outside. The recruits opened bleary eyes well before sunrise with the nearby church ringing six bells to notify the town's folk of the hour as an unfamiliar Corporal entered the billet to rally the men into life, 'Ups ye gets lads' snapped the man, 'Corporal Mathias Skinner is here to makes you into soldiers'. Mathias Skinner had served the 17th regiment since a boy, similarly to Zeke Turner he had been taken into the Regiment from a towns orphanage but the similarity ended there, close to thirty years of age Skinner stood at six feet in height with his lean figure giving him a ungainly and unwieldy appearance and a permanent sneering expression, his blotchy skin bore the scars of a heavy case of small pox contracted as a child and despite having served the Regiment for over fifteen years Skinner had yet to experience overseas service somehow managing to win the favour of influential officers and remain within more comfortable postings, he trusted no one and none trusted him. As Skinner strutted around the billet room, Zeke's eyes followed his movements cautiously, Zeke was familiar with this practice and was presentable by his bunk side almost immediately, the others however, less used to the practice took more time as the Corporal paced the length of the room kicking the bunk of any man who had yet to show enthusiasm to the day, the Corporal singled out the youngster James Walsh who as expected for his age had neither the wit or wisdom to jump into life when spoken to by a superior. Skinner abruptly moved to Walsh's bunk who laying lazily with one hand supporting his head and the other covering his eyes from the morning sunrise moaned at the Corporals orders, Skinner lunged at him grasping a tuft of his bright red hair, 'Now when I says up boy, you gets up' howled the Corporal as his loud bawl caused spit to fly from his mouth into the face of the bewildered Walsh forcing the few who had not yet sprung to life to do so as the fiery Corporal Skinner put the fear of God deep into the heart of each man present. Skinner yanked the youth from his bed with such force the bunk shook and titled with the momentum, Walsh tumbled to the straw covered stone floor with Skinner wasting no time in carrying on his fury dragging the bewildered lad to the exit and out of sight of the remaining six.

A minute or so passed as Walsh re-entered the billet stumbling through the doorway whilst spluttering for his breath, his upper body soaked through, directly behind him strutted Skinner pushing the drenched recruit towards his bunk,

'Stand by yer bunks!' bellowed the Corporal with the two fellow soldiers bolstering his authority on either side of him.

The seven stood firm and straight in front of each bunk and Walsh despite the warm morning breeze stood shivering and dripping wet on the straw that sparsely covered the flag stoned floor, all but Zeke Turner who'd witnessed this type of bullying too many times before stood too scared to do anything other than whatever Skinner commanded.

The pause lasted barely a few seconds before being shattered 'Outside now!' Skinner again bellowed as the lads scrambled past the bawling man and the two accompanying soldiers.

Once outside the file was gestured towards the right wall of the barrack square and formed up in line nervously waiting Skinners next move. On crossing the parade ground Will noticed the now half empty water barrel that had contributed to Walsh's soaking and thought to himself how long before this Corporal chose his next victim to intimidate. The seven recruits patiently waited for Skinner and his entourage made their way towards them, Skinner appeared from the billet now much calmer told the file that they would begin the day by learning the drill and manoeuvre techniques required by each man to position his self within the company. For hours Skinner mercilessly drilled the file of seven, turn left, turn right he hollered until the monotony of it had drummed itself into each man and with every mistake a recruit made Skinner would single out and beat young Walsh for their punishments, Will winced as Skinner rained vigorous blow after blow upon Walsh for the files slightest misdemeanour. At mid day after almost six hours of relentless drill Skinner allowed the file a brief period of rest, none of them had yet eaten that day although for Will, long periods without sustenance was no new thing. Skinner disappeared for an hour leaving the recruit's time to rest upon the cobbled parade ground and the file was given permission to take water from the nearby half empty rain water barrel, the men scooped the cool water to their faces and wiped the sweat from their necks.

Sitting squat upon the cobbled ground Zeke Turner piped up addressing the whole group 'He'll tell you it's for your own good boys for he wishes to break your spirit' he spoke 'and do not cross him neither, this man has the authority to make a hell of your wretched lives'. As the phrase 'talk of the devil and he shall appear' were ever true Skinner re-appeared onto the square striding towards the party 'Fall in line' he again barked without emotion, 'I'll share some words with you lads' Skinner growled softly and paced back and forth holding a coin between his finger tips, 'from now on' pausing a moment as he paced along the line of seven 'You all belong to me, you'll do as I ask, when I ask' he continued 'now do this and you'll become proper soldiers fit for the Kings armies'. Continuing around the backs of the men deliberately causing nervousness so very unfamiliar to Will, Skinner positioned himself behind Walsh and placed the coin into his hand 'There lad, a penny for your soul' he sneered 'and a good price for it too for you're worth no more than that, you understand me boy?'. This man clearly oozed hatred towards the recruits. As he continued to pace along the line his soft voice suddenly broke with a fierce snap 'If any of you scum should think of deserting me you'll find yourselves on the end of a rope' he spoke methodically as he continued to strut back and forth the line 'Desertion from His Majesty's army' he quoted as though the words engrained into his voice 'is a capital offence' he paused for a moment then continued staring hard towards Walsh. 'And for those of you with an idiot nature about yourselves, means hanging!' his anger and hate spilled from his mouth, 'Don't think you can runs neither' he continued whilst resuming his pace 'Mathias Skinner has his eyes everywhere'. The Corporal paused for breath briefly whilst continuing his tempo around the file 'Now, let us continue in your transformation into fine soldiers'. The file stood like small children waiting for instruction as Skinner toyed with them forcing them in the days heat to stand firm, each mans eyes stared directly into nothingness as the Corporal strutted back and forth on front of the seven, 'If any man moves' he growled and making level with Walsh his arm swung outward with his thin birch cane pausing level with the youths neck, instinctively Walsh cowered away from the oncoming blow as Skinner held his force shy of contact but by now his order had been broken, James Walsh had disobeyed Skinners direct order and would now pay the price.

Will and the others knew what was to come, in a casual manner Skinner squarely faced the youth, nose to nose he stood and from the corner of his eyes Will could see Walsh shrink with fear whilst trying desperately to stand firm in accordance it the Corporals wishes. Holding his position for what seemed an age Skinners face twitched with a nervous affliction as he turned away, believing this torment over Walsh breathed a sigh of relief when suddenly Skinner swung and punched Walsh hard and square in the stomach. Walsh collapsed on the parade ground floor doubled up in pain, groaning with agony and clutching his stomach, instinctively Will moved to assist the injured lad. 'Fool if you do' whispered Zeke, 'he'll have you next'. Helplessly, Will relaxed his tense muscles knowing Zeke to be right. Walsh lay on the ground clutching his stomach and crying with the agony of the blow as Skinner stood all conquering over him, 'Ups you get lad' he spoke lifting the boy by his oversized collar,

'Back in line' he snapped between clenched teeth. Walsh coughed and spluttered a little blood from his lips as he hurriedly fell back into his place, Skinner watched triumphantly over the broken lad with a spiteful smirk upon his face.

In time to come Skinner would regularly abuse his position of authority, confiscating personal items purchased by the file for his own use or to resell back to them. The file grew to despise Skinner fearing amongst other things his sadistic nature and unpredictability.

After a long day spent on the garrison parade ground finally the recruits were ordered to left face and march forward passing through a stone archway before arriving at the Regiments store room. Stacked high with neatly folded tunics, breeches and accoutrements the men were address by an elderly clerk to provide his name as it was checked against a heavy clerks ledger, Will had never had the luxury of new clothing and shoes, even when he could get them as cast off's shoes were the height of comfort in his poverty stricken life. The file stood in line under Skinners direction as a tailor's assistant measured the men and fitted them each with new cotton undershirts and scarlet tunics with lace edging the likes Will had never dreamt of.

The file was ordered to discard their personal clothing and don the heavy cotton breeches and undershirt provided to them as each man was required to make his mark in the ledger upon receipt of each item. The Adjutant called out the following as each mans arms were stacked high with allocated items reeling off the articles with a long drawn monotony, 'Woollen hose one pair, cotton stockings two pairs, canvas trousers long one pair' the clerk struggled to keep up hastily penning the items into the ledger, 'Boots, leather two pairs, cotton undershirt one, woollen waistcoat one, long heavy coat one, felt hat one, soft cap one'

The quartermaster of the store addressed the men collectively informing them that the equipment issued was now each man's responsibility, loss or damages would be charged to the recruit and thus deducted from his pay, the file was instructed to sign his mark as to witness such.

The party moved outside either wearing or carrying their equipment and was ordered to return to their billets.

As Will made his way to his bunk he noticed his neighbour Zeke already present by his bunk carefully laying out his newly allocated equipment. Looking upwards Zeke advised Will to make a mark of his own upon his belongings as the loss of someone's kit would quickly be replaced by that which belonged to the naïve. Taking note of him, Will borrowed a small lead pencil from his mentor and carefully marked his initials into his clothing as best he could given the tool to do so. The recruits lay in their bunks admiring the intricate needlework on the cloth that manufactured the Kings uniforms, Zeke produced cotton and thread from his personal belongings and started to re-stitch each tunic button tightly, 'The loss of even a button will be deducted from your pay' he remarked. With nearly twenty years service with the colours Zeke began to teach the file the tricks and techniques of how to treat and prepare equipment as to survive the rigours of a soldier's life, an extra stitch here or a fold there to make the cloth fix into a permanent position.

The following month was spent largely on the parade ground practicing drill manoeuvres until each man had instructions firm within his head and the unit could move in unison.

Zeke Turner, when asked this purpose advised his comrades that in times of battle each mans life may depend upon his swiftness in executing an order, the recruits learned the timings of the army by heart and by the time the month was out could move in unison into any form the Corporal ordered. By mid October the long hot summer had finally given its last and the cold damp autumn air moved southwards bringing the fall of the leafy trees. The file spent its' free time within the barracks gambling what valuables they had with a set bone dice until finally receiving the pay and bounty offered over a month ago by Sergeant Lucas. Appearing before the Regimental pay clerk, to each mans dismay the bounty that lured them the weeks before in the tavern whilst listening to Lucas had not accounted for the clothing and sustenance each had received, even the drink from the night at the tavern had been deducted from their bounty leaving from a promise of three guineas and eight shillings the pitiful sum of just four shillings.

The file felt they had been tricked despite the small consolation that they had all been regularly fed and clothed to a good standard and had lodgings provided in a warm and reasonably comfortable environment. It was a bitter pill to swallow but the file knew they would not live so well without the Army providing the security of their billet. The Regimental pay clerk advised that each man would receive a weekly allowance of nine pence after stoppages—made payable every fortnight, as Will made his mark against the heavy ledger signing for the pay he'd received the ever present and watchful Corporal Skinner then removed a further penny for the benefit of the Regimental agent.

Back in the recruits billet Will stared at his open palm counting as best he could the remaining coins, whilst each man had dreamt of the rich bounty promised the reality of the situation bit hard, the lure of wealth, riches and fame had fooled them all except Zeke who had seen tricks similar to the recruits of the 6th Regiment many times before but for now no there was no backing out or escape for they had all willingly committed to the lengthy period of enlistment. Skinner had readily reminded them at all hard occasions the consequences of desertion and Will began to accept his decision to enlist when Zeke sweetened the bitter pill with the raw fact that none amongst them had been better fed, clothed or quartered before this time.

The file had been refused permission to leave the barracks and perhaps, Will thought the Regiment had lost too many recruits after the bounty was paid before to risk it again. The Allen brothers had quickly spent their pay upon cheap gin peddled at the barrack gates, passing it around the file each man took a generous swig before the bottle made its way to the next. Whilst laying about their bunks idling away their time until next required to parade, John White on having received so little of his promised bounty stared into his open hand and complained bitterly to the file, the impressionable James Walsh who had already began to despise the system after a series of hard beatings he had received from Skinner joined in with this mutinous talk.

As the atmosphere in the barrack room worsened, Zeke who until now had remained silent carefully listening to the file's whinging finally spoke up, 'Quieten down lads, such talk will only end in trouble for us all'. The young recruits well aware of his experienced nature stopped their grumbles and listened as he spoke. Removing his smouldering pipe form his mouth Zeke began his monologue 'You made your decisions as free men did you not? you even swore an oath to such to the magistrate' he paused a moment as the words rested on the minds of his fellows, 'Lucas did not deceive you, for you heard what you wanted to hear, you've sought tales of adventure and fame and that my friends, is what you'll find soon enough you can rest assured of that, not one of us has been tricked by any other than himself'. The six youths each stared down at the dirty straw floor knowing his words to be true.

Looking squarely a Dan Allen, Zeke advised him to save his cheap drink till a time when they were not so hot headed. With tempers calmer, Zeke stood up and moved to the empty space in front of the bunks and he turned his back to the six lads pulling his cotton shirt over his head and revealed over two dozen deep red scars that marked the width of his broad back. In lowering his head Zeke revealed the extent of his old wounds, the youths sat silently on the edge of their bunks gawping open mouthed at the scarred mess upon his back. Giving the lads enough time to absorb the wounds Zeke dropped his flimsy shirt and faced the lads, 'Anger comes with youth boys, I was once as you are now until the Skinner I knew whipped it out of me, take my heed and learn to curb your tongues, if Skinner or any of his cohorts had heard your words then you would surely be flayed as I was'. The room remained silent as Zeke continued, 'Skinner and his kind are the backbone of the army, this type are born for His Majesties service for they knows no better, discipline comes in two forms to him, the lash and the rope, he'll worry not which you gets but cross him and he'll be sure you face at least one them'. The uneasy silence continued across the billet room after Zeke had raised the fear of god in the youths, Dan cursed then gave out a laugh as he flopped flat onto his bunk.

Sam Coles snapped irritated at the twin, 'Pray Daniel, tell us what does amuse you so much? You think this predicament light' he spoke stern faced as the others started to chuckle at Coles stern expression, before long the group including Coles himself found itself laughing collectively at the situation.

The months of October and November brought the harsh north winds across the country, during this time the file had learnt drill, been issued with equipment and had the principles of musketry explained to them although none had yet to handle a musket and by early December the seasons change had brought the first snows of the winter, from the billet window Will watched the snows settle on the parade ground and form peculiar shapes on around the wooden frame of the window as the winds swept the powdery snow upwards along the sill. The billet had little ventilation and the rooms dampness lingered long in the cool air reminding him well of his times past constantly living in such harsh conditions, was this life any better? he asked himself in a moment of self thought, he'd been well fed and quartered certainly, his peers had bonded well with him as he had them, for now at least, he had few regrets on his decision to enlist.

Zeke used his wealth of knowledge and somehow procured a brazier from the militia quartermaster, once lit it would at least take the chill from the room for during this cold period the soldiers were issued with an extra blanket and a pair of black tarred high canvas leggings to supplement the cotton canvas trousers issued for the summer months.

Time spent over the winter quarter went quickly and soon the file was assigned to the Regiments companies merging at the garrisoned town of Berwick on the Scottish borders, Skinner informed the file they would join the remainder of the Regiment there to bring the Regiment to full strength and until they receive orders to depart he would increase their drill to bring them up to Regimental standards.

The short winter days were mostly spent on the parade ground and despite the issue of the leggings Skinner had forbidden the file to wear them, daily drilling the group in the winter mud and filth that pooled around the barrack square, Skinner constantly bawled at the condition of the white uniforms allocated to the recruits. 'Walsh, Snow, White! You are a disgrace to yourselves and the King's uniform' he screamed across at the file, 'Make yourselves presentable to me this evening, I have a small favour to ask of you'. Returning to the files billet the group fell upon their bunks 'What do you think he wants from us Zeke?' James Walsh asked nervously, Zeke calmed his fears as best he could, 'Skinner is nothing but a bully to you lad, you should stand your ground to him and he'll leave you well alone but tonight he seeks to trick you and by falling us out early he thinks we'll idle the day away' Zeke continued to speak 'but Skinner my friend I have encountered your kind many times before, I know your games and I know your intentions too well'

Will pondered Zeke's words carefully and considered to himself the implications of his statement, as much as the bond of the seven had grown strong Walsh had proved himself a soft target to Skinner, If this Corporal ceased to vent his anger on Walsh then surely another would soon take his place, feeling the guilt of his fears Will vowed to himself that he would side by the youngster in whatever he chose. Zeke warmed a kettle of water over the embers of the billets brazier, 'The man wants you presentable for him tonight lads so blacken your boots and whiten your breeches as best you can, you best not give him any more cause to persecute you further'. Will bunged the drain of the trough that served as ablutions for the file as Zeke carefully poured the boiling water into the stone sink, 'strip lads' Zeke instructed the three, 'What?' Will questioned his mentors words,

'You'll need to soak your breeches and scrub the grime from them. Will, Walsh and White removed there whites and plunged them into the steaming bath, prodding them with vigour the water darkened with the filth of weeks of wear. Coles and the Allen brothers blackened the boots of the three that would present themselves in and Zeke pressed the scarlet tail coats under the weight of the stacked straw mattresses while wrung breeches hung on sticks around the roaring brazier the three dressed for parade in readiness for Corporal Skinner's request, finally Zeke tied the hair tight into a greased queue complete with tidy black lace ribbon to finish. Instructing the three men to stand completely still the lads were dressed for fear of unnecessary movement might spoil the group's efforts in smartness, Zeke paced round the three running his eyes from head to toe meticulously picking a loose thread or speck of dirt from the uniforms the three so proudly wore. Satisfied with their efforts Zeke gave leave for the three to depart for their dreaded appointment with the Corporal.

The sun set late in the clear sky followed by a sharp frost that settled on the high rooftops, the three made their way to Skinners rooms in readiness for his task, a sharp knock to the locked door was followed by Skinners voice bluntly ordering the three to remain outside, after a minute or so Skinner yelled the file to enter his billet room. The lads peered cautiously into the Corporal's quarters, a single bunk dominated the room lit with large tallow candles set upon shoddy wooden furniture, 'Come lads' he spoke in a calmness unfamiliar to the recruits 'Come further into the light I wish to see you in all your glory'. Will smiled inwardly to his self, Zeke was right it seemed as Skinners expression dropped on seeing the impeccably dressed soldiers,

'Seems you fellows have some sense after all' he commented, 'Now if you can oblige old Mathias a favour'. The three looked on puzzled at the Corporals choice of words wondering exactly what he meant.

Skinner led the three through the back rooms of the barracks and into the stable block at the rear of the structure, 'I need this area clearing by midnight lads so get to it and no slacking now else I'll be disappointed in ya's, I'll be checking in soon enough'. The three lads stood alone in the stables as Skinner returned to his own billet room, 'we'd best get to it' declared John White as he retrieved three shovels from the corner of a stall and began to shift the dirty straw from within, 'You think to do this labour in our uniforms John?' Will spoke up concerned to Skinners designs on ruining their efforts,

'Well thought Will' Walsh contributed to the conversation instantly removing his tailcoat and waist coat laying them over the side of the panelled stalls. The three shifted the straw into the centre of stable and after hours of hard and heavy work rested satisfied with their accomplishments. It seemed though not a moment had passed when Corporal Skinner returned to the block to assess their progress, the silence of the night soon shattered as he made his arrival felt, 'What in god's name?!' yelling at the three as they lay with their backs to the heaped straw, 'you think to serve his majesty naked boy' singling James Walsh out for his wrath. The three jumped to their feet in the presence Skinner and prepared themselves for the wrath the Corporal had in store. Skinner stood dominantly in front of the three as they struggled to dress themselves correctly, hastily fastening buttons of their tunics his eyes made for a banded iron bucket that served the stall nearest to him, the Corporal grabbed the bucket slopping its putrid contents as he swung it towards the three.

It was Walsh that bore the brunt, now soaked in filth Will winced at the rancid water that dripped from the three as Skinner grinned his toothless smirk. 'Best get yourself out of those filthy clothes lads, I can't have you on duty looking like some heathen savage can I?'. The three waited with confusion and uncertainty to the Corporal's next move, 'Strip boys, you'll be scrubbing for the rest of the night looking at the state of yers'. Under the Corporals orders the Will, White and Walsh removed their outer clothes that dripped with sour water stacking them in a pile at Skinners feet. 'Walsh!' he barked, 'oblige me and launder these filthy rags fit for the Kings uniform will you, there's a good lad'. Walsh's youth and naivety betrayed him, certain that whatever he did Skinner would punish him he remembered Zeke's words earlier and refused the Corporals order.

Skinners eyes widened in furious anger, 'I'm not asking you boy! I'm telling you . . . now get to it'. If Walsh had stood his ground things might well have ended differently, but the snap of Skinners voice jumped the young lad into action as he gathered the pile within his arms and waited for the next instruction. 'Right boy' Skinner spoke, 'outside is the water barrel you'll be needing for your task, follow me and I'll make sure you do a fine job for your fellows benefit'

Will's mind cast back to Walsh's drenching on their first encounter with the hated Corporal and it didn't take much thought to predict the nights outcome for young James Walsh. The two worked tirelessly forking fresh straw from the loft above into the empty stalls, neither man spoke but collected his thoughts to poor Walsh who outside suffered alone at the hands of Corporal Skinner, the silence shattered as Skinner's arrived into the stable block from the freezing winter night. 'Left, right, left, right . . .' he shouted as he and Walsh marched into the vicinity of Will and John. Both looked upwards in pity at the sight of Walsh, humiliated at the hands of the hateful Corporal, the boy stood soaked through with the slop bucket wedged on his head.

'Halt!' Skinner yelled, clearly frightened Walsh stood disoriented within the stable block waiting nervously for the next instruction. Skinner addressed the two as they stood ready with their shovels 'Take this pathetic specimen back to your billet, you can claim your clothing tomorrow'. Walsh, now too scared to move waited long after Skinner had departed before removing the bucket, Will comforted the lad as he showed distress at the punishment he'd suffered. 'Come James' Will assured the boy, 'You've stood your ground with him, If Zeke is right you've had your last from that bastard'. Walsh was called to Skinners account early the following morning, although Zeke accompanied the rural lad in his duty to assure him Skinners hatred would not resurface in the presence of a seasoned soldier, for now at least the seven would be safe as Zeke made his presence known whenever Skinner had designs on the files sufferings.

By the last week of January the file was ordered to combine with its company and march northwards to the Scots border town, during the last few hours spent in their billet the seven recruits reflected their few months with the Regiment and particularly the spiteful Corporal Skinner, each man openly hoped he would not be joining them on the march north.

The files last night was spent quietly within the billet with the rooms candle stubs flickering in the cold air as each enjoyed the company of his comrade's presence. Suddenly the wooden billet room door shook with a bang, 'Opens up' came the all too familiar voice. 'Hell, It's Skinner' mumbled White, 'come to torment us one last time no doubt' he added. Walsh who sat nearest the door rose to let in the outsider, the moment he raised the latch the door swung inwards with a force smashing Walsh hard in the face. Skinner staggered into the billet, dead drunk and carrying an empty bottle of spirits, pushing Walsh aside without any care he staggered towards the party as they sat about their bunks. 'Gives up your drink to old Mathias' he cried.

The file stood up as on parade with exception to Zeke who having lost all respect for Skinner stared fast at the space between his knees with contempt for the Corporal, 'Clear out Skinner, you've no business here' Zeke spoke showing little reverence to the man. Ignoring the comment Skinner directed his drunken rants at the remaining six lads 'come on fools, I needs drink!' he slurred before swigging the last few drops of his cheap booze

Dropping the empty glass bottle on the stone floor it shattered into tiny fragments, James Walsh stared madly towards Skinner swaying besides the bunks, wide eyed with fury he lowered his head and charged Skinner mid body, unsteady the Corporal took the force unexpectedly as the two crashed into the nearest bunk toppling it to the ground. The might of Skinner far outweighed Walsh's small size and although blind drunk he quickly overwhelmed the youth pining him down on the straw floor. Uncontrollable and mad with rage Skinner began to choke the helpless lad, the Corporal consumed in a fit of fury, mumbling incoherently and frothing with madness as Walsh desperately tried to wriggle free. The remaining youths too scared to intervene for being the next recipient of Skinner's wrath sat rooted to the floor when Zeke moved with speed to intervene into the fray swinging his booted right foot into the Corporals hate filled face.

With a sickening crash Skinner released his grip from the youngster's throat and fell to the side of Walsh, 'Get him up and get him outside, quickly' the unconscious Corporal groaned as the seven lifted him from the floor and carried him outside,

'Take him to the stone watering trough over the yard' Zeke ordered, 'lay him by its side, he's so drunk he'll think he fell onto it when he wakes'. The youths jumped into action quickly and did as Zeke instructed laying the unconscious Skinner down beside the frozen water trough, James Walsh was the last to return to the billet but not before spitting on Skinner's unconscious body and delivering a firm kick to the ribs, Skinner groaned on receiving the blow as Walsh felt wholly justified in his actions paying back the Corporal for his endless bullying.

Inside the billet the seven quickly straightened the room to its previous order, Zeke removed his hard black leather boot to reveal an already bruising foot 'He'll fare worse than I me thinks' he chuckled.

*   *   *

Chapter Two

The Tweed

After a brisk breakfast the seven men paraded outside with full equipment, Skinner stood ever present and stared hard towards the party with deep contempt, his eyes swollen and purple in bruised colour, his body stiff from the blow given by the redeemed James Walsh, to the seven he'd been paid his dues. Will breathed a sigh of relief as they realised the dreaded Skinner would remain, for the time being at least within the militia's barracks

The file was now assigned to a new sergeant who'd arrived the previous night at the barracks with two files of private soldiers raised from Somerset County. The sergeant was introduced to the seven as Sergeant Vaughan, who under the command of Lieutenant James McPherson would lead the soldiers north to Berwick and merge with the Regiments other companies.

The Church behind the barracks sounded nine bells as the thirty men marched outwards to barrack square and towards the crossing at the river soar, Zeke remarked they would be expected to march thirty miles a day in order to meet the Regiment as swiftly as he'd heard Lieutenant McPherson wish.

The last snows of winter had fallen a few days prior but the cold winds prevented any reasonable thaw, the turnpikes although clear of snow had in places copious amounts of mud to hinder the troops movements, making it difficult for all to remain in a relative formation. The horse backed McPherson typically rode well ahead of the company's loose formation allowing the accommodating Sergeant Vaughan to fall out the column into a more practical method of movement, occasionally the Lieutenant would return to his ranks and the file would temporarily fall back into line if only for the benefit of the present officer.

By night fall the party made camp at Normanton village on the Nottinghamshire border not many miles from the Allen brothers' home parish, Sergeant Vaughan had managed to secure a dry barn for the night and arrange with McPherson's consent for a local farm to deliver bread, cheese and mutton to supplement the meagre soldiers ration.

The barn that provided the night's shelter was a dank and draughty building, the recruits pilled dry straw high to insulate what little heat could be generated amongst the men, Coles remarked the farm had probably turned out pigs to provide occupancy for the soldiers, 'Better than the ditch' replied Zeke who had no doubt endured a night or two in far worse accommodation.

Will sat squat on the filth strewn straw floor, his back against a supporting timber post, he'd wrapped both his issued blankets around himself for warmth, Wisely, Zeke suggested as he had done they place their knapsacks under their backsides to keep them from the damp ground.

The long days progression had taken its toll upon the party, barely had the last man finished his evening ration before the barn was silent with its slumbering exhausted occupants. As was now usual, the file woke early to the sound of the returning company picket guard, the group of men consumed whatever food was left from the previous nights ration before forming up outside the barn entrance, Vaughan addressed the men that a long days march lay ahead in order to make schedule after Lieutenant McPherson rode into the camp and briefly spoke with the Sergeant and his corporals before riding into the distance.

Sergeant Vaughan properly fell the men from formation as soon as the officer was out of vision and started up the drummers beat to keep the men in relative time, the village lanes although still muddy from the heavy snowfalls the week previous showing some signs of drying out at least giving the men the chance to remain steady on their feet. Weaving in and out of the rural countryside the company fell out of line for a half hours rest, each man watering from the nearby brook, Will consumed a crust of bread given to him by Zeke as he had the sense to preserve his food and the generosity to provide it to his fellows knowing he could never guarantee his next meal. Subsidised by some winter berries gathered from the frosted bushes, the file continued its long march northbound reaching the outskirts of Rotherham town just before sundown, at least this nights billet would be more comfortable than the last and the company had the opportunity to lodge within an Inn on the Nottingham to Wakefield road. McPherson had provided the Inn's landlord with prior warning in order to keep stock on sufficient ales, arriving almost an hour past dusk Will and his comrades unloaded their packs into a secured stable and rested in the tavern warmed to the roars of the open fireplaces.

The Inn was void of custom except the red coated soldiers, Zeke explained to his curious friends, 'locals and Redcoats rarely mix . . . often have I seen a bloody mess left behind after a volume of drink was consumed by the two'. Zeke drank from his tin tankard and lit his freshly filled pipe from a slow match resting by the fireside, 'The landlord would be well paid to ensure his usual patrons frequent elsewhere tonight' sucking on his pipe to ignite the moist tobacco he paused a moment before continuing

'The gentleman officer will be held accountable for any damage done here tonight and questions from the local magistrate would be the last thing he'll need'. Will and the others raised their eyebrows at Zeke's experience and knowledge of such matters, 'twenty years teaches you a thing or two' he continued wiping the residue of his drink away from his dry lips.

More liquor was produced by the landlord and his wife who would see their profits from this night far outweigh a month's worth of takings from the village patrons they'd normally entertain, the company would spend the night consumed by drink till both purse and tankards ran dry.

The following weeks march was much the same as the company of men marched proud through villages and hamlets of England's counties, locals would cheer and young girls giggle as the company of smart red coated soldiers proudly stood to attention at the smallest opportunity.

Like a plethora of peacocks the men showed their audience the British army at its finest and himself a gentleman soldier within his very own glorious 17th Regiment. Travelling northwards through the East Ridings, occasionally the company would spend the night in some distant farms outbuilding but more often McPherson had pre-arranged dry warm quarters at an Inn or travellers hostel and after twenty days march the company had made good time approaching the border to Scotland at Berwick town by the river Tweed.

McPherson made good use of the garrison there, billeting the company in the new Regimental barracks of the absent 25th Regiment.

The Regiment of the 17th had been garrisoned at Berwick for over a month waiting for replacements and recruits to complement the battalion to full strength, during the course of the following week the file watched new arrivals swell the battalion's ranks to over four hundred men.

One such arrival had filled the file with dread, the morning had been its usual busy, the men sat whitening their leather and blacking their boots when through the garrisons main gates marched a company of men led by the dreaded Corporal Skinner, 'Sergeant Skinner by the looks of it now lads' spoke Zeke coyly casting his glance sideways.

Skinner had spied the seven almost immediately and made his way towards them the file sat uneasy waiting for Skinner's sly words,

'Well lads, looks like the march kept you intact' as none of the file bothered to look Skinner in the eyes, each continued to work upon his equipment half ignoring the Sergeant yet retaining the protocols of being addressed by a senior rank.

Skinner frustrated by the lack of response held the upper hand over the seven, 'these lazy times have grown ye fat, I have just the task to test your bodies', with that final comment Skinner strutted back to his own file and proceeded to yell them into order, 'Looks like he's not finished with us yet' Zeke spoke.

This vengeful Corporal had every authority to make a hell of each man's life and James Walsh cursed knowing his ordeal under Skinner may well return, 'Worry not lad' Zeke rested his hand on Walsh's shoulder, 'he'll be well watched by us, besides' he continued 'Skinner was so drunk he'll not have remembered the payment he received from us'.

The company spent a further six weeks billeted in the border town attached temporarily to Captain William Darby's company, the seven men were assigned to a labour party under the hated Sergeant Skinner in re-building a wooden foot bridge that crossed a narrower part of the river tweed.

The traditional showers of April came late in 1772, the party often spent the days of May sheltering from the squalls under the work details heavy oiled water proofed canvas bivouac. Darby's engineers were running behind schedule and the party was ordered to labour on regardless of the poor weather, battalion carpenters and smiths prefabricated the structure and the seven men would spend hour's waist deep in the freezing cold river driving the timbers to the muddy embankments, the twisted boughs of the ancient oaks leered overhead, snatching at those who laboured beneath. As darkness fell the rains came hard biting into the bodies of the already drenched men, bare-chested the party bore the bleak weather desperately as the engineers pushed to complete the structure, the rains fell so hard the dammed river struggled to cope with such volumes of water.

Walsh the youngest of the seven found the labour too much for his boyish body, stumbling frequently in the river beds thick mud, ever watchful Zeke requested to Skinner that work stops until at least the rains had subsided, however as the details officer had returned to the battalions barracks Skinner declined Zeke's plea citing it would undermine Darby's wishes to complete the works, Zeke however knew the real reason was that Skinner would again see the file suffer, his eyes easily betrayed his hatred for the seven lads, he would now have his revenge. Zeke on realising Skinner's vengeance gave up his plea and made his way to the banks edge and scrambled down the slippery mud slopes to the swollen rivers turbulent edge, hastily gathering a coil of inch thick hemp rope he tossed it towards Will 'tie yourselves together' he yelled the driving rains lashing against his face, Will did as Zeke directed and passed the rope onto the rest of the file, 'This river will not contain itself much longer if this rain doesn't give' he spoke returning to the deep swirling waters. The group had worked hard against the rivers strong swirling currents to secure the heavy timbers when without warning the upper part of the high embankment gave way and collapsed cascading its sides into the already rising river.

As the torrent of mud and fierce waters gushed downstream towards the party, the seven men desperately attempted to flee its wake

'Hold the rope' yelled Zeke, his voice inaudible over the commotion straining timbers. Scrambling for the river bank it became each for themselves as the incomplete wooden sub structure felt the full force of the tidal flow easily unseating it as though made of matchwood, the shattered bridge crashed towards the party as they desperately scrambled towards the swirling rivers edge. Smothered by the muddy waters and smashed timbers Will felt himself enveloped by the onslaught of the tidal fury, barely able to keep upright himself he watched Walsh struggling to keep with his feet, the young lad rigid with shock and fear stared wide eyed at Will as though waiting for instruction on what to do, 'Move! Move now!' yelled Will.

Over Walsh's shoulder he saw a huge support timber begin to topple as debris and fallen tree branches roared downstream and smashed into the unsteady structure. Confused and shocked by the situation, Walsh rooted himself to the spot, the youth turned to face the large beam as it toppled and crashed downwards onto his body striking him squarely in the head and attempted to shield himself with his arms from its crushing blow.

The others who had seen the strike were powerless to help as Walsh's boyish frame crumpled under the force of the debris and sunk beneath the raging torrent, the sight of his hand aloft the swollen river was the last any would see of the youth as the debris carried him with momentum downstream faster than any of the group could move. Will attempted to intercept Walsh's position but soon failed as he himself fought against the swirling current and debris that raced downstream, Zeke shouted for him to leave him and save himself else the file would at this rate lose two of itself but ignoring Zeke's instruction Will scrambled toward the area where the youth had submerged desperate to pull Walsh from the depths, cold and exhausted at fighting the currents flow he himself slipped into unconsciousness and sank into the depths of the muddy torrent.

It was Dan Allen who pulled Will, half drowned from the river a hundred yards from where he had submerged, the brother was lucky to have found him as the river swept away everything in its path, as the rains continued to lash down Dan having somehow gotten hold of the rope with the help of the remaining labour party pulled him to the muddy embankment to safety.

Will regained consciousness after a sharp whack delivered to his back by Dan, coughing and spluttering the foul waters from his lungs, he lay on his side and spewed his guts clean of the murky brown river. Slowly sitting upright, dripping wet and shivering frozen to his bones, Dan and Sam Coles crouched beside Will and with arms under each shoulder pulled him clear of the deadly river, Sam Coles continued to slap his back hard with each cough Will mustered. As the groups reached the top of the embankment, the three collapsed and saw Zeke, furious at Skinner's inaction yell and curse towards the Sergeant regardless of his authority over the file, Thom and White sensibly barred the way anticipating Zeke's anger prevented him from reaching the cowering Sergeant Skinner and subsequently the lash that would be his punishment for venting his fury at the man responsible for this disaster.

With the bridge washed away the separated party spent the remainder of the wet night on either side of the river, Will, Dan Allen and Coles sheltered under the engineers wagon, whilst Zeke, Thom Allen and White huddled together under the drenched canvas now vacated by Skinner now absent from the tragic scene.

By the early hours the storm finally broke and its rains subsided, although the river was still to fierce to attempt a crossing the labour party had formed itself into two search teams to look for Walsh's body. Will remained by the party's camp, exhausted and barely conscious, Coles remained with him until the search party returned.

Zeke found the boy at first light tangled up amongst fallen branches a mile further down the river, his twisted and contorted body looked peaceful and content with his eyes closed as though asleep, his body unmarked save a small purple bruise that formed on his forehead. Wading chest deep to reach the young boys body, Zeke carefully untangled him from the barbs of the tree branches and cradled his limp body like a babe and strode the slippery banks to lay the young corpse at rest. The remainder of the party gently raised him from Zeke's arms and carried the lifeless body to the slippery grass embankment and placed it carefully inside a grey woollen blanket. John White stitched the sides of the cloth to enshroud Walsh's body, together the party carried the corpse back to the wrecked construction site and placed it at rest inside the wooden wagon that held the labour party's equipment.

The remainder of the file sat near the wagon acting as the duty of comradeship became James Walsh's final honour guard, Thom Allen built a fire for the six to dry their drenched and muddy clothes as the men sat in silence each reflecting their own relationship with Walsh. Seven had taken the Kings shilling those months past, now on this dreadful day stood one fewer now bonded by grief and pain caused by a man intent on their destruction. Thinking to himself how little he knew of Walsh's life before enlistment, Will pondered James Walsh's brief life, speaking rarely of his life before his time with the Regiment only recalling Walsh was born and raised in the eastern county village, he thought hard to remember the snippets he'd heard.

Walsh had worked with the village woodsmen between assisting his father in barrel making, hard labour had given Walsh the beginnings of a good physical shape although his youthful looks and mannerisms gave away his tender age of the sixteen or so years he claimed to be. Walsh had told his comrades of his reasons for enlisting into the Kings army, a village girl had accused Walsh of fathering her child and at such a young age, James Walsh had no desire for responsibility to fatherhood or marriage to a peasant girl. And if Walsh desired anonymity, he'd found it, laid to rest on the high muddy banks of the river Tweed, wrapped in a damp woollen blanket in an four feet deep unmarked grave, his bones soon to be lost in time.

The remaining six of the file paid their respects to the youth whilst the educated Coles struggled to offer a decent prayer for this wasted young life. Will placed a plucked wild flower on Walsh's shroud as the six men covered his young and innocent body with the soft earth dug from his grave.

Captain Darby, upon hearing of the disaster abandoned his project, Coles remarked that if the bridge had been finished it may have been monumental to Walsh's tragic death but this was not to be, the loss of time and materials to the army far outweighed the loss of James Walsh's short and tragic life. Directly after this tragedy, the file was discharged from Darby's company and merged back into McPherson's ranks under Sergeant Vaughan. The day following Walsh's death, the file sat around the bunks within their billets, Zeke removed the belongings stacked under his mattress and carefully opened his knapsack, removing each item from its contents Zeke placed them upon his bunk "Tis customary to draw lots for a dead man's belongings' he claimed, but none of the youths seemed too fazed by this statement as Zeke gathered six stands of straw from the floor and clenched them tight in his fist.

James Walsh's personal possessions were meagre, a pair of bone dice, a tinderbox and flint striker, sewing kit, a penny whistle, a corn dolly and a felt pouch containing three penny's.

Will drew the whistle although he had no skill or inclination to play it he would place it amongst his own belongings as if it had been with him for years, despite never being one for sentiment Will felt obliged to treasure this item as some testimony to a life lost so young, Zeke took the two dice and with them the six spent the night quietly gambling the few coins they had accompanied by a pitcher of hard ale Dan Allen purchased from a merchant trading his wares to the garrison. Typically Sam Coles sketched the poignant scene, Will glancing upon his work noticed an absent space amongst the party purposely left to accommodate the lost seventh member of the group.

After a few further days at Berwick the battalion was ordered to advance to Edinburgh, Colonel Charles Mawhood the most senior officer in the Regiment was keen to form his Regiment to a full compliment in readiness for an overseas posting, the Regiments colours would be presented and honoured to the ranks and officers that served, a significant moment in a soldiers life Zeke spoke relaying his own experiences of such in days gone by.

The first signs of the summer had begun to appear as the temperature rose and thawed out the last of the bleak weathers bitterness. Mesmerised by the coastline of which Will had never before seen he felt the fresh sea breeze pierce his long tailed redcoat and the salty sea air sting his dry parched lips. The highlands looked a bleak place to be, miles upon miles of brush and scrubland covered the landscape as far as the eye could see whilst small colonies of wild flowers desperately clung onto life in this desolate terrain.

A further three days march and the company would reach the capital Edinburgh, its tall spires that in dominating the skyline looked familiar to Will, at this distance the silhouette could be mistaken for his home town but this town was like none Will or any of the county lads had seen, huge by comparison he wondered what types occupied these lands as the Regiment marched the final league towards its destination.

The garrison formed part of the capitals ancient castle, with its battlements leering over the fast growing new Georgian capital and its thick stone walls perched high on its granite base the castle watched menacingly over Edinburgh's skyline.

With the settlement of a protestant monarch onto the throne and the Jacobean rebellion crushed, Edinburgh and the outlying areas although losing independence with the act of union in 1707 had prospered well economically.

An expanding local wool trade had provided the city with an almost infinite supply of high quality wool as the towns numerous frame knitters turned the raw material into fine clothes and materials and commercial docks had given Edinburgh the opportunity to export its wares quickly to the wealthy merchants to the south and empire beyond.

The company finally arrived at the castle late afternoon, instructed into their assigned thatched billet within the castle walls the six men rejoiced at the end of a six hundred mile march, celebrating the end with a bottle of local whisky procured on the final stretch of the journey. The barrack room billets differed little from those around Magazine Square back in Leicester where the file had enlisted and trained, the barrack itself however was overwhelming to all, constructed of granite block and mostly built into the volcanic base on which the Edinburgh castle stood proud. The castle barracks itself could easily accommodate three or four Regiments if required, a large stable block by the huge entrance gates, stabled over a hundred horses for a sizable detachment of Dragoons.

Lieutenant McPherson's company spent the next two months within Edinburgh, the company drew from an almost endless flow of recruits, until at full strength the battalion compliment stood well over five hundred men, some like Zeke Turner had re-enlisted into the ranks but most were fresh and youthful, all ages appeared in the company, boys for drummers, experienced former soldiers for the junior non-commissioned ranks. Zeke, not wishing to take any more responsibility than necessary kept quiet when a senior sergeant had asked for volunteers to become junior corporals even though it would increase his daily pay well above the ranks of a private soldier, the files loss of Walsh to its compliment was already a severe blow to the remaining six men. For Zeke had grieved too many times before to become attached to these boys, for now his obligations to the file ended with their survival, he'd lost many fellows similar to Walsh on the fields of battle and knew very well while he served within His Majesties Army he would continue to lose men, friend was term rarely used by Zeke, comrades certainly but friendship came at a price and not one he was willing these days to consider flippantly.

The file had served almost a year within the Regiment, and McPherson's company finally began to learn skill at arms with the long land pattern musket. Individually the men of the company were given an unloaded second grade musket with which to familiarise himself with and after two full days spent shouldering the weapon until like foot drill it became a second nature to the user.

On the third day, the company learned to manoeuvre with present arms and were each issued each the seventeen inch forged steel bayonet and accompanying leather scabbard in which to sheath it, the men were instructed how to attach the blade to their leather waist belt, although those near Zeke paid more attention to him than the musketry Sergeant. McPherson's company finally started to look like professional soldiers, a far cry from the early days when the illiterate struggled to tell left from right.

The time eventually came when the senior Sergeants felt the recruits where ready for musketry practice, the troop were taken out the barracks accompanied by two horse pulled wagons containing powder, shot and the muskets themselves. The Sergeants formed their company's against the rural hillsides a few miles from the castle barracks and Corporals from the company sectioned the men into groups of ten finally issuing the lines a musket and five rounds of cartridge each. Zeke's file stepped forward to a flat upon the hillside marked by a series of short white pennant flags, the remainder of the company stood fifty paces behind as the musketry sergeant went through the loading procedures.

The group was instructed to remove one cartridge from his pouch and hold it firmly upright within his grasp, placing the cartridge top in the teeth the men were instructed to bite the top away from the remainder of the cartridge. Whilst gripping lead ball between the teeth a measure of powder is poured down the length of the barrel and the lead ball spat down the bore falling on top of the powder charge, the remained of the powder placed into the priming pan of the trigger mechanism and the paper wadding thumbed into the entrance to the barrel. The muskets ram rod was drawn and placed in the tip of the barrel then firmly rammed down the length of the barrel securing the complete charge into the base of the muskets barrel, the rod was then to be returned to the underside of the barrel and the firelock presented forwards.

Sergeant Vaughan asked the men individually if he understood the orders, after each man acknowledged the drill the sergeant issued them each a flint from a cloth bag instructing him to wedge it under the dog lock mechanism of the firing action and secure the holding screw into place. 'Right then lads, let's see what we've learned then, Load arms!' yelled Vaughan as each man in turn drew his weapon to his front and perched the middle part of the barrel by his left hand, the Sergeant called command to each movement as the file worked in unison and obeyed his instruction. Will bit hard and tore the thin paper shroud around the combination of lead and powder, tightly holding the lead ball between his teeth he poured the measure of the black powder into the barrel. With the lead shot firmly grasped in his teeth he spat the ball into the barrel, the bitter taste of black powder and greased paper resident in his dry mouth. The remainder of the powder poured into the open pan of the musket and the frizzen plate that would generate the spark once the flint struck was pulled back in readiness to discharge its wares.

The file collectively drew the long ram rod from underneath the muskets furniture and placed it ready into the top of the long steel barrel, Vaughan's eyes checked the soldiers action and when satisfied gave the order to ram the charge home. Releasing the thin steel rod it fell under its own weight compacting the paper wadding hard onto the measured black powder and lead ball.

Looking sideways Will noticed at several in the line nervously drop their rods and hastily pick them from the ground hoping their Sergeant would not pick them out for punishments. Now wracked by nerves Will's right hand shook with excitement as the rod was replaced and the muskets hammer was cocked in readiness to fire, finally Vaughan gave the order, 'Pre-sent' he barked the word drawing the word of command into a clear and concise order, 'Arms' he snapped quickly. The line raised their muskets to shoulder level in unison, Will felt the heavy barrel strain his arms as he desperately steadied the weapon, placing his index finger into the trigger guard and felt the slight pressure of the sprung mechanism resist his index finger as he prepared to fire his deadly weapon. 'Fire' bellowed Vaughan and Will slowly squeezed the trigger, click, he felt the lock mechanism release and the hammer slammed down striking the open pan of the weapon, a spark lit the powder and instinctively he closed his eyes to the blinding powder flash, his right cheek felt a sharp burning sensation as the powder ignited in a bright flame. Together, the muskets cracked loudly as the powder ignited the larger charge within the barrel, feeling the kick of the heavy musket into his right shoulder and catching him off balance he steadied himself somewhat embarrassed by his inexperience but Will was not alone in this unexpected result, the line staggered as the line of muskets recoiled from the blast. Ahead the long grass to the files front shuddered as the muskets spat the flaming lead ball into the hillsides slopes.

With the air pungent with the rotten smell of burnt powder Sergeant Vaughan addressed the file 'Good work lads' he commented, 'now again, till you can do it by your heart content' the Allen brothers both fuelled by adrenalin and excitement smiled amongst each other as Vaughan ordered ground arms and went through musketry drill over and over again.

By the end of the exercise all ten men in the detail were proficient in volley fire from the long smooth bored barrels, Vaughan accounted a professional soldier should fire three or four rounds per minute and with regular practice the detail would soon achieve this, 'Modern warfare' Vaughan continued to deliver his speech 'requires only that you present and level your arms to the enemy'.

This statement confused the recruits somewhat until Zeke informed him that with massed and concentrated fire the enemy should wither and fall under such devastating musketry. After discharging the five allocated rounds, the men of the line were dismissed and made their way back to the remaining company whilst another file stepped forwards to begin the same well practiced instruction.

Glancing at his right thumb, sore with an aching numbness Will shook his hand to distract the pain from his mind as the rejoined the company and sat upon the grassy hillside until each file had handled the muskets sufficiently to satisfy Sergeant Vaughan's standards of musketry.

Lying lazily upon the hillside, the file watched onwards amused by the swallows and swifts that dived deep into the valley below, turning sharply with each thunderous boom as the details in training discharged their muskets into an imaginary enemy.

McPherson's company left the hillside mid afternoon and returned along the ancient stone roads towards Edinburgh town, with faces smeared with the residue of black powder the file reflected on its development into King's Soldiers and as colonial tensions rose in the Americas, soon their skills would be put to test.

The company ate well within the garrisons cookhouse and shortly after returned to their billets, Sergeant Vaughan entered the bunk room and issued the men with their pay in full, the Sergeant informed the file they would be granted a leave of absence from the Kings duty for the night allowing the file if they so wished to leave the castle barracks. This would be the first time the group left the company's presence in almost a year and Zeke's soldiering experience proved as ever invaluable, a hot iron was placed in the billets glowing brazier and Zeke mixed starch with a little water in his mouth, rinsed and spat it on the items to be pressed before running the hot metal over the seams, 'Removes the lice' he informed the lads, 'ironing out the bugs'. With a month's pay in their purse the six men spent time grooming themselves and gathering each other's hair back into the fashionable tail behind the head to be tied with a length of black lace ribbon into a neat bow before embarking from the barracks down towards Edinburgh's drinking houses. Vaughan met the file at the garrisons gatehouse were a picket guard stood watch down the cobbled road towards the old town, 'Easy yourselves tonight Gentlemen' Vaughan advised, 'I need not remind you that a city can be a dangerous place' a statement Will needed not reminding of. The six men gestured acknowledgement to their Sergeant and in their smart well presented crisp white shirts, red tail coats and soft scarlet caps proudly displaying the number seventeen the men of McPherson's company set down castle hill towards the nearest taverns.

Edinburgh was a rapidly expanding city, the act of union had forged strong ties with England and prosperity provided the Lothian district with surplus cash to expand its size to accommodate the growing industrial population. New buildings still undergoing extravagant construction merged seamlessly with the old town, George Street named in honour of the monarch, with its clean sandstone blocks stood in the heart of the new town, perfectly laid out in symmetrical design these buildings of grand design flowed gracefully from its side streets contrasting the old town that had stood at the base of Edinburgh castle for centuries. In the old town however, multiple level buildings of medieval wooden construction loomed over the old and narrow cobbled streets, with a fast growing population of over fifty thousand inhabitants the old town reeked of poverty and the stench of humanity that comes with it, Will had seen much poverty in his time but this reached a new depth. Thom Allen had commented that he found it difficult to comprehend why the poor crammed themselves into such small spaces when the countryside had an abundance of space, Will who had grown up in similar although smaller surroundings to the city they found themselves within tried hard to find the words to satisfy such a simple question as the rural lads gawped in wonder of the cities delights. Poverty stricken, the poor peddled their wares on every street corner, fruit sellers challenged the men to try a apple or two from a basket laden with fruit and weavers plied their trade from cramped shop fronts, each floor of each wooden building overhung the lower one restricting the natural light given from the setting sun.

The file soon found what they'd aimed for, the Candle Makers tavern, the nearest tavern towards the cities heart with its small slate roofed the building stood on the far side of Candlemakers Row, graced by small cheap frosted glass window panes, the house leaned forwards into the street and its red door daubed with old flaking paint lay open enticing those who would pass by. The tavern split itself into two rooms with a serving area and cellar access in between, each room was accessed by a similar door to that of the entrance except its condition had not weathered so badly. Eagerly, John White was the first to enter the building, followed by Zeke, Coles and Will while the Allen brothers chanced their luck with cheap whores that took a fancy to their smart uniforms and the coins within their purse. White led the file to the lesser of the two rooms and made his way to the nearest unoccupied table with two tallow candles at either end providing a flickering of low light combined with the faint but sickly smell of rendered animal fat.

The crumbs from a loaf of bread was swept away by Zeke as the six removing their soft caps sat and decided on how they would start the evening. An auburn haired serving girl appeared and poured pale ale into six tankards and placing a coin towards her the girl scooped the fee into her palm and blessed the group a joyful evening, now with their tankards charged the file raised their vessels not caring for what was spilt and toasted the company's better fortunes. Zeke leant back against the wall, sucking on his sweet tobacco listening to the youths chatter as they recalled the memories of the previous year.

As darkness began to fall across Edinburgh, the old town gave way to a far seedier kind of life as thieves, peddlers, tinkers and whores replaced the honourable and civilised society and the dark back streets and alleyways became a hive for corruption and vice.

The six soldiers being newly paid spent heavily on their entertainments and soon attracted these types, gamblers and whores tried to ply their tricks and wares on the naïve soldiers and only the experience of Zeke prevented them from being fleeced of their pay and valuables. Will sat uneasy as some local lasses eyed him and his friends from a near table, John White had noticed the attentions too and gently elbowed him in between the ribs with a brash comment about his probable bed for the night, the group laughed at length to Wills obvious nervousness. Confidently, John White wasted little time in approaching these women and straddled the long bench, White began his tireless banter much to the amusement of his comrades who watched his efforts from the comfort of their snug.

The file consumed pitcher after pitcher of ale and the night passed into the early hours of the next day, laughing, drinking and smoking rich scented tobacco purchased from a peddler. Eventually John White having spent all his coin returned with his wanton bedfellows to the table hoping to ply them with more ale, no one minded the extra company as White's efforts amused the file with plenty of entertainment. The two local girls merry with strong alcohol giggled and flirted heavily with the file and in sensing Wills embarrassments playfully taunted his polite manners. Inexperienced with such attentions he squirmed as the buxom girls flaunted their bodies blatantly towards him mischievously aware of his naivety. Whilst Zeke's age and wisdom gave him a good judge of character he playfully allowed the group to enjoy the harmless fun given by these types despite them consuming the majority of every jug purchased but eventually with coin expended the six men released the interest of the women who left the tavern to pursue frolics elsewhere much to the irritation of White who having lost the chance with his bedfellows admitted defeat to the cost of three shillings pay.

The file took the long walk towards the barracks as the morning sun began to rise over the distant ocean, full of merriment and song Will felt the brotherhood of soldiering. A new family had been gained in the most unlikely of circumstances, the bond between the group had grown strong over the many months they'd spent together and despite the tragic loss of one of their kind the six men had gained a harmony most knew little of, they'd grown to depend upon each other and trust one another with their lives. This would be a bond to serve them well.

For the next few months the file saw the battalion grow in its complement and Will remarked on the youthful looks of the new arrivals oblivious to time he'd spent with the colours he'd now entered his nineteenth year. The 17th Regiment with its new arrivals stood at ten full companies with each company holding forty men, the Regiment finding good use for all comers recruited to the ranks, orphaned boys as young as ten years of age became drummers and pipers, those with height joined Captain William Brereton's Grenadier company, for the most however a red coat and 'Brown Bess' musket would suffice to make them soldiers with the numerous companies of line infantry. Sergeant Vaughan had often pressed Zeke towards a junior company position, to the Sergeant an old soldier would be invaluable in a Regiment full of newly enlisted soldiers and until now Zeke had resisted the pressures only finally agreeing when the Vaughan suggested separating the six into newer less experienced files.

Well over five hundred men now occupied the castle barracks in Edinburgh, the once spacious surroundings now gave way to cramped musty billets as each dormitory burst at the seams with eager young men enlisted into the 17th Regiment. On acceptance of the Corporals rank Zeke was issued a gold coloured embroidered epaulette to indicate his position in McPherson's company and the ranks received new blood to bring it up to strength, although the six would keep them at arm's length at least until they had proved their worth.

Summer passed into the fall season and the fine weather at last began to turn, with daily musket drill though rarely with shot McPherson's company became proficient in skill at arms and complex battle field manoeuvres. Each morning the companies would parade to be inspected by the senior sergeants and dismissed as each saw fit, at harvest time the company was hired by local land owners to engage in fruit picking with each man paid extra for his duty, although the hours were long, the monotony and boredom of barrack room life was broken for the time being at least and the extra pay came in handy for the file, on receiving their additional pay each week the file pooled the extra coins together and enjoy the entertainments of old Edinburgh town or purchase a few luxury goods to make a soldiers life more tolerable.

By the end of October 1772 news came of the seventeenth's forthcoming appointment to Ireland, McPherson's company was detailed at Leith docks to assist in the early embarkation of the Regiments baggage and belongings.

Barrels of salted beef and pork were rolled along the quayside, stacked ready to be loaded onto the broad brigantines chartered to transport the battalion to Ireland. With access daily to the public life news came of civil unrest in the American colonies, Coles tried his best to explain the situation in the new world as best he could from what he'd managed to read in the available printed news sheets. Coles talked without end attempting to enlighten the others with the crown's policies in colonial America although to the remaining five Coles amused himself more than his audience who regarded the whole affair as some distant quarrel that affected their lives so little.

Together, the six men rolled barrel after barrel along the quayside towards the awaiting ship, her tall masts held furled sails tight to its timbers as she lay alongside the commercial docks. Sailors and merchantmen worked busily between the file, dashing in between the soldiers as space became available, mules harnessed into a cradle slings hauled high over head to be landed on the decks and herded below into the ships hold, the bustle of the port moved at a terrific pace as trunks, crates and barrels of provisions were loaded onto the ship in readiness for the advance companies departure to the Irish province. The six took time from their labours and drank heavy from their canteens, red faced with exertion in the fresh ocean breeze Will caught his breath as he rested his arms upon stacks of wooden crates, sweat running freely down his spine and soaking into his cotton shirt, his warm breath caught the cold air providing him measure of the cold morning. Thom Allen removed his boots and rubbed his toes to circulate the blood and Zeke took the opportunity to light his ever ready pipe, drawing long and hard on his preferred scented tobacco before offering it to his comrades. White and Dan Allen sat amongst the high stacked crates with legs swinging beneath them as Sam Coles drew his sketch book from his belongings and with charcoal salvaged from the billet rooms brazier outlined each characters pose, the sketch dated October 1772, Leith Docks.

The file eventually returned to the billet at sundown, a heavy days work complete the file now too exhausted to do anymore than lay upon their bunks and rest tired bones after an exerting days labours. Arriving too late for supper, Zeke managed to scrounge mutton and beef platters as a late meal and before long the file slipped into the nights silence, as the hush befell the billet Will opened his eyes wide as the billets door was kicked inwards without warning, 'Turn out . . . get up and get fell in!' yelled Vaughan aggressively

Instinctively the six jumped to attention, grabbing his tailcoat Will stood in front of his bunk quickly fastening the pewter buttons and adjusting his felt hat. 'Corporal' Vaughan addressed Zeke formally 'Account for your men'.

Zeke Turner knew exactly what had happened as he'd seen this behaviour before, 'All present Sergeant' he replied to the anxious Vaughan. Sergeant Vaughan swiftly left the billet room caring little for the confusion amongst the ranks he had caused.

Will and the others looked perplexed towards Zeke. 'Looks like desertion to me lads' Zeke calmly stated 'We had best hope it's not one from our company'.

A sharp whistle blew from the outside parade ground and the battalions drummers struck up a beat, Zeke ushered the file to form up into company order outside.

The bright moon shone down upon the parade square silhouetting each company against the cobbled ground as seldom seen Officers were observed discussing the situation amongst themselves with senior

Sergeants furiously pacing the lines of each file desperately counting their companies strength, the men from McPherson's company where counted by Vaughan who informed his officer all present and correct clearly showing signs of relief through his otherwise tense features.

The file learned Captain Leslie's company was missing two men, both newly enlisted at Earlstowne, a half day march west of Berwick. The seventh company had lacked recruits into its ranks falling far behind the other companies in strength and the officer had instructed the files nemesis to fill the ranks by any means possible, Zeke felt it highly likely the two absconders had felt the familiar wrath of Skinner.

McPherson's company would assist Leslie in the hunt for the fugitives, the company was ordered to make ready with full field kit and equipment, the six returned to their billet and hastily packed their belongings into their small packs and knapsacks ready for the advance at first light. As dawn broke both companies formed in triple line at the garrisons main gates, the gate guards swung open the heavy barred doors revealing the breaking sunrise over the chimney smoked skyline of Edinburgh, the towns silence broken to feet of seventy men marching in unison down from castle hill towards the southern gates of the old town. The two companies soon reached the outskirts of the city and broke formation into single file, Zeke's junior rank now privileged him to company orders, he revealed to the file the absconders had confided with a third man within Leslie's company revealing their proposed destination, the combined companies would make for the small town of Dalkeith with hopes to capture the two deserters there.

The hundred soldiers arrived in Dalkeith at midday flanked to the right by a squadron of mounted militia, crossing the sweeping stone bridge that spanned the river Esk the town thrived from. Both companies' officers rode well ahead of the seventy or so men who now fell under the command of the senior sergeants.

A tall granite Celtic cross marked the market place of the Lothian village, the arrival of English redcoats brought painful recollections to the elder generations, window boards slammed shut fearful of the army's presence for the Jacobean rebellion of 1745 was still fresh in the memories of Scotland. The soldiers stood around in groups resting their weary arms on their land pattern Brown Bess muskets, the still winter air bit into the flesh of any one foolish enough to stand idle for too long.

Vaughan broke his company into four groups of ten men and fanned them out towards the southern perimeter of the village boundary whilst Skinner detailed his men to search the village market place and move eastwards towards the outlying and distant dwellings. The Sergeant having returned from a briefing with McPherson ordered the file to move towards the southern farms and heath lands on the Old Berwick road.

The file moved slowly through the thick heather scrubland lifting each step high to avoid the boggy ground underfoot, Zeke placed ten yards distance between each man as the file edged its way towards a distant farm dwelling rising upwards from the market town, through the winter fog smoke from the stone crofters cottage drifted high above the thatched roof as the line of redcoats approached.

The silence was broken suddenly by a commotion from the distant patrol, the heads of the red coated soldiers snapped back towards the noise, one of the fugitives had bolted as Skinners company approached an abandoned stone outbuilding. The helpless refugee stumbled and fell through the brush in his haste to escape the advancing line of infantry, Skinner ordered his men to fix bayonets as they made ground on the half starved, freezing wretch. As the file turned towards the event, Will could see only too clearly the events that unfolded before him, the exhausted fugitive knowing his chance of escape had gone sank to his knees with his back to the oncoming soldiers, his filthy cotton shirt torn on the thorny bushes that had hindered his escape.

'Shoot him!' cried Skinner as he furiously raced towards the captive and the soldiers that surrounded him, the ranks from Skinners Company stood still uncertain that they'd heard the order correctly, Zeke and Sergeant Vaughan upped pace towards the incident knowing what Skinner was capable of in his blind fury. Increasing his stride through the bog, Will struggled to keep pace with the rest of the file but all too late, Skinner snatched a primed musket from the nearest soldier and pulling back the hammer discharged his shot squarely in to the back of the prone captive. The musket spat its lead in an explosion of flame from the barrel, the fugitive's body jerked forward then slumped face down onto the cold muddy ground, his ragged torn shirt smouldering from the close proximity of the muskets powder discharge, Vaughan and Zeke well ahead of the rest of the file checked pace, too late to intervene Skinner had found his prize.

The second fugitive screamed from the collapsed cottage 'Don't shoot, don't shoot' he blurted out his words desperately hoping against a similar fate as Skinner swiftly turned to face him directing his steel bayonet at his belly, he advanced on the second man who fell to his knees pleading for his life. Of this Will was certain, if Vaughan had not been present this man would feel the cold blade plunge deep inside his gut but Skinner knew the eyes of Vaughan were upon him and hesitated from delivering the fatal lunge.

Skinner swung his musket into the helpless man's face, reeling sideward he became hysterical as the soldiers picked him from the ground and shackled him in irons. Zeke rubbed his brow with his thumb and index finger and as his head dipped down Will sensed the frustration he felt once again with Skinners personal injustices.

The march towards Edinburgh was quiet and solemn, the sun began to set by mid afternoon and the cold crisp moor lands became illuminated by the bright moon. A thousand thoughts raced through the minds of the six knowing Skinners seniority would protect him from justice as the two company officers had received report from him that the fugitive refused to yield and had been shot as a last ditch attempt to subdue him. Will asked Zeke why Sergeant Vaughan had not intervened in Skinners report to Clayton but Zeke himself struggled to explain in simple terms the procedures of a military tribunal and courts martial in a case where justice had been administered in the field, 'No sane man will testify against a sergeant and besides who would care about the welfare of a deserter?'

Will shrugged his shoulders at the answer, trying to find a humanistic argument against this Regimental system, Zeke continued 'we've crossed Skinner before and suffered his wrath, would you care to cross him again for you know at firsthand what he's capable of' Zeke ended the statement tucking his cold pipe inside his woollen waistcoat as he moved up the line of soldiers bringing the pointless conversation to an abrupt end.

The two companies arrived back at the castle around midnight as a hard ground frost settled on the turnpikes and pathways of the town. The garrisons guard took the prisoner from the returning party escorting the pitiful man inside the castles ancient medieval cells. The files billets had stood unoccupied all day holding a chill about the air as Daniel Allen struck his flints into some shaved goat hair kindling picked from his backpack and after several attempts eventually the flame took to the dry kindling of the room's brazier. The damp straw crackled into life as the glowing embers smouldered and give life and a little light into the otherwise darkened room, taking flame from the brazier John White lit the candle stubs and the billet became home once again to the six as the file settled down for the remainder of the night.

Zeke woke the billet at dawn the following morning, the battalion had been ordered to a full order parade and the file was given an hour to prepare for Regimental inspection as dirty boots were polished, creased shirts pressed and hair waxed, dressed and tied, Zeke checked and double checked each man before turning out on parade knowing well what was in order for the battalion that morning. This was an impressive sight for any man to see, McPherson's company fell in line with each man carrying his full weight of equipment, the Regiment's complement of ten companies formed into a hollow square with drummers and the tallest of Grenadiers wielding eight foot halberds on each corner. In the centre of the square lay a wooden stave frame made from long ash poles tied together to form a pyramid shape, the captured fugitive was escorted from the guard house and without noise or complaint strapped to the structure. The prisoner's hands held high and bound to the heights of the fame whilst his ankles spread far apart and roped to the base. With all ranks and company officers present, Captain Clayton read from the Kings regulations and the articles of war charging the prisoner with desertion announcing the punishment to the man who now shivered uncontrollably with fear and cold combined. The fugitive was to receive ninety lashes for his desertion, Zeke whispered into Will's ear how lucky he was to receive such a mild punishment, a harsh court-martial would have sentenced the prisoner to over two hundred, lucky? Will thought, lucky would be to not get caught.

A drummer from the prestigious grenadier company was selected to administer the punishment and in tearing open the prisoner's shirt, the feeble thin cotton tore to reveal his milky white skinned bare back. The punishment began as the drummers rolled their sticks onto the tight skin of their instruments as the lash lay motionless in the hand of the administrator until Sergeant Skinner signalled for the punishment to proceed.

'One' yelled Skinner through gritted teeth, The drummer twisted his body to gain a momentum of force and like a coiled spring swung the lash across its victim's body, the captive yelped with pain as the leather straps of the lash cut deep into his back. All those present could see the damage done by the first blow alone and winced at the anticipation of the next strike, a series of blood red lines formed across the pale back of the prisoner as Skinner called for the second stroke to be dealt. The man cried with pain as the lash bit hard into his already bleeding skin, Skinner dramatically drew out each call to prolong the moment as the prisoners back arched to avoid the leather knots of the cat.

By forty lashes to man passed out through pain, Captain Leslie called for the flogging to be stopped despite a protest from Skinner that the prisoner had received less than half of his punishment, examining the prisoner a Sergeant of the Grenadier company shook his head towards the drummer indicating this vile spectacle finally over. Barely alive the prisoner was cut loose from his bonds and carefully placed face down on the hard ground, his flesh merged to a messy pulp of blood, skin and tissue, the likelihood of anyone surviving such a harsh flogging was slim. The victim was doused by a bucket of salty water and by washing away the mess of bare flesh the parade could see the extent of the fugitive's punishment, the knots in the lash had cut deep into the man's back and with each swing tearing clumps of flesh from his body and oozing blood from his bare and open wounds soaking into the man's white canvas trousers. The prisoners comrades attended to his wounds as best they could carrying him away to his billet for treatment, this man's survival now lay with his comrade's commitment to tending his wounds, Will knew should anything similar happen to him he would be glad of the company he kept. The companies were individually dismissed from the parade ground and returned to their own billets, the general orders confined each company to their barracks as punishment to the Regiment for the fugitive's misdemeanour, the six men lay around smoking cheap rum laced tobacco whilst Coles oiled and restrung his violin in readiness for a more appropriate occasion.

The cold November hit Edinburgh hard, heavy snows prevented the battalion from leaving the town and thick ice set around the shores of the docks preventing anything but the heaviest of ship movements. By the end of the month the snow had fallen heavier than ever, shallow slate roofs strained as their inhabitants venturing into the cold outside struggled to clear the weight from the awkward stone tiles. The file used its time usefully supplementing their meagre pay clearing lanes and roads into the capital whilst the work was hard the extra pay came in handy for the soldiers to purchase provisions useful to a soldier, unskilled heavy labour came cheap in Edinburgh, the men worked tirelessly together to gain a few extra pennies. The extreme weather had confined the battalion to within the perimeter of the city walls, nights were long as days were short and boredom festered within the ranks as Zeke tried his best to keep the file occupied, competitive fist fights between companies best men would often be settled within the barracks backrooms with high stakes placed upon the winning outcome.

The Regiment's companies paraded daily as a method of occupying the soldiers abundance of time although as equipment was rarely used the time spent preparing it for inspection became less each day adding to the frustrations of already frustrated and jaded men. Rivalry between company's became fierce, as each sergeant tried to outshine the others in presentation the pride of each company was pressed hard into the ranks, Sergeant Vaughan was a soldiers soldier, he enlisted as had most of his fellow countrymen at an early age and progressed through the ranks quickly as the Regiment lost men through war and disease, in peaceful times however promotion came hard if at all, battalions were disbanded or at best reduced to half strength, a fate that befell Zeke with his previous Regiment. Sergeant James Vaughan chose wisely amongst his ranks for the best candidates to assist his soldiering duties and Zeke Turner fitted Vaughan's bill perfectly. A seasoned soldier who knew how to get the best from a man and the tricks the lower ranks might pull. Confinement albeit involuntary to barracks bred trouble, as the snows continued to fall heavy on the Lothian and surrounding districts, the billets and bunkhouses stank of stale sweat as men struggled to unfreeze the water pipes from the garrisons deep wells to the many hand pumps, lead pipes burst open each night and stone water troughs froze several inches thick with ice.

Soldiers tales became stretched bearing on the ridiculous at times as men thought of new ways to amuse themselves, tempers frayed and the inevitable fights took place amongst the staunchest of friends.

The Regimental Sergeants took it upon themselves to arrange prize fights amongst each company, the financial bounty for the victor was high, lucrative enough for a man to risk his life in a bare knuckle fist fight with a man more than capable of breaking ones neck with a single blow. Sergeant Vaughan asked each file for a volunteer to enter the unofficial yet highly celebrated contest, only John White seemed interested and with passionate persuasion from Sergeant Vaughan thus became the champion elect of

McPherson's company. White's physique owed much to his profession, apprenticed to a carpenter, White knew extreme heavy labour, with the weight gained from a regular diet and hard physical work his defined muscle tone showed it well. Stripped to the waist with knuckles bandaged in strips of dirty white cotton rag, John White looked formidable as a prize fighter, his shoulder length dark hair loosely tied behind him, with piercing deep blue eyes White took on the easy if not reluctant challenges from other files within McPherson's company that offered to give him experience in bare fist fights quickly dominating the company's fighting.

Vaughan favoured White to take the Regiments supreme title and bet heavily on him, success meant winning very high stakes for his gamble but as interest in the competition increased the secrecy of the fights became harder to conceal from the Regiments officers as the demand to watch the contests increased. Often a fight between company champions would be abandoned half way as an officer approached a little too close to the barrack rooms. John White's chance to shine as the company fight champion came soon enough.

Vaughan had arranged for White to fight a company Sergeant from Lieutenant Sawford's ranks, the files billet would hold the venue and bunks were hastily arranged to provide room for the ensuing brawl as over thirty men packed as tight as sardines into the small billet room designed to hold barely more than ten, the billets sanitary buckets where emptied, swilled and filled with snow to cool down the fighters during the breaks between fighting. The fighters were provided with a second to assist in between the rounds and in surprise to Will, John chose him to assist in between the bouts rounds. The fight began badly for White, felled twice in the opening round White insisted on continuing despite a series of painful small cuts and splits around his deep set eyes, cringing at the extent of his friends injuries Will swabbed the sores with goose fat to ease the split skin as White once again faced a series of blows from his adversary in the following rounds. Sawford's fighter stood over six feet tall, a mammoth of a man with the physical shape for the grenadiers but clearly without the speed or intelligence for the reputable company. Dazed, John White struggled to connect his punches to his opponent eventually using what feeble strength he had to protect his self from the rein of blows directed upon him until the third round was finally called. These types of fight would typically end with one man unconscious and at this rate White would not last the next round despite both bewildered fighters constantly baited and egged on by the heaving spectators who had waged heavily on the outcome, the final round started with the fighters thrown back into the fray to the cheers for the baying crowd. Now desperate, Will shouted to end the fight for the sake of White's injuries but his voice was unheard above the din of the maddening crowd.

White was sapped of strength, bloody and near blind with cuts and swollen eyes he stumbled around the ring falling to his knees as his opponent stood over his vulnerable body in readiness to deliver the next blow should his adversary attempt to raise to his feet.

The straw that once lay thick upon the floor had been cleared to a corner of the room to avoid the fighters losing their footing on the surface slippery with sweat and blood, in this excitement blind panic over ruled all calm and sense as a yell was heard from the rear of the billet, the crowd surged into the fighters area pushing their way towards the door in a mad panic. A tallow candle that illuminated the room had unsettled and fallen to the floor igniting the highly combustible materials that stacked the billets corners, with the light source extinguished the billet quickly became a dark smoky hovel as the occupants scrambled to the doorway to escape the rapidly expanding blaze. This room could not have been a better tinderbox, the bunks had been stacked together to maximise the floor space for the numerous spectators and the high piled straw was perfect to start the inferno, the dry tinder soon spread flames to the parched timber roof supports, within seconds the barrack room was in chaos. Men struggled to exit the blaze quickly and those too slow became trampled underfoot in the confusion as the occupants scrambled to get outside into the clean and breathable night air.

Outside, the snow continued to fall thick as the last of the rooms occupants dashed away from the scene in an attempt to avoid incrimination in this unlawful act, the file gathered outside having snatched what few belongings they had, Sam Coles complained bitterly that his knapsack had been crushed underfoot during the escape splintering his fragile treasured violin, as Coles muttered to himself regarding his petty loss. Zeke suddenly snapped 'Where's White?'. Dan spoke up claiming he thought he had seen White crawl to the exit early in the confusion but Zeke angrily snapped the reply to the brother, 'Where in hells name is he then?' adding 'The lad could hardly stand let alone save himself'. Having lost one member of the file already Will's instinct to protect those close to him kicked in as he turned to face the blazing inferno, the flames leapt through the falling thatch of the roof and the windows small glass panes cracked and shattered under the intense heat inside and Thom Allen encircled his arms around him forcibly preventing Will from entering the raging fire. Above the crackle of flame, timbers spilt and crashed to the floor as Will wrestled Thom's grasp free and made for the burning billets entrance. At the entrance to the billet room the heat quickly scorched his exposed skin as he turned to protect himself from the high temperatures. A barrel of icy rainwater stood to the left of the door and hurriedly knocking the wooden lid from it, Will smashed the thick layer of ice and soaked his cotton shirt sleeves liberally giving him a small fighting chance of withstanding the enraging flames he was about to enter. Will took a deep breath and covered his mouth as best he could with his drenched shirt sleeve, the room was a haze of smoke and flame but as the billet had been previously cleared for the fighting Will did not have far to search for White.

John White's unconscious body lay curled in a foetal position to the left side of the room just a few yards from the doorway, Will ducked to avoid the spiting flames from the well established burning roof timbers and tumbling straw thatch. Hot charred timbers and smouldering ash fell about him as he struggled to make his way to his vulnerable friend, as the smoke choked his lungs, his watering eyes made it all the more difficult to see in an already obscured room.

Knowing his best chance of survival was to stay low to the floor Will dropped to his knees and began to fumble his way across the darkened room, feeling the floor with his finger tips he desperately grasped for a human shape, suddenly success as his palms touched his comatose comrade. Placing his arms around White's waist, Will dragged the heavy mass towards the exit as the roof supports creaked under the strain of the roofs weight, the weakened frame struggled to hold itself as the far end collapsed onto the stacked bunks. Frustrated at the lack of progress Will screamed at White to help him in his struggle but this was a useless call, White already battered from his adversaries blows had succumbed into unconsciousness in a room full of chocking acrid smoke and fumes, as Will began to lose hope a figure appeared beside them quickly followed by another, Zeke and Thom had dowsed themselves and entered the rescue half expecting to be recovering Will as well as White. The three lifted Whites heavy body and dashed a swift departure from the room as the burning roof timbers finally collapsed seconds after they cleared the doorway.

His rescuers carried White a few yards clear of the building and gazed with horror to the extent of his injuries now evident in the brightness of the moon light, his once thick black hair scorched bare on his right side, his skin blistered around his eyes and forehead and his hands curled into a claw like shape, this once strikingly handsome lad had transformed into a figure of horror. The clean air caused Will to cough heavily as his lungs cleared of the acrid smoke as Zeke assessed White's injuries shaking his head on close examination, charred skin peeled away from his flesh as the heat seared deep into his bones and his muscular chest blistered into a huge and ugly red sore.

By now the garrisons Guard had arrived upon the scene and Captain Leslie had formed a line of men to attempt to douse the flames however this was a token action since the building once the home to the file was gone, the roof finally collapsed into a smouldering pile of debris within its centre leaving the exterior wall to slowly crumble into the inferno. Leslie continued his men in drenching the timbers to prevent the smouldering ashes from flaring up and igniting once again. Vaughan appeared besides the party and rested his hand gently on Zeke's shoulder, 'pity the poor lad, a fine soldier indeed' gazing down at Whites dying body 'best get him moved to shelter quickly'. White was carefully placed in a canvas hammock and carried to the garrison's infirmary but little could be done for him, with shallow breath he lay upon his back for three days never once waking. The remaining five of the original seven men who enlisted under Sergeant Lucas at Leicester took turns in replacing the damp linen strips on his wounds until finally some change occurred in his condition. On the fourth day White opened his eyes, Sam Coles was present and immediately sent for the rest to come quickly to the infirmary, Zeke, Will, Thom and Dan rushed to his bedside and in turn each man asked John how he felt offering soft words of encouragement towards his recovery, White smiled as best he could although he knew his time was now upon him, clearly in intense pain his eyes glazed in frustration of trying to speak but no words came from these cracked and parched lips. Coles poured a little water from his canteen into White's mouth but he could not keep it down, spluttering the fluid he turned to Will, smiled and slowly closed his eyes, with that final moment John White passed into the eternal sleep. Will bowed his head and removed his soft winter cap as the others followed suit, Zeke gave White the final dignity and covered his disfigured body with a thin blanket and left their friend to his peace.

The five left the infirmary and made their way silently to their allocated temporary billets, the fire had consumed much with only a few personal belongings salvaged by the file but Will had saved nothing, his belongings now consisted of the clothes he stood in less his tail coat, Will had been lucky to save his life let alone any of his issued equipment. The losses would be deducted from the files pay although Sergeant Vaughan had collected a total of fifteen shillings from other companies to ease their loss but Zeke elected the fee would be used to ensure White a decent burial by most standards, his loss had been appreciated by not only the file but by those of Vaughan's company too, in solemnity none of the remaining five attended Whites interment although between them they made sure his burial to be with dignity and with fitting memoriam Zeke carved Whites initials and a Celtic cross into the hard stone of the barrack room walls, now immortalised in time White's presence would forever be a part of Edinburgh castle.

Over the next few days Will received a new tailcoat and other replacement equipment and in their temporary home the five prepared the new equipment to the battalions standards, whitening leather, blacking shoes and softening the felt hats to the seasoned shapes of a professional soldier, searching through the charred remains of their billet, Will recovered only James Walsh's penny whistle amongst the ashes, wiping the tarnish from its once shiny exterior Will tucked the instrument into his tunic and thought on, of all the things to survive the blaze, a dead lads belongings only remained, ironic yes, but to Will the trinket would remain for now a keep sake to both Walsh and White as he continued his life within the ranks.

The weather improved as January gave way to February, the long expected thaw brought floods to the outlining countryside and the docks at Leith sprang back into commercial life as the heavy ships of His Majesties Royal and Commercial Navy smashed through the weakened pack ice. Sam Coles sketched often during the final days at Edinburgh most notably the new roof as it went reconstruction over the shell of the files former billet, being this time sensibly relayed with slate rather than the thatched insulation that blazed through the billet rooms. Within a week the Regiment was ready for its departure from Edinburgh and the Companies turned out in full parade for inspection, the Regiments Colonel, Charles Mawhood stood present in his full military regalia as junior staff officers dashed around the authoritarian figure whilst he carefully inspected the ranks along the garrisons large cobbled square.

All ten companies paraded in full kit as respective officers positioned themselves in front of the ranks, their gentleman's swords presented squarely towards the Colonel as he and his adjutants walked the endless line of red coated soldiers, company Sergeants barked orders incoherently to the untrained but to the professional soldier each sound was a given signal to carry a manoeuvre. In turn each Officer proudly presented his own company for inspection, Darby, Clayton, McPherson, Scott, Tew, Sawford, Leslie, Seymour, Collinridge and Brereton, as the gentleman officers took their turn to display their troops to the Regiments commanding officer. Will was more than aware of inter Regimental rivalry as he'd heard Zeke often criticise other units for sloppiness but now he felt fierce pride within his own file and company, under Zeke and Sergeant Vaughan, McPherson's lads were the pride of the Regiment. Zeke cracked a wry smile from the corner of his mouth as he looked across the ranks of his company, full with pride and honour his file stood firm to attention, now the epitome of the professional soldier, in unison leather soled feet stamped the ground hard on command of the senior sergeant, hands slapped the dark mahogany woodwork of the now familiar Brown Bess musket and firmly presented their arms to the Regiments most senior officer.

This was a moment Private Will Snow felt a responsibility and pride to himself, his comrades and to his glorious Regiment.

In order of precedence Captain Brereton's Grenadiers led the parade from the garrison as drummers beat the Regimental march, the companies in all their magnificence marched proudly down from the castle at Edinburgh to its busy docks, with this grand spectacle crowds lined the narrow streets of the old town gazing at such impressive grandeur, stay dogs ran alongside the endless line of smart red coated soldiers barking and yapping in excitement and snapping at the heels as the men marched perfectly through the winding cobbled lanes. Zeke stood with authority on the flanks of McPherson's company as the battalion formed up into line along the quayside, the docks already alive with activity harboured over a dozen ships ready to transport the company's across the seas to the

Regiments next garrison. The long wooden gangways connected the quay to the tall mast sailing ships, ordered to remove their bayonets from the muskets the company was assigned to board an allocated vessel.

Lieutenant McPherson signalled Vaughan to embark his men aboard a transport and the files formed in a single line and the signal was given to board the ship, carefully Will trod the steep wooden boards towards the upper deck of the ship firmly grasping the thick twisted hemp ropes either side of the planks and in glancing down he watched the last loads of provisions be hoisted aboard the moored transport vessels as the gangplanks were dragged aboard the laden ships ready for the signal to depart. The long lines of red coated soldiers flowed steadily into the abyss of the lower decks via a steep narrow stepped ladder, Zeke's file in turn was given the order to go below desks after passing their muskets and cartridge boxes to a detail of Marines governed by a smart uniformed Naval officer. The narrow opening to the lower deck gave cause for all to bow their heads as they entered, after adjusting his eyes to the low light Will removed his felt hat and slid his equipment from his back cradling it within his fore arm, together the five men placed their equipment against the sloping sides of the vessel 'McPherson has given word for all ranks on deck' Zeke spoke 'So claim your bunks and let us oblige the gentleman officer' he added.

The lower deck had no natural light other than the narrow access hatch above highlighting the fine dust within the still air, Coles rummaged around his knapsack until he found what he was looking for, a tallow candle to illuminate their new quarters 'Ships and fire don't blend well lad' said Zeke in his usual sarcastic tone, pre-empting Coles desire to provide light to the darkened hold. With the officers orders in mind the five men made there way back up the slatted ladder and onto the bright sunlit decks, rows of men stood at the sides of the ship as the last of the Regiment embarked from the quayside into the awaiting transports.

The company formed motionless in line as huge furled canvas sails began to drop heavily filling with the sea breeze and causing all underneath

to flinch at these unfamiliar sounds. Will tilted his head backwards to
see the magnificence of the ships towering masts, feeling a nauseous and
giddy at the distance above as nimble sailors darted around the rigging
balancing upon thin timber spars with extreme agility, their dexterous
hands moved along the cross masts and unfurled the remaining heavy
canvas sails ready for embarkation to the seas.

Sprightly sailors scaled the network of intricate rigging with ease,
running from side to side past the bewildered soldiers as orders were
given to cast off. The thick heavy mooring cables dragged through the grey
waters to be hauled aboard as the slow moving hulks towed by longboats
slowly eased from their moorings and departed the from the quay side, the
strong ocean breeze soon filled the huge canvas sheets as they absorbed
the brisk marine winds. The ship lowly listed and eased away from the
quayside towards the convoy escort that lay anchored a quarter mile off
shore, the second rate ship of the line HMS Brilliance watched over the
departing voyageurs as the transport ships gained speed she dropped sails
and positioned herself off the starboard sides of the fleet.

Fair and favourable winds speedily sailed the transports and her
escort around the northern shores of Scotland and across the Irish Sea to
Donaghadee, a coastal fishing port too small to take the large brigantine
transports each company was disembarked off shore in lime washed long
boats a file at a time and rowed the last half mile of ocean to Irish soil.

The Regiment's companies quickly mustered and moved southwards
towards Dublin just a few days march away, on route Sam Coles talked
endlessly along the roads to the provincial capital city, either amusing
himself or his comrades Will cared not to ask but the chirpiness and
enthusiasm in his voice amused all that listened, a knowledgeable source
on most matters Coles kept the files spirits high with his political satires of
current events and not one tired of his talk, although very few understood
it to the level Coles would have wished. Having failed to replace his violin
lost during the billet fire, Coles enquired to Will for Walsh's tin whistle
and picked a tune fitting for a company of marching soldiers, Sergeant

Vaughan felt the company's moral lifted as Coles played and objected little to the lapse of order the senior officers might have preferred.

The Irish weather had favoured the march, the traditionally wet early spring months had offered little more than an occasional light shower making the heavy woollen tail coats of the soldiers more comfortable to bear, all but Will who had replaced most of his lost equipment in Edinburgh complained bitterly of the state of disrepair of their uniforms and belongings, despite soldiers with a tailors skill repairing as best they could thinning elbows and leather soles most would have long disregarded their shoddy clothing, knapsacks split and burst their stitched seams as the soldiers crammed their treasured belongings into any available space.

Irelands commercial roads gave the Regiment good progress towards the walled city of Dublin, Leinster county's rolling green hills guarded the sunken lanes leaving the countryside unspoiled by the expanding industrialism that had began to scar the rural landscapes of this beautiful land, for most this would be their first time away from the mother country, for many, a country some would never see again.

*   *   *

Chapter Three

The Boyne

The Regiment made camp on the outskirts of Dublin by the middle of April 1773, a year that would see widespread civil unrest in the American colonies and come to play a huge part in the Regiment's future histories. As the company arrived at its garrison it found their service would not afford the luxury of purpose built garrisons that Berwick or Edinburgh had provided, the past turbulence of this catholic nation stood ever poised for an uprising and forced the crown to station scores of readily available Regiments and Corps in the event of any rebellion against the crown. The comfort of warm militia garrisons were given to the fashionable cavalry Regiments and despite the 17th's seniority to other Regiments this meant little when it came to any order of precedence, the light Dragoons had already garrisoned within the walled city and the 17th were left to find billets as best they could in and around the surrounding area.

Sergeant Vaughan tried his best to billet the ranks of McPherson's company in private houses or inns but the hostility caused by years of military occupation left little welcoming to the weary troops desperate for warm billets for the night and eventually Vaughan reluctantly gave in to a lost cause and set camp with the company under temporary canvas along the edge of Summerhill two hours march from Dublin. The company saw little of its Officers whilst at camp, only occasionally Lieutenant McPherson ride into the company's camp and briefly spoke to Vaughan on matters of the battalion's movements. Active service in Ireland had reduced a soldiers pay by a penny a week, a shilling and four pence was drawn from the Regimental pay clerk fortnightly and often spent quickly on strong drink provided by travelling peddlers to the newly paid soldiers keen to indulge in some small luxury. The monotony of soldiering began to show in the strained patience of the ranks, restricted in their movements the soldiers began to bicker amongst themselves as weeks of boredom and endless drill frustrated the company, Zeke kept his file busy finding labour for the five on a nearby farm three miles from the encampment, the daily income afforded the file a dry billet at a nearby farm cottage rented privately from the absent English landlord, the single roomed thick stone walled abode kept the men dry and warm during the showery month of May during which the five men arrived at dawn every morning at the nearby farms high walled entrance waiting for the farm manager to allocate each man his task. For the remainder of the month and into the next together the five worked rebuilding the crumbling dry stone boundary wall that isolated the English landlord from the tenant farmers. The heavy labour kept the men cheerful as they unloaded a large wooden cart of reclaimed stone into groups according to size, ready to be skilfully laid into the collapsed wall, Will watched with fascination as Dan and Thom Allen who familiar with this type of work layer stone after stone into a interlocking network of rough rock so well fitting the thinnest coin was hard pushed to fit the gaps. The file worked from dawn till dusk seven days a week and for their efforts in addition to regular daily pay the dry billet was a welcome reward for the labours each man made.

Daily after dusk Zeke led his file back along the muddy tracks towards the tenant farm house to receive their pay, he had negotiated eight pence per day for each mans labours and although individually they received only six pence, but no one objected to Zeke's management of the extra pay used to procure necessities for the file to survive with some comforts, rather than waste their additional pay on cheap gin, Zeke procured extra blankets enabling the file to discard their moth eaten and thread bare ones issued on their enlistments.

For most of the dry summer months the five men laboured on the farmstead only required weekly to report for company duties, with such a heavy military presence in the area any potential threat of uprising had been pushed well into check and the extra hands hired from the Regiment provided plentiful labour in the harvesting of the summer crops, the two brothers revelled in their work happily leading the team of huge dray horses along the plentiful fields of wheat. Whilst Thom and Dan obliged their skills in the crop gatherings Will, Zeke and Sam Coles put to work laying new hedgerows along the field edges, hacking the thickets of bramble that weaved in and out of the trees, often Coles took the time to draw these local scenes in his ever expanding sketch book.

Towards the end of the harvesting season Thom and Dan skilful with arable labour retained their employment on the farm whilst Zeke, Will and Sam worked labouring for a local mason in repairing the walls and roof timbers to a crumbling and derelict outbuilding currently under renovation. The strong August sun burned the exposed naked backs as Will and Coles hoisted the timbers upwards towards the waiting craftsmen, the two lads secured the thick ropes around the oak beams and heaved on the pulley that attached to a block and tackle, in such searing heat the men could only manage a few hours work before exhaustion demanded a rest from the high scorching sun. The final heavy truss resisted all it could to prevent itself from moving into place before being slowly guided to rest by the masons above. Almost in position the heavy timber began to swing violently as the two soldiers struggled to hold it steady enough for it to be lowered onto its carved fitting, Zeke stood high on the lashed wooden scaffold directing the beam as the weight of the oak strained against the ropes. The Mason called down and urged the two to lift just a little higher and Will and Sam heaved the dead weight as the half ton timber edged towards the stone walls. Guiding the weight into its proposed final position, the mason signalled the pair to slowly release the ropes as the mason levered the weighty lumber home into the prepared slot, the giant rafter perched precariously high on the stone wall as the exhausted men breathed a sigh of relief now the heavy timber finally lay in position. Above, the Masons discussed the works amongst themselves leaving Coles and Will to rest their aching arms, from the corner of his eyes Will glanced upwards and saw the unattended beam jolt from its crumbling moorings and slip downward towards the inside of the structure, on impulse he grabbed the coiled rope at his feet in an attempt to stop the timber falling further, the hemp rope grasped in his hands pulled tight as the slack was taken up by this falling giant.

With hind sight Will knew his efforts were idiotic, the thick cord burned through his fingers as the pulley above fought to cope with the plummeting half ton weight, Will held on as the rope ran burning through his grip, the pain in his hands became unbearable and releasing the rope the timber crashed to the floor. Will stared at his unfeeling palms as blood oozed from open wounds caused by the friction of the uncontrollable cord, a moment passed perhaps only a few seconds then the pain hit hard, holding his palms open he yelled in agony.

Coles rushed to his aide and Zeke scrambled down the tall ladder to assist and grabbed a pail of water to soothe hiss pain, plunging his bleeding hands into the cool water gave only a moments respite to his agonies, then the real pain came burning like hell the wounds cut deep into his flesh, his clenched fingers made no response to commands and the lightest flinch caused extreme torture.

Zeke endeavoured to ease the fingers loose from the closed grip they'd involuntary adopted as each movement caused Will to recoil with incredible intense pain. Coles urged Will to rest on the stone building blocks as the pain began to ease a little and Zeke poured rum from his canteen bottle into his dry lips, 'It'll be light duties from now on lad' Zeke tried to make humour of the injuries, 'invalided out of service before you're a hero'. Will appreciated his friend's dry humour chuckling at Zeke's relaxed serenity whilst trying to take his mind away from the acute gravity of his injuries. As Coles bandaged Will's hands with cut linen strips as fresh blood soaked into the bindings with each movement he made and as Zeke correctly predicted Will became invalided temporarily from service and convalesced at the Regiments head quarters, spending most days of the late summer amusing himself by watching the militia companies drill relentlessly outside the city walls perimeter until his wounds healed sufficiently. Thwarted by his inabilities to rejoin his comrades and barely able to complete the smallest of tasks, frustrated Will could bear his confinement no longer and pleaded with the Regiments colour sergeant to be allowed to return to his company.

The duty Sergeant finally gave in to Will's petitions if only to save him the constant annoyance of his requests and gave permission for Will to accompany Captain Leslie's company back to McPherson's camp as the Regiment began to merge its companies back together. Will returned to his file meeting up with the camp at Summerhill, making his way through the canvas bivouacs towards finding his friends, hordes of summer flies buzzed through the hot and stifling air as he searched through the pockets of men for his own file, his target lay with their backs towards him, in the centre piece of the group a small fire flickered beneath a spit holding a hare poached by Thom and Dan who no doubt had many times snared such quarry. Approaching the group Will crept silently to surprise his comrades, Zeke lay upon his back, his trademark pipe smouldered blissfully under his cocked hat and Dan sat cross legged gazing into the flames with a ear of corn dangling from his mouth. Will stepped light footed as he reached his friends crouching carefully behind the slumbering corporal, the noise of his movements drowned by Coles never ending chatter.

As he approached Will pulled hard onto his corporals felt cap crushing it downwards over his eyes, the startled corporal jumped to his feet his vision still obscured by the floppy felt hat as he fought to remove it from his head. The remaining three men turned around to the commotion seeing Will doubled up and laughing heartily at Zeke's flailing arms as he struggled to restore his sight.

'Will, You're back!' Coles joyfully exclaimed rising to his feet to greet his friend firmly shaking his hand, Thom and Dan jumped up from their relaxed manners to welcome their returning comrade with open arms. Zeke finally pulled the hat free from his head and ruffled his lank greying hair, 'You young rascal' he spoke and grinned through his tobacco stained teeth and he threw his arms around Will's shoulders with joy at the file being complete again 'it's good to have to back'. Thom Allen poured a healthy jug of cider and handing it to Will as the others toasted his return, the five men gossiped till the early hours, now gratified at Will's safe return.

The long run of well paid labour on the nearby farm was coming to an end as the harvest reached completion, Will's hands had healed well although a deep red scar had embedded itself along the length of his palms, movement of his fingers was slow and stiff but the surgeon who treated the wounds assured him there would be some stiffening but little lasting damage. Whilst the others toiled with the last of the fields harvest, Will found light work minding livestock on the far meadow of the farm land, requiring his presence for muster at dusk and dawn only, his skin bronzed as he spent the final summer days basking in the bright sun. A narrow brook twisted carelessly through the meadow with a weather bleached trunk of a long fallen tree bridging the shallow running waters, the work was easy for him as the sheep went about their business grazing the lush green grass of the pasture. Dangling his bare feet from the fallen trunk into the cool waters, the flowing brooks wash ran high up his ankles as he swung his legs back and forth like as though he was a carefree child, suddenly a voice called out surprising him to it's whereabouts, swinging round to determine its direction he lost his balance and slipped from the trunk, flailing and falling sideways into the flowing stream below.

Will hit the pebbled water's edge splashing the flowing waters high over him, scrambling to his feet the only damage was to his pride, his heavy soaked breeches pulled low around his waist as he slipped on the smooth worn stones again falling down into the waters, the voice called again and resting on his knees too wet to care he looked upwards to the banks edge with his vision blinded by the bright afternoon sun. Squinting his eyes in the bright light Will determined a human shape laughing at his predicament and brushing back his wet hair through his stiff fingers Will shielded his eyes from the glare of the sun to see better who this company was. A hand reached down to help him up the high bank and reaching out Will grasped the open hand, his wounds forgotten his grip had no strength as his weight pulled his grip free and again he plunged backwards into the flowing stream and finally he gave up his efforts and lay backwards as the flowing water rushed over him, caring little for his embarrassments or clumsiness. Will laughed at the comedy of this situation as the figure climbed carefully down to the flowing waters and leant over his prone body, 'Are you alright?' the sweet voice spoke as a soft hint of a southern Irish accent graced her words, 'I didn't mean to scare you' she continued

Will rested on his elbows and gazed at the beauty above him, with the soft flowing curls of her Celtic red hair dangling loosely around her pale freckled face Will struggled to find a sensible thing to say only mumbling his replies to the ever apologetic girl.

The two sat on the streams edge as Will stripped off his wet shirt and laid it on the lush grass to dry, the girl introduced herself simply as Keira telling Will her family farmed near the village of Ballivor, this beautiful girl was around Will's age perhaps a year or so older, she spoke of the long days she would spend walking the streams pathway and how the lone figure astride the fallen trunk had intrigued her enquiring mind. She had known of the English soldiers and their camp at Summerhill after her father had warned her to avoid their types at all costs, perhaps the innocent boyish figure of Will swinging his legs playfully into the stream had displaced her father's myths of the Kings soldiers and inquisitive to Will's being she had approached the soldier with youthful curiosity. Keira's family had farmed around these lands for several generations, renting the lands from an English landlord the family enjoyed the prosperity of sheep farming enjoying a fairly wealthy status in the community.

Will's experience with the opposite sex was limited, the Allen brothers and John White had often frequented prostitutes in the Edinburgh brothels but Will had listened too much to Zekes tales of the pox and the cures offered by Regimental surgeons to risk a two penny thrill with these whoring types. The pair sat along the fallen trunk dangling their feet as Will had done into the waters below, the hours went by as the two talked of aspirations and desires from their simple lives, as the summer sun edged towards the horizon she announced she had to return to her village and the two waved their goodbyes as each walked in opposite directions. Keira turned and called back after him in her soft Irish voice, 'I'll see you tomorrow then?'. Will raised his hand to acknowledge her request his grin broad across his face.

The four miles along the road to the camp took longer than usual despite Will's sprightly steps, Zeke greeted Will with a jug of watered beer enquiring how his labours went that day, Will made no talk of his encounter preferring to keep his encounter to himself but Zeke had noted to himself the buoyancy this lad had about himself.

The following day was hot, the hottest of the month so far and even with increased humidity Will rushed early to the meadow missing the files breakfast in his haste to meet his new acquaintance, he sat himself in the exact same spot waiting for Keira's promised return, an hour passed, then two as his heart began to sink thinking how stupid he'd probably made his self look with his bumbling words and lack of high intellect and conversation. He lay backwards and tipped his felt hat over his eyes closing them to the sounds of the countryside when a familiar voice called to him, 'You came back then?'. Will sat bolt upright to see Keira a few yards away holding high her skirt as she made her way through the long grass towards him, 'I've brought us some lunch to share' she spoke, 'It's not much I know but I didn't think you would have any with you'. Keira sat down beside Will and unwrapped a cloth that held a rich fruit cake, 'I baked it for you earlier' she spoke, 'It's why I'm a little later than I wanted to be'.

The two shared the meal in the lazy summer heat and Keira learned of Will's life before enlistment having never experiencing the deprivation of a crowded town life or the squalor it breeds, she enquired to Will on his life in the English towns and his times with the Regiment, Will told her of his father who had all but abandoned his children in favour of the bottle, of his brother Joseph and sister Rebecca and of the new family he'd gained within the Kings army and Keira grinned as he told her of the tales of his good friends and their times together. Keira looked surprised when Will told her of his illiteracy, although he'd had some schooling his education had been brief, Keira promised to return the next day with some simple books for Will to study and somewhat embarrassed at his lack of education in front of a middle class girl Will agreed if only to politely satisfy her insistence.

Over the next few days Keira pushed hard for Will to learn to read and write and although he often became frustrated by his lack of progress Keira patiently insisted on his perseverance despite the annoyance Will felt at his failures.

The two lay amongst the long lush grasses of the meadow as the afternoon sun warmed their backs, With Keira's resolve Will managed to read and write to a relative degree and although his hand was slow his legibility and understanding improved vastly.

Whilst concentrating hard on his written words Keira took the quill pen from his hand and scribed a passage on a fresh sheet of parchment, Will stared hard at the drying ink trying to make sense of the flowing text he read out loud the words—*I am falling in love with you*—

Will hadn't realised the gravity of what he'd spoken as he continued to dumbly stare open mouthed at the words as Keira laughed at his boyish naivety, suddenly the realisation of what Keira had written hit home and he turned to her silenced by the moment, the two stared into each others eyes for an age before Keira broke the silence 'Well why in God's name don't you kiss me then' she spoke firmly yet softly, again Will became lost for words and sensing his embarrassments she leant towards him pressing her soft lips into his as the two locked together in an embrace falling backwards into the soft meadow. The two lay in each other's arms unawares to the pale azure sky's giving way to dark stormy clouds that encroached on the horizon, Will and Keira failed to notice the distant summer storm clouds that enveloped them as they lay entwined in one another's arms.

As the slow rumble of rolling thunder crept towards the couple, Will sat upright now suddenly aware of the looming darkness as Keira sat behind him stroking his long dark hair, 'We'd best find cover before this storm hits us' Will exclaimed suddenly and leading her by the hand the pair ran towards the edge of the meadow whilst the heavy rain fell about them as they made for cover of the trees reaching the sanctuary of the canopied forest, the electric sky illuminated the dark sky quickly followed by a tremendous clap of close thunder as the arduous rain crushed the tall grass around the meadow as the eye of the storm passed directly overhead. The violent storm made it impossible for the two to move from the shelter of the tree boughs, now marooned Will and Keira fell asleep in each other's arms to the sounds of the thunderstorm swaddled by the tall tree's above. Eventually the storm eased enough for the pair to emerge from the safety of the woodland and reluctantly the two parted once more, Keira kissed Will lightly on the lips praying a swift return tomorrow.

Will returned to Summerhill camp much later than normal that evening missing the Regiments muster at dusk, Zeke paced aggressively towards him on his arrival, 'Where in God's name have you been lad?' Zeke snapped his annoyance evident in his eyes. As Will struggled for an adequate answer to the obvious question when Zeke gave him no further opportunity, 'Vaughan wants to see you, I'm to escort you to his bivouac immediately' Zeke sternly uttered whilst ushering Will towards the Sergeants tent. Will knew he was in trouble, he had taken advantage of his light duties and would now pay the price. Zeke approached the Regiments senior Sergeants tent sternly advising Will to wait outside as he entered the large canvas and dropped the flap behind him leaving

Will outside to ponder his fate. A minute or so passed before Zeke and Sergeant Vaughan appeared, formally the Sergeant advised Will he would be charged with failure to report at muster and deducted a month's pay on account, as further punishment he would be required to appear before the guard at dawn in parade order ready for his punishment detail. He stood dumbfounded at the penalty, the loss of pay he could cope with but tomorrow he was scheduled to meet again with his love Keira, it was no consolation when Zeke advised him that if Skinner had gotten his way he would be under arrest for desertion as the hated Sergeant was all for issuing a warrant for his seizure to face a trial by general courts martial, Zeke had negotiated with the Sergeants Vaughan and Skinner for leniency by exampling his character and good conduct thus far and he'd negotiated well in his absence but Will however, thought otherwise.

The two returned to the files canvas shelters but neither spoke, the clear moonlit sky illuminated the camp as the two walked through the rows of bivouacs as company men lay around drinking and gaming their time away. Zeke held Will back a moment before the two entered the files immediate area and spoke 'If you're thinking of desertion lad, you've no chance' looking him firmly in the eyes he squeezed hiss upper arms, 'The provost guard will hunt you down and you'll be on the end of gallows as soon as they find you, just take your punishment and put whatever troubles you behind you' but Will shook himself away from his Corporals grasp and entered the files canvas frame, closing his mind on the trouble he'd found himself in. Dan, Thom and Coles nodded with acknowledgement on the two men's return but said nothing knowing the stupidity of wasting the opportunity of his light duties. Zeke slept the night outside the bivouacs entrance less Will should take his absence he would be there to bring him to his senses.

At dawn Zeke roused the file with a pot of fresh coffee and bread ration, 'You'd better get ready for muster lad' Zeke spoke into his ear but Will was in no mood for this day, he'd thought of nothing else but his appointment with Keira now ruined by his late return to camp the night past. Will dressed and loaded his equipment into a parade order never once speaking and made his way to the picket guard on the fringe of the company encampments, Sergeant Vaughan formally greeted him tasking him and two others on punishment detail with digging new company latrines, the three men where escorted by the guard to the rear corner of the camps large field where each man was issued a shovel and tasked to dig a series yard square holes. He toiled hard that day, much harder than the other two men despite the uncomfortable aches in his scarred hands, the punishment details guards sat lazily on the perimeter occasionally raising a cocked hat in some casual attempt to observe the men's progress, unable to focus on his task Will found his mind on the meadow where he was due to meet up again with Keira, praying she might realise he was detained beyond his wishes. His punishment was given as ten days heavy detail and each day required to labour on company orders spending the long days with menial and tedious tasks, peeling potatoes for the company cooks one day and digging ditches on the next, Will resented the stupidity of his actions but knew to reveal the true reason would incur a far greater wrath as the Regiments standing orders forbade fraternisation with the population.

On the tenth day Will arrived at dawn for his punishment and found the duty Sergeant had released him from his sentence and allowed to return to his regular duties and as the file was absent from the camp still working the tasks assigned to them by the tenant farmer Will seized fates opportunity and rushed back towards the meadow his mind playing out the moment of seeing his beloved Keira once again. Although knowing the likelihood of her being present at the meadow was low he clung to her words that she would often walk the fields and hoped desperately that he would find her, he reached the brook and frantically short of breath scanned the area for his love.

Waiting all day until it became obvious that she would not be returning and Will reluctantly made his way along the pathways to the camp in time for the evening muster, despondent he sat beside the blazing camp fire and struggling to speak the words in his soul he eventually confided in his old friend what had troubled him so badly. Zeke offered no words of encouragement Will desperately sought only blaming him as the others did for his foolishness in ending a rare and comfortable existence, Zeke was far more occupied with the return of Skinners interference in the files matters than of Will's troubled heart, yet Will still pined for the love he'd lost and Zeke knew the troubles that faced him. Now concerned if nothing was done Will might well desert the company in search of his sweetheart and as always he felt the responsibility for his men. Zeke found reason for the file to venture towards the area of Ballivor and despite Will's assurances to his friend that he was safe to travel alone Zeke was insistent that all five travel with him to the far flung village in fear of him absconding once his heart began to overrule his head. Zeke trusted Will like a brother but the passions of a man can easily control the head, a desertion would tarnish the company's reputation and he alone would be held responsible for the files loss.

The four followed closely behind Will speaking lightly amongst to each other as he trailed the stream northwards to its parent river, the Boyne. The tiny village of Ballivor lay two miles north of the sweeping Boyne river, the file rested on crossing the footbridge that spanned the green waters and watched momentarily as local fishermen set nets and traps for eels on the waters edge wading chest deep amongst the tall reeds for their quarry, these rural Catholic lands where unfamiliar to the file and their presence gave the local population good reason to scowl at the five red coated soldiers as they entered their village. The party made its way up the slopping hill side towards the small set of houses dominated by the ancient stone church, Zeke elected to keep himself and the others behind for fear that their soldierly presence would cause alarm and offend the villagers, Will walked the dusty road towards the central collection of the community and uncertain of his next move this lone soldier paced the area hoping Keira might see him as the eyes of the villagers watched carefully of his movements ever cautious to his presence.

A three storey building of modest wealth and style sat at the hub of the few buildings in the village, with black iron railings that guarded the dwellings boundary its large modern sash windows offered illumination to the occupants within and his instinct felt sure this would be Keira's home, how long would he wait for her was anyone's guess. Looking back down the hill side he saw his comrades sat upon the roads edge and from the safe distance Zeke's eyes kept watch on his movements still wary of his unpredictable desires. Gathering his courage, he stepped towards the house, a high brick wall ran parallel to the building leading to the rear access behind, knowing his place within the social classes he walked along the path to the rear and entered the small cobbled courtyard. Pulling his waistcoat downwards in an attempt to present himself better and dressing his cocked hat to a move formal position he glanced at his reflection if the buildings windows, finally satisfied with his appearance the nervous Will lightly rapped the rear door.

He waited a few moments but no answer came and impatiently he knocked the door again, nervously concerned that perhaps he didn't knock loud enough for anyone to hear him he struck the door a third time when the upper part of the door swung outwards a few inches catching him unawares and forcing him to lean backwards else be struck by its outward swing.

If his friends had seen the bumbling mess he had transformed into they would barely be able to control themselves with laughter, he stood wide eyed and frightened by the presence of a plump rosy faced cook who quickly eyed him up and down and with a deep scorn spoke so fast Will could barely understand her words, 'There'll be nothing for you here' she scolded in her thick set Irish accent, 'especially for your beggaring kind' as the heavy door slammed in his face leaving him bemused by the incident.

In removing his hat Will stood shocked and speechless upon the doorstep unsure of how to recover this failing situation when again the woman snatched open the door, 'Do you want some food? Is that it?' she snapped before he could utter any of his pre-rehearsed speech, 'You can have some goose eggs if you want them? That's the best I can do for you' the woman continued to scold him as she disappeared back into the kitchen. The woman presented a wicker basket of brown eggs to Will who had yet to utter a word, dumbfounded by the situation he held his felt hat as a sign of respect to this Irish woman who took it as a symbol to place her wares into his upturned hat. 'a handful of eggs and that's all I can spare, now be off with you before I call the master of the house!' and with harsh passing words the door slammed shut and the iron latch clicked down into place.

Will stared down at the contents of his headwear, the woman had threatened the wrath of the house master and knowingly after his period of punishment he could ill afford another run in with the Regiments provost guards, he slowly turned away he looked upwards hoping for hopes sake that Keira would be gazing down at him laughing as she had done the day they first met. Alas, the windows stood empty and with it his chance and plans fallen to ruin, he walked back down the side entrance to rear yard and stood for a moment perplexed by the ruination of his dreams, seeing Will return Coles shouted up to him and waved him down to rejoin the party on the roads edge. Clutching his hat he approached the four who rose to their feet enquiring about his encounter.

'Eggs?' Dan Allen spoke, 'we've come all this way and you've returned with eggs?'. His brother Thom fell about laughing and replied 'at least he's the foresight to think of our supper'. The four laughed as Will stood like a fool cradling the contents in his hat as the others fell about with hysterics at the stupidity of the situation. Will grabbed an egg from the basket and threw it towards Dan hitting him in the chest as the shell exploded into his clean white waistcoat splattering yellow yolk over his smart uniform, this now made Will laugh, enough eggs for each he thought and delivered a bombardment towards his friends.

The five men walked slowly along the tracks back to Summerhill camp, laughing and joking at the times and adventures they'd spent with each other, Sam Coles followed a pace or two behind quickly outlining the scene in his jotter for completion back at the files billets. For some time yet Keira was never to be far from Will's thoughts, her flowing red hair and beautiful bright green eyes brought fond but short memories to him, Will would never realise but his love had spent days waiting for her soldiers return but her father furious at her involvement with an English soldier had banished her to the house until the soldiers garrison left the area, later she would be found with child, Will's child.

By late September, the Regiment broke camp at Summerhill in readiness for overseas duty, the months in Ireland had been comfortable for the soldiers of McPherson's company during which their bronzed skin stood bold against the crisp white cotton undershirts and bleached linen trousers. The season's rains started the day McPherson and Leslie's company rejoined the remainder of the Regiment at the fringes of Dublin city, private billets arranged by the Regimental officers offered reasonable warmth and shelter as the weather turned against the closing season with the damp golden leaves carpeting the roads leaving bare trees forlorn and pitiful against the skyline. The five men billeted in a private house and allocated the back rooms of the building, the space was cramped but dry as the Irish winter drove hard against the thick walled building, the mistress of the house offered to launder the men's clothes for a half penny a day leaving the five men ample time to repair their uniforms and equipment for the pending expedition to the overseas colonies. As the days grew shorter and nights longer Sergeant Vaughan would often join the file in the evenings preferring the company of the seasoned soldier to that of the recruits that increasingly filled the ranks, together the group discussed the news of further rebellion in the Northern Colonies and the implications it would have on their next garrison, Vaughan felt it likely that the Regiment would be re-fitted for duties in the America's but not before time most felt as in having no new equipment since enlistment the condition of their clothing had passed mostly beyond repair.

The battalion formed at Phoenix Park in Dublin by late spring to be formally inspected by Colonel Mawhood and his staff, the ten companies returned an impressive compliment of four hundred and seventy six rank and file in number. With the end of the 17th's garrison in Dublin the men of the Regiment where given a day to settle their affairs and debts before they moved some seventy miles southwest to Kilkenny, the march was uneventful although some losses were incurred through sick and lame struggling to keep pace with the long line of marching soldiers and its baggage wagons.

1775 saw yet more disturbances in the Americas whilst the 17th waited for news of its pending embarkation overseas and casual labour was hard to be found as the wet Irish weather hindered the local economy and the larger quantity of labour offered to the local men over the occupying British Army, occasionally the file might find work repairing roads and turnpikes connecting the town to the outlying villages but the abundance and bountiful employment of the previous year was long forgotten.

The 17th Regiment embarked for Galway by early summer, inspected daily in preparation for duty each company was formed in line with its Corporals and Sergeants present on either end, for the first time in over a year the Regiment was issued ball for its musket drill, with the increase in live fire exercises Zeke muttered this was a sure sign of the dangerous and turbulent times ahead as resistance from the rebellious colonists in the Americas had reached a new height requiring the need for further military presence in the new world. The 17th would form part of the British Legion and embark for the Colonies after its forthcoming refit of campaigning equipment. Typically Zeke was always the first of the file to awake, his priority lay within the files kettle ensuring a hot beverage for his men as they awoke, Today the 17th would be fitted for campaign overseas, briefed by Sergeant Vaughan at day break the companies corporals each returned to the men and advised them to present their equipment to the quartermaster at the battalions headquarters.

By mid morning the long line of soldiers waiting for new issue of wares was beginning to move, Will and his friends reached the front of the line and five men were summoned forward to the waiting battalion orderly, their old utensils and apparatus handed over and checked against the thick leather ledger Will recognised from his initial allocation many months ago. His old rigid goatskin knapsack now replaced by a soft canvas bag with the Regimental number 17 fastened on its deep covering flap, his leather wear reissued and two pairs of straight lasted ankle high boots allocated to the men on return of the well worn and cobbled ones that lately fell apart at the seams. In addition, white heavy canvas trousers replaced the linen types and the cotton undershirt now came with an additional black neck stock, the red tailcoat had been modified by fastening the tails higher up behind the wearer allowing more freedom of movement at speed. The traditional three cornered felt hat remained the same but new replacing the worn.

The most significance change to the soldiers' equipment was with their muskets, the cumbersome long land pattern musket which they had drilled with endlessly was replaced by the shorter pattern version of the Brown Bess, now several inches shorter in length, these new firelocks received grumbles from the older soldiers who by experienced nature had become familiar with the length of the long land pattern and struggled to wield the new issue shorter version with the skill and flow previously. Zeke was amongst those seasoned campaign soldier's who favoured the old firearms over the new issues, 'The army will have us kiss the enemy if this bayonet tip gets any closer' he joked as his wit never failed to raise a smile amongst the men as they prepared their new kit as they had done many years before. Government contracted tailors could never quite stitch the strained seems as well as needed giving need for the men to stitch extra thread on the inner seams of their clothing and sew around the polished pewter buttons that always managed to ping off when you would least expect it but now re-equipped the 17th looked the pride of the British army, their bright red tunics showed no signs of wear or having been dulled down by seasons of harsh weather, their brilliant white canvas trousers stood contrasting the scarlet red tunics with white lace facings of the line infantry Regiments, in passing inspection the men of the 17th gave a hearty cheer to the officers who had led them this far.

The old town of Galway bustled with the arrival of the new Regiment, street sellers and shop keepers bartered with the men as the demand outstripped the supply and pushed the price of goods higher than most could afford. The cheapest of items became more expensive than any basic soldiers pay could afford, soldiers bought whatever wares they could find to supplement their existence on the campaigns in the new world, the five of the file grouped together its coin to gain extras such as candles, tallow, wax and pitch sharing the costly burden amongst each other.

The early months of the fall season brought heavy Atlantic storms across the ocean, secured for the night from the harsh gales Will and his comrades listened the violent sea's crash against the western Irish coast line from the files tavern billet positioned alone on the cliffs edge, the inns weather board shutters rattled against the stonework as the fastenings struggled to hold the boards in place, the five men sat silently by the fireside collecting their thoughts staring into the warm glowing fire as Will watched the blaze dance as the strong winds blew down the chimney stack subduing the flames into the hearth. As the storm raged the Inn sat empty for all but the five men and the landlord, it would be a fool that ventured out needlessly on such a harsh and bitter night, the howling winds swirled around the outside of the lonely tavern protecting the occupants from the fierce Atlantic weather. The last of the candles flickered in the pool of molten wax the five men retired to their bunks, Will wrapped himself in his thick woollen blanket and in listening to the sound of the storm lashing against the roof tiles and shutters as he drifted into sleep.

The following morning brought some respite to the cove after the fierce storm had passed during the night leaving a trail of destruction in its wake, once mighty trees had fallen like matchwood onto whatever lay in their paths and slate roofs lifted from their fixings lay collapsed within the buildings they once protected. The storm had claimed many lives and many livelihoods, the violent high tides had brought severe flooding to the region with large tracts of land lay underwater for miles inland.

The small fleet of fishing boats that worked the bay around Galway had been obliterated beyond any use, wrecked on the surrounding coastline the vessels lay crushed high on the encircling rocky cliff sides, livestock lay dead in the sodden fields as the fierce weather tallied its claim to its victims. The file was called to duty to guard the damaged properties from looting, Will observed the destruction to the once beautiful countryside, an ancient village church tower lay in a randomised heap of fallen masonry, this ancient Celtic monument had stood for centuries only to be destroyed in a single devastating night.

Men, women and children wandered the countryside numbed by the carnage and destruction around them as Will and the others appreciated these losses incurred to the local people and the long term effect it would have on them, their homes, possessions and futures all erased on that terrible night. Lieutenant McPherson arrived at the village by midmorning instructing Sergeant Vaughan to assemble the company along the distant beach front, a Flemish merchant ship had wrecked along the northern rocky coast and floundered on the regressing tides a mile down from Galway bay, the company was ordered to assist in salvage and recovery of any valuable items and protect the wreck from looters.

Sergeant Vaughan led his company as it quick marched along the sandy beach now stripped bare by the gales and leaving the beached hulk of the merchantman helpless by the tides edge. Crossing the exposed beach the strong seas gusts blew a damp sea mist mixed with fine grit and sand along the desolate coastline chilling those exposed to the bone, Will held tight onto his felt hat and raised his collar of his red coat to protect him somewhat from the cutting breeze that whipped about them as the company advanced towards the outlying wreck. In the distance scavengers picked through the spoils of its cargo far along the coast line and Vaughan ordered that a volley be discharged to warn the looters away. The muskets snapped black powder high above the heads of the scurrying thieves scattering them up the cliffs edge out of harm's way from the armed soldiers. The beach now deserted save the thirty men of

McPherson's company paced along the smoothed sand that washed flat by the brutal ocean waves, the file approached the smashed hulk seeing the tall masts snapped clean from her hull she lay helpless like a beached whale stranded on her side.

Remnants of shredded canvas sail hung down the lower side of the hull allowing a fairly easy access to the tilted decks that once housed the smashed barrels and chests that now lay strewn around the proximity of the wreck, the Ocean had done her damage and reminded both soldier and mariner alike how fickle a mistress she could be. The once valuable cargo now lay in tatters, worthless and drenched, spilling liberally from smashed chests, the company sorted through the destruction for what may still hold some salvage value. Sergeant Vaughan arranged his files to gather what could be saved whilst Zeke's file was tasked to enter the ship to search for any bodies or improbable survivors. From the fore of the ship the nimble Thom Allen quickly scaled the tangled mess of hanging sail using it to climb to the upper decks of the vessel, disappearing from sight Thom returned after a moment as the remainder of the file waited eagerly for news of his findings, the strong wind carried his voice far away so in waving from upper decks he signalled by hand the area to be safe. 'Up yer goes lads' Zeke spoke placing a hand on both Will and Coles shoulders as they stared upwards at the creaking hulk, 'There may be some bounty to be had!' he laughed with his comical attempts to urge the lads onto the wrecked ship. Zeke ushered the pair to remove their felt hat and tailcoats as Will carefully laid them across a splintered barrel he tugged the ropes checking their fastenings for security, these sodden twisted hemp cords brought painful memories to his scarred palms as he scaled the timbers towards the sloping decks.

On reaching the top Thom leant his hands downwards to assist Will in boarding the fragile wreck as he pulled himself over the ship sides. Once aboard Will held on tightly to the smashed upper timbers of the galley until he found his bearings since his unsteady motion made it more difficult by the listing angle of the precarious hulk,

Thom's brother Dan followed Coles leaving Zeke alone on the beach eager to receive news of the situation on deck, 'no sign of life' Will shouted down to Zeke as he eased his way across the carved wooden balustrades to the ships wheel house and the decks below.

Zeke yelled through the bracing winds for the four men to venture further into the wrecks hold, the ships listing position made it difficult to manoeuvre through the littered gangways of her upper decks, the doors to the aft of the ship swung freely creaking on their hinges to reveal the darkness within. Will grasped the fallen mass of rigging enabling him to hoist himself to the rear of the ship, the slippery decking planks making it difficult to keep steady footing on the uneven surface, on reaching the doorway he held tightly on the splintered frame pulling himself inside and gaining a clear view to the cabin space, the tilted position the wreck had found itself in had moved most of the contents towards the doorway giving the explorers chance to steady themselves once inside.

The once comfortable captains' room stood ruinous with smashed fixtures and furnishings littering the interior of the cabin beyond any hope of salvage. An opening in the centre of the room gave way to the lower decks and yet more destruction within, Sam followed Will and peeked into the depths of the ship as the two Allen brothers scrutinised the devastated room for valuables and salvage. Descending a steep ladder Will and Sam lowered into the darkness beneath, with little light the pairs vision was limited until Sam removed his tinderbox from his knapsack striking his flint to ignite an oil lamp hanging from the low ceiling.

The darkness lifted a little but not nearly enough to illuminate the deck any further than a few feet from its source as the pair ventured precariously along the slanted room the lamp revealed racks of expensive cloth that lay soaked and spoiled across the wooden planks.

With destruction similar to the previous room the two men carefully made their way to the far end of the wrecked ship.

Will examined several chests prising their flimsy lids loose with his long bayonet, sampling the bitter powdery contents on his tongue

Will guessed tea though long ruined by the effects of saltwater. The pair moved further along the low ceiling whilst Coles held the oil lamp high to increase illumination, Will squinted as his eyes adjusted to the varying light conditions whilst the hull creaked and groaned a death rattle as the ships strained timbers struggled to hold its unbalanced weight. Evidence of the crews being lay around but none of life, personal belongings to the lost crew lay smashed and broken strewn across the sloping planks, thick canvas hammocks swung from the beams obscuring an already limited vision as further the two ventured into the ship passing more and more damage as they made their way along the middle deck.

The entrance to the main cargo hold of the ship lay at the far end connected by a narrow ladder leading downwards to the murky abyss, the two paused a moment and stared down into the void below, partly flooded as the remnants of the oceans high tide swirled beneath them. Sam squared up to Will, 'I think you had better go first' he reasoned to his friend, 'I can make sure you can get out if anything happens' he added to justify his logic, Will gulped and again looked into the hold hearing only the cold swirl beneath him.

'Hold the lamp high then' as he confirmed his willingness to descend the ladder, Will eased his way down the tilted ladder into the gloom and darkness that dominated the ships cargo hold, Sam leant downward into the hatchway providing some light to the dank area as the cold sea waters churned around the hold's tilted bow carrying half submerged barrels and chests along with other shattered debris.

Standing knee deep in the chilly sea waters Will quickly ran his vision along the cargo hold for anything of value, the darkness made it difficult to determine the rooms contents when feeling a movement against his cold soaking legs he looked down, a dark buoyant shape barely visible in the obscurity bumped into him repeatedly as the flowing waters swept about his legs, leaning down to feel the object, his hand dipped into the icy waters as he poked the floating shape to identify it closer for value,

The object rolled in the water revealing the stone cold the touch of a stiff and bloated corpse, the body with eyes and mouth wide open starred directly at him. Startled, he jumped from his skin, his yelp causing an already tense Coles to cry out with fear and quickly disappear from view. In panic Will scrambled back up the slippery ladder tangling his feet around the wooden slats in desperation to escape the bloated horror below, Coles was already half way along the deck before Will himself reached the top of the ladder, with heart racing he clambered along the wreck to the upper deck of the ship desperate for breath, bumping and crashing into everything that littered his path.

Coles stood at the entrance to the decks the oil lantern long since discarded, 'What in god's name was it?' his trembling voice enquired, speechless Will shook his head frantically as he struggled to regain his breath, the two gathered composure as the Allen brothers appeared at the lower decks entrance and looked to each other puzzled by the shouting and commotion below, Will looked at them embarrassed by the fear he exhibited, 'Err' he mumbled, frantically trying to regain his lost composure and dignity, 'Nothing down there save the dead' deepening his voice to reclaim some of his lost manliness. Coles laughed at Wills attempt to make light of his fears and the four progressed back towards the upper deck and leant over the ships side to the waiting Zeke. 'Will's just pissed himself' Dan yelled laughing aloud at his own words, 'Aye, the two ran like girls' Thom added. Zeke looked puzzled at the private joke the two shared, whatever happened forever remained a mystery to him but the four adventurers giggled for hours afterwards as McPherson's company continued to scour the surrounding area of salvageable goods.

Later the Allen brothers returned to the depths of the ship to recover the drowned corpse deep within the hold, the body emerged wrapped in a canvas sail sheet cut for the purpose, with little dignity in death the wrapped body was lowered down to those on the ground, the corpse placed besides the wares that had been recovered from the wreck, Zeke guessed the body belonged to the merchant who'd financed the voyage, too greedy to leave his profits he had paid the ultimate price by stubbornly staying with his goods whilst the crew sensibly took to the safety of the vessels long boat. Loaded onto a cart along with the very few unspoilt goods the company had managed to salvage from the lost ship, this body whoever he may have been would find rest in an unmarked grave, his once valuable commodities now scattered and lost along the desolate west Irish coast line.

An attempt to salvage the wreck itself soon proved fruitless, the damage to the hull was beyond a temporary repair as the Atlantic tides approached its victim once again making the wreck unsafe, the company was forced to abandon the ship to the seas as the her tides swept around her hulk, the stricken vessel soon became lost to the tidal surge. The company returned to the files billets and the file drew their ration from the company stores, a pound of salt beef each pooled together to make a large stew more than enough to satisfy the hunger of the five, the landlord prepared the meal in exchange for a serving of the rich broth and the promise the five would purchase their beer from him rather than the travelling tinkers that worked the bay.

As the evening edged towards midnight finally the five sat by the warming fireside alone, Dan Allen pulled from his pocket a silver pocket watch taken from the corpse within the wreck that day, 'He'll not need it where he's going' he commented, Zeke and Coles both examined the time piece noting its markings clearly making it of solid silver manufacture, etched on the outer casing scribed markings only the educated Coles could read well enough to translate.

Zeke remarked the inscription would make it less valuable on the open market but a pawnbrokers shop was a sure avenue to fence such an item without raising suspicions in its being, although the value redeemed would be less it would prove to be the safest and quickest way to dispose of the valuable item without raising suspicions. Zeke and Coles removed as much of their issued clothing to pass themselves away as skilled tradesmen, Zeke knew two soldiers attempting to pawn such a rare item would reduce the value offered to them even perhaps bringing in some unwanted questions as to its rightful owner.

The two returned after an hour passed, the pocket watch had been valued at two guineas however the broker had suspected the item to be ill gotten and offered them only sixteen shillings. Insulted, Coles at first refused the offer but the wisdom of Zeke had realised the sooner the item was fenced the better and reluctantly Coles agreed the sale of the silver watch by bargaining a hocked violin into the arranged agreement. Coles eyes lit up on seeing the tatty instrument quickly removing the cheap gut strings of the instrument restringing it with better quality types he'd salvaged from his fiddle lost in Edinburgh, a moment or two of tuning and the string instrument played as sweetly as ever, the good spirits lifted by the return of Coles skill and entertainments.

*   *   *

Chapter Four

The Charles

Athlone, a western commercial port town on the fringe of the Atlantic Ocean bustled with men from the 17th Regiment in readiness for the campaigns in the Americas.

Soldiers idled away their time in the small billets that overflowed with red coats eager to enter the escalating conflicts of rebellion in the new world, with the new short land pattern muskets issued to the file as row after row of red coated soldiers loaded his equipment and belongings into the cramped allocated space beneath the decks of the chartered transports that would ferry the 17th across the oceans to the new world.

As the file formed silently on the upper deck, the flotilla of heavy transport ships gently drifted away from the rugged coast line towards the cold barren seas westwards, huge white gulls soared overhead baited by youthful soldiers with crusts of stale bread until far from land they finally gave up the opportunity to scavenge and abandoned the fleet to sail alone, by nightfall the rugged and rocky shoreline of Ireland had faded into the vast seas behind. A detachment of Royal Marines patrolled the decks policing the restlessness of the company's eager soldiers as soon the long voyage ahead bred boredom and frustration amongst the ranks, the men gambled their pay away on trivial wagers, tempers soared as the cramped conditions took their toll on these jaded men, violence erupted frequently as men confined to the lower decks lashed out at anything and everything that disgruntled their already foul moods. Encouraged by those who knew his musical skills Sam Cole's abilities with his regained instrument calmed the fiercest of tempers and would save many other wise destined for the lash.

The bleak Atlantic weather crashed against the sides of the sail driven slow timber vessels scattering the fleet far and wide, the troops inside already frustrated by the lack of space grumbled at the length of the westward journey, confined to the lower decks most men lost all sense of time and purpose and Zeke on several occasions enforced the disciplined role he so much detested.

The strong ocean storms detained the Regiment's arrival at Boston harbour by several weeks, land finally sighted on new years eve of 1775 but not until the arrival of the new year did the 17th receive orders to disembark along the appropriately named long wharf on Boston's eastern harbours, the transports one by one slowly positioned themselves alongside the lengthy wooden harbour, heavy ropes secured the vessels tightly to their moorings as scramble nets lowered over the sides provided the men means to descend onto the boards of the dockside edge. Passing equipment to the first men ashore, the file disembarked the ship and formed up along the quayside under the watching eyes of the provincial guard. McPherson's company marched to the centre of Boston town much to the cheers of the loyalist population, who saw the reinforcement of troops as clear indication of General Lord Howe's intentions to break the lengthy siege of Boston by the rebellious continental army.

The scene of much political turbulence over recent years, the loyal Bostonians gazed and gawped at the endless line of red coat infantry as they formed orderly columns on the expanse of grass before the town customs house waiting to be billeted within the town. Will gazed upwards at the elegant and fashionable structures that occupied the town around, these tall wooden dwellings appeared far roomier than the crowded slums he'd lived amongst over his twenty years.

With painted timbers that coloured the area brightly, the bareness of trees dormant over the winter months would surely bloom into vibrant colour come springtime. The area soon filled with soldiers whilst company officers talked amongst themselves deciding how and where to best billet their men, Boston had seen much restlessness over the last few years and now lay firmly griped the under siege by the Continental army that surrounded the peninsular. The siege of Boston had begun in April of the previous year after colonial militia men had bloodied the nose of General Lord Howe's predecessor General Thomas Gage forcing him to withdraw his troops into the safe perimeters of the peninsular of Boston town, Gage had attempted to break the siege at nearby Breeds Hill but the casualties sustained by British troops proved too heavy and the attempt failed with substantial loss of life. With the inactivity of the following months by the crown armies, feelings towards His Majesty King George where strained and sympathies were small, the men sensed as much as groups of local men from varying walks of life communed on the streets cautiously noting the movements of the battalion's men wondering if this increased presence might turn the siege in the loyalists favour. The Regiment's senior officer Colonel Mawhood, had instructed his company officers to billet the Regiment around the pastures in the town's centre should no accommodation be forthcoming and although the population of Boston was greatly reduced with the pressures of the siege, a decent billet became hard to find. Sergeant Vaughan returned to the company after speaking at length with Lieutenant McPherson,

'It appears lads' he addressed his company whilst shrugging his shoulders 'we are to make camp here on the pasture square, McPherson will endeavour to find suitable billets on the morrow but for now our beds lads, lay upon the ground'. As the quartermaster's Regimental stores were yet to be unloaded from the transports still tethered by the quayside subsequently, the company's shelter for that night at best would be the clothes and equipment on their backs. Coles grumbled 'For nearly two months we've travelled and these fools can't even find a bed for us' the file prepared the ground as best they could given the circumstances.

Sergeant Vaughan dismissed the men out of line giving strict orders prohibiting the fraternisation with any local businesses until the regiments clerks could ascertain the situation better, movement from either side had been slight as the British garrison languished in the confinements of the besieged town.

Will sat squat on the damp grass as the weak January sun dipped behind the tall wooden houses causing the seasons chill to consume those that stood motionless, whilst temporary bivouacs constructed from bayonet an arrangement of gathered woollen blankets created a makeshift shelter, the camp sprawled across the once picturesque greens of Boston town, hundreds of newly arrived redcoats trampled the lush grass into a sea of soft brown mud as men argued to find a pitch accommodating enough for the cold night ahead. The night chill bit fiercely into the bodies of the men despite dozens of fires lit for warmth. Will's bones ached as they had throughout his youth reminding him harshly of his home town and the conditions he thought he had escaped, huddled together for warmth the five men lay under their blanket bivouacs sharing their daily ration of watery rum to warm their bodies from the cold January air and prepared themselves for what little sleep that might be had.

The following morning brought a heavy frosted dew to everything that lay motionless overnight, Zeke boiled coffee on the communal blackened kettle and shared it amongst the men of the file as Dan poured what little was left of the rum into the boiling camp kettle hoping to bring warmth to the bones of the five.

The hostilities in the surrounding areas made it restricting for a permanent base of military operations, Colonel Mawhood briefed his senior staff to the advancement of the Regiment to a more agreeable environment. Sergeant Vaughan ordered the company into a double line to be led proudly with drums beating and fifes playing from the exposed land on Boston common to a more suitable and permanent billets within the besieged town. The 17[th'] Regiments ten company's marched northwards through the peninsular towards their new semi permanent residencies on Hollis street at tip of the town sedge. The siege of Boston had taken a heavy toll on the area, buildings scorched by sabotage, looting and vandalism stood as they'd been left with the occupants long since departed and the cemeteries seldom used until recently showed signs of heavy occupancy as the cost of war settled its debts. For most a communal grave would be their final resting place as disease soon wrought havoc amongst the cramped defenders garrison.

Prior to rebellion Boston had prospered well, its inhabitants had numbered twenty thousand but the threat of war and the prospects of a lengthy siege had reduced the town population to less than six thousand citizens loyal to the crown. Those who had shown allegiance now existed only as victims of war, with either business interests to protect or too little money to secure passage out of the harbour these loyalists went about their days as best they could despite the continuing threat of the besieging revolutionaries.

The men of the 17th occupied the redoubts along the tree lined Orange Street, the inner line of defences strongly prepared for any forthcoming assault though the siege had reduced itself to now little more than the occasional raid or pot shots from snipers positioned on the hills surrounding the town. The file was assigned a stint of guard duty on the remote picket lines of the defences, Will and Thom Allen drew their lots being allocated the hours of dusk till first bell of the new morning.

The January chill brought heavy frost over the earthworks, the deep trenched fortifications and bastions provided some cover from the winds that whipped across the harbours inlets and fortunately the Regiment's provisions had by now been unloaded from their transports, small mercies that the men were provided a more purposeful shelter.

Starring into the darkness across Jamaica plains Will stamped his feet hard on the frozen ground beneath to bring some warmth to his chilled body, despite being issued with a winter coat the cold crept into his skin and brought shivers to his bones. Amused by the patterns made from his warm breath against the sharp air he glanced towards Allen as the darkness played tricks on his over active mind, 'Thom' he whispered but received no acknowledgement to his words, 'Thom!' he repeated himself this time a little louder. Thom Allen slowly looked sideways towards Will 'What is it?' disturbed from his light slumber by his words, 'Can you see anything?' again Will whispered his voice towards his friend, 'Only the inside of my eyes' Allen casually replied pulling his hat back down over his face, 'Now keep quiet else you wake the entire bloody town'. Hearing a sharp noise in the distance Will turned directing his firelock and bayonet into the void

'Hold and be identified' he cried out as he felt the icy hand of fear upon his back, Thom jumped to attention fumbling for his musket as Will challenged the darkness, 'Hold I say, hold or I'll fire' he cried again with an edgy nervousness in his voice and his hand shaking violently upon the trigger of his musket.

'Best be pointing your weapon towards the enemy' came a familiar voice from the darkness, 'Zeke, you cursed fool! I nearly blew your damned head off'. Will relieved by this false alarm held out his arm and helped Zeke down into the narrow trench.

'Next time lad, you'd be best to prime your musket before presenting it in the face of your enemies', he kicked the boots of Thom Allen and chastised him in doing so, 'Next time when the lad calls a stand to, do as he says, It may just save your life'. Zeke unloaded his equipment, resting his own musket against the redoubt, 'I've brought you a hot brew' he spoke whilst pouring the liquid into three tin cups. The men leant against the trench wall sipping strong black coffee as the three gazed across the neck that linked the town to the mainland, 'Your watch will be done inside an hour so I'll stay here with you to guide you back'. Relieved from guard duty just after first bell was struck, the silence broke the crisp still air with its timely alarm, promptly the new guard relieved the old and Zeke led the two tired and exhausted men back to the billets allocated to his file.

White frost formed on the sides of the tight canvas sheets that covered the deep trenches of the picket lines, the mornings cold fires were rebuilt and relit to thaw out the bones of the sleepy soldiers and drummers walked amongst the narrow streets with heavy baskets of bread loaves issued as the soldiers daily ration, not pausing their rounds for a moment for those too slow to claim it. Will and Thom sat under their doubled woollen blankets, Zeke had excused them early muster roll call on account of their late picket guard duty whilst Coles and Dan Allen would take their turn the coming night as the men of the company did duty on perimeter guard.

The siege of Boston had lasted far longer than the garrison's commander General William Howe had anticipated, unbeknown to his intelligence the rebels that surrounded his army where dangerously low on gunpowder and supplies and in no position to withhold a break out should the inhabitants have mustered the courage or initiative to commit to an assault. Howe's inactions would cost the inhabitants of the town dearly, allowing the besiegers much valuable time to strengthen their positions around the higher perimeters of Boston town. His network of intelligence however had brought news of proposed fortifications of Dorchester heights overlooking the town and harbour, British sluggishness and inactions would eventually allow the rebel army time to strongly fortify the heights, the high ground granted to the besieging army prevented the British gun boats from elevating high enough to reach their targets and dislodge them from their commanding positions.

The 17th by now had been in active service for almost a month, contained by a force of short enlistment militia and ill disciplined locals, British senior staff officers had urged a proposed break out of the garrison but General Howe aware to the fate of his predecessor held caution, unsure of his enemy's strength he declined to commit his army to a similar humiliating defeat as the one suffered a Breeds Hill six months previously. With this inactivity came frequent gossip and rumour of evacuation from the siege amongst the ranks as news arrived of the rebel army's invasion of lower Canada and the internal uprising of the French Quebecois, Will and others spoke heartily of making a fight of the situation stating the rebellious militia would clearly be no match for the might of King Georges armies, history however was dictating otherwise, the garrison at

Boston stood surrounded by the unorganised local militia blockading any commerce arriving from the mainland, the army relied upon its relief from the sea but a hard winter had frozen the port thick with ice hindering any but the largest of vessels free movement into and out of Boston's harbour. The besieged army slowly starving faced little option than to sit out the siege else evacuate the colony to the rebellious army that held them to ransom, fortunately the flow of sea borne commerce was still controlled by the dominant Royal Navy thus allowing the town to receive provisions by sea although with the bitter weather the harbour could take but a few ships to unload the much needed supplies, opinions for most was that soon enough the rebellious enthusiasm would diminish and the siege would falter.

Something strange happened during these idle first days besieged within Boston town, at first Will assigned it to the monotony of being cooped up in limited space but soon the others began to notice it too, Sam Coles usually despised his guard duty but lately he'd not only stopped complaining of it, he'd been given to volunteer for additional watches. Whilst Dan and Thom often joked at Coles social airs and graces but now Will took a curious interest in Coles apparent change of behaviour, often, he noted Coles preoccupied with thoughts deep in his over active mind. Soon enough the two drew a watch together as they patrolled the length of Boston's streets, choosing his moment when the two stood alone Will pressed home his curiosity, 'Sam my friend' Will spoke nervously, 'does something trouble you'. Coles, lost in a day dream took a while to answer such the simple question, 'Such as?' he replied his eyes still fixed across the street corner the two patrolled, 'I know not Sam' came Will's reply having expected a more positive and informative answer 'but lately you've seemed hindered with other matters'. Coles grinned and took his gaze from whatever had caught his eye, 'There' he spoke enthusiastically 'Over there' he said. Will followed Coles line of sight knowing not what his was supposed to see amongst the massing crowds that obscured his view, 'Do you see her?' Sam spoke stretching his neck over the heads of people that went about their daily business, 'Her?' Will replied 'a woman?' pausing 'what is so special about a woman?'. Coles returned his vision back upon his target 'for six days now' he spoke transfixed by his fascinations 'she walks this street at this time every morning, I know not where she lives nor do I know where she goes but with such a vision of beauty no man could wish meet another'. Will thought over the meaning of Coles words and now intrigued himself stared hard into the crowd expecting to see the goddess Aphrodite herself, 'and there she goes, until tomorrow for then I shall glimpse her once again' Coles spoke. Mystified by the event Will spoke 'You mean to say you've been coming here for six days straight, pulling a four hour watch but a moments sight of some woman?'. Not just some woman my friend' Coles returned to his normalities 'the most fine looking woman a man could ever gaze upon, I have admired her from afar as she strolls this street with her three friends and tomorrow I shall intend to address her'. Laughing aloud Will spluttered his words, 'tomorrow?' he spoke 'and how do you expect to do that exactly?'. Coles faced his friend and spoke enthusiastically 'You'll help me do it Will, I have it all planned out'. Will attempted to make some sense, bewildered by this swift encounter, 'you mean to say you have yet to speak to her?', 'Not exactly, no' Coles replied 'but she looked at me once, at least I think she did'. Overcome with a fit of giggles Will enquired on how two impoverished infantrymen could concoct a plan to introduce themselves to someone they have never seen closer than ten yards,

'I have it all worked out Will' Coles revealed the plan to his friend, 'today I intend to write poetry, you shall memorise its words and tomorrow deliver it to her on my behalf. Will closed the conversation with a simple phrase 'Shall I now? then God help us all'.

Later that afternoon Coles and Will secluded themselves in a quiet room of their billet as romantic words flowed smoothly from Coles well educated mind, the trouble however, lay with Will and his inability to remember such complex verbiage, over and over the two rehearsed Coles dramatic prose until finally by the late hour Will had cracked it, not one mistake, not one error, Will repeated verbatim as Coles dictated his choice of chosen words.

The morning sun shone over the hills that surrounded Boston town, Sam Coles awake hours past sat excitedly waiting for his friend to stir, as Will pulled on his breeches and dressed himself for the day he noted Coles added appearance, slick oily hair, combed tight into the fashionable queue of the day, clean shaven but then Coles always was, an impeccable soldier one could not be found within fifty miles. 'Here' Coles handed Will a length of black ribbon 'tie this and we'll go'. Will dropped his shoulders with despair, 'you still plan to go ahead with this idiocy then?', 'Of course' Coles replied 'today Is a day of destiny, now come, we've not a moment to lose'. Will stood behind his friend and combed his hair one last time before securing the lace into a neat bow behind his head, 'All tied Sam' Will assured his friend of a job well done ending his words sarcastically 'for Queen herself should trouble herself to overcome your charms'.

The two men reported for duty as Coles had done so for the past week, the sergeant of the guard looked Coles and his grandeur up and down as he briefly inspected the two before they began their watch, 'You on a charge lad?' he muttered in remarking on his smart appearance as he penned their names into the guard house ledger, Coles smiled, his heart raced as he and Will drew closer to the moment he felt he'd lived for. Together they stood apparent on the corner of the same street Coles had been assigned to watch over the past week, the crowds thickened as the hours grew long, 'There, there she is' Coles said pointing across the street identifying his distant love 'no go on my friend and do your best' he finished pushing Will into the general direction and the crowded street. Will fixed his gaze onto the would be recipient of his message and reluctantly paced across the street, speaking to himself over and over again the words Coles had drummed into him the night before. His target stood middle and left of the group of four that Coles identified and Will pushed through the crowds never daring to take his sight from his intended recipient less he lost his chance in the crowds. After the struggle to reach the group, Will presented himself to the ladies and started his rehearsed speech, or at least attempted to. Bumbling and butting, the hours spent in rehearsals flew absent from his mind, the words he'd spent hours reciting now long since gone, he stood awkwardly in front of four complete strangers who detecting Will's ill ease giggled amongst themselves as he blurted out some attempt at Coles fine diction. Desperate, Will gave up and gave an embarrassed explanation in defence of a plan gone terribly awry. Coles, oblivious to the disaster that had unfolded grinned like some love struck schoolboy and attempted to look dashing, fascinating and charismatic knowing the gazes upon him, the four girls listened in fits of giggles as Will explained with some added colour the events of the last few days.

The elder of the girls gave reprieve and spoke to Will humbly, 'if the truth be told young master, your friends presence has not gone unnoticed to us neither, pray please introduce yourselves and enlighten us to your names?'. Will smiled broadly, as from the jaws of defeat he'd snatched victory and the relief showed as he had done his friend proud. His nerves now settled Will gestured Coles to his side, as Sam presented his self to the ladies with charm as Will spoke formally 'Ladies, may I take the pleasure to introduce the honourable Samuel Coles esquire, gentleman soldier in His Majesties armies', Sam concluded the introduction 'and may I present Mister William James Snow, ditto to the cause'.

The elder of the group politely replied 'then may I have the honour of introducing myself and my sisters to you too, my name is Mary, and this is Katherine, Elizabeth and Jane' she ended with a polite curtsey. Will took a mental note of the girls as their names became known to him, all of perfect prettiness he could well see how Coles had gotten so smitten with these girls. Mary, to Will's judgement, placed her in her late twenties, Beth perhaps two years younger and the youngest being Jane, barely an adult. The real beauty of the family however was Katherine. Perhaps of equal age to Coles the two looked well matched, educated, somewhat more refined than the usual types that frequented this quarter of the town, the two fixed eyes upon each other as Will held awkward small talk with the three remaining sisters.

The moments passed and Mary sensing the need to return to their business drew the encounter to a close, Coles barely took his sight from Katherine's eyes 'Can I see you again?' he asked after her and Mary delivered the reply on Katherine's behalf, 'I think we would very much like that young sir as Mary obliged them with their residence's whereabouts, unlike Will, Coles could retain his memory well, this would need no memorising for he intended to make his acquaintance further at any cost.

The two men ended their guard duty and returned to their billets, Coles neglected to reveal to any other his secret and Will was trusted not to divulge his privacy to the remainder of the file, for the rest of the day the file idled away its hours until required to face muster that evening, with an hour of daylight left Sam hurried himself back to the billet to prepare for his evening liaisons, as smart in appearance as ever Coles asked Will to check over his attire, his uniform neatly pressed the way Zeke had taught them upon first enlistment, his brasses shinning he stood the pride of the Regiment as he waited for the hour to arrive.

With a leave of absence granted, Dan and Thom often spent their evenings in some local tavern drinking away what little coin they had preserved since receiving their last pay and Zeke, although fond of brewed ales sought a quieter company on most occasions, a small flagon of ale returned to his room and the company of whoever sought it.

'You alone tonight lad?' Zeke enquired, 'Aye, That I am Zeke, save your good company on these dark and dreary nights' Will replied. 'And what of Coles?' Zeke asked 'I fear his appearance does not mix well with the brothers tonight'. 'Of Coles I know not Zeke' Will answered attempting to deny any knowledge of his friends whereabouts, 'ha ha, come lad' Zeke was not convinced of Will's account, 'It takes more than that to fool me, a lady is it?' Zeke suggested. 'I cannot say Zeke, for Sam's business is Sam's business' Will said avoiding eye contact, Zeke laughed and wiped away the froth from his whiskers, 'You need not have to say anything Will, your words told me already but I hope Coles be careful for I fear Howe will abandon this town and leave its inhabitants to face the consequences of supporting the loyal cause, If Sam Coles attaches himself to one that is tied to the town he'll face a dilemma I should not wish upon any'. 'Ah let him be as is Zeke, tis just some harmless fun' he added, 'If that's all it is then I have no concern but you had best keep a careful watch on his emotions, I have seen the best of men undone over a broken heart' Zeke ended the conversation returning to his pipe.

Over the next few days Sam Coles reverted back to his usual self, now as disinterested as before in his guard duty and ever glib with his tongue but Will was privy to otherwise. Coles had revealed an escalation in his relationship with Katherine, or Kate as he now referred to her, spending as much time together as possible, the two had fallen madly in love giving cause for Will to turn Zeke's words over and over in his mind. What if Howe's army should abandon Boston, should he relay Zeke's concerns to his friend or let its course run naturally? troubled by this dilemma Will kept tight lipped to Coles over their Corporals predictions, his confidence was to be kept and the probability of the army evacuating this town was slight, or so he hoped.

The men of the 17th Regiment, ever keen to capitalise upon the opportunity for adventures and glory had been selected in a forthcoming raid to secure information on enemy dispositions far beyond the perimeter of the defensive lines, the battalion called for volunteers to advance towards the heights surrounding high ground to gain information on the besieging army's strength.

The file eager for action duly opted for the adventure that lay ahead of them, Captain Leslie was to lead the small reconnaissance party up towards the summit of the nearby heights to gain intelligence on the rebel numbers, positions and movements. Leslie's selected men removed all campaigning equipment save their cartridge pouches and firelock tool, a sharp new flint was made available to each member ensuring a clean strike to the frizzen plate along with twenty rounds of cartridge supplied to them individually. The chosen men, excused duty that day spent the hours prior to nightfall preparing their skirmish equipment for their forthcoming reconnaissance of the enemy, Zeke ran burnt cork over the metal of his musket and bayonet to dull down the shine of the steel encouraging those accompanying his to do likewise, save a glint from the moonlight reveal the party's intentions.

At midnight the reconnaissance party boarded three long boats assigned to cross the frozen low tides across the sand banks, the narrow boats rowed the short distance towards Dorchester Neck with the proposal to reconnoitre Dorchester village itself for enemy activity. At midnight the company moved across the low tides towards their destination. The long narrow row boats crashed in the loose shingled beach halting the momentum with a jolting force, steadying his hands on the rough splintered timber edge Captain Leslie drew his sword from its ornate scabbard and silently signalled the party to advance inland towards the cover offered by the tree lined slopes towards the summit, together the mixed company cleared the long boats wading the last few steps through the shallow waves that lapped the shingle beach, the crunch of pebbles under foot masked by the crash of the waves upon the shore line.

Leslie instructed the men to form a staggered line as they advanced the shallow gradient at the foothills of the heights, the dark night sky provided the perfect cover for he advancing red coats, silently this composite company progressed towards the summit with the youthful Captain Leslie standing firmly at the head of his troops as the dull glow of the enemy camp fires flickered in the distant valley. Silently, the progressing line reached the heights, a few trees provided cover at the top of the position as the company formed a skirmish line charging their firelocks ready for any contact with their foes as the officer scanned the distant horizon with his field telescope and made notes of enemy temperament and strengths in the valley and hills opposite but closer yet silhouettes merged from the distance towards the British scouting party.

A small group of rebels began moving upwards to the crest of the hill oblivious to the reconnaissance above, Leslie needed to act fast and now knowing the full extent of his enemy's number the officer ordered his company to retire back to the foot of the hill for a swift evacuation back across the low river and to the safety of their own lines. Five men would need form the rear guard and Zeke eagerly volunteered his file to delay any advancement of the rebel scouting party should they discover their actions.

Zeke spread his men thin across the sparse tree lined ridge and in kneeling behind a fallen tree trunk Will charged his musket with shot and slowly eased back the hammer ready to fire his weapon at the advancing enemy. The darkness amongst the tree's made vision impossible at further than forty paces, Zeke passed amongst his file and instructed them not to advance and pursue the enemy under any circumstances for fear of the file losing sight of each other amongst the shadows and firing upon each other in the confusion, 'Anything that moves to their front is your enemy, I expect you to treat it as such and blast them to kingdom come' he whispered before moving on to inform the next man. Coles lay ten yards to Wills left and the two Allen brothers to his right whilst Zeke prepared himself centrally in readiness to withdraw the file should things go badly for the ambush. The chatter of the rebels advance party moved towards the line of the waiting trap and Will could now see the shapes of four men who scouted far ahead of the enemy lines, moving directly towards him Will prayed the enemy would turn away or at least divert its movement away from the death trap that lay within its path, his first time in the face of the enemy fear entered into his mind, kill or be killed he said to himself over and over again convincing himself of the righteousness of his forthcoming actions.

Still the scouts advanced, slowly yet carelessly the four figures trod through the crisp fallen leaves towards the waiting red coats muskets. The targets stopped for a moment barely twenty yards directly to Will's front, the advancing scout party huddled close together whilst one drank from a bottle and another drew heavily on his pipe, the party converged and paused to determine their direction sharing the tobacco with its smoke lingering in the cold night air. With emotions new to him Will spoke softly to himself 'Just turn away' his breath deep 'turn away and you'll be safe for I do not wish you any harm'. The five concealed redcoats crouched set in an extended line of each other waiting for the right moment to discharge their muskets with devastating closeness at their victims, with shallow breath Will felt the beat of his heart pound against his chest, the long barrel expanded from his arms like a deadly extension to the soldiers body as he focused his aim towards his target. Still praying silently to himself for his adversaries to return to their own lines Will felt the strain in his joints as he held his position fearful of the enemy observing his movement and wondering if the anxiousness would ever diminish when facing these deadly situations, his tense body readied itself for the moment, despite the cold night his linen undershirt clung to his body against his damp and clammy perspirations.

The centre man now just a dozen yards in front of the trap stopped for a moment, staring hard to his front his eyes met Will's and hesitant in disbelief his eyes widened as he realised his party had blundered into the trap, Will stared down the long barrel of his musket with the prone figure fixed squarely within his line of fire, the target shifted desperately to escape before the trap became sprung but with no time to call a warning to his fellows Will squeezed the stiff trigger of his firelock, with spring released the flint and snapped down against the metal of the muskets primed pan, his eyes blinded by the flash of bright burning powder impeded his direct vision, the pan smouldered for a split second then fizz-crack finally igniting the touch hole to the primed barrel.

An explosion of bright orange flame spewed from the cold steel barrel spitting its contents into the darkness and slammed into the chest of its intended victim, as gunpowder smoke obscured the view to his front, the cracks of fellow muskets filled the night air with a violent din followed by the screams and cries of other victims. The smoke hung in the still air slowly dissipating into the night, wide mouthed with shock Will rose from his knees and re-charged his musket with the precision he had learnt through years of practice, within a few moments the musket was presented to its next target, he scanned the distance for his next victim but the ground lay still save the lingering trace of smoke and the faint smell of burnt powder.

Motionless the four bodies lay clustered together on the cold damp earth as each of the file had found his mark silencing the scouts that lay before them. Zeke cautiously moved through the line to inspect the victims of his successful ambush and with bayonet ready the Corporal examined the bodies,

'This one is still alive' Zeke whispered and silently he gestured Will and Dan to break cover and move his position, 'Carry the prisoner back Captain Leslie, he can decide what to do with him' he instructed the two before informing Thom and Coles to recharge their muskets and form another line thirty yards towards the shore.

Will shouldered his musket and lifted the wounded prisoner to his feet, Dan attempted to assist only to be told he'd much practice in carrying the helpless on dark nights. Dan looked puzzled at Will in making no sense of this comment but made use of himself by levelling his musket protecting the three as they made a speedy decent towards the safety of the long boats. Reaching the beach Will released the helpless prisoner over to the crew of the remaining long boats as they cast off towards the lights of the harbour.

The crew rowed for all its worth across the low tides of the bay and Will looked back towards the heights for signs of his remaining friends hearing only the familiar crack of discharging muskets. The Coxswain sensed Will's anticipation leaning towards him reassuringly, 'Fear not lad, the crew won't leave without them, it's Captain Leslie's orders'. Upon arriving at the safety of Boston town's peninsular shores the officer greeted the two as they made their way from the shore line into the protection of the camps perimeters, Leslie shook both men firmly by the hand enquiring to the whereabouts of the others from the file, the excited officer promising them half a guinea each on the safe return of the remaining men.

Back towards the coast line of the heights, musket shots echoed through the thin tree lines as Coles, Thom and Zeke snapped only black powder as quickly as they could manage, to fully load the entire cartridge would give any pursuing rebels ground the three could ill afford to spare, by snapping only blank shot would keep rebel heads down and convince the enemy into believing the ambush party consisted of larger numbers than the few that it had. Tricks like this bought the withdrawing skirmishers valuable ground as they scrambled down the hill side to the safety of the waiting long boat for evacuation back to the security of the British lines. A north shore mortar battery had been placed on standby to cover the party's retreat and Will prayed the battery would have the sense not to open fire whilst British men were still unaccounted for. Peering across the bay to the wooded hill side that stood isolated in the darkness, Will scanned the rise carefully for signs of movement towards the beach, Captain Leslie had ordered the remaining boat to stand on alert with muskets primed and bayonets fixed in anticipation of hostiles pursuing the stranded British soldiers. The thin picket line of redcoats manned the towns perimeter and waited patiently for the return of the last boat and on hearing the faint crunch of steps through the pebbled shores Will eased himself over the parapet of the trench redoubt, Captain Leslie gave order for the line to present their muskets over the fortified barricade as the noise became apparent to all, glaring down his muskets barrel towards the dark shores a faint voice called out, 'Hold your fire, 17th coming in' a familiar voice called towards the line, Will exhaled with the relief of his friend's safe return as a jubilant Captain Leslie praised the five men in orchestrating the successful action and withdrawal in the face of the enemy and congratulated Zeke and his men personally.

The file later learned the reconnaissance company had encountered a rebel scouting party attempting to advance to positions over Dorchester Heights, the captive prisoner although shot clean through the stomach and not expected to live had given much information to his captors the strength and intentions of the rebel army. This intelligence was prepared and given promptly to General Howe who's staff now estimated the enemy to number over twenty thousand troops with a further reinforcement of heavy artillery captured from the British garrison at Fort Ticonderoga, currently moving across country to turn the siege against the British stronghold.

Until this news became widely known the spirits of the besiegers however was far from broken but now the British defenders faced a rude awakening to the gravity of their captivity within the town, this would be a hard and difficult enemy to dislodge from the surrounding areas and General Howe and his staff planned an heavy assault to remove the enemy form the heights at Dorchester and despite echoes of similarity of Breeds Hill less than a year before. This time the 17th Regiment would remain to defend the town from possible enemy counter attacks whilst the British main assault would land on the shores of Dorchester Neck and drive head long into the enemy lines with desires on crushing the enemy artillery that occupied the surrounding summits. Over the next few days available small ships packed into the many wharfs of Boston loading troops in readiness for the attack, men of 17th breathed a sigh of relief knowing the casualty rate was expected to be high.

Howe's inadequacies had given the enemy valuable time to fortify the heights against any attack causing rifts between his general staff on the best plan of action to raise the siege. Mawhood's Regiment merged in to a brigade commanded by Earl Cornwallis and would remain in Boston to man the redoubts and forts that guarded the entrance to the town, the 17th combined with the 40th and 55th Regiments watched the flotilla of barges anchor off shore and out of effective range of the enemy artillery.

The invasion fleet waited patiently for favourable winds to direct the assault speedily onto the shores but despite the fleet's tolerance, the weather only worsened bringing violent squalls to the surrounding area. After three days of terrible and foul weather Howe called off his attack and abandoned any hope of regaining control of the heights, for the loyalist citizen of Boston, this latest failure to relieve the siege brought the final act of British occupation of the town and reluctantly Howe called his staff to announce the evacuation of the peninsular and withdrawal to the Northern Province of Nova Scotia for refit for the forthcoming summer campaigns. As the news filtered down to the ranks, Will could not help but feel pity for the beleaguered citizens abandoned to their fate once their presence had left, although some might gain passage to the Northern provinces for most this would mean abandonment of their livelihoods and homes.

Once confirmed, news of the evacuation sank Coles like a stone, ashen and lethargic yet full of temper verging on eruption Coles removed himself from the presence of his friends, 'Leave him be a while Will, we always knew this moment would come' Zeke spoke up. Feeling helpless to the situation himself, Will could only imagine the emotions Sam Coles faced right now, his bond of friendship wanted so much to seek out his friend and offer some kind words but even Will knew in circumstances such as these nothing would or could console him at this moment.

Nobody saw Coles for the remainder of that day, his return at midnight brought concerns amongst all in his file, his personal situation now revealed to the group and even Thom and Dan Allen offered some comfort to his shattered soul, 'Sam' Will whispered as he sat down beside him 'We'll think of something, I promise'. 'There's no need' Coles replied, 'I have taken matters into my own hands, we plan to marry tomorrow and the army will evacuate us together as man and wife'. Having overheard Coles comments Zeke drew his pipe from his mouth and spoke up, 'I knew this would happen lad and foolishly I thought you had more sense than this' he spoke calmer than expected, 'I let you be thinking your head firmly upon your shoulders now you announce your marriage to a girl you've known just weeks'. The file sat in silence as Zeke continued to explain how such plan would convince no one as scores of Bostonians would try many similar tricks to gain a passage to safety. Coles stood to his feet aggressively and refused to listen to any logic to make him see sense, Zeke in sensing his determination reluctantly agreed to speak to

Sergeant Vaughan on adding Cole's future bride to the list of Regimental wives. With Zeke absent the remaining four went about arranging Cole's marriage the following morning, typically Thom and Dan obliged the drink and Will was asked to assist Coles with his preparations for the event, the two guineas given to the file by Captain Leslie would serve the party well for entertainments and the four raced ahead of themselves in excitement, but Zeke's return later that night brought Cole's hopes and dreams crashing back to earth.

Reluctantly, Sergeant Vaughan had agreed to petition the forthcoming marriage to McPherson but from Zeke's tone Will knew the outcome would not be favourable, Coles however, still holding the hope that this would secure passage for his bride to be insisted the event be celebrated in all its finery, 'Zeke' Sam addressed his Corporal 'As Kate has no father to speak of, I would very much like you to give my bride away'. Zeke looked awkward at this suggestion but in seeing the delight brought to Cole's eyes agreed, 'and Will, you sir shall be my best man' Coles added with jubilation. Excitedly Will accepted the honour but pondered the concerns Zeke now faced, taking him aside Zeke explained his worries in confidence, 'See lad, although Vaughan can be very persuasive the matter lies with the regimental clerks, I recall my time in the 6th regiment when a sergeant married a negro girl just prior to the battalion's departure from the Caribbean, the clerks sensed the marriage a sham and refused her passage' he whispered his words carefully, Will listened with concerns to the outcome of the story 'Go on, tell me what happened?' he spoke. 'There are some memories lad I do not wish to relive and this tale is one of them, the Sergeant now torn between his love for his wife and his duty to his ranks boarded the vessel as his new bride screamed from the quayside and begged for his return but the sergeant could not, for his a position responsible to his men and leaving them would set them a poor example, so simply he stood firm and proud, stiff upper lipped you might say as the ship loosened its moorings and departed the shores for old England, the following morning they found him stone dead in his bunk, some said of a broken heart for rumour had it his bride was expectant with child and no truer tragedy could be had on that painful voyage home'.

Will looked on open mouthed on hearing Zeke's tale, 'you think the clerks would similarly deny Kate passage?' he questioned

Zeke rubbed his chin 'that my friend is in the hands of others, now come, if there's a marriage to be had let us enjoy the celebration as best we can eh?' trying to uplift the dampened spirits.

The two returned to the file, as Coles paced the room delivering a choice of poetic phrases to his disinterested audience of Thom and Dan, together the five drank well into the morning hours until the new days light splashed the night sky. Coles led the file towards a small Presbyterian church, though neither bride nor groom a pious nature the two had convinced the minister to marry them with utmost haste. Kate and her sisters arrived a few minutes after the file and having little religiousness about them the service was conducted simple and brief much to the delight of those present, on payment to the minister the group left to begin their evening of celebrations at the nearest tavern. Having the foresight to bring Coles violin with him Will urged Coles to play a few lively tunes much to the excitement of the party as the party danced into the night, Though the group toasted the pairs fortunes, Will with a heavy heart looked onto the eyes of the newlyweds knowing the troubles they faced ahead but for now, they lived the moment, in good and joyous company he swallowed his ale and gave a mighty cheer to Mr and Mrs Samuel Coles, the happy couple.

The long night was spend drinking and dancing until Zeke with his character wink suggested to Coles he should consider obliging his bride with his husbandly responsibilities, Coles laughed and in shaking his friends hands firmly bade them goodnight as he led his bride towards their wedding suit.

The remaining four strolled back to their billets but for Thom and Dan the night was still young and chanced their fortunes with the bride's sisters pressing to capitalise on the romance of the day, Zeke however would have none of it insisting the file return together less their luck run dry. The four wandered giddily through the back streets to their beds, laughing and singing amongst themselves as they went, today had been a good day Dan commented but Zeke and Will knew trouble brewed on the horizon.

Sergeant Vaughan arranged for Coles to be given light duties in the circumstances but for the newlywed couple time was running short, in a week's time those who petitioned the Regiments clerks would be required to draw lots for the few available births aboard the vessels scheduled to evacuate them to safer lands, Coles chose not to speak on the matter immediately changing the subject matter whenever Will or the others approached it, Zeke advised to leave him be, he knows the risks, it was Coles prerogative alone to discuss it as and when he chose. As time drew closer citizens of Boston grew ever more desperate to evacuate the peninsular, space on civilian transports exchanged for a kings ransom as fears of rebel retribution escalated amongst those sympathetic the crown, seemingly abandoned to their fate, Coles complained with disgust in the policies of the crown and ranted with ardent passion.

Will noted a different side to his personality fired with detestation towards the inhumanities of his parent nation towards the very people he felt they should protect, Coles was changing in personality, no longer a man of arts he became consumed by the injustices of mankind.

Until the final evacuation could be arranged the garrison would consolidate its positions as best it could within the besieged fortifications, a direct assault by the rebels would certainly prove costly to the defenders and although with enough manpower the defence could withhold it positions, the heavy losses involved would almost certainly bring about questions of Howe's ability to command his majesties armies in the colonies. For now the garrison would be fixed to its defences around the fortified perimeter line until the evacuation could be organised, occasionally the rebel sharpshooters would lay claim to a victim foolish enough to expose himself above the network of fortifications at the southern end of the town but for most the lives led were nominal.

The 17th and its company's moved back into Boston town after a hard week entrenched in the outer perimeter defences of the peninsular neck, scattered amongst varying billets McPherson's company occupied the derelict or abandoned houses of the western quarter of the town. Loyal Bostonians went about their daily business as best they could despite the occasional harassment from the besieging rebels, commerce flowed and even with a soldierly garrison of nearly eight thousand troops prices remained affordable to even the most impoverished.

Will raised a query to Coles why the colonies began such rebellion against the crown, Coles revelled in the question and for once the men around him listened with a genuine interest to his debate rather than drifting into disinterest after a minute of his chatter. Sam Coles had kept a keen eye on the politics of the colonies, explaining that the wealthy land owners felt unrepresented within English government, some colonists wanted unrivalled independence from the crown whilst others felt the answers lay within a fair and equal representation, a wise man however could see the real interests in these vast lands, the cost of recent wars in the ever expanding colonies has left a huge deficit in the purse of the Kings treasury, some might say the cost of protection from England's old enemies came high. Zeke bolstered Coles words speaking with clear hatred of an underhand French involvement in these wars, an Englishman's natural enemies he spoke are often found on the field of battle.

The file changed billets frequently within the town, rarely spending time in anything other than abandoned houses belonging to now departing colonial merchantmen and Will had himself noted the degree of freedom given to the individuals who inhabited these colonies, although often bonded to a master the citizens came and went with little restrictions to their normalities, far different to the lower class poverty existences provided in England. Life for the common soldier however was deteriorating, the ration drawn from the Regimental stores lacked much in the way of freshness as commodities began their transferral towards the British controlled forts at Halifax, fruits and vegetables usually procured easily from the country side became nonexistent as the siege squeezed the available resources dry. Whilst those Officers who could afford to do so spent their time in comfortable private billets, the rank and file of the besieged army sheltered amongst the diseased masses rife with smallpox, typhus and flux.

The ranks amongst the 17th where reduced as much as any by the disease that spread quickly through the unhealthy plagued town as the endemic outbreak reached almost biblical proportions the muster roll of the Regiment returned only one hundred and forty eight of a return taken in Ireland of nearly five hundred able soldiers less than a year before, this extent of disease claimed from all walks of life and at this rate of sickness the garrison would be hard pressed to man its inner defences adequately let alone push the war towards the half trained volunteers of the rebel armies. Trade and crafts flourished despite the limits on the available market, the harbour received a few goods daily and items far beyond the expense of the working classes in England became easily affordable although not always available.

Will on receipt of his pay purchased a block of pressed tea from a loyalist merchant desperate to sell his stock rather than let it fall into the hands of looters knowing the withdrawal to be imminent, moulded into a tablet twelve inches tall, six inches wide and an inch thick the embossed block demanded no more than two shillings, back home such luxuries where far beyond his reach.

The five men sat on the wooden porch of their billets within an abandoned townhouse along Greene Street and Zeke tipped a company drummer boy to bring a kettle of boiling water to the men outside, breaking of the corner of this novel beverage dropped the chunk of pressed tea leaves into the steaming pot, Zeke had sampled the flavours of fine tea whilst stationed in the Indies and Coles had enjoyed the refreshments as a youth in his privileged upbringing. But for all, this was a drink now to savour, the hot kettle having been left to infuse a while was finally poured and the steaming liquid filtered a thin strip of linen into the files drinking vessels. Slowly, Will sipped the pale fused liquid as shown by the elegance of Coles gentlemanly gestures, the bitter taste lay in mouth as he swilled the contents around his teeth before swallowing the contents into his stomach, 'A gentleman's drink' Coles raised his tankard high as a toast to the party of five gentlemen soldiers, 'Good health to one and all', but elsewhere, the effects of disease spread quickly through the besieged ranks, despite better conditions offered to the officer class two company officers had succumbed to the Typhus epidemic shortly after withdrawing into the cramped squalor of Boston's quaysides.

Captain Sawford of the 6th company and Lieutenant Maguire of Mawhood's general staff had both succumbed to the terrible disease, the losses to the ranks had been enormous by comparison, Sawford's decimated company had been disbanded and the remaining files became merged with others desperately in need of replacements, with such losses affecting both rank and file an Ensign of the Grenadier company purchased the Lieutenancy commission from Maguire's meagre estate shifting the hierarchical chain of command upwards, In the Indies, Zeke spoke 'the surest way to promotion was to survive six months garrison duty.

Burial party's daily dug new grave pits for those succumbed to the effects of illness, for the officers a formal burial was organised but for most, their ends came tossed into a communal pit covered with quick lime and hastily filled with the cold earth, the 17th lost many valuable and experienced soldiers during the worst of the siege as men Will had served with for nearly four years met their end in this diseased town and soon forgotten to the passages of time. For Zeke however, all this was a part of war, it would be foolish to expect to die quickly at the hands of a clean painless bullet wound, his previous posting with the 6th Regiment had cost them heavily to tropical diseases with very few falling at the hands of their enemies, it was small consolation to the soldiers that today his enemy was suffering as much as he.

With the towns economy quickly failing, firewood started to fetch steep prices as did other necessities, abandoned and damaged buildings were torn down and stripped of their valuable timbers for fuel to maintain the defending garrison whilst Howe's preparations for withdrawal where being finalised. Parties of men axed and hacked the elegant carved dwellings for anything that would combust for fuel, little escaped the destruction as the frozen men sought warmth within their camps and billets.

By early march 1776 the garrison at Boston was preparing for withdrawal northwards to reinforce the threatened Northern provinces while the improving early spring weather gave the rebels cause to probe deeper into the thinning British lines and the previous small skirmishes now developed into lengthy stand offs as both sides sought an advantage over his respective enemy around the defended perimeters of the harbour town.

On Howe's direct orders two companies of the 17th positioned themselves in anticipation of an expected enemy assault as the remainder of the Regiment prepared for evacuation to the growing number of naval vessels entering the quays around the town.

Zeke's file having shown good form and discipline at the engagement at Dorchester Heights was requested to position itself in a holding line outside the perimeter defences of the town towards the Roxbury Hill road, the Navy's gunboats would bombard the flat plains directly in front of the town preventing a full scale assault of the town as the thinning garrison boarded the ships for the evacuation. Captain McPherson spread his men thinly across the westerly road towards the collection of ruined houses at Roxbury village, a boundary stone wall would provide cover for the file until the signal was received from the remainder of the company to withdraw. The enemy opened the mornings fray with a fierce launch from heavy artillery emplaced around the occupied Dorchester heights, heavy round shot pierced the winters air crashing hard into the frosted ground before them, the earth shook violently as the frozen earth leapt smashed high from the ground as the cannonade ricocheted across the flat plains gaining momentum towards the defences. Men close enough to receive the barrage soon withdrew to the safety of the dry stone wall as the spinning round shot bounced along the ground throwing shattered stones through the air and claiming victim of those inquisitive enough to keep exposed for too long. As the picket lines cowered behind their protection, Royal Naval gunboats anchored off the mouth of the Charles River returned fire across the killing grounds before them preventing the rebel forces from advancing into perimeter suburbs. The thunderous roar of heavy cannon rumbled from the distant harbour and echoed across the deep valleys that surrounded Boston town, the men checked and rechecked their muskets as the damp air might misfire the powder without any warning. To protect his muskets powder pan, Will lay a square of leather hide over the lock of his weapon as the winters sleet drove hard soaking him and the ground he stood upon. Thom Allen was the first to spot movements observing Captain Leslie's company led by Sergeant Skinner positioned to their right discharge their muskets into the tall grasses either side of the wide tracked mud road.

The crack of musketry poured a black putrid smoke across the vision of the staggered line, Will squinted to see what lay ahead when suddenly the distance ahead lit up with fury, 'down !' shouted Zeke as the file dropped to their knees behind the safety of the stone barricade as the enemy gunners smashed canister shot containing hundreds of lead balls across the open lands between the wooded slopes of Roxbury hill and Boston town as advancing rebel minutemen darted across the low tree lines towards the thin line of redcoats. Will presented his musket towards the closing foe and squeezed the trigger mechanism, the hammer snapped downwards igniting the powder in the pan with an unfamiliar muffled fizz, 'Misfire' Zeke shouted towards him, 're-prime only your pan! not your barrel as your bullet will still remain' he added knowing the sounds of battle and the sound of damp powder. Too frequently had Zeke seen the effects of panicked soldiers under the stress of battle, drilled into instinct a misfire would lead the user to reload a fresh round onto the existing one stuck fast within the barrel, often the barrel would explode as the two lead balls collided under the force of a double powder charge. The result? never pleasant.

Opening the pan and with hands shaking in fear Will blew hard into the muskets pan to clear any spoiled gunpowder removing his muskets small pick tool he dug the burnt congealed powder from the barrels touch hole ready to again prime his weapon.

He snatched at the cartridge box at his side fumbling with the stiff leather flap to the contents within, ammunition fell from the pouch into the mud at his feet as Will tussled to grab a cartridge with his stiffened cold hands.

Finally pinching the paper twisted top he bit hard into the lead ball, spitting the unneeded lead shot at his feet and pouring the measure of powder into the open pan. With little time to clean the fouled touch hole Will prayed silently that his trusted firelock would do its duty to him, standing tall he presented his musket a second time towards the direction of his hidden enemy, drawing the hammer back with his hard calloused thumb his index finger felt towards the hook of the steel trigger, without the care to aim he again fired his weapon across the field of tall grass. 'Bloody hell Will' Dan shouted over the din of gunfire, the gravity of a second misfire became apparent, 'is there any point you being here?'

The line of infantry poured volley after volley towards the invisible enemy in a desperate attempt to cause a degree of pain to the enemy as they had done to them, knowing at such excessive range and with little aim the muskets would do no damage to the hidden rebels save prevent an open advance across the vacant plains. Now under a constant heavy barrage from the heights Skinner began to withdraw Leslie's company into the perimeter of the town abandoning the defences in the wake of the enemy's barrage.

Zeke took this as his signal and began collecting his line of men from the stretch of stone wall that offered some relative safety from the hot metal splinters, Will had yet to successfully discharge his musket now concentrating on the probable fouled black powder deep within the length of the steel barrel he failed to notice the men either side of him leave the cover in favour of the better defended town. Zeke stooped low on reaching

Will as he busily picked his muskets barrel clean, 'We're moving out lad, this place is due to be blasted to Kingdom come' and grabbing him forcefully by the tunic collar the two men bolted for the safety of the towns lines, Will glanced to his left to see several men from Leslie's company motionless at the foot of the stone walled ditch cut down by the violent volleys from the rebel artillery.

As the last two men sprinted along the exposed wide road that lay littered with spent and shattered cannon balls being they vaulted the parapet to enter the trench, the engagement had cost the defenders a dozen lives without any sight of the enemy, tempers soon flared at the frustration of this ghostly opponent and accusations flew of company's firing upon each other in the confusion of the skirmish. Unsure of the enemy's numbers and movement the British line reformed along the deep breastworks dug at the town edges and catching his breath Will leant against the parapet as the line presented their muskets over the protective earthworks

With the immediate panic resided Will removed his hat and examined his head wear, poking his index finger through a clean bullet hole that penetrated the dome of the soft black felt Will stood perplexed a moment, a few inches lower he thought and he would be resting with the dead along the shallow drainage ditches that ran along the flat farm lands. Staring to towards Leslie's company he glared towards Skinner, his mind cast back towards the vengeance he had wrought to his file, although he could not be certain, Will considered the hatred Skinner held towards him and his friends. Zeke suddenly piped up instantly grabbing Will from his thoughts

'Draw your bayonets lads, could be bloody work ahead'. The company in perfect unison unsheathed their steel blades and with sharp twist snapped the bayonets onto the socket end of their muskets. The parapet of the defences now faced its adversary trimmed with seventeen inches of cold steel patiently waiting the enemy's advance, the tables now turned any advance from the enemy would be met with a volley of lead and would cut the attack to pieces.

Squat along the foot of the trench the thin line of redcoats waited for any sign of movements along the distant tree line, Will delved into his cartridge box for a tally of his remaining ammunition, empty . . . the leather flap that secured its contents had worked loose, his two dozen paper wrapped combinations of powder and shot lay scattered across the plains from which he had just escaped, 'Damn it' he exclaimed, 'any spare shot?' he called to his fellows either side of him. Zeke pressed a loose handful of ammunition tightly into his scared red palms, 'Just make sure they count eh lad' said Zeke before peering cautiously over the parapet as Will secured his ammunition inside the drilled wooden holes of his leather bound cartridge box.

For over an hour the line waited with patient discipline for the imminent assault from the enemy, the land before them lay still save the occasional flight of jet black crows that morbidly investigated the dead that lay beside the previously occupied stone wall. Still the enemy had yet to show itself but despite occasionally launching a harassing volley across the surrounding flat lands, the anticipated assault failed to materialise and under McPherson's direction Sergeant Vaughan issued warning to retire to the inner defences.

Numbering off the remaining men, the Sergeant stood the ranks down and instructed every even numbered man to withdraw to the perimeter of the town ready for evacuation. This was the moment Sam Coles had dreaded, instructed by Sergeant Vaughan to make his way to the Regiments headquarters, Coles and his bride would draw lots to secure passage to the north. With the evacuation now imminent Engineers of the 64th Regiment had packed powder barrels around the general staff headquarters at Fort Hill, if the bastion was to fall to the enemy General Howe decided it would lay ruinous in the hands of Washington's advancing army.

With civil order showing signs of collapse, the evacuating troops came under strict orders to refrain from looting and pillage on threat of public execution by hanging. The provost marshals men kept a close eye on the departing troops for any breach of conduct by menacingly enforcing their presence but as discipline amongst the starving citizens was crumbling and ragged mobs of soldiers and sailors rampaged through the distant fringes of the falling town, houses of suspected patriot families where fired and looted, the presence of the provost did little to deter the mobs bent on destruction of this hell hole that imprisoned them for the past months.

The file was assigned guard to the office buildings that governed the arrivals to Boston's long wharf, being one of the few companies that still maintained its military discipline amongst its ranks, the men watched as dozens of fleeing townsfolk and soldiers tramped through the holding yard, the greed of humankind evident as soldiers and citizens over laden with their treasured valuables packed into the holding yards until passage could be gained.

'In defeat' remarked Zeke 'an army becomes little more than a reckless mob' noting the absurdity of men negotiating heavy furniture through narrow back alleys towards the harbours only to abandon it once there. Coles arrived at the headquarters with his bride Kate, the tension apparent he asked for the file to accompany him to the clerk's office as they and others in a similar position decided their fate to chance.

The long line waited restlessly outside the clerk's office, to Will things did not look good but optimistically Coles reasoned his chance as good as any, surely he concluded, his position in the military would count for something but Will could think of little other than the Sergeants tale relayed to him by Zeke. The clerk announced that due to the higher than expected demand, the draw would take place only once all regiments and baggage where aboard their vessels and accounted for, 'Cutting it bloody fine aint he?' Dan quipped but Coles failed to acknowledge, the tension obvious in his eyes, 'we'll be together my love, we've nothing to fear' he spoke placing his arms around his wife for security. Eventually the clerk called the first group forward, Coles peered over the heads as the group ahead placed their hands into a wooden box and drew a small piece of folded paper, decided simply, the few lucky ones shrieked with jubilation, their lives secured they skipped past the queue towards the quaysides.

'Next ten' the clerk called the line forward. Coles ushered Kate forward as the clerk instructed the group to draw their lots and Kate placed her delicate hand into the depths of the box and slowly drew it out, the folded piece of paper contained one of two lines, 'To Go' or 'Not To Go'. With eyes fixed upon on Kate, she opened the folded paper and stared down towards the words and slowly read them aloud.

'Not to go' she gasped as tears began to roll down her pale complexion, Coles looked on in shock 'this cant be' he exclaimed angrily 'there's been a mistake, there must've been a mistake' he reasoned but the clerk was uninterested for he'd been witness to these emotions all day, 'Next ten' he yelled over the commotion keen to end this spectacle and signalled the party to vacate outside.

The file attempted to soothe Coles and his bride, but for Coles there was no consoling, shattered he broke down in tears as his bride of just three weeks was led away by the guards. Coles, restricted by the guard separating him from his bride yelled over the noise of the quayside 'I'll find you Kate, I promise I'll find you'.

But Kate did not hear his words, her head buried deep in sorrow she was ushered back into the masses that gathered for the chance of reprieve as the last of the ships left the wharfs. 'What now?' Will asked Zeke urgently, 'I know not lad but I feared this day would come' Zeke replied as he ran his fingers across his stubble chin 'we'd best get Coles away from here, I fear his sanity this moment'.

Towards the end of the wharf Officers and administrators struggled to cope with the surging rabble of refugees desperate to secure passage on the Royal navy's transports out of the colony, the crowd heaved back and forth as Officers and ranks struggled to maintain order within the panicked inhabitants of the colonial town, with bayonets drawn the crowd was kept at bay as the final loads of baggage where loaded aboard. As space aboard the fleet became limited looted goods were abandoned on the wharfs edge as its inhabitants gave up their gains in favour of a position within the evacuations, stacked chests and barrels fell from the high harbour wall in the freezing harbour waters, no longer did the value of goods matter as the value of life outweighed the expensive items salvaged from the towns stripped homes and warehouses. The withdrawal now in its final phase left deserted streets on the southern tip of the town and squeezed into an ever tighter area the men of McPherson and Leslie's company's would guard the entrances of the docks until the remainder of the battalion boarded the transports moored in Boston's many wharfs.

Those without the means to secure passage wandered the lonely streets contemplating their fates at the hands of Boston town's new occupants elect as cheap two penny whores blind drunk on large volumes of spirits abandoned by the army jeered and whistled the five as they slowly paced the ghostly quiet streets leaving Boston in the hands of the enemy.

Although none at the time knew it, Howe had negotiated the towns evacuation free of harassment in return for leaving its government buildings intact, as a bargaining tool Howe edged on caution giving orders for the administrative buildings to be packed with powder it seemed likely now the retreat would be bloodless. The dominating presence of heavy artillery from Fort Ticonderoga enabled the besiegers to place devastation in any point of Boston town and harbour and Howe concerned of his reputation as an effective commander needed to evacuate and evacuate quickly. The company became one of the last to leave Boston, moving into the now empty holding area, the town stood around them in eerie silence, occasionally a shout or scream would break the stillness giving a haunted feel to the few men that remained. Sergeant Vaughan liaised with Zeke on manoeuvring the company aboard the last remaining ships that occupied the abandoned wharfs, by dusk the signal came for the last departure and McPherson's men lined the gang ways to the transport that would ferry them northwards to the rendezvous at Halifax.

On deck, Will stared across the rooftops of the abandoned town as the last of the winter sun set over the horizon and the town plunged into an eerie darkness. Over a hundred men crammed aboard the vessel and struggled for space whilst the Regiments baggage filled the hold and crew quarters forcing the ranks to stand on the upper decks, typically the rains began to fall quickly soaking those exposed and a morbid silence befell the ship as the last of the fleet drifted eastwards negotiating the high sand banks of the harbours tides, demoralised, Will and his friends now stood on the decks of the very same troop transport that brought them to the besieged town barely three months ago, losses to the defenders had been high not only in human costs but more so in reputation as this professional army of King George had withdrawn in the face of an irregular militia army with only a hand full of the rebel fighters taken for the price.

These wounds cut deep for the men of Howe's army, these ranks had fought against Europe's finest troops often in the face of overwhelming odds but the Boston campaign however, had proved a disaster for the highly trained and highly disciplined British army as they withdrew by sea along the jagged coast line of Massachusetts. The evacuation fleet of flat bottomed barges and tall mast warships drifted through the night on the high spring tides away from the abandoned town, those bewildered inhabitants who had chosen or been forced to stay within its limits wandered a ravaged ghost town in the face of the advancing continental rebel army. Coles only words since leaving his Bride Kate summed up the British failings at Boston . . . with tears welled in his eyes he spoke just a few words, 'Hang your head in shame Howe, hang your head in shame'.

*   *   *

Chapter Five

The St Croix

Despite the tactical loss of Boston, the flotilla of ships landed at Nova Scotia in reasonable spirits, the losses after a lengthy siege at Boston had been so great to so little gain and already stretched thin by skirmish and more so disease the 17th garrisoned briefly at Fort McNab in Halifax Bay and waited replacements from their mother country.

Having disembarked, the 17th marched the short distance to Pleasant Point on the southerly tip of Halifax, the Regiment camped in the bleak and desolate grass lands around the south point of the town, if conditions in Boston were bad then Halifax became hell, the biting north winds raged around the thin canvas tents rendering them all but useless as the soldiers fought in vain to set camp on the Atlantic plains.

Realising the fruitlessness of the attempts, Sergeant Vaughan had directed orders to dig pits in which the soldiers would receive some degree of shelter from the harsh squalls of the North Atlantic seas. The frozen ground made it difficult to penetrate the deep frosted layers of earth, with shovel, pick and bayonet the file sweated long and hard in driving snows until the pit stood ten feet square and four feet deep, company sappers provided fresh cut pine trees to lay atop the pit and with the frozen sods of earth these temporary hovels provided an adequate shelter from the falling thick snow. Dan Allen kindled a large fire in the centre of the pit with a small hole placed in the sods to vent the cramped subterranean bunker, with warmth at last the five men removed their red tunics and lay them on the hard earth, the file received its ration by late afternoon as the snows fell thick across Halifax bay and consumed their meagre offerings in silence. This hovel, by far the most dismal the five had lived in over their years together barely provided enough shelter from the elements to be classed home, the men positioned their blankets around the narrow fire pit to receive some benefits from the shouldering embers. As the flames subdued into the charred logs and the light dimmed into the faint orange glow of the blaze, the file stared silently into the flames and leaving his familiar tobacco for his friends to share Zeke left the bunker for his briefing of the company's orders.

Later Zeke returned having collected the files evening ration, covered from head to toe in thick heavy snow he shook his outer clothes free of the ice and snow that formed on the faded red wool of his uniform, the sight looked fairly comical as this well seasoned soldier stood like an abomination at the bunkers entrance. Isolated within the bunker, Zeke's return shocked the remaining four oblivious to the conditions outside, commenting on the heavy snow fall Zeke spoke 'This long winter will delay the campaigns a while lads, McPherson claims we'll be stuck here a for months yet'. Stripping down from his wet outer clothes Zeke swigged from the tall leather flask of bitter rum before handing it to Will to share amongst the file, the ration raised a warmth inside him as he gasped and drew his hand across his mouth and passed the flask around the file as the men settled down for the night ahead.

Will woke early to a strange sound amongst the pit, Sam Coles with his back rolled to the dying fire muttered incoherently to himself, touching his forehead he felt the cold clammy skin of his friend, the fire now subdued somewhat to just a few glowing embers leaving the bunker in semi darkness and chilled to the night air. Placing Coles discarded blanket around his shoulders Will re-stocked the dying embers with dry firewood. Outside, although the fall had ceased, but over two feet of compacted snow and ice settled around the camp and as temperatures plummeted to freezing a hard crisp surface.

The night was still and crisp and the air dry within the files subterranean hovel, wide awake and concerned with Coles well being Will made to the entrance of the pit, narrow peering into the dark night, Will shocked by the hostility of the environment lowered the heavy waxed canvas sheets over the doorway and weighted them with sods and rocks to prevent the bitter winds penetrating the snug dugout but for the reminder of the night he barely slept, transfixed by the embers within the fire pit he strategically placing dry logs around the dying sides of the fire to keep the constant warmth strong as he dozed with a keen eye on his friends health.

Zeke woke his usual early, surprised by Will active presence he enquired to him how he'd slept, Zeke's rasping voice disturbed the two brothers who took Zeke's early morning growl as a signal to arise to the day., as the group stirred only Coles remained asleep, 'Sam' Will called to him but Coles lay dormant within his grey woollen blanket, 'Coles!' Dan too tried to rouse him but still no movement came from the curled figure, Zeke crouched down besides the shivering shape as he lay in a foetal position protecting itself, easing back his blanket Coles clutched the edge with too little strength to object, 'This lad has the fever' he spoke alarmingly, the remaining three stood silently as Zeke called for boiling water from the fires embers. Thom and Dan Allen had never understood Sam Coles, between them they had so little in common they rarely shared a similar opinion but now kneeling besides his sickly weak comrade the brothers soothed his brow with strips of damp linen warmed in hot water from the files kettle pot. The differences between the file may have been great but in testing times they became like brothers, never to falter. Zeke quickly dressed for the poor weather and ventured outside seeking permission from McPherson to request a visit from the Regimental surgeon but returned alone with grave news that camp fever ran rife thorough the ranks and the surgeon and his orderlies where stretched too thin amongst the increasing cases to attend to all but the most severe cases, McPherson however, had persuaded the surgeon to at least give direction to Zeke in how to contain the case until he could be examined. Taking instruction carefully on the best procedures to treat the victim and break the fever, Zeke had seen fever run through the ranks many times before and instantly knew the symptoms that could lay claim to a man's life inside two hours. Will and Dan carefully positioned the delirious patient upright resting his frail body against their knapsacks to support his dead weight whilst Thom restocked the fire into a roaring blaze with thawed peat blocks cut from the frozen ground. The stench of burning peat filled the dug out as the small vent hole failed to cope with the smouldering damp earth beneath, the pit sweltered under the heat as the heat raised the air temperature higher in an attempt to sweat the fever from Cole's body, the four men now bare-chested could barely cope with the intense humidity within, each taking turns to freshen their lungs with the sharp cold air outside.

For a week Coles drifted in and out of consciousness, shivering cold one moment then fiercely hot the next, delirious with the ravages of violent fever his four friends nursed him through the sickness until finally the fever broke and Coles condition improved enough for him to take a little softened biscuit with sweetened tea from Will's diminishing block. The fever had taken its toll on Cole's health, constantly coughing this youthful sprightly lad had aged considerably by his illness, his spirited youth now long gone, his optimistic outlook which had kept the file in good company now lay lethargic and silent, staring into nothingness Coles barely uttered a word whilst lost in deep thought, Will tried to convince himself and the others the reasons for their comrades sluggishness

'His fire is dampened by the painful times he has suffered, surely his good spirit will return soon enough', he looked to justify his friends lack of interest and motivation but Coles sat isolated, saying nothing to assist Will's pleas but Zeke had seen the effects of typhus too many times before on distant campaigns where poor sanitary conditions bred the ravenous disease, those that died were usually the lucky ones he thought to himself as the ravages of violent fever had vicious ways of changing men's temperaments, more often for the worse.

The long winter ended with a sharp rise in temperatures, the northern winds shifted and thawed the last of the snows from the harsh landscapes and by late April the weather improved enough to resume the campaign season in full and decimated company's received replacements from the home lands and newly appointed Regiments made their first appearance overseas, the forthcoming invasion into New York and the Jerseys would be their first blooding in these rebellious lands.

Colonel Mawhood's 17th Regiment now formed part of the 4th brigade along with the 40th, and 55th Regiments under over all command of Major General Grant as forthcoming months restructured Howe's forces. The company less those still invalided from service formed ranks along the commons of Halifax town and observe Sergeant Vaughan instructing replacement recruits in the tricks of foreign campaign, to who his enemies might be and how best to survive the hardships of these lands. At distance the company's appearance looked the pride of the British army, on closer inspection however, uniforms began to fray, white laced cuffs torn, breeches split beyond repair and the hard wearing black winter leggings lay in rags around the wearer's legs.

Whilst the seasoned soldier did his level best to keep pride intact within their Regiments, for five years of service to the kings colours Will and his file had received only twice a new issue of clothing, a far cry from the 'gently and comfortably clothed soldiers, Sergeant Lucas had promised the impressionable lads on enlistment but morale kept high nonetheless, talk of the forthcoming invasion into the rebellious colonies would lift the spirits of the army after the disastrous siege at Boston, men talked of scores to settle and the final crushing of the rebellion in the coming summer months.

The file stood idly around the edges of the camp gazing at the precession of newly arrived soldiers, Dan pointed out to the file the strange green uniforms of hundreds of newly arrived troops, 'Hessians' Zeke spoke with a respect clear within his voice 'Germanic mercenaries and fierce warriors too, hired from the Prussian states' adding 'Be glad the Kings purse is deep and these men fight on our side' he quipped with a serious but light hearted tone. Will gawped at the strange appearance of these 'warriors', rarely under six feet tall, these moustached soldiers had a fierce menace about them and now amused by their strange and foreign appearance he thought to himself how Coles would appreciate the spectacle more than any, Coles however, was still absent from the file recovering in the regiments hospital after the effects of camp fever that decimated the ranks regardless of status or bearing.

Over eight thousand Hessians would merge into the Howe's army in preparation for the summer campaigns that most felt would crush the insurrections once and for all.

Previously, General Washington had thwarted Howe's every move during the long siege of Boston and fearful of enemy intelligence infiltrating the British command Howe ordered the 17th to move towards the expanding town of Saint John in the territories towards Lower Canada in an attempt discover the source of Washington's abilities to outmanoeuvre him.

With the arrival of replacements to the ranks the 17th regained its effective strength and Grant issued command for Mawhood to lead his Regiment to its destination and with winter firmly behind them the warm spring soon brought colour and life to the countryside, thick evergreen pine and spruce trees towered overhead as the column of soldiers marched through the countryside. Arriving late in the evening the advance camp had already been set much to the relief of the weary foot sore soldiers. Coles had rejoined his file on the last leg of the march having hitched a lift with the brigade's baggage wagons, welcoming their friend back into the fold Coles remained as silent as he had the last time the file had seen him, his usual chatter missed by all, his spark long since departed.

The region of New France and had troubled the English for years, although the bitter fought French wars had secured Nova Scotia and gained Quebec as a protectorate of Britain's expanding empire, French Quebecois insurgents had regularly terrorised loyal British colonists in the harsh isolated wilderness lands. Local Indian bands aided the British in their fight against the French but in these uncertain times the Indian nation lay split between its alliances to the crown and to those that sought to overthrow it.

The Ojibwa and Oneidas tribes had retained their loyalties to the crown but in these uncertain times, several trappers personal accounts had it that Penobscot Indians had sided with the Quebecois militias and began a series of raids against remote loyalist farms, the 17th would move north from saint John and establish its presence in an attempt to bring the tribes back to the British heel. Whilst smaller Indian bands had long served alongside the British forces as light auxiliaries and occasionally fighting in their own right against enemies of the crown, the unpredictability of these rogue nations caused enough concern to warrant investigation into the largely unsettled lands west of Fredericton and along the winding St Croix river.

Seymour, McPherson and Leslie's companies now combining one hundred and twenty men received instruction to scout west from Fredericton towards the small fur trading post of Hartland along the Saint Croix River and re-establish relationships with influential tribes of the area that might pull smaller bands into order. The three companies advanced in column through the wilderness roads towards the small outpost that would offer the column some shelter and sanctuary for the night. These unsettled lands proved difficult to travel as the coherence of the columns order began to crumble, sensibly to speed movement the three companies fell into line formation just five abreast as the road turned into a track that loosely followed the course of the river. Zeke commented on the environment being ripe for ambush, "'Tis a good thing we're not packed tight' he spoke, 'We'd be cut to pieces should be receive fire now'.

Although the high midday sun struggled to penetrate the thick evergreen canopy above the moisture remained trapped on the forest floor causing humidity to rise uncomfortably as the men struggled with the weight of the equipment carried about them. The officers gave orders for the companies to fall out giving a brief rest along the narrow tracked pathway, much to the relief of many exhausted men who instantly fell to their knees with fatigue. Will swigged cool water from his wooden canteen, swilling the contents around his dry mouth before spitting it at his dusty feet, Thom Allen removed a half loaf of bread from his knapsack and broke the crust into five pieces for his friends to share and Zeke predictably lit his long stemmed pipe and sucked the smouldering tobacco into his lungs before customarily offering it to the others when Zeke paused a moment and stared towards the front of the column, 'Something's afoot' he spoke trusting his soldierly experience to give him prior warning of anomalies in hostile lands. The five men looked over the heads of the line as they rested the few minutes, the companies had employed four Métis Indians to scout the way ahead, finding something strange ahead they returned to deliver the information to the three officers, 'Bloody hell' Dan spoke up alarmed by their presence, 'where in God's name did they come from?' he asked with alarm, 'They joined us some ten miles back' Zeke replied as he pulled his pack onto his back anticipating the urgency ahead, 'Then why didn't you tell us we were being shadowed?' Will asked, Zeke settled his equipment on his shoulders and pausing a moment from his tobacco answered 'Because you didn't ask' he answered nonchalantly, Will looked on, stumped at the answer, 'A logic in its own right' Coles piped up, the first words he'd uttered since the column left Fredericton.

The officers signalled the company sergeants to a hasty briefing, 'Now is the time we get to taste our officers competencies' Zeke commented spitting a mixture of tobacco juice and saliva on the dank floor. Sergeant Vaughan made his way through the long line of soldiers to the file and knelt beside his corporal the two discussed the orders as directed by McPherson. The hired scouts had reported signs of an enemy presence ahead, although no direct sightings had occurred the scouts had tracked a good number moving through the forest towards the outpost that lay ahead and cautiously the officer's strategy would involve careful movements until more intelligence could be gained on the position. Vaughan raced back to the head of the line leaving his Corporal to direct his men as required. 'McPherson wants us up front' Zeke announced rising to his feet and securing his musket across his shoulder. The file collectively groaned at the short length of their rest whilst the remaining company still lounged from this arduous march, Will helped Coles to his feet and eased him into his equipment before passing him his musket 'Double up' Zeke called back as the two lagged a distance behind.

Reaching the front of the column the file fanned out to the left flank of the main body, the three officers rode at the lead of the line of redcoats and Sergeant Vaughan led a selection of marksmen to the right cautiously patrolling the hostile area they now entered.

'Keep ten paces between each man' Zeke ordered his file as he spread across the line as five other members of the company quickly joined the file to bolster their effective firepower should any attack be forthcoming. The flanking guard of well spaced men trod lightly through the undergrowth, lifting his feet high, Will felt the snags of thorny brambles entangling his feet and caring not to loosen the barbs his motion pulled them clear as the depths of the gloomy forest thickened. To keep level with the column the line of ten checked its pace keeping sure and firm sight towards the main body of infantry, 'Don't lose sight of your markers' Zeke whispered along the line to his wards, 'and keep pace with the others' he continuously instructed his men as they moved forward through the wilderness. The file stepped fifty yards left of the main column keeping watchful eyes ahead and Sergeant Vaughan's file all being well, would guard the right flank.

The darkness of the forest lifted occasionally by bright beams of sunlight breaking through the high canopies but the most the movement was through the dark obscurity of the ancient tall forest. The forest floor stank of decay, damp and rotting hulks of fallen tree's making a straight line of movement impossible as the line tried to keep cohesion, Zeke leading the files front called a halt to the advance signalling his men to squat for cover whilst Vaughan trusted his corporals experience in assessing the situation.

The line lay still for a few moments whilst Zeke gauged the files position for a potential ambush. Sitting perfectly still Zeke honed his soldering skills to the surroundings as the faint smell of burning wood smoke tickled through his senses, every man of the line watched for his signal knowing that men like Zeke Turner did not live by luck alone. Now confident the area ahead was secure from the enemy, he advanced the line slowly towards a clearing in the distance just barely visible through the gloom, as the line moved forward the source of the smoke soon became apparent. Zeke signalled an all clear to Sergeant Vaughan who in turn rose his men from their concealed positions and signalled them to cross the exposed trail to merge with his own line. Zeke and Vaughan carefully scrutinised the clearing ahead and concluded their actions, four men drawn from the Sergeants lines would return to the column for the advice of the officers wishes. The selected men skilfully darted through the undergrowth and into the shadows beyond to relay their findings. Zeke signalled his file to spread ranks as the clearing was perfect killing ground for ambush, Coles, Will and the two Allen brothers made their way to the forward position, finding at the feet of the two a wide eyed pale corpse that lay propped against a tree stump clutching his bloody guts, shot clean through his stomach the injured victim had crawled from whatever lay ahead to die alone into the dark forest, Sergeant Vaughan examined the body for clues to who may have killed the man, 'Bloods fairly fresh, I doubt he's been here longer than a day' Zeke remarked, Sergeant Vaughan directed the advance party, 'The four of you go ahead and scout the clearing,' instantly the four quickly unloaded their knapsacks and prepared to move towards the thickening grey smoke, 'Nice and slow lads, keep your wits about you' Zeke commented confirming the gravity of the possible ambush.

The four travelled a further hundred yards through the dark forest before the bright sunlight gave a clear image of the destruction that lay before their eyes, as the party advanced cautiously from the forest into the clearing the cause of the drifting smoke came apparent. The timber walled stockade stood ghostly silent within the clearing, abandoned of life the fort spewed smoke from within.

The file positioned itself either side of the stockade entrance and cocked their muskets unsure of what lay inside, thick smoke from the smouldering log cabins drifted across their view and watering the eyes of those who witnessed the carnage within its boundary limits. The heavy timber doors of the stockade lay wide open revealing a score of bodies that lay scattered in every direction, around the collection of charred and vandalised wooden cabin's, the occupants it seemed had fought hard to protect their homes before falling under the enemy's violent attack.

Satisfied the perimeter was empty of the attackers Will turned to face the deep forest behind and waved Zeke up towards the area, the Corporal dashed across the clearing reaching the four that poised themselves alert at the forts entrance, 'All quiet it seems' Will advised, 'not a living soul about'. 'Aye, it looks a bloody mess in there' Thom added as Zeke visually assessed the carnage. Zeke gave orders for his remaining men to advance from the tree line towards the settlement moving in double time to the massacre that stood before them. The mounted officers brought the remainder of the column in to view ordering them to fall out prior to the clearing and secure the area for any threats that still may be present, the five men of the file walked through the dead brutally cut down as they had fought to protect their homes, with respect they carefully lifted his feet as not to disturb their twisted and contorted bodies but these victims desired no respect as mutilated they lay in the days heat swarmed by flies. Sergeant Vaughan entered the compound and made direction for the file, 'Spread your file Zeke, search for survivors and clues to who committed this butchery' he instructed his Corporal. Zeke ordered his file to search for survivors amongst the dead that littered the area around, the outpost had been hit hard during the attack and by whom was at this stage anyone's guess, on entering the scorched log cabin they soon found the answers they were looking for. The main central building of the outpost had been ransacked throughout, its contents and furnishings trashed beyond hope and in all the destruction towards the rear of the structure a small wooden door lay ajar from its frame, Will nervously peered inside the opening and quickly turned away in disgust at the horrors within.

The men of the outpost had fought gallantly against their attackers, however these people were traders and trappers not soldiers, their primitive and antiquated muskets gave little chance of fending off a concentrated assault and now shot and speared, the defenders lay mutilated within as they fought their last action, as these brave men had died to protect their homes the women and children had secreted themselves in the forts storage room at the rear of the building and undiscovered the attackers had fired the building's roof as a final act of destructive vandalism. The thatched straw roofs had gone like tinder once flames had caught hold, those left inside chose to face their end by burning to death rather than be cut down as they fled.

The silent remains of the occupants lay huddled together on the dirt floor as babes in arms suffocated at the mother's bosom.

Will looked on with a sickened feeling at the horrific sight within before shouting Zeke over to his findings who paced towards the macabre scene rubbing his bristled chin commenting as he strode on the brutality of the maiming, despite his years soldiering Zeke showed clear signs of distress as he witnessed the tragedy inside the small room cupping his hands over his nose and mouth in disbelief. The two brothers glanced inside but despite their harsh and brutal upbringing had no desire to expose themselves longer than necessary, Coles on the other hand, paralysed with shock stood broken hearted and despondent at the brutality that confronted him. As the file moved away fresh faced and inexperienced soldiers eager to see what the file had discovered peered inside, some retching at the sight while others turned away in disgust with neither the stomach or morbid fascination to see anymore.

Around the rear of the cabin lay more slaughter, pigs, goats and fowl lay within their pens with their throat slit, dogs had been skewered and anything of value smashed beyond use during this terrible orgy of violence. McPherson stood aghast at this cruelty and conferred with his brethren officers on the best tactical option, the full days march back to the Regiment's garrison at Fredericton would leave the column more than vulnerable to whatever attacked the outpost with such ferocity, so as to protect the column better Seymour and Leslie would return immediately to Fredericton leaving McPherson and a handful of experienced men from Leslie's company to defend the outpost.

The departing men immediately fell in and moved swiftly back towards the track that brought them there leaving just thirty men to secure the wooden stockade from further attack, lessons learned at Boston on the urgency of disposing of the dead put the majority to work digging communal pits in the baked stony earth. Soldiers piled their equipment and heavy redcoats in the centre of the smouldering community and stacked their loaded muskets in readiness for any return of the enemy and went about removing and ordering the dead for a speedy burial once the party had finished. Will turned to a commotion coming from a trader's cabin, miraculously amongst all the carnage a survivor had been found, though barely alive a young girl no older than twelve years of age had been scalped and left for dead amongst her kin folk, too weak to be returned to civilisation the girl drifted in and out of delirium as the file moved her from the harsh days heat into a temporary shelter at the centre of the stockade. Coles still unfit for heavy duty nursed her as best he could under the difficult circumstances, offering his patient a little water to her parched lips and soothing her last moments with lamented tunes picked out on his treasured violin but the odds of survival drew slim for the young girl and realising her suffering McPherson directly instructed Coles to make her last moments as comfortable as possible after witnessing such atrocities at the hands of the enemy whilst Sergeant Skinner argued fiercely with Vaughan over the loss of one man to care for such a hopeless cause, the girl would be lucky to make daybreak he insisted, Vaughan quietly reminded Skinner of his seniority within the Regiment almost to the verge of humiliation of the lesser ranked sergeant. Skinner scowled at

Vaughan as he instructed him to return to his own party and make himself more useful in rebuilding the defences of the stockade.

The treaty of Paris and Huberusberg thirteen years previously has ended the wars between France and Britain in the northern colonies gaining French Canada to expanding British interests in the Americas, although the French presence was accepted in these lands the uprising against the crown in the southern colonies had given rise to discourse from the French population.

Yet unbeknown to the defenders a combined raiding party of Penobscot Indians and Quebecois militia had hit the outpost hard bent on killing all the inhabitants as a warning to the expanding British interests in the surrounding area.

Zeke was still despondent at the sadism committed to the outpost and although he'd seen warfare many times before this brought a whole new level to the atrocities a man was able to commit to his fellow man, 'Warfare is changing in these modern times' he spoke indirectly to those around him, 'These people cared not for politics or representation, only for the meagre existence they could forge out in these inhospitable lands'.

The days sun began to dip over the tall tree's casting long shadows across the clearing, Sergeant Vaughan ordered picket guards on the high timber walls and the smashed lumber gates that swung freely from their fastenings repaired to withstand another attack should it be forthcoming. The outpost that housed a community of fifty men women and children now stood sparsely defended by a force of less than thirty as the defenders prepared themselves for the night. Thom Allen questioned the sense in dividing the column in the face of the unknown enemy and Vaughan subtlety reminded him of his position within the ranks, "tis not your responsibility to question a gentleman officer lad, no matter how unreasonable his decisions may be', Allen took this lightly knowing even Sergeant Vaughan had doubts to the officers preference.

Now putting his men to good use Vaughan ordered huge lumber piles to be stacked on the fringe of the dark forest, 'Come nightfall we will light em bright to illuminate the clearing, It affects the enemy's sight' he said clarifying the reasons behind this.

Sergeant Vaughan was no fool, he had served with the 17th longer than anyone could remember, 'married' to the army they said and a true soldiers soldier, Vaughan had enlisted as a boy to the end of the war of Austrian succession and for nearly thirty years he'd travelled with the colours far and wide across the empire, 'Sergeant Vaughan is an old breed of soldier' Zeke remarked to the file,

'With luck some of you may live to see his age'. Being born in rural Ireland James Vaughan had little trace of his natural accent, a veteran of Louisburg, Quebec and Wilhelmstahl Vaughan had soldiered well during his career, well enough some said to retire on the proceeds of bounty he had accumulated over the times but Vaughan only knew the army, his family it was said lay on the field of battle. Will had taken little notice of his Sergeant till now seeing Zeke as the epitome of professional soldiering, his mentor however respected Vaughan's type and in Will's eyes if Zeke thought highly of him then he was a good man to have in ones presence.

At dusk the ranks drew lots on guard duty, the Allen brothers drawing the first stint of their watch from ten till two bells, Coles and Will would relieve them till daybreak. The deep blue summer sky passed into darkness, lit with bright stars and a moonlit evening the beautiful night sky gave little hint to what was coming. Vaughan ordered the lumber piles ignited as planned, casting shadows amongst the trees making the inexperienced guard jittery and uneasy, several times calling a stand to on their watch. As the last of the daylight disappeared over the trees the timber gates closed to the dark forest that surrounded them and Will snuggled down by the file's fireside staring into the embers that burned brightly before closing his eyes to catch a few moments rest. Although it only felt like minutes, after a few hours Zeke shook him by the shoulder urging him awake, 'Wake up lad, tis your turn for watch' disappearing to fetched Coles who had spent the evening nursing the young girl under nearby canvas, reluctantly leaving her side for his allocated guard duty. The two men climbed the short wooden ladder that led to the narrow parapet above, Will patted Dan on the shoulder, 'Go rest friends' he softly spoke 'your time is done'. 'Aye' replied Thom 'all is calm, tis quiet out there, although some jittery fool keeps calling a 'stand to' at the slightest noise'.

Thom and Dan Allen withdrew from the narrow ledge and descended the short ladder to the files warming fire, Will glanced down as the two lay under their woollen blankets and settled down for the remainder of the night. The full low moon shone brightly across the clearing as the series of camp fires dwindled into smouldering ashes, Zeke made an appearance at the top of the ladder, 'If they are sure to attack it's now so keep your damned eyes open' he offered few words of encouragement to the two bored sentry's.

The dead of night lay still with the distant trees swaying gently in the summer breeze and the raging pyres died down into a faint glow as the last of the timbers smouldered away, 'Will' whispered Coles, 'I can hear something', 'Oh hush your nerves will you, you're as bad as those recruits behind us' Will answered whilst resting against the timber palisades.

'Stand to' Coles snapped, 'What spooks you now Sam' Will replied. 'Stand to will you', he paused his breath to listen for the slightest sound, begrudgingly Will sighed as he picked his musket from against the stockade when tipping his felt hat backwards he heard a feint noise come from beneath the parapet, the noise came again and this time louder, his voice snapped at the sentry's positioned to the left, 'You heard the man, bloody stand to wont you!', the men on the left wall jumped into life at his authoritative words. Ever cautious Will peered over the side of the parapet, the darkness below obscured his senses as the full moons long shadows made it difficult to see past the ditch twelve feet beneath them. He stared long and hard for his eyes to adjust to the darkness beneath and just as he was turning away he heard the familiar fizz then crack of a musket discharging to his left.

Coles yelled at Will to move back to cover of the parapet when suddenly catching him unawares the tree line lit up with a vicious volley of rifled musketry. Will dropped instinctively to the low ledge that supported him as lead balls thudded against the thick timbers, a moment's hesitation longer and he would've been hit by the shower of hot lead from the distant tree line.

Ever alert Zeke cried towards the two 'are you hurt?' he enquired upwards, 'Just my pride' Will yelled back over the din of discharging gunpowder, the two men readily presented their arms towards the trees and releasing their cocked hammers simultaneously the two fired their shot high to adjust for the falling trajectory of the bullet. Of the two sentries distanced to their left, one lay slumped over the timber logs that protected the stockade from attack his musket still rested by his side, the other too scared to do anything but cower behind the safety of the wall. Bent on hands and knees Will crawled towards the position as still the sound of bullets slammed into the outside of the wooden structure, pulling the dead man down from the stockade he noted the man's musket primed and ready for use, If this was to be a long fight a spare weapon might well come in handy he thought taking it back towards Coles who sat busy ramming home his next charge destined for the enemy.

Beneath the parapet hurried soldiers rallied to their arms ready to face the unseen foe, protected by the thick timbers of the stockade Will heard a dull thud against them, not a sound of the familiar bullets but of a scaling ladder placed against the stockades walls, waiting a second or two Will raised his musket and presented it over the parapet precisely into the face of the oncoming attacker.

Without thought he squeezed the trigger of his weapon . . . crack, his pan ignited and flashed the charge directly into the face of the bewildered assailant, the closeness of his enemy startled him as the shot slammed into its victim, the man hovered a moment before cascading backwards down the wooden scaling ladder and with his feet tangled midpoint the body hung suspended until gravity played its part and tumbled the corpse to earth. With a wall breach imminent the two men could not load their muskets quickly enough so Will drew his bayonet from its scabbard and snapped it secure to the smoking tip of the weapons barrel, the socket twisted into position with a sharp click barely in time to receive its victim scurrying up the ladder to the parapets edge.

Will glanced right to see Coles wrestle his foe from the thin ledge of the parapet and throw his screaming body to the inside of the stockade where it was quickly dispatched by waiting bayonets of the soldiers below. The Allen brothers darted up the short ladders to the parapet to assist their two comrades and Zeke directed from the ground points were the attack was most likely to penetrate, Will and Coles stood firm on the height of the stockade whilst Thom And Dan made their way towards them, Coles ferociously lunging downward at any who dared scale the ladders outside.

The first assault fizzled out leaving three casualties, one dead and two lightly wounded on the British side and an estimated count of six dead from the enemy. Vaughan mustered his men, ordering any burning camp fire extinguished save the light from obscuring the vision of the defenders and advising the men to don their familiar redcoats so that during the ensuing attack the enemy might not be mistaken, despite the warmness of the summer night not a man objected to his order knowing the confusion of battle only too well.

A Company drummer boy distributed fresh cartridges and water to those who requested it and Zeke withdrew his men from the parapet in order to prepare them for another assault. The five lifted ammunition from the young drummer's felt hat carefully placing them inside their cartridge pouches and taking a moments respite Will uncorked his canteen and gulped heavily from its contents before passing it around his four friends, 'Finish it' he spoke to the last of the drinkers before twisting his bayonet loose from his musket and wiping the congealed blood into a rag from his pocket, Coles silently took the remainder of the water and poured it around his sweated neck before handing the empty container back to Will.

'Back to it lads' Zeke spoke being the first to climb the ladder back on to the parapets heights and the five men positioned themselves at even spaces along the square wooden fortifications, Zeke trusted his men with his life and after five years together that time would well be upon them. The thin line of redcoats perched on the edge and waited patiently for the next assault, Lieutenant McPherson paced the clearing surrounded by a half dozen men ready to plug gaps or stem a break through. The cracks between the thick lumbers gave slight vision into the darkness beyond, for over an hour Will and his comrades waited silently till without warning the tree line again lit up with a volley of musketry, again Will heard the dulled thuds of lead hitting the tall timbers protecting him from his enemy. The men waited again for another volley then rose themselves in unison presenting their deadly weapons at the dark forest beyond, the five men uniformly snapped their powder spitting lead across the short space between the fortifications and the forests trees.

'We need to keep a sustained fire' Zeke said, 'Will, Sam, present your muskets when Thom, Dan and I reload'. For the next few minutes the file poured a constant fire towards the enemy as the seasoned soldiers managed to discharge an impressive four rounds a minute. 'Keep your heads down lads' yelled Zeke to his men, 'the next assault is imminent and I'm going to need every man jack of you ready'. Through the gaps Will squinted to observe the movements of the enemy ahead, the enemy in good number began wheeling a four pound field gun from the cover of the trees on the furthest part of the clearing, 'Bloody hell' he paused 'they've got artillery', Zeke snatched a glance over the low parapet to confirm Will's claim and took one look before calling to all that could hear him to present arms simultaneously upon the field piece as the gunners elevated it to its firing position.

'Now!' Zeke yelled as the well drilled line of redcoats rose over the parapet and presented their muskets on their target. 'Choose your targets' Zeke screamed as the side of the stockade aimed their deadly muskets towards the dreadful target, 'Fire!' he yelled through the rage of the din above. The north side of the stockade erupted with spark and flame, the soldiers bullets found their mark throwing dead and screaming artillerymen from the guns carriage, the field gun sat unmanned across the clearing as gun smoke drifted across the fort. The gun stood silent across the clearing towards the forest's edge, now the redcoats had found its target none would be foolish to man the gun until the defenders had been subdued. With the immediate threat removed the file relaxed a moment when without warning the far side of the stockade erupted in a ball of flame as splintered timbers scattered across the perimeter of the log cabins.

Whilst concentrating on the northern assault the rebels had brought a second gun into place bearing towards Sergeant Skinners position, unnoticed the rebels had blasted round shot into the stockades gates shattering them across the defended area leaving a wide gap between the stockades circular walls. Men cried in agony as the iron cannon ball smashed through the stockade gates like brittle matchwood splintering amongst the defenders. The dust and smoke settled across the distant side of the stockade as Skinner stumbled through the smoke, bleeding heavily from his face, hatless and his sergeants' epaulette's torn from his tunic he collapsed over a headless torso of one of his fellow defenders. Zeke paused a second taking stock of the situation signalling to his four friends, 'All of you, get down now' the four men leapt from the parapet onto the hard ground beneath, 'Come on' he cried as the five swiftly made their way towards the breached timbers, 'We need to plug that gap'. Together the five raced across the yard to the breached gateway, on reaching the gap Will observed Skinner standing to the left of the breach yelling obscenities towards those around him, bleeding superficially from his legs the hated sergeant collapsed at the sight of the five rushing towards him 'Please don't hurt me' he whimpered, delusional after the shock of being physically blasted from his position 'pray have mercy for sweet old Mathias'. The file ignored the pathetic figure as he collapsed face down into the dust snivelling to himself for fear of his life.

The men took positions either side of the breach and quickly studied the tree lines for the artillery piece, Zeke identified the position of the gun that caused so much destruction to the defences, the five quickly reloaded their muskets and presented towards the gun, 'Fire!' Zeke bellowed as the five slammed their shot at the gunners exposed while reloading the cannon. With the professional soldiers accuracy the enemy fell under the hail of fire as the redcoats hastily discharged their weapons in the face of their enemy. The gun stood silent with the crew mortally wounded as the file breathed a quick sigh of relief. As the Redcoats reloaded it was now the rebels turn to open fire, unlike the disciplined volleys from the defenders the enemy took open pot shots at the besieged guardians of the ravaged stockade. 'Keep your heads down' Zeke ordered, 'I need every one of you alive' he added carefully aiming his shot towards anything that moved from the tree line. 'He don't half state the bleeding obvious' Dan Allen quipped and Will smiled at the wit and cheer of his comrades despite the desperate situation they found themselves in.

McPherson directed his men to cover the breach allowing the five to withdraw a little into the perimeter of the stockade but after an hour of battle ammunition began to run low, Dan Allen called the young drummer boy for more ammunition from the company baggage wagon, the sprightly lad scurried over to their position dropping a wooden box at their feet prising open the sealed lid with his small sword as each delved into the case for more cartridges. As the file packed their cartridge boxes Dan passed his canteen around as they caught their breaths after the wild moments of gunpowder exchanges, 'Rum?' Coles queried as he swallowed too much expecting the contents to be water, 'Aye, the best' he replied as Coles handed the canteen to Will who gulped a heavy mouthful followed by a long gasp as he drew the cuff of his coat over his mouth.

The fight had quietened down by now to only the occasional rifle shot coming from the tree line, 'They're regrouping' Zeke shouted staring out into the void ahead, 'We've not seen the last of this yet' he added.

Will poured the last of the water from his canteen over the hot barrel of his musket and brushed any fouled powder from the pans touch hole, it was now over two hours since the opening shots of the engagement which gave cause for him to discharge his musket over thirty times towards the enemy. His thumb swollen and calloused he gently rubbed his right cheek reddened and sore with powder burns from the edge of his dry powder blackened mouth to the lobe of his ear, untying his long hair he gathered it up back into a tight group and retied the lace into a bow around it save it singing any further from the powder flash from his muskets pan.

The bright full moon shone across the night sky as the exhausted garrison stood on alert for yet another attack, Zeke was uncannily right, another attack came just prior to the dawn sunrise. McPherson wandered amongst his men asking for their welfare, 'All's well with us Sir' Zeke commented as the officer drifted from group to group. The lull in the fighting gave the defenders some time to repair the gap within the stockades breach, anything that would hinder an assault was used to obstruct the six foot wide splintered hole caused by the enemy's now redundant cannon. The attacker's inexperience in professional warfare had cost them dearly, by positioning their two small field cannons away from the protection of the forest made access to the pieces a killing ground for the precision shots of the well trained and disciplined redcoats as the bodies of those who'd attempted to reoccupy the guns lay spread thick along the ground, none nearing the pieces closer than five yards.

Six hours after the initial assault the sun began to rise over the horizon forcing the assaulters into their last chance of successfully over running the outpost and the experience of the redcoats knew almost precisely when the final assault was coming and prepared to present their arms fully in the face of the enemy. The south side again bore the brunt of the assault with each man ever eager to face the rebels with their long sharp bayonets but wisely Zeke kept his file close to the weakened breach of the defences knowing the enemies strategy. If the enemy could get a number inside the stockade the effectiveness of the musket would be rendered useless and the fight would resort to bloody hand to hand combat, with overwhelming superiority the defenders would soon be overrun and the fort taken once and for all. The crack of enemy muskets that filled the air signalled the start of the rebels last assault on their quarry, Sergeant Vaughan steadied his remaining men in the face of the enemies final advance. Positioned on the parapet above the hastily repaired breach on the south side of the stockade the five men poured their shots into the advancing attackers but Zeke was right, with too fewer ready muskets the advance of enemy made steady progress into the defences of the outpost. Although much slower to load the attackers armed with rifles had good aim on the defenders forcing them below the safety of the palisades, the redcoats could barely raise their heads to reply to the fierce fire.

On reaching the perimeter once again the assault ladders leant against the barricades, only then could the defenders position themselves to return fire on the attackers. At the main gate Will discharged his musket time and time again as the assaulters desperately tried to gain entry within the perimeter defences, 'Ammunitions running low' Dan called to the frantic drummer boy below, 'That's the last lot' the boy replied as he scurried up the short ladder to the platform above, 'Best make em count Sam' Will added, 'We'll be using steel before too long'. Will fumbled around his cartridge belt for his charges, only two left, priming his pan with his penultimate round he carefully followed the path of his opponent as he chased across the clearing towards him and with a sharp crack his musket fired its wares towards the assailant, slamming fiercely into his body the man continued to dart towards the stockade, blood squirting upwards from his shoulder wound before stumbling to the ground in a cloud of dust, quickly he recharged his musket and presented one final time to his enemy. Pulling the muskets hammer firmly back he squeezed the trigger sharply claiming yet another victim, 'That's it for shot' he shouted, 'Me too' replied Dan Allen as the sounds of discharging gunpowder faded across the stockade, the musket now became useful for what every soldier feared most, the bayonet.

Will shook his arms to relax the musket that would now receive the enemy even closer, Still the enemy came at them and Will lunged forwards, his bayonet pierced the chest of the vulnerable man, his body twitched as Will sank the full length of steel into his soft flesh. Struggling to pull his bayonet clear of the sinking body Will yanked the blade from the torso losing and his footing slipped backwards to the ground, winded and breathless he lay with pain in his chest wondering at first if he'd been shot, Zeke knelt down besides him crouching next to his spread body, 'you'll be needing this' he said handing him his musket and rubbing the palm of his rough hand across his long hair before returning back into the fray.

Will gazed toward the parapet above as Coles violently swung his musket at all who dared to appear on the parapets edge, one of his victims dropped from above landing with a large thud next to the dazed lad who in slight shock stared into the wide open eyes of the dead attacker that now shared the space around him. Quickly rising to his feet, Will looked around at the last of the furious assault dissipate around him, a few redcoats stood behind the temporary barricade delivering shot towards the withdrawing enemy as they fled back towards the safety of the forest tree line. Making his way up the ladder to the parapet Will concerned himself with his friend Coles, wild with fury he cornered the last of the invaders who despite being badly wounded sank to his knees pleaded for his life as he clasped his hands together for mercy.

Sam Coles, now enraged with hatred lunged forward with his blood soaked dripping bayonet, this enemy, a mere boy sat prone on his knees pleading for safe quarter found none. Lunging forward he pushed his steel tipped musket hard into the boy's chest, his eyes widened as the steel passed through him pinning his young body to the timbers behind, deep in the blood lust Coles withdrew his bayonet and lunged again and again into the bloody corpse before him. Will rushed across the parapet towards his friend, 'Sam' he called placing his hands on Coles shoulders 'It's over'. Coles swung round towards Wills direction, his eyes untamed with fury Will dodged the might of the musket as the berserk soldier lunged towards him. 'It's over Sam' Will spoke as he forcibly yanked the musket from his arms and threw it to the ground. Coles sank to his knees sobbing at the carnage around, the dead lay thick at his feet, more than half a dozen had died on Coles cold steel with more dead at the foot of the stockade outer walls.

Zeke stood besides Will as the two looked on at Coles and his state of collapse, resting his hand on his shoulder he spoke softly to him, 'Battle does a strange thing to a man' offering his open hand he helped Coles back to his feet.

By mid morning the defenders felt safe enough to venture out to the perimeter outside, the dead lay thick at the base of the stockade with a count of ten inside, the toll had been bloody, the defenders had lost sixteen to the assaults that night, ten to the barrage that decimated the southern wall. Skinner recovered his superficial wounds to be active in presence by noon strutting about like some hero. Sergeant Vaughan reported twenty eight dead amongst the attackers with both field guns abandoned in the hasty retreat. Exhausted the file sat shaded from the high midday sun resting their tired bones from the night's battle. Coles edged away from his friends and sat besides the body of the girl he'd nursed the day before, his knees high under his chin he rocked back and forth with motion as his head sank into his knees. 'Leave the lad to make his peace with god' Zeke commented to the others, Coles fury had alarmed his fellow file, considered the 'gentleman' of the group his behaviour had upset the harmony of the file, 'He's not the lad we once knew' Thom spoke harshly, but Zeke interrupted his complaints 'such a chain of events changes a man' himself having seen men break under the strains of battle many times before.

For the remainder of the day what was left of the defenders waited for Mawhood to send relief troops to the decimated garrison, Coles sat alone and when approached by his friends moved away to a quiet corner of the stockade in solitude. Brereton's Grenadier company along with two companies of the infamous Hessians relieved the battered survivors at dusk, the reinforced garrison was now sufficiently manned to strength giving little probability of another attack, the stockade's new troops allowed the bewildered survivors time to rest until daybreak and the long march back through the forest to the border town of Fredericton and the much needed supplies it held.

Sam Coles spoke little during the weeks spent at Fredericton and then the larger garrison at Fort Saint-John, whilst the four frittered their pay on cheap drink, gambling and the many prostitutes the town quartered, Coles however preferred his own company fishing the quiet backwaters for wild trout and salmon, the four often returned to the billet to find freshly caught fish left for them by their subdued comrade.

Whilst the army built its strength for the forthcoming invasion into the southern colonies the company rested itself lazily along the rivers edges, drinking the days away or preparing equipment for inspection by senior officers, the fray along the St Croix river had given rise to promotions within the 17th Regiment, Lieutenant McPherson was gazetted to the rank of Captain leaving his old position vacant until his replacement arrived from England, Lieutenants Tew, Seymour and Scott also received the rank of captains of their respective companies, whilst Zeke himself was offered the rank of Sergeant within a depleted company refilled with fresh recruits. Predictably Zeke declined the offer, again citing his preference with his men in McPherson's company and Will privately enquired to him on the wasted prospects of the Sergeants role within one of the refitted company's, Zeke as nonchalant as always joked 'you lads wouldn't last five moments without my watchful eye over you', Will chuckled at his Corporal's comments realising only too well that his mentoring had kept the file together and saved the lives of them so many times over, they all knew Zeke's presence held the five of them tightly together, a seasoned campaigner knew the noble art of soldiering as though it was his life, for Zeke Turner, this son of a Dorset smuggler who had been adopted into military service from such a young age, campaign soldiering was his life and without the bond and camaraderie of Regimental life Zeke would stand alone in this world, it was his life blood and lately he needed his fellows as much as they needed him.

Coles had kept distance between himself and the others in his file much to the annoyance of Thom Allen, though each man had on several occasions attempted to console their friend into what troubled him so the bond between the five showed signs of fragmenting beyond repair. To aid in his self imposed isolation Coles regularly volunteered for additional guard duty, spending hour after hour alone by the camps perimeter guard house, Will often took hot drinks to Coles whilst he laboured in his extra duties but often found the previous beverage untouched.

As the summer months arrived the advance party's broke camp and formed up alongside the remainder of the Regiment, Coles had rejoined the file but his personality had changed considerably. In times before Coles would use any opportunity to press his education and intelligence onto the others, to outsiders it was seen as patronising, to those who knew him, this was just his way but these days Coles rarely spoke, tortured by his inner pains Will could clearly see the turmoil within his mind, presently his manner had altered beyond recognition, often before any periods of silence would be soon filled with Coles opinions and doctrines of the world they shared. Now Sam Coles sat alone and in silence, troubled by the horrors of warfare and loss.

Howe's invasion against the congressional army required a large amphibious landing, in amassing troops at Staten Island within Richmond County south of New York, Howe hoped the strike into the heart of Washington's army would smash the rebellion once and for all, the 17th now reinforced to a battalion strength marched westwards along the Bay of Fundy to the harbour town of Jonesport to rendezvous with the waiting invasion barges. The Province of Massachusetts Bay was one of thirteen revolutionary colonies declared in rebellion against the crown by King George, ever watchful the 17th and the accompanying squadron of light dragoons trailed across the countryside towards the waiting fleet. In loose marching formation the company advanced steadily along the long roads that linked trade routes from New Hampshire towards Nova Scotia, occasionally resting at sparsely inhabited hamlets and villages that lined the winding roads offering shelter and hospitality to travellers. The company rested for the night at the village of Eastbrook, a tiny gathering of typically weather boarded colonial buildings with a current population of less than fifty families, the village consisted of a general merchant who enthralled at the arrival of paid troops hastily opened his shop to the eager soldiers more than willing to buy his overpriced luxury goods. Whilst the squadron of Dragoons commandeered the Smithy and outer buildings the 17th where left with whatever billets they could find, the small Inn offered little room and knowing his few available rooms now commanded a high value placed a price higher than most could or where willing to afford. Will and his comrades joined the long line for shelter at the local church, the small singular roomed whitewashed Lutheran building crammed with a few rough wooden seats were soon cleared to make way for the numerous soldiers, the five sat at ease towards the rear quarter of the wooden floored church, the warm summer months dried the surrounding lands of the dampness that desperately clung to the earth but to these seasoned soldiers a dry billet was more than preferable to a night blanket on the hard country earth. Sitting cross legged upon the untreated wooden floorboards the file shared cold bitter tasting coffee from the communal camp kettle and passed a loaf of flat bread amongst themselves each man breaking an equal share from the small loaf.

Coles rarely spoke about his troubles in these difficult days but Will the closest of the four to him knew him far better than to leave his friend to suffer the anguish within his soul. Pressing at every opportunity for an angle into his minds anxiety, Coles either humoured him or dismissed it out of hand requesting he be left alone, his sketch book untouched since their arrival at St John, his fiddle not played since the defence at the St Croix River. Discouraged with his lack of progress Will abandoned his efforts for the night at least and tilted his black felt hat over his eyes and began his docile slumber after the days march leaving the disturbed Coles staring vacantly into his minds turbulent void. The sun set past nine bells as the occupants of the church fell into a silence within the envelope of its dark embrace.

Just prior to dawn Will awoke amongst the sounds of the company men stirring, stiff from the days long march combined with a uncomfortable night's sleep on hard but at least dry boards he arched his shoulders back stretching the tension from his strained muscles, widening his bleary eyes, noted unusually he was the first to awaken amongst his file, Zeke sat with his back square to the walls as he'd slept all night and Dan and Thom Allen lay curled with their backs to each other as though co-joined together.

Will ran his calloused fingers through his long greasy hair in an attempt to make himself more presentable to the day, scanning his sleepy eyes around the dim room, his senses rudely awakened on realising Sam Coles absence. Calming his concerns, he hoped against logic that Coles would be found outside gathering his rations from the company wagons, until his logic noted the early hour of the day, Will pulled on his tailcoat and trod carefully through the still slumbering soldiers who gained advantage of these extra moments sleep before the company would be called to muster. Silently pulling open the wrought iron latches that secured the churches double doors, Will stepped out onto the boarded front porch and quickly scanned the village for his missing comrade, with no life signs obvious he swiftly paced towards the Dragoons stabling hoping his presence might force Coles to emerge from his sanctuary. The morning summer sun rose quickly over the distant horizon and soon illuminated the village and its surrounding area from its shadows, standing in the small village centre clearing again Will scanned the horizon for his missing friend, the air was still and silent save the sounds of the horses occasionally baying at the tethers that secured them to the stables. The bright orange sun shone fiercely into Wills eyes as he shielded them as best he could from the glare that lit the village into new life.

With no sign of Coles forthcoming, Will returned to the church again silently stepping through the dozing men that occupied every available space in the church room. He carefully picked his steps towards his comrades and leant towards Zeke, who although appearing to sleep always kept on constant alert for the unexpected, sensing Wills presence Zeke acknowledged his approach with one eye open gave an enquiring look. Will crouched down by Zeke's side, 'Coles has gone' Will whispered, 'Damn it' the Corporal replied with seriousness in his rough voice, though he had almost expected Coles' departure sooner or later, 'You've searched outside?' Zeke pressed Will for as much information on the situation as he could.

The Allen brothers stirred from their sleep unawares of Coles' departure, Zeke quickly hushed instructions to the group, 'You have an hour at best before anyone notices he's missing, the three of you have little time to find him before Vaughan starts asking questions, I can tell him I've sent you foraging but you need to be back inside an hour for the ploy to hold tight'. Knowing the fury McPherson would hold on finding one of his company deserted Will nodded his understanding of Zekes plan before signalling the two brothers to accompany him outside. Once outside Will quickly explained to the brothers the predicament the file now found itself in, pondering a moment to consider Coles condition, It could be that Coles needed to be alone rather than spend the night cooped up with the remainder of the company, Sam Coles had remained loyal to the file even with the recent episodes that troubled him so deeply, for now though Will shouldered the responsibility of with finding his missing comrade before the Sergeants of the company realised his absence.

A rapid judgment gave Will enough clues that Coles was unlikely to make direction back towards the road from whence they had come, the road south stretched far into the distance, wandering across the meadows and skirting around the distant woodlands. Knowing he needed to act fast the three men raced towards the copse of trees that lay a few hundred yards to the south of the village.

Chasing through the long summer grasses the three men reached the thicket wishing for Coles to emerge from his hiding, the woodland lay silent save the morning song calls of high perched birds and the three men cautiously entered the wooded grove losing sight of the village the remainder of the company still quartered within. If the four men did not return by morning muster the Regiment would be delayed in its rendezvous with the fleet at Jonesport quays, the provost would be turned out to search for the fugitive and the punishment would undoubtedly end in the rope for the captured man and the lash for the others as a deterrent for anyone foolish to consider absconding from the crown army. Pacing a few yards into the coppice Dan whistled the two towards his position. Making haste Will jumped towards the situation eager for a trace of Cole's whereabouts, there he found Allen crouched besides the thorny bramble bushes, 'What is it?' he enquired as Dan's body obscured the view, Dan turned slightly revealing the contents of Coles knapsack scattered liberally amongst the undergrowth, his violin smashed and splintered, his sketching journal lay open and damp with the morning dew penetrating its loose pages. 'Curses!' Thom exclaimed arriving on the scene.

Dan quickly gathered up the salvageable belongings pointing towards the signs of a struggle within the proximity of the area, Will instinctively leveled his musket opening the priming pan ready for any trouble that may occur, the three men crouched to the soft ground holding a silent position to listen for any noise of humanity above the natural sounds of the woodlands and now ever more conscious of the diminishing time Will's mind raced back to Zeke who with quick wits should stave off enquiries to the missing file but time was running thin and Coles whereabouts had still not been established fully, now in panic he hatched a plan that would either find Coles or at least account for his absence.

Dan, Thom and Will cleared the coppice and returned back to the billet at the village, by now the company was active and breakfasting in the glory of the morning sun that drenched the village square, Zeke in spotting the three paced across the meadow towards them fastening his red tunic along the way. Sergeants Vaughan and Skinner stood watchfully as the four men met a short distance outside the village, Zeke with his back towards the camp addressed the file, 'I knew you wouldn't find him' he shook his head with these despondent words, together the men made towards the waiting Sergeants, 'Vaughan is furious and Skinners not helped either with his remarks about ill discipline within our company, there is talk of our file being broken up and merged with other companies'.

Will checked pace with these impacting words as the two approached the file with indictment to the files ascendance, with quick thought Will lied as to the events at the coppice, 'Coles is dead' he addressed the two sergeants, Zeke with his wisdom knew Will's words to be false but remained silent as Skinners expression dropped from glee to frustration, 'What happened out there' Vaughan demanded to know, 'I don't know for certain' Will replied formally 'But it looks like he's been butchered out there' adding with some confidence as Vaughan visibly fell for the account. Dan added to the tale 'There was a fight of some sorts, Coles must've wounded or killed at least three before they got him' as Zeke interjected that he had sent the four out as a forage party, bolstering the wild story they told. 'Aye, it was all but over by the time we got on the scene' Thom spoke, 'Not a shot was fired but the bayonet drew a heavy toll on the rebels'. Zeke realised the three might easily get carried away with the heroics of the make believe action silenced the file before the story verged on some brave and gallant action in the face of overwhelming odds. 'Best return to your billets' remarked Zeke to the three men, 'We'll be moving out before long', with this news the three strolled back towards the church tittering to one another on how Sergeant Skinner had been foiled at the further loss of vengeance upon the file.

Alone, Zeke continued to discuss the files loss with the two sergeants placing some dramatic emphasis on the unknown enemy that seemingly patrolled these lands emphasising the vulnerability of the Regiment in uncertain lands. It seemed the ruse worked as Skinner stormed towards his company yelling to his men to fall in line.

Sam Coles held a privileged upbringing, sheltered from the everyday squalor and violence most endured his place in the ranks had lasted longer in the ranks than Zeke had expected, once a valuable member of the file his demise had been swift, Zeke had hoped in time Coles would confide to his comrades the troubles bore by him but time was something the file had little of.

The summer campaign was fast gaining momentum and the 17th were to play a critical part of it. Zeke pressed the three to the events out in the woods, Will stood by his words uncomfortably keeping up the pretence of Coles disappearance, knowing Zeke to see through the charade he offered these words of comfort, 'There was nothing more you could have done lad, Coles became consumed by his demons' he addressed Will directly, 'I have seen many times what warfare can do to a man, for his sake he best make for the unsettled lands westwards for else now if he's caught by the crown there's hanging for sure' and now with his head bowed between his knees Will pondered Zeke's sensibility while struggling to contain the emotions of losing yet another of his compatriots in this bloody campaign. The file knew Coles was filled with dread and consumed by hate to the forthcoming advance into the southern colonies, for King George's army one man's pity cut little sympathies in these troubled times and his lethargy would be punished by those that disciplined the ranks. From Zeke's wise discourse the remaining men recognised that if Coles stayed with the file then fragment it surely would, needing to regain his soul Sam Coles had disappeared from his brothers realms.

By the time the 17th were mustered for the continued march the squadron of dragoons had swept the area in patrol for whatever had brought Coles demise finding only his torn scarlet tunic tangled in the briars of the outlying woods. With this new evidence it was sufficient to Captain McPherson that the account given was genuine and proved to him that hostile rebel forces operated within the area and the 17th without sufficient support would be prone to attack from any threats nearby, with the ruse upheld the company officers losing valuable time already urged a swift movement away from the village with fears of a return in numbers of this make believe enemy, McPherson sincerely commenting to Zeke that the file had lost a good man that day. Away from the company's presence Zeke chastised the three lads on how close they had come to a companywide search for the missing file, only Zeke's quick intellect and persistence that the experience and professionalism of the three soldiers had saved them from Skinners accusations of desertion . . .

The Company muster roll would list Coles as killed in the face of the enemy but as to his real whereabouts his comrades could only guess, whilst Will and the Allen brothers had elaborated with their story on the findings at the coppice, the torn red frock coat found by the Dragoons had concerned them to the possibility that Coles indeed had been caught unawares by the continental rebels and succumbed to the fight that ensued, with the village now fading into the distance any thoughts of confirming their fears had dissolved with the urgency of the forthcoming invasion of the southern colonies.

The 17th made good progress towards the harbour at Jonesport, making the rendezvous in good time to board the barges in the harbour in preparation for Howe's imminent invasion, the huge fleet of ships and transports followed the rocky island coastline along the Bay of Fundy towards the southern colonies that challenged the crown's authority. On approaching the small harbour, the 17th Regiment was met with tall ships that anchored in the grey seas of the bay, Will counted over a hundred vessels with more coming into view as the Regiments company's travelled the last leg of their journey southwards, this was a sight to see for all concerned, the largest fleet assembled in modern times in preparation for general Howe's assault deep into the rebel armies.

The fishing docks at Jonesport proved too small for the barges to navigate and so via long boats manned by sailors of the Royal Navy the men of the 17th made way to the pebbled shores and waded through the surf to board the small vessels, Will and his file waited patiently for their turn to be called forward an take their places in the boats that would ferry them to their waiting ships.

Sergeant Vaughan stood ahead of the line signalling each party from his company forward as the long boats began their push through the choppy

Atlantic waves that crashed high upon the shale beach, eventually with a nod from their sergeant Zeke signalled his file towards the convoy of boats relaying back and forth to the barges.

With quick time the four men reached the stony beach and with instruction from the boatswain boarded the unstable craft, the oarsmen heaved the boat through the waves and with a mighty push cleared the beach and set for the fleet anchored a mile from the coastline. Ten soldiers crammed into each longboat the oarsmen rowed hard against the tides, the bow of the vessel rising high onto the oncoming waves that fought to push them back to shore, looking either side Will noted an upturned craft crashing back against the shoreline with drenched red coated soldiers flailing as the waves swept them back to the beach, the sailors yelled at the novice soldiers who's inexperience had upset the boat as it reared high through the colliding waves, 'General Howe would wish us Marines it seems' Zeke laughed as the comedy of the situation led to fits of laughter amongst the file.

Within an hour the long boats approached the fleet at anchor, first rate ships of the line menacingly leered overhead as the small ferry boat navigated its way towards its allocated transport, approaching the dark hulk of the ungainly craft a cord net tossed downwards towards the longboats party, with astounding agility two crewmen scaled the net towards the decks of the ship straddling atop of the broad beams of the vessel gesturing upwards to the waiting soldiers below, 'Ups we go lads' cried Zeke over the din of the seas swirling around the ship hull, Will unsure of his footing stepped carefully into the rungs of the rigging and hoisted himself towards the ships flat deck, with a few strides Will clambered over the sides and stepped down onto the planked decking of the barge.

The file stood on the broad deck braced by the Atlantic winds that filled the sails of the flotilla as the last men of the 17th Regiment boarded the numerous transports ready to join the fleet poised off the coast line, Sergeant Vaughan numbered off him men accounting all present and correct in the company ledger. As sailors climbed the high rigging above,

Zeke typically took opportunity to light his pipe in the shelter of the ships forecastle sucking heavily to ignite the crammed bowl of his rich scented tobacco.

The heavy canvas sails unfurled by the nimble sailors dropped downwards of their spars filling instantly with the strong breeze of the ocean, within a moment the hulk that served as their transport to the fleet strained at the cables that tethered it to the oceans bed.

The grand fleet was scheduled to rendezvous off the coast at Nantucket Island, the barges carrying the men of the 17th Regiment came into position with the horizon lined with the white sails of over eighty vessels poised to advance on New Jersey, below deck the file sat amongst others from the McPherson's company gambling their time away or preparing their equipment for the forthcoming landings, as the transport barges slid alongside the huge fleet calls from above ushered the men on deck to witness such an impressive collection of his majesties navy, Will savoured the moment with pride as he was now part of this great moment in history that would surely crush once and for all the rebellion in the colonies.

Amongst the flotilla of ships went smaller vessels carrying orders for each transport to make haste towards the sound at Staten Island, with this order came word of a declaration of independence from the crown colonies, in all thirteen colonies had signed the affirmation renouncing ties with the mother country, no longer would the army be containing rebellion, now escalated to a new level this was formally a war of Briton against Briton, friend against friend and brother against brother.

*   *   *

Chapter Six

The East

The mid July morning was broken violently with an opening barrage from the naval ships of the line, shaken in his cot Will raced to the upper decks to catch a glimpse of the cannonade that shook the air so brutally, the early morning sunrise blazed across the ocean adding to the fiery redness that accompanied the guns flaming hot barrels as they poured heavy round shot across the bay onto the distant flat lands of Long Island.

Zeke appeared presently on deck all too familiar to the viciousness of a naval gunnery barrage, in handing Will his redcoat he spoke his wisdom once more 'You'd best gather up your equipment lad, If the weather holds we'll be ashore before noon, this barrage is just to soften them up a little'. Will had learned to trust his corporals sagacity, silently slipping his coat over his chilled shoulders he returned to the lower decks to gather his equipment for the forthcoming landings. Thom and Dan Allen sat by their mess bench rasping sharp stones down the length of their bayonets in preparation for the enemy that defended these strategic lands, Will stared deep into the actions of the two brothers, no longer where these the boyish lads he'd enlisted alongside so many years ago, both brothers and Zeke had become his new family and they as surely he did also begin to show signs of stress and weariness on their campaign hardened bodies. Contemplating the reality of their lives together struck a chord in Will's soul, seven had enlisted at Leicester nearly six years past, now only four remained, he wondered how they would fare with the campaigns ahead now the formal continental army massed for the first major engagement in the summer campaign.

Zeke's hand patted Will's shoulder as the file readied itself for its muster on deck, 'Vaughan will call us to arms soon' he spoke 'clear your belongings, It's doubtful we will be coming back'. The four men gathered their possessions and equipped themselves for the roll call and allocation to the waiting long boats that lined the hulls of the transports, each man in turn checking each other to secure the equipment needed for the campaign. McPherson's company waited patiently on the decks of the transport barge for the order to disembark, standing in lines of three abreast, Sergeant Vaughan paced back and forth the ranks in readiness for the gesture to board the longboats below, the ships Boson watched carefully through his spyglass for the signal from General Howe's flagship HMS Eagle for a change in signal indicating the invasion to go ahead as instructed.

The company filled the upper decks of the transport ship poised in a moment to launch the huge sea borne landings that would re-establish the crowns presence within the troublesome colonies, finally news came of Howe's decision to defer the assault until his network of intelligence had ascertained the nature of the enemy he now faced, Dan spoke with annoyance 'this hesitance will surely cost us dear'. With a heavy sigh of despair Sergeant Vaughan called his corporals to heed and informed them of the judgement and decision to stand down until further orders were received and Zeke formally addressed his file assigned for the invasion, 'Stand down lads, they'll be no movement for us today' as spoke disappointedly as the company began to return below deck to their quarters and despite the fear of war resting heavily on his mind, Will resented the restrictions of life aboard the cramped vessel and on returning their muskets to the ships quartermaster the company departed the upper decks to their mess below and the monotony and frustrations of General Howe's waiting games.

To ease the monotony of the confinement Zeke allowed his file freedom of movement throughout the anchored vessel, although with the company restricted to the ship there was little to do other than gamble away the long hours below decks.

Over the following days the company waited eagerly for the order to disembark for the landings on Staten Island, by now the fleet had massed to its capacity of the coastal shores totalling more than two hundred war ships and smaller vessels, each crammed with soldiers waiting for order to advance ashore.

The Royal Navy gun boats patrolled far into the mouth of the Hudson river up keeping an almost constant barrage of cannon fire on the entrenched continental army in the surrounding peninsula forts and finally Howe's staff signalled the invasion to proceed as directed. McPherson's company was called to order and formed on the decks as the long boats beneath positioned themselves for embarkation. Standing at the head of the file, the ships quarter master reissued the muskets to the long lines of Redcoat soldiers patiently waiting their instruction, with a honed instinct, Will immediately opened the pan of his weapon to inspect it for fouling and rust, reaching into his cartridge case he fumbled for his pick tool to clear the touch hole from pan to barrel of any burnt powder residue that may hinder his muskets ability to discharge its shot, should the company face resistance from their enemies once ashore a man needed to rely on the effectiveness of his weapon, unscrewing the clamp that secured the flint he replaced it with one fresh and cut clean securing the screw to hold it firmly in place. Towards the front of the line lay a large wooden chest containing greased cartridges ready for issue on departure to the longboats beneath.

Zeke poised formally at the front of his file and assisted the men over the side of the transport vessel into the waiting boats beneath, on passing the last man Zeke cleared his legs from the ship and lowered himself into position along the narrow galley as the longboat crew pushed clear of the hull and outwards to the sandy beaches that lay on the distant shore. The warm summer zephyrs blew low clouds steadily across the bay and gave a temporary reprieve from the strong sunshine that sweltered the soldier's backs underneath their heavy woollen redcoats. As the oarsmen heaved away gaining speed against the swirling currents, the warm summer breeze blew cross winds over the soldiers who patiently took position in the fast boats, being towards the bow of the boat Will could see scores of craft already landed on the sandy beaches of the designated landing point on Staten Island, tiny red figures ran from the shoreline towards the shallow cliffs that overlooked the bay as scores more long boats crashed onto the sandy shores disembarking their passengers. 'Brace yourselves' the pilot shouted above the noise of the surf crashing onto the beach, 'we're about to land'. The long boat crashed onto the pebbled shores of the landing zone jolting its occupants forward, instantly the naval crew leapt from the boat and using the crafts momentum hauled the longboat high above the tides edge onto the soft sandy beach,

'Out we gets' Zeke shouted at the file to quickly disembark the landing vessel and muster with the rest of the Regiment already positioned higher up the beach, 'Hardly the assault we though eh lads?' Zeke spoke as he continued to fumble through his pockets for his pipe, the file cleared the craft as it was hastily turned around in the crashing waves ready to ferry back for the next wave of soldiers ready to be landed.

The men shouldered their muskets and paced towards Sergeant Vaughan who already had organised his company into column ready for McPherson's order to advance inland. Vaughan addressed the file with a friendly smile and Will listened in carefully to what the campaign would entail, 'Mawhood wants the brigade to form up inland immediately' as he briefed the file with McPherson's orders of the day, 'we're to move inland and wait for the last companies to arrive'. Whilst waiting for instruction to advance inland, Will wondered to himself the whereabouts of this new and organised enemy that challenged King Georges authority in the colonies,

'Don't you worry Will lad' Zeke reassured him, 'General Lord Howe does not bombard the shores for nothing so fear not and we'll get our revenge for Boston this day yet'. The file stood patiently for the last of McPherson's company to join the column and join with Mawhood and the remainder of the Regiment and by late morning these restless men finally moved off the beach that was by now crammed with soldiers, supplies and provisions patiently waiting to be organised by the landing beach masters lay unmoved upon the beach head as staff officers checked and rechecked the paperwork that came with the supplies before instructing auxiliary to load them further ashore. As the company moved inland, the soft sand that covered the golden beaches gave way to grassy tracks that led away from the cove and onto the high plains and woodlands that filled the island.

The town of Richmond had remained loyal to the crown despite dangerously isolating itself in doing so, the islands Loyalist population lined the roads and pathways leading towards the town cheering the endless line of Redcoats that began to occupy the terrain. The company neared the main camp and McPherson rode excitedly amongst his men having marked the encampment of the 17th, leaning downwards from his powerful steed he spoke at length with Sergeant Vaughan instructing him on where to position his column, Vaughan signalled his corporals to move forward through the open fields that enveloped Richmond town and towards the canvas city that over shadowed it. In the distance the 17th Regiment's flying colours indicated the camp hastily being erected by auxiliaries and engineers, miles of bleached white canvas gave a clear indication to the size and determination of Howe's campaign to regain control of the colonies and smash the colonies treacherous 'declaration of independence' from the Crown, to individual eyes it seemed the entire army of King George was mustered on Staten Island and as far as the eye could see the land crammed full with soldiers going about their duties. The company joined its parent Regiment and Will observed the bright Union colours of the 17th's standard that flew proudly in the breeze, he had not seen their pride since the Regiment left Edinburgh so many months ago, the Union flag emblazoned with gold edging flew fully in the stiff ocean breeze. With the numerals XVII embroidered with pride in the centre this moment stirred Will's patriotism to the glorious Regiment in which he served.

On entering the camps picket ropes drummers from Brereton's Grenadier Company welcomed McPherson's men to the beat of the Regimental drum and a hearty cheer. Looking far and deep amongst the men of his Regiment, Will accounted for familiar faces he had served alongside for all these years past, the few seasoned and experienced soldiers stood out easily amongst the new recruits that filled these ranks depleted by war and disease, he wondered to himself how many of these new lads would live to see his age, 'his age?' he thought to himself, he was yet twenty five years old but he knew only too well campaigning had taken its toll on him physically, whilst still fit and relatively healthy now he knew this campaign had aged him and his friends prematurely, his bones ached more now than they ever had done before and his once pale soft skin had tanned and leathered to the bleak and harsh climes in which he now served. As he gazed across the ranks his eyes caught Zeke as he busied his self amongst the men, fast approaching forty years of age, in these times this was an age to be proud of considering the life expectancy of a soldier on campaign duty, he mused briefly to himself that should he ever reach those years whilst serving in the ranks it would be by a miracle, how had Zeke survived so long? Will considered to himself, Coles, Walsh and White had gone from his original company and replacements had merged into the ranks, of the company he enlisted into only the lucky remained as sickness and disease claimed as many lives as the enemy's musket and cannon.

Zeke Turner had served under the Kings colours in some form for nearly thirty years, where had it got him? Will raised the question to himself, seemingly to most nowhere but Zeke would have it no other way, his family was alongside him now, to return to a civilian life would have meant alienation in society to the likes of him after living an army life for so long, the army was his blood, the army was his life, he knew no other. Passing through ranks of McPherson's company, Will trod through the men that made up the ranks of the Army and the men to deliver a decisive blow to rebellion that stirred within these colonies, now with the foothold on the mainland secured soldiers prepared themselves ready for transportation across the straights that separated Staten island and Long island and the enemies fortifications, the naval transport barges began to line the shorelines ready to hastily transfer the invasion forces onto the rising slopes on Long island. The atmosphere around the tented city grew in excitement as the forthcoming assault grew closer, the naivety of replacement troops stood out as their keenness for battle betrayed their inexperience in warfare and contrary to this seasoned soldiers made solemn pacts with each other to care for their affairs in the event of their end on the battlefield, the dead rarely retained their dignity in death. News came that the 17th was to play a supporting role in the forthcoming battle as the main assault would be made by the Kings Hessian mercenaries in an attempt to drive the rebel army from the island and beyond, under General Grant's 4th brigade the 17th formed the second line alongside the 40th and 46th Regiments, in reserve the 5th Regiment held the brigades baggage wagons whilst the brigade proper awaited the turn of battle should it be required.

The younger ranks showed signs of disappointment at the news, revenge for the humiliation at Boston would have to wait another day as massed men watched the first line of the assault prepare for the landings at Gravesend bay on the south eastern tip of Long island. The harsh lessons learned at Boston provided General Lord Howe with reliable intelligence to his enemies' strengths and dispositions, Staten Island had proved loyal to the crown and provided such information to Washington's troop positions around the defended inlets that might hinder the British landings, General Washington positioned batteries around the bay commanding over the area Howe's advance would hope to achieve a foothold on, the immediate success of the landings lay with the abilities of the Royal Navy to suppress the guns that had the ability to devastate the assault as it waded ashore.

The morning of the 21st of August saw the familiar barrage of the Navy begin with a turbulent fire onto the positions of the continental army that dug in high on the surrounding lands overlooking the proposed landing grounds. The bay around the islands inlet lit up with thunderous fire from the frigates that anchored themselves within, heads turned towards the proposed landing grounds as round shot whistled through the dawn skyline smashing into the defenders positions overlooking the bay east of the small town of Gravesend, Will shuddered at the thought of what the defenders were living through, huge clumps of earth threw high above the impact of the dug positions turning them in to the living hell now visible across the straights as the barrage gave a clear indication to the suffering the enemy endured, Will stared across the straights and felt compassion towards the enemy as those caught in open space where shot to pieces as heavy round slammed into the earth, despite the harsh brutality of war Will thought no man deserved the hell of this bombardment and the thought of being buried alive under the falling earth and debris settled uneasy on his mind. The Royal Navy's barrage lasted long into the day and its monotonous rage quickly lost the attention of the ranks awaiting instruction to begin the assault, rumours passed along the lines that the invasion would start at midnight that evening.

As the midnight hour approached McPherson's company was issued with ammunition and stood ready for orders of embarkation once the first wave was ashore on Long Island, Sergeant Vaughan formed his files into three lines and waited for Mawhood's order to descend the winding tracks towards the beaches and the invasion barges that would ferry the assault across the seas. Signalling the start of the seaborne assault the barrage from the anchored frigates ceased as quickly as it started and the invasion began in earnest with the endless lines of red coated soldiers trailing down towards the beaches to board the flat bottomed barges that would carry the assault towards the enemy. The company stood watching as the huge camp abandoned by its inhabitants emptied leaving barely a skeleton of itself behind, the midnight darkness gave a ghostly aura as the chatter and noise of restless soldiers faded into an emptiness.

The cloudless moonlight gave an indication of the scale of the assault as the straights between Staten and Long islands became filled with slow moving barges crammed full of red coated soldiers dedicated to the assault, staring across the bay the four men of the file commented on what lay ahead of the attack, Zeke piped up with observance 'This Washington fellow has fatally given Howe the chance to face him head on'. Will glanced sideways to Zeke pressing him for elaboration to his words, Zeke continued 'These rebels have the skill and passion to defeat us at every turn and now his ragged militia army faces us directly Howe has the upper hand and the opportunity he has sought since Boston' his monologue was interrupted short by Sergeant Vaughan's arrival, greeting the file informally, Vaughan spoke to the collective 'It seems your actions have reached the ears of Mawhood's general staff'. Zeke's instincts yet again pre emptied Vaughan's words as he turned from the cliff top and gestured the others to follow him to the files tents to reclaim their equipment, Sergeant Vaughan paced alongside the file as they walked the short distance back towards the encampment to be greeted by Captain McPherson and several nervous looking men from other companies of the Regiment.

'General Howe has instructed Mawhood to construct a composite company of chosen men to accompany Brigadier Robertson's Loyalist troops in the attack' Vaughan informed the file, Captain McPherson added to Vaughan's instructions 'I see no reason for you not to take this honour in the field Zeke' he spoke ever eager to prove himself on the field of battle. With this assignment the file quickly grabbed its equipment and moved towards the massing men of the regiments that had been assembled to the first line of the assault and down the narrow tracks to the shores of Staten Island. The file moved loosely through the long line of troops waiting for orders to board the returning barges and onto the rallying point for Robertson's loyalist company. Arriving at the head of the line Thom saw the files nemesis bawling orders at Staten Islanders who had volunteered to give fight to the enemy, 'It's no wonder these colonists want shot of us with fools like Skinner in charge' he spoke with contempt for the Sergeant and as the file drew closer to the company, Skinners voice became clearer, the four chuckled to themselves as the Sergeant elaborated to the militia his heroic actions against the enemy at the St Croix River 'single handed I fought scores of em with me bear hands after all me company lay dead or deserted' he recalled his own version of events the four knew only too well.

'Pish' yelled Zeke with contempt over the silence of the captive audience, 'you cried for your mother all through the night' as he cupped his hand around his mouth directing his voice. Silence fell across the gathered men. Skinners head snapped towards the direction of the four, furious that someone might challenge his bravery, with fury known well by the file Skinner raced towards the direction of the heckle pushing through the crowd ready to strike any that dared to question his accounts, the militia parted as Skinner yelled 'What blaggard dares to call the brave and noble Sergeant Skinner a liar?!'

Will's grin dominated his expression as Skinner's eyes made contact with the four, with his face flushed red with embarrassment and the frustration clear, Skinner paused his wrath and ceased re-enacting fearful of the ultimate humiliation, insolence the atmosphere became tense until Zeke drew heavily on his clay pipe and raised his eyes to meet Skinners, 'perhaps the brave sergeant would care to relay his tale from the beginning?', Skinner visibly uncomfortable twitched as he struggled for a way to resolve his predicament 'Damn you Turner, damn you to hell' Skinner spat his hatred towards the four sharply turning his back and pushing his way through the crowd that stood silently watching the confrontation between the group. With Skinner gone the four burst into howls of laughter, 'I would give a years pay to see that again' Dan Allen said between howls of laughter, 'Well done Zeke, no man could have done any better' Will slapped the satisfied Corporal on the back as the four chuckled amongst themselves.

By dawn of the following day the first line of the invasion was ashore Long Island with no resistance from Washington's army, the slopes of Long Island massed with Howe's Hessian and British soldiers ready to advance inland to face their enemy. Captain McPherson joined the composite company in time for their embarkation of the invasion barge, the low riding barge crammed with troops made its way with the receding tides from the shores of Staten Island and the short distance across to Long Island. The barge made a steady progress across the bay although Will kept a keen eye on the waves as they lapped the sides of the vessel, bitter sea salt stung his dry lips as the barge rowed slowly towards the beaches of the landing zones. A few yards short of the beach the company was ordered to disembark the barge to hasten its return for the next ferry of troops, with a heavy splash Will leapt over board into the surf up to his mid rift in the cold Atlantic waters and collectively the men waded ashore holding their muskets high to protect it from the sea, led by Captain McPherson the company gathered on the dry sands until the company was accounted for on Vaughan's muster roll. The four men huddled together removing their sodden redcoats that weighed so heavily on their shoulders, Sergeant Vaughan joined the party and share a smoke from Zeke's pipe advising them to McPherson's instruction,

'When the officer returns we'll form the light company to Robertson's loyal militia, these colonial lads are unbloodied and you will add a steadiness should they falter under fire'. Zeke nodded at Vaughan's instruction knowing the collapse of a line in battle could turn the fight one way or another, after the siege of Boston, Howe had faced humiliation at the hands of Washington once already, to do so again would see his immediate recall back to England, Lord Howe was determined to gain a decisive and final victory in this forthcoming campaign.

McPherson returned to his composite company that waited its orders for a swift embarkation from the landing beaches and onto the tracks that led inland towards the proposed battlefields. The company paced the tracks from the beaches to the flat lands that levelled the tops of Long Island, thousands of troops massed from the earlier landings occupied the views east across the small township of Gravesend and south of New Utrecht, while columns of red coated soldiers patiently awaited their commanding officers orders, the green jacketed Jaeger mercenaries from Prussian Hess and Cassel districts distanced themselves from the regular troops of the Kings army, forming green pockets in a vast sea of deep scarlet red.

Sergeant Vaughan led his troops towards Robertson's Regiment of militia that formed loosely on the left flank of the massed troops whilst mounted Dragoons trotted into position on the right. The thirty men that formed the composite company would act as light infantry teasing the enemy when they encountered them into battle that mimicked a European style of warfare rather than the irregular styles that suited these rebel Americans' so well. Vaughan instructed his company to discard their equipment save a light skirmish order of musket, cartridge and canteen with the brigades baggage wagons and prepare to advance into the territories held by the enemy, Zeke paced the line of militia that would accompany the red coats addressing the loyalists on tricks that might save their lives when encountering their foes ahead, Will and the two Allen brothers primed their muskets in readiness as McPherson advanced his men past the Dutch settlement and towards the heights that dominated the island. Howe's main assault would move towards the town of Flatbush and drive Washington's army northwards to Brooklyn and force a final surrender and end the rebellion once and for all.

As the advance made steady progress towards the heights Robertson split his force from the main body in order to check the left flank of the enemy should they attempt to break out of Howe's bottle neck. The selected men of the 17th Regiment accompanied by an equal number of loyal militia increased pace a half mile ahead of the advancing columns spreading themselves thin to lessen themselves as targets should the enemy spring ambush on the skirmishers. Led by Captain McPherson, the order directed itself towards a tavern that stood alone on the empty road, the Inn long since vacated by its owners looked a likely opportunity for ambush, Zeke paused the advance and silently signalled this file to move on the flanks of the tall wooden building giving cover to each other as they strategically advanced towards it. The skirmish order came within a hundred yards of the Inn, Skinner broke his men away to the right mimicking Zekes movements, pausing an equal distance from the abandoned building. Zeke pulled the flint of his musket back to the ready position, 'any closer and we become a good target so prepare yourselves as best you can'. The men under Zeke's command simultaneously clicked the locks of their muskets as he pointed to Will and silently gestured him and the Allen brothers to scout ahead of the staggered lines and investigate the seemingly building. Closing a few yards at a time Will studied the weathered tavern in detail for anomalies or evidence of any life, the Inns large ground floor windows boarded tight with winter shuttering whilst the smaller upper floors smaller obscured by leaded glass would give a perfect opportunity to rain lead down on the advancing troops, nervously he paused a moment in the long dry grasses and glanced back to Zeke and the remainder of the line for instruction to continue this uncertain advance. Zeke held the line steady and signalled Skinner to advance men as his own had done.

Mathias Skinner had served the Regiment for longer than any cared to remember, his experience in battle however was to the extreme limited, having wrangled comfortable administrative positions within the battalion he was hated by the ranks and despised by his superiors and with his bitterness consuming him, he blamed anyone but himself for his failings and often chose a soft target to vent his personal vendettas. Skinner had secured the rank of sergeant as the Regiment formed itself into battalion strength and desperate for seasoned soldiers Colonel Mawhood had finally listened to his petitions for promotion, his lack of professionalism however had repeatedly led cause for his company to falter far behind the others in prestige and accomplishment.

Will turned his attention to Skinner as he raised his men in unison and advanced them towards the building, Zeke shook his head waving his arms frantically for Skinner to stay in position and advance only a small portion of his line towards the Inn but Skinner took little notice of a rank beneath his own continuing to usher all his men towards the abandoned building ahead. Glancing his vision back towards the Inn, Will ran his eyes down the length of his muskets barrel as Skinner openly moved his men across the lands directly in front of their target, his weapon trained steadily on the building the advanced line could do little more than watch as Skinners naive eagerness betrayed a textbook advance on an unknown position. Zeke cursed loudly at Skinners incompetence, Will clearly heard the choicest of words directed at the sergeant and smiling at Zeke's humour he stood up amongst the grass only to be yelled himself to return to the cover it offered. 'If Skinner wants his glory let him have it lad' as Zeke advised Will to stay low until the area was secured.

As Skinner closed the last forty yards the obvious trap was sprung, a burst of fire emitted from the boarded building into the vulnerable troops led by the sergeant. Will watched in horror as men crumpled under the withering fire that spat from its secreted positions around the enemy held tavern, scattered men in disarray raced back towards the safety of the main column leaving the wounded and dead to lie abandoned in the tall grasses that now became the killing grounds of the company and the loyalist militia.

Acting quickly, Zeke moved the remainder of his men up to Will's forward position ordering his men to lay covering fire in a desperate attempt to keep the enemy's rifles at bay until they secured a dominant point over their enemy.

With the right side of the assault now collapsing, Zeke's handful of men stood alone and vulnerable to the secreted enemy fortified within the building, Sergeant Vaughan made his way towards Zeke's men unseen in the covering grass that would offer so little protection if the enemy should train their weapons upon them, 'Tell me what you've seen Zeke' Vaughan asked his Corporal,

Zeke replied with contempt for his nemesis Skinner 'What I've seen Sergeant, is a fool that lead his men into certain death'. Vaughan stared into Zeke's eyes for a moment finding it hard to disagree with his chosen words before returning to the moment at hand, 'I've send word to McPherson to bring up the horse artillery, we can smash em out', Zeke replied with the immediate in mind 'How long do you suppose that will take James? there are men dying out there'. For the first time ever Will heard Zeke refer to his Sergeant by his Christian name, to others the context of this moment was as insignificant as Skinners continued failings but to Will, he saw this as an event when survival outstripped the formality of rank, these men levelled as soldiers not of hierarchy and protocol, the bureaucracy of an army mattered little when hot lead spat around one's ears.

'We can wait here no longer' Zeke continued to update Vaughan with the very real situation they found themselves within, 'there are wounded men out there and once these rebels realise our predicament we'll all lie amongst them'. 'Very well Zeke' Vaughan replied, 'Can you move yourselves to a better position?'. Dan Allen leant into the conversation as the skirmish line watched for movements within the enemy occupied building, 'there's a blind spot on the far left side, no open windows that I can see' he advised the two, 'Good, lad' replied Vaughan, 'Zeke, see if you can lead your men around the rear, go in swift with the bayonet for once you close there'll be no room for a musketry exchange'. Zeke agreed to the plan and pushed gently upon Will's back urging him to scout ahead of the dozen men that lay cut off from the main body, until the heavy guns could be brought into effective range the few soldiers were alone in this quandary, to wait for relief would take time and as Skinners flight had panicked the militia they were supposed to support broke into disarray and fled back to the safety of the massed line. 'Easy lads, nice and slow and no damn heroics' Zeke offered some comfort as the group prepared to move, 'What fool do you take me for old man?' Will replied 'Whatever I am I ain't no hero' he assured Zeke of his sobriety in the gravity of the dilemma. Zeke smiled exposing his yellowed tobacco stained teeth, 'I see I've taught you well boy, now go and God's speed to you'.

Will and the Allen brothers along with two of the militia snuck through what little cover the area offered, 'and be careful lad, don't let me down' Will smiled at Zeke's last words and moved the scouting party ahead and towards the left side of the killing grounds. The men that remained fired their muskets into the slat boards that protected the Inn from the elements splintering the timbers as the lead shot slammed thorough the dry weather boards, Will dashed to avoid a lead from the enemy that pursued his movements dropping hard to the ground as soon as his friends muskets had fired their last. Timing their movements to coincide with the covering fire, Will and the others made slow progress to the blind side of the building until they left the firing arc of Zeke's protection. The five attackers gathered and took stock of the situation ahead, assessing the death trap that lay before them Will took a short swig from his canteen before offering it to the two loyalists that accompanied them. The elder of the two slurped heavily from the vessel wiping his sleeve across his dry lips passing it to his comrade and tore a stalk of long grass from its root and placing it in the side of his mouth, 'How long have you served?' the younger of the two asked Will directly displaying a distinct west country English accent, Will looked shocked at the dialect spoken to him, 'which county are you from? he asked curiously, 'Somerzet' came the reply, 'Taunton town' the younger added. 'You're brothers?' Dan suddenly took notice in the conversation, 'Thom' he whispered the attention to his brother. 'That we are friend, we sailed from England barely two years ago, worked a farm for a while then thought best tried our luck in the colonies, long before this foolishness started'. ''Twas better times then, much better times' the other brother added. The Allen's chuckled at the parity of their circumstance, Dan laughed and fell onto his brothers shoulder 'Perhaps that's what we should have done brother'. 'Aye' Thom added, 'but still we'd have ended up drilling a musket either way'.

Leaving the four to their small talk Will assessed the area in front of the Inn, out of the protection of Zeke's cover the last thirty yards would mean a dash across the unprotected flank vulnerable to the enemy's fire, whether the rebels had the foresight to train their rifles and muskets to the rear of their defences they would have to risk the gamble but for now the five needed to close the distance between them and the blind side of the Inn. Will steadied the nerves of his wards 'Remember Zeke's words lads, no heroics . . . we'll rally round the back and catch em as they flee, draw your bayonets lads there's no time for shot' he instructed. Will looked into the eyes of the two militia that thus far had stuck to Will's tails, 'I need you to stay calm lads' he spoke softly to the two, 'Once we start moving keep moving, no matter what happens keep moving understand'. The two nodded at Will as they prepared for the race across the last few yards towards the Inn.

'Go!' Will shouted as the five raised themselves from cover and sped across the last few yards, the two loyalist brothers paced to the right of Will with Dan and Thom to his left. With good space between the five the gap towards the rear of the tavern closed to twenty yards when the rebels within realised the rear assault. With almost point blank aim the enemy presented their volley in their direction.

Will's ears began to ring with a high pitch, the event that followed played out in almost slow motion. With eyes focused on the feet of the Somerset lads running ahead, his vision blurred as he felt a sudden heavy thud towards the right side of his head, dizzy, his footing faltered as the men temporarily in his ward sped ahead leaving him staggering to his knees as his vision began to fail him. With hindsight Will would look back at this moment with sketchy confusion, despite the summer heat his immediate thought was that the summer rains had begun as his blood poured from his crown down into his eyes, concussed by the bullet that shaved his skull Will became confused, staggering in an imaginary forest that surrounded him, as his vision failed his last recall was fumbling for his felt hat fearing himself improperly dressed in the face of the enemy, with that Will lost consciousness and drifted into a dark and painful sleep. Will briefly regained awareness as Zeke towered over him, hoisted over his shoulder Will's body bounced like a rag doll as he carried his limp frame towards the Inn he had bravely attacked. Zeke kicked open the door and scanned the floor for space to position his wounded friend, outside Dan and Thom herded a handful of prisoners into a small corral that previously tethered the patrons of the Inns steeds.

Drifting in and out of consciousness Will caught just a few words uttered by Zeke as he supported his patients head against his backpack. 'You'll need to do better than that if you ever want a make corporal's pay lad'. Will coughed and spluttered as Zeke sponged a little water into his parched dry lips before wiping the congealed dry blood from his bullet grazed skull. His assault had caused confusion amongst the defenders who panicked by the loss of their escape route fled towards the rear door onto the waiting steel bayonets of the Allen brothers and the two loyalists, whilst several defenders had escaped many had thrown down their arms and surrendered without a struggle fearing they face their end at the hands of the advancing red coats. As the assault advanced the rebel resistance crumbled in the wake of the pressing Hessian Jaeger attack on the heights to the east pushing Washington's army north and towards a desperate stand along the small forts that barred the roads to Brooklyn and the heights that commanded the position over Howe's ultimate prize New York.

Sporadic gunfire sounded across the island the rebel army so desperately defended, in disarray the rebel commander hastily withdrew along the north road leaving hundreds of prisoners in the hands of the British army. Zeke sat with Will into the night as he waited patiently for the Regimental surgeons orderlies to make their way through the wounded most in need, Will's minor head wound would eventually be treated but after the Hessian's had attacked at the point of steel those with medical knowledge was diverted to any but the most hopeless cases. With numerical superiority of five to one, the attack smashed through the rebel lines with momentum that found large numbers of resistance isolated making them easy captives for the advancing British waves.

By the early hours the battle had moved far north of the initial contact giving opportunity for the army's baggage to catch the advancing army, Sergeant Vaughan managed to arrange for a minor orderly to check over Will's head wound, although Zeke knew the wound slight in comparison to the usual battlefield injuries, in these climes infection had the right to take a man's life as much as any bullet. With little compassion the orderly ran his filthy blood stained fingers across Will's scalp, 'He'll live' the orderly commented directly to Zeke, 'his head will hurt like hell once he comes round so keep him still for the day', the examination was over and the orderly moved over to the next patient across the room, clutching his stomach the man looked ashen in colour, almost drained of life Zeke recognised him as a man of Skinners company cut down in a hail of lead when the trap was sprung, the orderly took one look at the wounded man and shook his head 'hopeless' and moved along the room to the next patient.

The walking wounded made their way to the Inn seeking some protection from the elements as the winds brought a chill across the battle fields and with them word came of a complete route of the rebel army. As casualties massed outside the Inn, room inside became a precious commodity, as soon as life vacated the dying, the body was carried outside without compassion and the space reoccupied by the next desperate case. The lower floor of the Inn became full with the stench of death as the hopelessly wounded were placed on any available boards, army surgeons commandeered the back rooms of the Inn as a makeshift operating room, sawing limbs smashed by shot or stitching stomachs ripped by blade. Will again slipped into a deep slumber and Zeke rejoined Dan and Thom outside, the three shared the tobacco from his pipe and paused a moment and strained his eyes hard into the darkness, focusing on a discarded pile of amputated limbs casually thrown from the makeshift surgery's window he spoke casually, 'Gentlemen, the horrors of war do not cease to amaze me' he commented shaking his head in disgust at the flippant disregard for cost of human dignity.

The three returned to Will's side to find the two loyalists tending his needs, Will's eyes barely open sensed his comrade return and enquired to their position in the battle, 'The day is all but won lad' Zeke calmed him, pressing his smouldering pipe in between his lips, Will again coughed as the slight smoke filtered down into his lungs, raising himself upon his elbows Will felt his head and the filthy ragged bandage that bound his wound, 'What happened to our advance?' he asked, Zeke joked a moment, 'In light of your bravery lad, General Howe has requested you join his chiefs of staff' he grinned, 'your actions have become legendary in these lands'. Running his hands through his this blood congealed hair, Will's ability to amuse Zeke remained strong '"Tis about bloody time says I' adding 'though I fear I am best needed here with you fellows' he chuckled. The men sat with Will for a few hours until Sergeant Vaughan called Zeke outside on urgent Regimental business. Standing upright, Zeke grinned his toothy smile towards Will, 'Rest your eyes lad, the sooner your back amongst us the better' he spoke before leaving to meet with Vaughan.

The Inn, although ransacked by the rebel army still held a cache of alcohol for those who knew where to find it, Dan drew his bayonet and disappeared from the presence of the group soon returning with a bottle well hidden under the floor boarding, 'He can sniff it out you know' Thom joked as his brother returned twisting the cork bung loose from the bottle. Dan sniffed the bottle before passing it to Will, 'ah' he exclaimed 'gin, the ruin of many a good man' he spoke as he handed the bottle over. Zeke returned to the group after an hour's absence, 'We're returning to the Regiment' he spoke with a serious tone in his voice, 'Robertson's furious with today's events'. The two loyalists perked their ears to Zeke's words passing the now half empty bottle back to Dan and pressed the Corporal for further information, 'It seems our friend Skinner has hanged himself this time'. The group sat in silence waiting for Zeke to elaborate his words further, 'Robertson has called McPherson to account for the collapse of his line and McPherson holds Skinner responsible for the deaths of his militia'. 'The bastard has his comeuppance at last' Will muttered, 'a long time coming but finally we'll be shot of him' to the agreement of his friends. As the company prepared to withdraw the two loyalist brothers wished the file well and returned to their own company, Zeke's parting words seemed apt as the two left the Inn, 'If you've sense about yourselves lads, you'll leave this fighting well alone and go back to your homes while you can, today we we're lucky, for tomorrow it may well run out'.

The file gathered its muskets for the trek back to the Regiment camp as Zeke continued to speak on Skinners fate, 'McPherson wants those present at the Inn to deliver evidence of Skinners incompetence in the field', 'He's been stripped of rank and placed under arrest until we've all given our accounts of the event'. Dan Allen was the only man to add to Zeke's words although his choice seemed to fit the thoughts of all 'Not before time either, that bastard had it coming one way or another'. The four men travelled the winding track back towards New Utrecht where the Regiments headquarters and staff billeted, passing the endless line of movement northwards the file saw the extent of the invasion Howe directed in these lands. As far as their eyes could see troops massed behind the front line in readiness to exploit the breakthroughs the first line had punched through the overwhelmed defences.

Robertson's assault, combined with the Hessian attack on the heights had proved to be a diversion to Howe's battle plan, the main advance had swept east and north of the island encircling the remaining rebels tied down defending the passes that linked the Long Island towns and villages.

For once Howe's desire to face the enemy with traditional European warfare methods had proven decisive in his victory, facing massed volleys from the ranks of the British, the rebels had withered under tremendous fire and with so little experience many had fled in blind panic. General Washington was to learn a valuable lesson at the price of his fledgling army, it came to pass that the battle at Long Island had cost the continental general nearly three thousand of his precious and valuable troops, the largest portion now prisoners in the hands of the British awaiting transport to the prison hulks moored far off shore, from this Washington had learned to face the enemy on his own terms and the forthcoming winter would give him the opportunity to bloody Howe's nose as the rebellion faced the loss of New York and control over the Jerseys. For now though, the battle was not yet over, remnants of the rebel army held on in remote pockets hindering the general advance across the island and the final stage of the battle plan at Brooklyn, Howe hoped to drive Washington's army into the sea and force a surrender of his entire army.

The file drifted amongst the walking wounded and the scores of prisoners being herded into the former Dutch township that now crammed with soldiers and auxiliary troops supporting the assault. Utrecht, long since vacated by the population left its commercial enterprises primed for looting, the army's provost patrolled the dusty streets heavily and by presence alone kept order amongst the ranks, looting had been a capital offence in the Kings army and its harsh discipline held the British army in check whilst Howe, keen to curry favour with colonists loyal to the crown enforced this policy with an iron rod. Approaching the fringe of the town, provost troops under the administration of staff officers attempted to organise the huge volumes of prisoners massing in the open land around the settlement, Zeke turned the file towards a detachment of riders to enquire to the whereabouts of the 17th's camp

'How fairs the day?' a rider leant from his saddle enquiring with the four to situation from where they travelled, Zeke tipped his hat back and ran his hands across his sweating brow, 'well enough' he spoke in a sombre tone with no real desire to pursue the conversation into small talk 'We're making for the 17th, can you direct us?'. 'Aye' the rider replied twisting in his saddle he pointed east of the town 'a mile at most, I see they are moving north mind, you had best hurry'. Zeke nodded his acknowledgement to the horseman and pushed on along the dry roads the skirted the northern part of the town heading for the advancing column, the four walking side by side, with muskets slung casually over their shoulders the file made for the Regiment ready to rejoin its ranks. The file found the Regiment at rest on the road towards Bedford village, the heights taken the previous day by the Hessian division gave a clear view over the carnage of the battle, a trail of abandoned equipment gave good indication to the speed of the British advance through the rebel defenders lines, the heavy cannon once well dug into the defences lay abandoned by their former owners as stragglers of the British advance trawled amongst the dead and dying looking for anything of value to be pilfered before the provost arrived and began to clear away the debris of war. Zeke reported the files return to Captain Leslie Company who noted their return and dismissed the four from duty, 'Rest yourselves tonight men, the enquiry shall begin on the morrow, you'll need a clear mind for the court martial'. The file took receipt of Leslie's salute and made for the camp occupied by the regiment. 'Bloody hell!' Will exclaimed, completely astonished of Leslie's statement 'a court martial?'. 'So it seems lads' Zeke confirmed, 'whether Skinner wrangles out of the charges remains to be seen, battle confuses the mind so if we're obliged to bury the bastard we need to tell the officer exactly what we saw'.

The 17th remained in reserve for the remainder of the attacks on Washington's last defences and acted as temporary guards to the prisoners filtering back towards the British second line, stripped only of arms the lines of fugitives governed themselves as they herded into the stockades that surrounded the settlements until clerks organised them into transports. By dusk, the pursuit maintained by Howe's subordinates dwindled to a halt giving the rebel army much valuable time to regroup for another days fighting, stragglers drifted back to their own units displaying the effects the battle had on tired and exhausted bodies. A long day by any means, ended with silence amongst the ranks as the composite company of the 17th dissolved from Robertson's Loyalist brigade and merged back to their respective lines. That evening McPherson had expected a heroic return after being given the honour of leading the advance on the enemy defences, the reality however, found him facing an official enquiry into the actions that cost Robertson's reputation dearly after his militia collapsed and fled in sight of the enemy. The file sat amongst themselves in thought to the following day's events, Dan produced the remainder of the bottle pilfered from previously from the Inn, uncorking the bottle and generously swigging its contents, 'I'll leave you with yourselves lads' Zeke spoke up, 'I'll return shortly with our ration'.

Will, Thom and Dan soon finished the remainder of the gin when Dan produced another from his knapsack, 'you didn't think I would leave any behind did you?' as the three drank generously from the bottle. As the sun set over the bay, the camps fires drifted smoke across the area, Zeke returned with a meagre ration procured from the Regiments baggage wagons, 'a stale half loaf and a cut of cheese is the best I could do' Zeke said as he dropped his bag into the circle of the three, 'I need to find Vaughan in readiness for what tomorrow brings' adding as he made his way back to the main camp leaving the three alone in the fading light. For the next hour Will, Dan and Thom sat alone from the remainder of the company sharing amongst each other the last of Dan's gin until the bottle finally ran dry, Dan piped up as he swallowed the last of his find 'we should go and find Skinner'. 'Aye, let's find the bastard' replied his brother quick to add. Will should've known better than to fall in with the stupidity of the idea, an empty stomach and little sleep since they'd left Staten Island contributed to the bad judgments that lay ahead.

The three strolled through the camp which filled itself with pockets of tired men from the remnants of the companies that had seen action that day, rarely in more than groups of five, this gave an indication to the decimation the campaign had brought so far, not by battle but largely by disease and sickness, the battalion had seen itself re-equipped twice since arriving in the colonies but in less than a year the five hundred rank and file that sailed from Athlone numbered now barely two hundred, the 17th now found itself a skeleton of its former glory and its effectiveness in battle compromised by the number of muskets it could field. For now the 17th Regiment would be used to guard the large number of captives taken during the battle for Long Island. Silently the three made their way towards the temporary open air stockades built to house the prisoners, with barely a guard amongst them the rebel army sat squat on the barren ground staring at their victors in silence and pondered their fate. Will looked carefully amongst the captives noting above all the ordinariness of his foes, drably dressed in civilian clothes this rebel army that had caused the British army so much trouble showed no uniformity, these men looked as English as those he had grown up amongst, weavers, bakers, tanners and wrights, these wretched souls sat patiently awaiting their fate at the hands of their captors.

After the debacle at Boston, parliament had declared the rebel army as traitors to the crown refusing them any rights as prisoners of war, the usual fate for treachery would lead to the gallows but the sympathies amongst loyalists would tumble to levels the British could ill afford, the fate for most of the captives would be transferred to the navy's prison hulks anchored off shore until the rebellion was finally brought to heel.

There was some irony in finding Skinner shackled amongst the looters and thieves rounded up by the provost, under close guard the former sergeant lay with his back to a timber post staring into the nothingness between his manacled feet. Naked save his filthy canvas trousers, his previous aloofness had long been abandoned as his eyes glanced upwards towards the three walking towards him. Skinner struggled to his feet straining at the irons that restricted his movements, 'Lads, lads . . .' he pleaded with open hands 'there's some foolish talk of old Mathias facing a court martial tomorrow'.

The three stared at Skinner with contempt as he pitifully appealed to his peers, 'I know we haven't always seen eye to eye but lads come now, I'm asking you to help me out just this once, twas the others that refused my orders not I that gave them wrong'. Will's mind flashed back to every moment of pain Skinner had caused the file, from tragic young Walsh at Berwick to the troubled mind of Coles in Boston and Lower Canada, he raised his line of sight to meet Skinners who stood pathetically before him with open hands pleading for sympathy. For a brief moment Will truly felt sorrow for his nemesis, humanity was capable of many things but none he felt deserved Skinners predicament.

'Come Will' Dan broke the silence leaning into his shoulder all the worse for drink, 'Let us leave this pathetic excuse of a man to his fate'. Thom spat towards Skinner who with his pitiful expression changed his tone realising his pleas now fell on deaf ears 'Old Mathias will have you for this!' he shouted his typical hatred towards the departing three, 'you'll see' his departing words rang in Will's ears . . . 'I'll finish you all yet'.

The walk back to the files tent troubled Will, Dan and Thom giggled at Skinners pleas and staggered through the camp fires as they crackled into the night, 'What do you suppose he means?' he asked 'finish us all yet?'. 'Worry not Will my friend' Thom dismissed his fears, 'you've listened to the ranting of a condemned man' although Skinners final words lay deep in his thoughts long after they returned to their camp, the brothers slipped into a drunken slumber soon after arrival giving Will the opportunity to speak privately to Zeke.

'You're a much a fool as when I first found you boy' Zeke bellowed as he heard the tale unfold, Will knew the gravity of what the three had done by the gravity of Zeke's final word, boy. Lad was a common term Zeke used in referring to him personally, but boy had a note of scorn about it. 'It seemed a good idea at the time' Will attempted to justify the actions of the three, but Zeke refused to hear his reasons 'What exactly you say to him?' he demanded to know. 'I cannot recall for certain' Will replied knowing any enlightenment would infuriate Zeke even more 'besides, only a few camp guards saw us and they seemed little bothered by it all', Zeke ended the night addressing Will sternly 'You're a fool to yourself Will, you have no idea how men like Skinner wrangle out of these situations, he knows the tricks needed to play, god knows he's done it enough times'. Zeke left the file to stew in the moment seeking his own company for the remainder of the night.

The morning sun broke across the camp quickly bringing life to those exhausted enough to sleep more than a few hours the hard ground allowed, Will not wishing to receive another lecture left the file to retrieve fire wood in readiness for the files breakfast ration. On his return both Dan and Thom had already bore the brunt of Zeke's temper as the group sat in silence waiting for the company's order of the day. Sergeant Vaughan appeared shortly after the ration was issued and ignoring all but his Corporal summoned him away from the file, Vaughan's temper was evident to the three as Zeke reasoned with him over the three's misdemeanour. On his return Zeke addressed all three directly 'Skinner has made accusations against you all, he's claimed you swore to finish him at the trial, McPherson has no choice but to discount your evidence against him'. Will interjected Zeke's words 'Bastard liar, we said no such thing, it's his words against ours surely that counts for something'. Zeke struggled to contain his anger towards the three 'one of the guards swears he heard you say it plain and clear' turning to retrieve his red jacket 'but if what you say is true it seems old Skinner has more allies than we accounted for'. 'Where are you going?' Dan called after Zeke as he pulled on his tunic and dressed himself formally for the enquiry, Zeke replied in a flat tone 'My account is still valid, It seems I am now the only reliable witness, If Skinner gets off and he will believe me, we're all done for now he knows you would turn Kings evidence against him'. Will gulped at Zeke's words as the corporal made his way to the drumhead court martial knowing them to be true.

With Zeke departed tensions rose fiercely 'We need to finish this now' Thom spoke in hatred, 'We'll do the bastard ourselves' Dan added viciously but a moment of clarity embraced Will as he used words that may well have been spoken by Zeke himself 'Where do you think that'll get us? It'll be us that face the drumhead if we kill him, for murder of an enlisted man means a capital hanging'

Dan raised his voice in anger at Will's sensibility 'What do you suppose we do then Will? He'll take us one by one and I'd rather take my chances against the enemy than face Skinner on the field of battle'. The three sat around the dead fire in silence waiting for Zeke's return, by mid afternoon the Corporal arrived back at the files tent, Dan, Thom and Will stood simultaneously as Zeke dropped his equipment into the dirt, 'Well? Dan pressed Zeke for a relay of the events but Zeke continued about his business refusing to make eye contact with either man, 'What happened? Thom now asked anxiously only to be met with a hard stare. Eventually Zeke broke the silence 'The court found no evidence against him like I knew it wouldn't, the only witnesses were myself and the militia and as I am associated with you my evidence is questionable and Robertson has washed his hands of it withdrawing his militia's support in the case against', 'So what happens now?' Will enquired. Zeke snapped his frustrations 'I'll bloody tell you what happens now lad, McPherson is furious, the whole incident has embarrassed him amongst his brethren officers and Skinners regained his rank and remains a free man' he blurted his words in anger 'you lads had better watch your backs from now on, if you think Skinner had vengeance before you've seen nothing yet.

Zeke sat by the cold fire and removed his tatty leather boots rubbing a damp cloth over the seams and after an hour broke the delicate silence that befell the camp, 'By the way lads, I forgot to tell you, Vaughan wants to see you all, you'd best get your parade order together quickly, you should have presented yourselves an hour ago'.

The three hurried to Sergeant Vaughan who sat inside his tent, 'Wait there!' the Sergeant barked on their late arrival, together they stood in the uncomfortable humidity for the remainder of the afternoon until Vaughan left his tent and approached them, 'I trust Zeke has explained the situation to you?', 'Yes sergeant' the three replied formally, 'You'll be on auxiliary detail for the time being, do you understand?', 'Yes sergeant' again the three replied simultaneously, 'Now get back to your file and report back here in one hour, your Corporal will replay your duties to you'.

Back at the camp Zeke instructed the three they would report as the Regiments burial detail for internment of the dead, 'now drop your equipment and get to it' he snapped as the three scurried off to their destination. Stripping off their red coats and equipment Will, Thom and Dan reported back to Sergeant Vaughan who directed them along the pass towards the Bedford Road, 'Keep moving and you'll soon find the detail, there's about a hundred customers patiently waiting for you' he finished with a wry grin.

Silence befell the three as they left the sergeant's presence, out of earshot Dan piped up 'Some damn justice there, a bloody murderer walks free and we're made to bury the dead'. The stench of the battle field gave a good indication to the intensity of the fighting, the pass that led onto the slopes beneath the heights the rebels had fought so hard to defend was littered with the wretched dead, Hessian Jaegers and Grenadiers had harried the defenders causing mass panic as the green and inexperienced rebel soldiers broke under a hail of musketry and bayonet, now twisted and broken the dead lay across the open field with contorted faces their fear evident and permanently fixed to their expressions, even in death the horrors of their final moments etched deep in their eyes.

The auxiliary detail had started to strip the dead of valuables, piles of corpses stacked in rows ready for a communal grave to be dug lay stripped of their foot wear, the dead shared together a final embrace until the earth consumed them for all eternity. The sun finally set as the detail camped by the roadside, given an hour's respite from their labours Will noted others from the burial party 'How did you find yourself here brother?' he asked politely to his neighbour, 'Me? Oh I volunteered for the task!' the man snapped sarcastically as he bit hard into his ration of stale bread, 'whatever you choose to call it the lad asked you a question' Dan gave back as good as they received. The man grimaced 'They caught me looting the dead' he replied with little remorse for his despicable actions, 'I've made a pretty penny today, till I was caught by the bloody provost and found myself here'. Will looked in disbelief at the morbidity of the man as he chewed on his blackened filthy fingernails, 'I managed to get a shilling of one just now mind, I must've missed it earlier' he could do little other than sneer at the man's melancholy, 'From what Regiment do you hail' the man attempted to make conversation reaching into his bag and producing a half eaten sausage, Will looked on in contempt at the man's behaviour '17th, McPherson's Company', 'Can't say I've come across you before' he replied offering a slice of his supper to the three. Wondering what exactly the man meant by 'come across' Will chewed the heavily spiced meat shared with him by his neighbour, the man changed the subject to his wares 'good meat huh?'. Will nodded as he swallowed the last mouthful, 'I've plenty more, it seems these rebels have lived off the stuff for days, I got that bit from those laying behind you'. Will sharply twisted to view what the man referred to, a few yards behind him stacked four corpses ready for burial at first light, 'Sure you don't want any more? the man pressed his offer to him. 'Suddenly I have no appetite' Will answered ending the conversation quickly.

The provost woke the detail before dawn, walking about the scattering of men who had struggled for a few moments sleep that night, Will felt a sharp kick to his feet, 'Up's lad, there's heavy work to be done'. Pulling his felt hat that shielded his eyes from the surroundings he sat upright to watch Dan and Thom grumbling at such a rude awakening as the provost Sergeant stood over the three as they scrambled to their feet, 'You've a few hours labour to do before the ration wagon arrives' the Sergeant growled, 'Now get to it!'.

The detail sprang into action at the bark of the order, throwing shovels at the feet the group each grabbed the tools and formed into groups for the day's heavy labour. 'Bloody fine state of affairs this is' Thom spoke as the three cut the turf from the ground, 'Aye brother, what justice is this?' Dan added. The rocky earth baked hard by the summer heat refused to yield to the labours of the three as the provost guard gazed over them, the sun rose across the heights that dominated the landscape behind, the three rested their arms on the shovels for a moments breath as summer flies and mosquitoes swarmed around them settling on their sweated bodies, Will slapped the bugs as they settled on his tanned skin, 'Damn this place' he snapped at the frustration of the swarming insects 'We suffer frost bite in the winter and tropical fevers in the summer, I wonder what man would wish to fight for this place at all'. The slumbering provost guard although appearing to be sound asleep yelled over to the resting group having listened to the three's complaints, 'Grumble all you likes lads, you're here now, there's little you can do to change this situation'. The details ration arrived late in the morning, Thom was selected randomly to assist in the boiling of the ground beef issued to the men leaving Dan and Will to complete the digging that would house the dead, the two sat by the pits edge swinging their legs into the hole below and quenching the thirst from their canteens, behind him approached the man who had shared supper with them the previous night, the man sat between Will and

Dan and delved into his pocket producing a roll of tobacco. 'Smoke?' the man offered the velvet pouch to the pair, Will interrupted the man's action 'Depends where you found it' he asked with contempt, 'Ah lad, your high morals will keep you poor evermore' the man turned to Will smugly, 'I have just the thing to raise your spirits' adding when from the inside of his waistcoat the man produced a tin whistle, holding it in his open palms his presented it to Will and Dan simultaneously, 'It's yours for six pence' the man tendered the item. Will snatched it from the man's hands examining it carefully, 'Where did you get this?' he demanded to know. The man ignored Will and continued his pitch, 'finest silver I fear, I could get more for it but I feel you would benefit the most from it, I have a fiddle too If you desire but that is in need of some slight repair'. Will lunged at the man grabbing his collar, caught unawares he fell into the grave only to be followed by Will who leered over his bemused body wondering what he had done to deserve such a reaction, 'Where the hell did you get this?' he demanded to know, 'Tell me or by god I'll smash your skull in'. 'Will!' Dan jumped into the pit pulling him from the cowering man, 'What's got into you in Gods name?' he said struggling to hold him back from the confused man as he cowered in the corner. The man jumped up as soon as opportunity arose, 'your friend needs his head examining, now let me out of here before I call the guard' he spat as he scrambled over the side of the pit quickly escaping Will's temper. Leaving the two standing chest high in the pit Dan faced Will and pressed him to his sudden actions, 'Are you possessed lad? Are you looking for the gallows?', Will shook himself free of Dan's grasp and stared a moment into his eyes, 'Do you remember when we lost Walsh?', 'Aye' Dan acknowledged 'what has that to do with anything?', 'That night when we arrived back at the billet, Zeke drew lots for his belongings', 'Aye, that I remember' Dan answered none the wiser to where this was going, 'I took his tin whistle and you took his tinderbox' Will explained further, the realisation dawned across Dan's face, 'Are you sure?'. 'That I am Dan, we need to find out how he obtained it' Will spoke with fury in his eyes 'although I have a damn good inclination already'.

The sentry approached the two as they clambered from the pit, 'your both dismissed from the detail for one hour, go find your mess and take your ration', Will whispered to Dan as they walked towards the wagons 'we'll take him tonight after sun down, we need to find out where he got that whistle', 'Are you absolutely sure that it's Walsh's whistle?' Dan again asked fearful of further trouble, 'Damn sure Dan, we'll speak to Zeke when we rejoin the company about what to do' he replied.

The two joined the long line of men assigned to the detail, some shackled, some not, the guard with bayonets fixed watched over the line as it slowly moved forward to the head of the queue, Thom, assigned to the ration wagon served the detail with a generous portion of boiled ground beef and a quarter of a loaf of bread as the line moved along finally receiving a draw from several oak barrels containing water before falling out in a loose gathering around the wagons. Thom sat beside the two as they consumed their meal, 'what troubles?' he asked sensing their tension, 'Show him' Dan addressed Will directly, 'Show me what?' enquired Thom pausing his meal a moment despite the pains of hunger that wracked his stomach. Will slid his hand inside his pocket removing the whistle, not saying a word he handed it to Thom, 'You're showing me a whistle?' Thom looked on with confusion as he returned to his meal, 'Who's whistle Thom?' Will asked rhetorically. Thom ran his loaf around the rim of his plate soaking up the globs of fat that separated from the meat, stuffing the crust into his mouth replied the words Will sought, 'James Walsh's whistle by the looks of it' as he chewed on his final crust. Confirmed by his brothers words Dan jumped to his feet, 'wait Dan' Will called up to him 'We need to choose our moment in this, else there's trouble ahead for us all for it seems our looter friend has had access to our baggage' Thom replied.

The three continued with the burial detail until sundown before being dismissed for supper by the provost guard, the men gathered around the ration wagon ready to receive their evening meal and the three timed joining the queue to coincide with the looter joining the waiting line, approaching behind him Will whispered into his ear 'We need to talk friend, fall out the line and walk with us and no harm will come to you', Dan directed the looter with a gentle push between his shoulders and with his hand firmly on his neck directed him into the darkness and away from prying eyes. Pushing the man to the ground Dan knelt heavily on his chest, 'for God's sake man, get off me, I can hardly breathe' the looter gasped. 'Quicker you tell us what we want to know the better it is for all of us then' Dan snarled, 'Where did you get the whistle?' Will demanded to know, 'I cannot recall' the man answered struggling to release himself from Dan's weight, Dan clenched his fist in readiness to strike the looter hard should he hesitate once more with the answer, 'Wait, wait, wait . . .' the man stalled for time, 'I found a man from the 17th just after you told me your Regiment'

Will cursed himself and realised he'd willingly told the looter his company and Regiment designation giving him opportunity to rob their belongings while they remained on the burial detail, ''tis poor luck for me that I chance to sell them to the men that they truly belonged to'. 'Who gave them to you?' Will angrily questioned the man, 'Ah, that I can tell you, a tall scornful man, said he'd been given them by an officer no less and tricked me himself he did too, told me the whistle was silver but tis nothing but cheap tinplate' the man continued to struggle as the weight of Dan's body pressed onto his chest contracting his lungs furthermore, 'Lads', the man pleaded 'Lets me go and you can keep em if you like, they mean nothing to me, I have a leather bound note book too but it was beyond repair to sell it for even a hapenny'. Dan swung his clenched fist into the jaw of the man knocking him out cold, 'Sam's journal . . .' he spoke 'and the sellers description sounds very much like old Skinner'.

The three spent the following two days with the burial detail before being recalled back to McPherson's company, travelling north the Regiment camped on the outskirts of Bedford village as Howe's advance stalled at the heights overlooking Brooklyn. With Lord Howe keen to sue for peace offered Washington the opportunity to revoke the formal declaration of independence from the crown, but in an act of insult refused by the newly formed 'Congress of the United States'. General Washington had used the time wisely evacuating his battered army across the rivers that linked the land masses across to the Jerseys in order to regroup.

Will, Dan and Thom spoke at length with Zeke regarding their accusations of Skinners theft, Zeke sat calmly and shook his head 'Your proof lads, is where?' he questioned, The three stumbled a moment before Dan broke the awkwardness of Zeke's lack of interest, 'That bastard has stolen our belongings, he's sold everything of value'. But Zeke didn't change his tone throughout, 'Like I said lads show me your proof and we'll do something, McPherson will need solid evidence in this matter, having wasted his time with the embarrassments of Skinners court martial I doubt he'll listen to anything you have to offer, besides you'll have to go through Vaughan first and he has no confidence in you currently'. The frustration flowed through Will once more as Skinners ability to slip from justice defeated the file yet again, Zeke leant into the fire stoking its dying embers and finished the conversation once and for all, 'If what you say is true and I doubt not that it is, your grind is with your corpse robber fellow more than Skinner and unless you can prove his part in this then you'd be best to leave this well alone now, if Vaughan sees your vendetta against Skinner he will only view this as a petty squabble over dead men's trinkets'. The file sat silently in the darkness as troops movements passed by in readiness for the next assault on the rebel lines, their bond of brotherhood was strained to new levels as Will seethed at the injustices done to him and his friends, Zeke moved from his position and settled next to him, 'Lad, I can see all this troubles you but trust me, Skinner's now on borrowed time now'. Will butted into Zeke's speech raising his voice in anger 'He's gotten away with this time after time Zeke, you think his time is nigh? tell me what justice lets a man kill his own and suffer no consequences for it?'. Zeke shook his head, 'Your patience is poor Will lad, do you think after all these years I have not seen similar actions in many men, granted Skinner has gotten away with more than most but it'll catch him in the end, bide your times and you'll have your revenge one way or another'. From the darkness a voice slurred towards the file, 'So you think so eh Turner?' the gloom gave way to Skinners form emerging from the night shadows, staggering towards them, the figure swayed into the files camp and sat on an upturned barrel, the fire's glow illuminated his face like the devil himself as he spat with contempt into the files presence, 'I should thank you boy, for you've made me invincible now' he addressed Will directly, 'You cannot touch me now for all the eyes of the Regiment will see you as the instigator of my demise'.

Dan and Thom having listened in silence to Zeke and Will's talk sat upright in readiness for a fight, on seeing the brothers move Skinner turned sharply towards them swinging his bottle of drink 'Ah' he exclaimed calmly 'so It's murder now then lads is it?' Zeke shouted at the Allen brothers 'Calmly does it lads, you know what he's capable of'. Skinner continued to slur his speech 'Capable? You don't know the meaning of the word Turner, many have tried to finish poor old Mathias and all have failed and found themselves as wretched as lost souls'.

Lowering his head between his knees Skinner emitted an array of emotions confusing all of the file, his rambling made little sense but brought fear and loathing into the hearts of his captive audience, after ceasing his mutterings Skinner calmly stood and leant towards Will lowering his voice to nothing more than a mutter he whispered with clear sobriety 'Learn from this boy, you'd do well to listen to your old friend Turner and forget your concept of justice for in this world you'll not find it' as he tailed off his words Skinner opened Will's palm and pressed within it a shilling 'I trust this is more than enough for your lost trinkets?' he laughed away his contempt and wandered off into the darkness as quickly as he came leaving the file in silence once again, sensing the anger brewing in the file Zeke defused the tension with this his solemn vow 'I'll see him done for lads, mark my words but for now we must leave Skinner be and let him slip of his own accords'.

*   *   *

Chapter Seven

The Hudson

Howe's plan to crush the rebellion once and for all stalled to a halt on the Brooklyn Heights, the momentum gained as the advancing Corps smashed through the defenders failed to drive Washington's army into the bottle neck as British generals dithered on the slopes towards the last defences of Long Island, not surprisingly General Washington used the hesitation wisely and withdrew his battered forces across the Hudson River into the safety of the mainland giving him time to reorganise his forces to face the King's armies once again. Frustrated at losing his catch, Lord Howe planned his strategy for the next campaign ever wary of the increasing professionalism of his enemy they gained each moment they evaded capture but for now the final drive into the enemy resulted in only minor skirmishing leaving the British forces in control of the Island but without a decisive victory Howe so desperately pursued.

The weather proved favourable to the rebel army, had the winds been otherwise the Royal Navy might have positioned itself in the mouth of the East River preventing the bottle necked army from escape but this was not to be, by sunrise of the 30th of August after a heavy night of fog the rebel army had vacated the Island under the very noses of the over cautious British. Vaughan arrived amongst his company as the morning ration was consumed by troops eager to drive the enemy into the sea, 'Stand down for now lads' he instructed the files 'there's no movement for us today'. Zeke carried on his business as though unsurprised by the days order, 'What's happened Zeke?' Will enquired with enthusiasm 'Has the fight ended?' as the file sat on the grass squashed flat by the movements of thousands of troops ahead and ready to face the enemy, 'It seems our worthy opponent has out foxed us once again' he spoke running his pocket knife around the bowl of his pipe, 'This rebellion has now evolved into a bloody war, Howe will set us to winter quarters soon and the enemy will capitalise on our inactions for we should've smashed em out by now, this part-time army is gaining experience on the field of battle which I'm sure in time will cost us dearly'. Will looked on as Zeke crammed his pipe with tobacco and lit the bowl from the embers of the camps dying fire, the realisation of Zeke's words had concerned him, 'how much longer would this game f cat and mouse continue?' he thought to himself as the British poured thousands of fresh troops and Hessian mercenaries in the colonies and the enemy seemed to evade capture time and time again.

News from the front lines soon filtered through arriving at the 17th's camp by mid morning, scouting parties from the main assault had probed deep into the enemy lines at Brooklyn Heights to find the entire defences abandoned, not a soul was left behind. With such sketchy news the initial reaction was to assume the rebellion had faltered, succumbed to the success of the British drive into the heart of the enemy but within a short time the realisation revealed a very successful evacuation in the face of defeat. To most it mattered not whether the war ended this day or the next but to a man of Zeke Turner's experience the enemy's flight would prove costly in the coming months 'This Washington fellow fights a new kind of warfare to what the King's Generals are accustomed to, we've seen his capabilities already and the effect it does to an army unfamiliar to these lands, wherever the rebels run too Howe will be keen to pursue and even the most disciplined campaigning army soon falters on foreign shores'.

The company rested over the following weeks until Howe's general staff decided its strategy in holding the area's vacated by the fleeing rebel army. New York thus far inactive in the rebellion was a significant part of Howe's strategy in controlling the large key towns in the rebellious colonies, as soon as the weather turned favourably, Howe planned to occupy the town with a large garrison of troops. On receipt of this news Dan Allen offered some reflective humour to the Regiments orders 'Let's hope Howe has learned well from Boston and denies the enemy the surrounding lands eh?', 'Aye brother' Thom added 'I doubt I could face another winter like the last'.

It took two further weeks for the British to react to Washington's withdrawal causing concerns from Zeke to be aired openly, 'if Howe seeks to better himself in these campaigns he should do well to face the enemy directly as those who wield the bayonet for a penny a day, a man of standing could dine well on the glory of success whilst the likes of us face an uncertain future in the coming months ahead'. Amused by Zeke's flippancy Will laughed nervously at his corporal's monologue, the truth of the words ran deep in his mind as even Will could see the future looked bloody for Kings men and rebel alike. Howe's decision to enter New York came as no surprise once the order came for the 17th Regiment to vacate Long Island, the mouth of the Hudson River filled with the warships and barges used to ferry the troops from Staten Island to Long Island the three weeks previous. Unopposed, the Kings army entered the town to cheers from its inhabitants keen to welcome and exploit the many red coated soldiers arriving into the town. The file disembarked from its barge at the dock on the southern tip of the town, the arrival resembled the landings at Boston and similarly billets where hard to come by, Zeke careful not to rely on Captain McPherson's arrangement of company billets immediately began to trawl the back streets searching for reasonable accommodation. The file wandered the back quarters of the town keen to find dwellings ready to capitalise upon the garrisoned army, it wasn't long before Zeke had secured private billets with an immigrant Yiddish tailor on Elizabeth Street in the heart of the old town and conveniently close to the Bulls Head Tavern which welcomed scores of red coated soldiers with open arms, the file having agreed a favourable fee with their landlord made way towards the Inn.

The tavern was packed tight with soldiers, the noise unbearable for the level of conversation but the landlord made little complaint as his business boomed as rosy cheeked soldiers fought for space in his tiny yet accommodating rooms. Dan and Thom purchased ales and poured the brew into their tankards raising their vessels high to toast their fortunes at finding such comfortable billets in an increasingly filling town. From the taverns small leaded windows, Will watched scores of soldiers pass down the street desperate to find a reasonable billet, secure with Zeke's leadership Will rested his hand on his shoulder and grinned to his Corporal, 'May times be good for us Zeke, we thank you for all you have done' he comically bowed to his superior in jest, Zeke swallowed the last of his tankard wiping the frothy residue from his stubble, 'Nay lad, think nothing of it . . . for I may well need your help one day for I fear these bones will fall long before yours' adding comically 'for I'll be wanting a grand and fitting burial from you'. Will laughed at his friends black humour 'aye but Men like you last forever', 'that may be true lad' Zeke replied with his quick wit 'but sometimes men like me do not always wish to last forever'.

The file drank away the coin in their purses leaving barely enough to pay their rent, departing the tavern at sundown Thom purchased a small bottle of ale for the journey 'Best familiarise ourselves with this town if it is to be our home a while' Zeke insisted the file take the back streets. Strolling the lanes and streets of the old town, Will noted the difference in building architecture to that of Boston, these unfamiliar structures looked different to all he'd known before, Sam Coles would quickly have offered the explanation to this but these days Will had to remain content with his ignorance of his new surroundings. Long into the evening soldiers continued to ferry across the East River that separated Long Island and New York, grateful of their early arrival in the busy town the four men walked along the quaysides as hundreds of troops poured into the harbour, the four watched as a crowd gathered around a public square were King George's statue had once stood proud, toppled several months past it had been picked clean for its valuable lead and melted down to make the lead shot that had troubled the red coats so much over the past year, the file was just able to see the lowering of the Congressional flag and be replaced with that of the Union to a huge roar of applause and cheering from both soldier and civilian. 'Don't' be fooled lads' Zeke commented 'these fickle types have no loyalty to us any more than they had to Washington's army' he commented as he turned his back on the crowds quick changeability. Will rushed after him as Zeke shook his head to the inconsistency of the towns fickle nature, 'Be wary lad' he spoke 'for once we leave these types will cheer the next army to arrive, whoever that may be'. The file left the scene swelling in the euphoria of its 'liberation' from the siege that threatened the town, casually strolling along the narrow lanes and streets towards their rented billets, the houses appeared and commercial buildings towered over the narrow pathways offering little light onto the paved streets below, the cramped nature in some ways reminded him of his home town of Leicester, a town that had changed much since his departure nearly five years past, industrialisation was changing the landscape of England faster than anyone could have imagined, his home town was now alien to him, home? he pondered these days became wherever the army took him and as long as he was bonded to his file he would be happy with his lot. Stirred by thoughts of his home town he gave a moment to his siblings, Rebecca and Joseph both now well into adulthood, Will hoped they had fared well with their lives, despite the years he had almost forgotten that they would had aged as he himself had done, no longer would they be the young dependants he left behind assuming that their father hadn't ruined their lives as seemed most probable to him.

Zeke led the file to the tailors house, wrapping on the door to arouse the owner to their return, the door opened slightly as the tailor took a glimpse of the men stood on his raised steps, 'Ah gentlemen' he exclaimed in a thick accent, 'I have wondered upon your return'. The tailor led them through the house to their room at the back, 'there has been some' he paused a moment finishing 'let us say, developments since you left us last', Zeke cut short the man's statement 'surely you mean not to cheat us sir?', 'no, of course not my friend' he replied 'but living space comes as a valuable commodity these days and I was not expecting such a high demand for my rooms'. Will rolled his eyes knowing the outcome of this would cost them significant more coin than they had already paid, 'I have been honourable to my word, you may stay here as long as you wish but I am afraid to secure your dwelling for the long term I will have to raise the rent somewhat'. 'Exactly how much?' Dan butted aggressively into the landlord's words, 'Ah my hot headed friend, only a modest amount, for I have turned away many gentlemen prepared to pay a much higher sum than we agreed'. Thom joined his brothers concerns, frustrated by the tailor's attempts to gain a higher fee 'How much more?' he demanded as tempers rose. 'Hmm, let me see, let me see . . .' he drummed his fingers over his bearded chin 'I am but a modest tailor only struggling to seek a living in these difficult times, shall we say a shilling a week . . . each?!' knowingly pushing his luck with such an extortionate offer. 'Pish!' Will snapped 'we can find better elsewhere' he turned back from whence they had come, Zeke grabbed his arm preventing him from ending the negotiations so abruptly, 'ease yourself lad' Zeke whispered 'let me handle this from now'. The tailor held the upper hand in these negotiations and he knew it only too well, the town was bursting with its new inhabitants, all of them increasingly desperate to secure decent accommodations. Zeke thought a moment and weighed up the probability of securing another billet at this late hour would be impossible, they had been fortunate to arrive amongst the first ashore in New York but curse his stupidity for allowing this to happen, 'Two shillings for all of us is all we can offer' he spoke sternly. The Jew knew there was yet more to be had from this deal, 'Gentlemen, gentlemen, I can lease this room for much more than two shillings a week, In fact a gentlemen officer is due to come back this very hour, for what now am I to say to him?' presenting his open palms to the file in an honest gesture and pressing for a final closure on the negotiations. 'Then I say three shillings a week for all of us, complete with board' Zeke matched his demands. 'Agreed' the tailor jumped at the offer and quickly sealed the agreement with a firm handshake with each of them, 'Of course gentlemen' he added as the bond of the contract was secured 'I will require two full weeks payment in advance'.

Leaving the four alone a moment, the Tailor gave them a few minutes to work their finances accordingly, 'We've been cheated!' Thom spoke angrily, 'Aye brother that we have' Dan added 'We should have walked away, better to look elsewhere than be taken by a trickster'. 'Hush yourselves a moment and be calm' Zeke reasserted his authority over the hot headed brothers, 'do you wish to scour the streets at this late hour looking for lodgings? you will do well to find space in the gutter let alone a decent billet, even if you do find somewhere you'll be paying the same . . . if not more for the army's canvas has yet to arrive so you'll be out in the open fields that surround the town and with the rebel's position uncertain you may well wake to a cannonball at your heads'. Again knowing their Corporal to be right the file delved into their purses for the required coin, between the four they pooled eight shillings and a penny ha'penny in loose coin, the landlord would take six leaving barely enough to survive until the paymasters arrears where settled, hopefully Will thought to himself before the current rent ran out.

The landlord reappeared with a steaming pot of tea, 'I have taken the liberty in providing you with this beverage, consider it a token of my generosity, now gentlemen, you payment please'. Generosity Will though, pah, the man had raised his rent fivefold once he'd realised there was more capital to be had, the sweet tea was tainted by the bitterness of being cheated once again. Unlocking the room that would house them all together the four selected a bed each, modest yet certainly more comfortable than most they'd shared together, Will unloaded his equipment onto his bed and relaxed taking in his surroundings, a shuttered window kept the room draft free and whilst expensive, the room provided a good degree of comfort for the file as they rested their tired bones for the night.

Will woke early as Zeke opened the shutters allowing the morning sunlight to pour into the room, still in his uniform he had fallen asleep still clothed and atop of his bedding, rather than wake him from his slumber Zeke had decided to leave the exhausted lad be than to stir him from his dreams. The landlord on hearing movement above prepared a breakfast for the file, coffee, black bread and smoked beef was left outside the room alerted by a sharp knock at the door, Dan opened the door to find the platter neatly served awaiting their approval and raised his eyebrows at the quality of the food provided, 'It seems for all our extortionate rents we have become privileged guests' he joked. As the sun rose over the horizon the town brought life into its streets, the noise and bustle quickly dissolved the silence that befell the night past as carts and wagons negotiated the narrow lanes that entwined the town and cries of commerce quickly shattered the peace. Zeke would need to report the files whereabouts to the battalion's adjutants and instructed Will to remain at the billet until they returned with their orders for the day, 'rest yourself this morning Will lad' Zeke spoke in slight jest, 'consider yourself on guard should our host try to raise our rents once again'.

Will sat alone in the room when a gentle knock came to the door, rising from the edge of his bed he opened the door to the landlord 'Ah, good morning' the landlord spoke 'I have excess hot water should you wish it, a few moments more and you can have it to yourself if you want' he continued in his thick eastern European accent, Wary of this man's ability to extract his coin from him Will enquired to the potential cost of this extra hospitality, 'Come now my friend, if you are good enough to pay me such an honest amount then the least I can do is accommodate you fittingly'. Satisfied with the landlord's honesty Will grabbed his haversack and followed the man down the winding staircase to the lower basement level of the tall townhouse, the tailor practiced his trade on a long table covered with fine cloth, a huge pair of shears used to cut the patterns lay across the table ready to begin their days work. He followed the man to the fire range on which was a large copper kettle of warming water, 'wait here one moment' the man spoke before yelling back up the stairs from where they had descended, 'Y'oni!' he shouted cupping his hand to increase the level of his call, the rest Will failed to understand as the tailor spoke in his native tongue unfamiliar to him, a young voice cried down his father followed by fast footsteps on the floor boards above, the man returned to face Will and spoke part Yiddish and part English 'A klog iz mir! That boy sometimes has a lazy nature about him, perhaps I should take my cane to him more often huh?'. The tailor continued to mumble to himself as he walked to the cutting table to continue his work leaving Will isolated by the fire range, after a few moments of silence the tailor spoke again, 'He won't be much longer now I assure you' most apologetically 'now I see your coat is torn some, remove it for me and I will repair it for you' sensing Will's hesitance the tailor laughed 'ha ha, I see my peoples reputation goes far, for you my friend, there is no charge'. Will slipped his coat from his shoulders and placed it on the table, examining the quality he spoke aloud 'Good, good . . . I see the garment had been well cared for, I shall have this ready for you by sunset at the latest but for now you may use my stove for the water is now almost ready' and glancing behind, him Will noted the bright copper kettle beginning to boil, 'My son will be here in a moment, he will tend to your needs' the tailor spoke.

The tailors son ran down the stairs and entered the workshop, stopping dead in his tracks he looked surprised at the soldier who occupied his father's presence, the tailor addressed the boy again in a tongue unfamiliar finally switching his language to English to inform Will that the boy would lead the way to a bath tub in the rear rooms. The boy lifted the hot kettle from the range wrapping the handle in thick rags to protect him from its heat, the boy gestured for Will to follow him through the rear door into the room beyond. Lit by several high windows the bright lime washed rooms appeared to be a laundry for the tailors fabrics, a large tin bath hung high on the wall which the boy with his tender age could not reach, the boy looked at Will and ushered for him to remove the tub from the peg that held it to the white plastered wall, Will smiled to the boy as he lowered it and placed it on the tiled red flooring.

The boy about seven years of age spoke for the first time but Will could only guess this meaning 'A sheynem danke' thank you perhaps, who knows? he thought to himself. Will placed his hand on his chest in an attempt to introduce himself to the boy 'I am Will, William Snow' he spoke slowly to the boy grinning broadly towards him, 'Y'onathon' the boy replied humbly as he lowered his head in respect. With acquaintances made, Will undressed his outer clothes as his new friend poured the steaming water into the tub and left the room, easing himself into a soak he relaxed and un-tensed his shoulders sliding into the hot bath water, he couldn't remember the last time he'd soaked these tired bones, the heat made him drowsy as he closed his eyes and drifted over the memories of his life.

Personal hygiene was limiting to a campaigning army, a flowing river or stream might provide some washing facilities but usually the camps kettle would offer little more than a strip wash at best, a rare opportunity to bathe like this was to be savoured and Will certainly took advantage of the opportunity, after an hour alone a soft knock woke him from his day dream. The boy had heated more water for him to rinse the grime from his body, Will sat upright slopping the filthy water over the sides of the tub onto the tiles floor, the door opened a little as the boys head peered into the room slightly, 'Ich hobn mer waser' he spoke in his own language.

Pouring the water over Will's back the years of soldiering washed away leaving his skin vibrant and youthful once again, the boy pointed to a collection of large whitened rags piled on a shelf next to where the tub had hung, 'Trukn sich mit, helfn sich bitte'. The more Will listened to the tailors son he saw some similarities in his own tongue, 'Danke' Will attempted to converse in this strange and foreign language, 'Ya, Danke' the boy smiled back at Will's attempt to communicate.

Will dried himself and dressed in his under garments before returning to the tailors workshop, the boy sat atop of his father's table watching keenly as the man ran his sharp shears down the length of a bolt of cloth, 'I am grateful for your hospitality sir' Will spoke politely announcing his entrance to the room, he gathered his long damp hair into a group at the back of his clean scalp and twisted a length of black ribbon securing it into place, his white undershirt clung to his still damp and clammy body as the heat from his soak radiated outwards from his clean and softened skin, 'Come warm yourself by the fireside my friend' the tailor spoke, 'I'll have my son make us some fresh coffee huh?' the tailor added and switching back to Yiddish the man told his son to prepare some food for them to eat together.

'He's a good boy really' the tailor spoke in softened tones 'although it doesn't do him good to hear it too often' he quipped with some humour. Formally the tailor elected to introduce himself 'My given name is Evron, Evron Abramowicz although here I am known as Eli, my son as you already know is Y'onathan or Y'oni if you prefer'. Sensing his need to formally introduce himself, Will returned the introduction 'And I am Will, William Snow to be exact', 'I know already Will, Y'oni told me whilst you soaked yourself, and besides your name is written in the lining of your frock coat' Eli laughed at his clever observations.

Y'oni stepped cautiously down the wooden staircase, carefully balancing a tray consisting of cold roasted chicken, bread and three apples for them to share, the boy poured the coffee into three fancy china cups before offering them most politely to his guest 'Gezunterhait an shalom!' Eli raised his cup in good health. 'Danke' Will smiled back at the boy, 'Ah, I see you have learned a thing or two about our language already?' Eli spoke as he bit into his lunch. Seeing these people as the better side of humanity Will reached for his knapsack and delved inside and pulled from it James Walsh's penny whistle, holding it to the boy he offered it as a token of his thanks for the generosity he'd been given, 'a gift for you' Will held the whistle towards the boy who instinctively waited for his father's approval before accepting the gift, 'Ein geschenk fur sie' Eli nodded with approval for Y'oni to accept Will's small gift. The boy reached out his hand and received his new bequest, placing it to his lips the boy wandered back up the stairs blowing into the instrument with clear gratefulness at his reward.

The two men sat on the table with their lunch between them, 'Come my friend, let us eat, for it will be a cold day in hell when a guest of a Jewish household goes hungry'. Eli enquired into Wills life before enlistment, and idled away the afternoon as Will recounted his adventures with the 17th Regiment with a particular resentment when relaying the injustices of Skinners hatred for the file, 'Trust me my friend' Eli calmed Will's frustrations, 'a man like this will find himself doomed eventually, this justice you seek will prevail, for God will assure it'. 'Zeke says fairly the same thing, that Skinner will tumble soon enough, but I cannot see how after all that's happened' Will petitioned to Eli's reasoning. 'I think your friend Zeke has a good level of wisdom, you should trust his visions in this matter' Eli replied. The conversation was broken by the files return to the house, 'Now I have work to do William Snow for these garments to not make themselves you know'.

Will met with the file at the room they shared and relayed his events of the day, the kindness shared by his host had impacted heavily on him and the others keen to take advantage of a long overdue bath singularly spent an hour or so each enjoying their soak in the comforts of their new surroundings.

The four relieved of duties with their Regiment spent the next few days enjoying their time with their hosts, they all took a particular shine the Y'oni who attempted to entertain the file with his new flute, although conversations between the two was limited through language difficulties Will had the patience to share his time with his young friend and Eli often watched the two interact as he shared at length his life and experiences with his similarly aged Zeke. The two bonded well together for both had seen much over their years, Will occasionally caught some of the conversation and was particularly taken by Eli's tales of his coming to the colonies. Eli had been born in Danzig, a northern port city in the then

Russian principalities, as a Jew, Eli and his family had prospered well under Tzarist rule but religious reform had troubled his families freedom to practice Judaism, the colonies Eli thought, would offer freedom to do such without intolerances that crept into his ways. Eli and Y'Oni had sailed to New York when the boy was but a baby, the child's mother had perished during childbirth leaving Eli to raise the boy alone, Will thought to himself how similar circumstances had led to such differing lifestyles, his own mother had died young leaving Will in his father's ward, he needed little reminding of his own fathers failings in paternity. Eli, although strict with the boy had provided a sound foundation to his life, with hard work and a little luck the family would do well in these lands.

With their time spent lazily amongst the narrow back streets of New York, the town's new garrison had swelled to bursting point, the main assault by Howe had again stalled on the verge of victory but for now New York was at least secure once again in the hands of the British army. With autumn fast approaching the lands forthcoming harvest would supply the army with food and fodder for the winter quartering, on extended leave the file rested and enjoyed the fruits of this colonial town a million miles away from the battlefields to the north. The first two weeks of September came uneventful to the soldiers garrisoned in New York, with the surrounding countryside now secured from Washington's continental army, the large proportion of soldiers moved northwards into the camps provided, although a huge drain on their purses the file elected to stay in New York town relishing the humanity and comforts provided by their host Eli. For a few coins more Eli offered to feed the file an evening meal and in exchange for his generosity collectively the four assisted him as they could and Eli in return made good repairs on their tattered uniforms. On each night after supper the four wandered from Inn to Inn, the long warm evenings made pleasurable and memorable times for them as they joked and laughed amongst each other enjoying their bond of brotherhood regained. Eli soon began to trust the four enough to provide them a key to his heavy oak door that secured it from the back street thieves that knew of his prosperity, keeping to his beliefs enough to forbid alcohol on his property, a small amount of kosher wine was permitted on the Jewish Sabbath but for the four, any strong liquor was to be consumed away from his home, the Allen brothers thought Eli's insistence a bind but Will having seen the effects of strong drink on a man would ensure his hosts wishes upheld.

September 21st 1776 was to go down in history as one of the tragedies of this colonial revolution, for many that night would lose their homes and some their lives. The four of the file spent the evening as most had done settled in the inns and taverns that prospered so well from the army's occupation, the soft gentle breeze brought a pleasant warmth through the open windows of the towns taverns, Will noted to himself the abundance of soldiers still billeted within the town even though the camps north of the island had established themselves for some time. As the late summer sun settled over the roof tops westward, the last of the days light brought obscurity to the candle lit room as the many soldiers drank heavily having received their pay earlier that day, the four having been present since late afternoon occupied a narrow table to the rear of the rooms, the Black Bull tavern had done well from the four who obliged to give Eli some privacy often frequented the Inn with its short distance from their billets. The initial shouts were dismissed as the usual rowdiness of soldiers who could not limit their drink in these lazy evenings, too much time on a soldiers hands often spawns the devils work Zeke would comment as fights and scuffles often broke out over the most petty of circumstances. For a time the commotion outside was ignored until over the din Will heard bells ringing the alarm for attention, initially the four thought a call to arms had been ordered against the few small pockets of rebel resistance was still doggedly holding out against Howe's advancing army. The taverns broad doorway was obscured by the patrons eager to catch a glimpse of what events unfolded outside and gave Dan little cause for concern, 'come lads, more drink for the night is still young yet' he spoke eager to refill his empty flagon. Thom, Zeke and Will failed to hear their comrade's request as collectively they focused on the panic that spread outside, Zeke rose from his seat as the tavern emptied with the arrival of the provost guard calling all available men outside,

'Blast!' spoke Will despondently on realising the significance of the provost arrival 'what business do they have here?'

Zeke kept his vision on what little he could see of outside, 'grab your kit lads' as he snatched his own from a communal pile on the floor 'there's trouble afoot', in an moment the group donned their equipment and followed the fast emptying rooms. Once outside Zeke was immediately accosted by a sergeant of the provost recognising his rank above the others around him, 'There's fire loose in the town Corporal, muster what men you can and make way to the gun batteries south and gather any stragglers you may find on your way' the Sergeant instructed him. Soldiers scattered in every direction, the sudden appearance of the provost guard had unsettled the atmosphere and with the panic set in by rumours of arson, small groups of men raced through the back alleys in every direction possible confusing the turns and alleyways as they ran into each other. Zeke soon gave up in mustering the panicked soldiers, either concerned for their own lives or eager to seek an opportunity for looting, the rabble quickly littered the streets to any degree of cohesion. The four men kept closely together, in the consuming darkness bodies of men wandered the streets seeking opportunity, too easily could they lose sight of each other in the panicked confusion as the roof tops above became back lit with the glow of orange flame. Being largely of wooden construction these buildings had stood for generations becoming increasingly cramped inside an ever expanding town. The warm summer months had dried the timber frames to precarious tinder, either arson or accident was of little concern now as the west side of the town soon blazed and the heavy acrid smoke began to fill the night sky.

Having paced the towns layout several times, the file knew these lanes and walkways well enough to deliver the provost sergeants request promptly, on the outside of the battery pockets of men gathered as they made their way on instruction to tackle the blaze now fiercely raging amongst the tall buildings. Noting the smoke blackened faces of some men busily passing banded buckets along the causeways, Zeke stripped to his shirt and put the four to work in the line that trailed into distant darkness. A Major from a highland Regiment arrived and added some order to the confused line falling out every third man to a detail that would be used to tackle the blaze where it combusted next, Will and Thom numbered off and fell from line along with a composite of every other Regiment Will had ever encountered, together they numbered less than forty, not three men of the same Regiment. The Highlander gathered the men around and in his thick Scots accent led the group north to where the fire raged fiercest, side by side Will and Thom kept pace alongside the Major who scanned left and right down each narrow alleyway they passed looking for an area to access the inferno.

The streets lay largely deserted bar the occasional lost soul and made a tremendous din as the flames caught the dry timbers and took hold across the rooftops, the heat intensified as the group made its way into the inferno to assess the extent of the blaze and tackle it in any way they could manage. 'Ah, tis dangerous business we're entering Will' Thom spoke as they turned into the side streets to face the blaze head on as the Major halted the group on the edge of Whitehall Street faced by the burning remnants of what once stood as the Fighting Cocks Tavern. The heat from the blaze hit those entering the street head on taking the breaths away of many to did not shield themselves from its intensity, a few yards down the lane a hastily retreating group of men realised their attempts to stop the spread of fire had failed and withdrew a distance to regroup. The officer leading the exhausted flight of men conversed with the Scotsman as Will listened in to news of the incident. From what he could gather from the sketchy conversation, just after sundown a small fire had broken out in the back rooms of the Fighting Cocks Tavern, panic had set in and in the rush to vacate the building the fire had been left to take hold unhindered and spread quickly amongst the dry timber walls, behind him Will heard mutterings of arson and sabotage but according to the officer anyway, at this stage the cause of the fire seemed accidental at least. On the advice of the withdrawing officer the Scots Major turned his party back to the battery garrison as the internal walls of the surrounding buildings began to collapse inwards, Will could not help but be reminded of Poor John White's demise back in Edinburgh, his memory reminded of the terrible injuries White succumbed to, he could only hope that nobody had found themselves trapped inside. Returning to the fire fighting party at the battery, the streets filled themselves with floating ashes lifted high by the seasonal winds, the roofs of unconnected buildings nested the smouldering embers until they too took hold and ignited the combustible roofs quickly spreading the flames along the skyline above.

Reaching the line of fire fighters that trailed into the dark streets that sprang from the jetty's and wharfs the fleeing party set panic into the discipline that held itself together so fragilely. Spotting Zeke seeking out their return, Will waved his arms frantically and yelled over the din of the advancing blaze as he and Thom returned, the officers authority strained as fearing entrapment by the advancing blaze men scattered while they could before the blaze sealed them into their doom.

The Highlander stood firm asserting his authority and seeking to bolster his control over the chaos stood himself on a level of packed crates ready for shipment overseas, although the gathering stood silent the noise levels became inaudible over the blaze that advanced through the town at such a fast pace, no one could blame a man for abandoning his post in such terrifying circumstances and soon the Scot had control over only nine remaining men after panic hit those that previously fought the advancing fire, 'Corporal, from who's Regiment do you hail?' the Major enquired with an amazing calm in such trying conditions, 'Mawhood's 17th!' Zeke replied proudly, 'Then I shall see he hears of your loyalty to a brethren officer'. Zeke bore his tobacco stained teeth and smiled, for only a Scot could make light of these terrifying conditions.

The battery fort at the southern tip of Manhattan Peninsular offered some reprieve to the advancing fires but soon the dark side streets illuminated themselves with the advancing firestorm as the flames swept quickly across the town, 'Sirs, we must do our duty and do it well, His Majesties Navy will deliver us passage should the rage bear on us too close' the officer addressed his gathering in order to inspire a little confidence in his jittery companions ever ready to abandon their post. The group entered the lower level of the artillery barrack rooms that attached themselves to the battery block, 'Look for poleaxes and the likes' Zeke shouted his orders to his fellow ranks, 'if we can make a break between the buildings the fire might falter'. This was a tall order for only a handful of men to achieve but if they could stall the fires advance somewhat their efforts would not be in vain.

The heavy lock from the barracks armoury received a point blank shot from the Scotsman's pistol and shattered blowing the banded oak door wide open and inside racked long rows of muskets and barrels of loose powder to be made into cartridge and charge. on the wall opposite hung several axes and pole arms which were quickly handed out to each of the men, Zeke grasped Will firmly by the shoulders and gave a clear and concise order, 'Listen lad and listen carefully, I'm giving you this task cus I trusts you with my life, loose powder can be a temperamental and fickle mistress so you need to dispose of it quickly, I don't care hows you do it now but once that heat enters these rooms this stuff is likely to go up and we'll all be blown to kingdom come, you understand?'

Will nodded in acknowledgement as Zeke gave his final instruction, 'Thom, you sticks with him, he'll tell you what you need to do, now hurry! There's no telling how much time we have should these winds change direction'. The armoury emptied as the party armed themselves and raced outside to assess their tactical situation of the raging fire, Will and Thom stood alone in the darkness illuminated only by a small lantern that hung freely from the rafters above, 'What's to do Will mate?' Thom pressed him on Zeke's orders, 'We're to move the powder Thom, Zeke says it's likely to blow if the heat reaches it' he spoke as he struggled to budge the nearest barrel, 'We'd do better to hurry Thom, these things aren't going to shift themselves now' he continued with a small dose of sarcasm at Thom's inactions. Thom realising the gravity of the situation dashed to Will's side and heaved his weight into moving the barrel, slowly the heavy barrel rocked from side to side as the two strained under its load. 'This is going to take an age' Will spoke as he regained his breath 'Aye' Thom added 'there's at least two dozen more yet'. It took ten long minutes for the two men to carefully move one casket to the safety of the far room away from the encroaching blaze and Will cursed the laziness of the batteries artillery men for placing such combustibles so close to the door, although in all likeliness any man would do the same save pacing the length of the barracks each time the ordinance was needed.

At this rate of movement the magazine would need ten men and an hour or more to remove the packed warehouse of its stock, in a moment of inspiration Will paused his efforts and stood upright easing his aching back, 'Thom' Will paused his friend a moment, 'we shall never make this task in time, we can however spoil the powder', 'You mean to render it damp?' Thom looked on 'and how exactly?'. 'Wait here until I get back, I won't be a moment' Will shouted as he raced out the door towards the blazing town.

As soon as he cleared the door the heat hit him head on, the fire now spread far across his sight as the winds increased and ignited the timbers towards the centre of the town. Fearing entrapment, Zeke and his fellows desperately tried to create a break between the buildings already alight but with only a handful of men his task was becoming increasingly futile. Zeke stepped back a moment from the flaming timbers and raced to Will on his arrival, 'How goes lad?' he enquired, ''Tis slow work Zeke, but if we can spoil the powder it may give us a chance', 'What plan do you have?' Zeke pressed intriguingly his breath laboured in the intense heat. Will huffed with exhaustion, the intense heat making anyone's breathing short, 'If we dampen the powder it may save us and the garrison should the flames reach us' he revealed. Zeke grinned broadly, not knowing whether this was in humour at such a foolish plan or admiration of a moment of inspiration, Will waited for his reaction to elaborate, 'See lad' he finally spoke 'there's brains in there after all' tapping his finger onto his skull, 'Now get back to the powder and wait for me there, I shall not be much longer' Zeke stopped his labours and sought after the Scots officer for approval of the plan leaving Will to return to the task at hand.

Arriving back to find Thom struggling alone with the barrels Will informed him of his intended plan, a moment later Zeke and Dan arrived bearing hatchets to start the task of splitting every barrel in the magazine, 'Best remove your shoes lads, any spark on powder in here will do us to kingdom come' Zeke said as he kicked off his tattered black boots, Dan dropped the thick bar that secured the magazine door and secured it firmly from the inside, handing each of them a hatchet Zeke swung his axe into the side of the nearest barrel splitting the rope and brass banding that held it together, the fine black powder poured freely onto the stone floor 'Let us hope General Washington does not hear of our loss lads, we'd be somewhat short on shot eh?' Zeke joked as the four began to smash open the barrels that filled the room. Will swung his hatchet into the long line of stacked barrels, the floor soon became awash with piles of black powder spread liberally onto the cold stone floor. As the four reached halfway, Zeke announced that they would need to draw water from the well in the next room and render this explosive tomb useless. The well that drew deep from the sea was primarily used for the gunners to swab the barrels of the artillery positioned on the bastions above, for now though the salt water would be liberally poured along the long magazine floor soaking into the fine grains of black powder making a thick but passive sludge.

Secretly, Will had enjoyed the destruction he was now licensed to cause, an act like this constituted treason that would bring the severest of penalties but this was sanctioned by their acting officer and the four laid into the remaining barrels with vigour.

Leaving the remaining few barrels for Will alone to break, Zeke Dan and Thom snatched several buckets besides the well that occupied the small room besides the magazine and tossed them into the dark abyss beneath, collectively the three drew the water from the sea and raced with speed back into the room now occupied solely by Will, 'As soon as your done lad join us, there's little time to lose here' Zeke called down to him who'd become lost in the destruction of the last of the intact barrels, exhausted, Will buried his hatchet into the final barrel as the last of the powder poured to the ground and rested his weary arms against the stone wall catching his breath a moment after exerting himself so heavily, 'No time for idleness Will, there's work to be done' Dan spoke slopping his buckets contents onto the gunpowder piled in heaps around the broken barrels. For the next hour the file poured gallon after gallon of sea water onto the powder littered floor until it ran thick with sludge, Zeke called a halt to the four's labours giving a moments breath to the tired and exhausted men that hopefully had saved the magazine from catastrophe. Self entombed inside the magazine, Zeke knew the repercussions should the fire reach the magazine with barrels of combustible powder stacked inside, with the magazine door barred to the world outside he could only hope those outside had succeeded in creating a fire break between them and the inferno that gripped the town.

Satisfied the majority of the barrels contents where now inert, Zeke called his men together and led them to the upper floor of the battery to gain an indication to the conditions outside. Reaching the tip of the winding staircase Will stood amazed at the blaze that had ripped through the western part of New York and beyond, the sky above glowed fierce red as the flames licked high into the nights darkness, the noise unbearable Will watched Zeke's lips issue instruction but heard no sound as the crackle and hiss of burning timers drowned out their voices on the battery rooftop. Following Zeke back down the winding staircase, the four gathered at the barred doorway ready to reveal the destruction outside, Dan tapped the fastened bar with the heel of a hatchet freeing it from its tight wedge, the bar lifted was the last obstacle to either safety or doom, slowly Dan creaked open the heavy reinforced door, an inch at a time until he became certain the yard outside was safe of flame.

Outside, gathered the remaining men who themselves blackened by smoke and exhausted had retired from the blaze having pulled the precarious burning timbers from the buildings. In a moments surrealism, Will stared down at his bare stocking feet, soaked with black sludge that ran high up his white breeches he realised the extent of his actions, whether anyone should ever realise the extent the file had achieved he cared not, for Will knew his quick thinking had possibly saved the whole town from total destruction and felt pride within himself as he looked back into the open door of the magazine illuminated by a sealed lantern that swung from the rooms rafters, he chucked to himself realising that over the last two hours he had dwelled at the gateway of oblivion, every variable was against them, the raging fire encroaching towards the battery fort, the piled gunpowder with its volatile temperament, the loyalty to stay and secure the magazine long after many would have fled brought pride to him and the file he belonged to, the Scots officer stood beside the group and stared on into the blazing houses that once bustled with life, 'You've done well lads' he spoke addressing none of them in particular, 'I shall see Mawhood hears well of this day'.

As the fire raged on, the night passed into dawn revealing the wake of the raging fire, although still well alight the fringes of the blaze had subdued leaving only charred and smouldering remains of what once stood as a busy harbour, from high on the battery position looked across the remains of the town observing organised groups continue to break the fire on the eastern part of the town.

'We've earned our rest for now' Thom spoke as the four gazed in silence across what once stood as tall rooftops but now as scorched and charred timbers held together like flimsy matchwood waiting to topple in the breeze. The large plume of black smoke trailed high and wide over the Manhattan peninsular and across the Hudson River westwards, 'Arson?' Will thought to himself, the Scots officer had thought different but a blaze of this magnitude surely could not have started from a single source?

Whatever the reason, Will's mind turned to Eli and Y'oni at the billets on Elizabeth Street, the fire had spread far beyond his line of sight and into the direction of their hosts abode, he prayed they'd found safety from the raging blaze or better still the fire had not reached that quarter of the town.

But for now at least, beneath the battlements of the battery the Scots officer, his smart uniform tattered and torn gave account of the night to the provost guard who swarmed the streets rounding up the slightest suspect for questioning as accusations of sabotage and arson spread through the town almost as quickly as the fire had itself. For the time being at least the mixed troop of soldiers that saved the bastion would have to remain at the battery after the provost had limited movements of all the town inhabitants, the destruction of the battery's magazine contents had caused the Scottish officer considerable time to explain and thus hindered the groups release from the garrison, but for now the file could do little until dismissed but cough and splutter their fouled and smoke choked lungs, 'Not using the time for your pipe Zeke?' Will laughed as he'd noted his pipe remained secreted in his tunic, the file had enough smoke in their lungs to last a lifetime it seemed.

Organisation came back to the town soon after midday, the engineers organised available men into work parties that began to tear down any unstable buildings, the Royal Navy positioned several gunboats and frigates off the Manhattan shores should the confusion generated by the blaze give Washington's army opportunity to capitalise on the disarray.

Those not commandeered by the engineers found themselves mustered for duty in readiness for high alert, the file given a few moments to gather their equipment made their way along the quays parallel to the destruction of the town, skirting north along the east edge and into the heart of what once housed the file in their comfortable billets. The town bustled with soldiers keen to rejoin their Regiments but until the area was secured to the satisfaction of the Provost Marshal, men, women and children gathered on the fringes waiting restlessly for the allowance of movement, on every street corner that had escaped the blaze Dragoon guards positioned themselves watchful over the souls that had lost their homes and livelihoods. Menacingly these troopers peered down on those that tried desperately to retrieve their belongings, the provost guard checking everyone's identity in the frantic search for suspects and scapegoats. The corner of Elizabeth Street thankfully had not succumbed to the blaze but the guard however had restricted access to the dwellings, Zeke spoke at length to a sergeant of the guard to allow them a few moments entry to retrieve their belongings, finally the guard gave in to Zeke's clever reasoning's, although relieved of immediate duty he'd petitioned to the guard that his unit was due for muster that afternoon, the sergeant too tired to argue having heard pleas of New York's inhabitants cautiously glanced left and right and satisfied this break of protocol had gone unnoticed gave Zeke the wink to advance down the street to their lodgings. A few yards in and Will saw the reason for the numerous guards posted around the town, although the fire had spared Elizabeth Street the looters had not, a profitable and wealthy district of New York had quartered many merchants complete with their gains of commerce, doors hung loosely on hinges and barely a pane of glass was left unbroken, the streets littered with personal belongings smashed beyond salvage as the looters had scattered on the arrival of the guard.

Whether soldier or citizen had caused the destruction, the damage was immense and Will's heart sank as the four paced towards Eli's modest home on the right hand side of the street, its painted gloss door had been smashed off its fastenings and been trampled as the looters fought for what valuables they could find, living humbly Eli and Y'oni had amounted some wealth and luxury over their short years in the colonies, in one fateful night they had seemingly lost everything they'd owned.

Zeke was the first to enter, cautiously he lifted his feet over the smashed furniture that could not easily be carried away by the thieves, a fine bureau that held Eli's commercial transactions had been prised open, to the looters worthless scraps of paper, to Eli years of work and livelihood lost. Will followed on behind Zeke along with the Allen brothers, Zeke stopped the file as they walked silently through the house reaching the back staircase, 'Hush' he whispered pointing up the broad wrought iron spiral stairs to the rooms they'd rented, the four heard footsteps above, heavy footsteps that sounded like several looters were still picking over the spoils. Will un-shouldered his musket and primed the weapon quickly, Zeke drew his bayonet and held it tightly in his hand ready to face whoever roamed the upper floor of the house, 'Stay here' Zeke instructed Dan and Thom, 'and ready yourselves for their flight' 'Aye' Dan acknowledged 'they'll not get past us' he added cocking his musket ready. Zeke carefully trod the winding staircase with Will's musket poised over his shoulder, reaching the top Zeke raised his hand stopping Will from advancing any further, the two waited a moment outside the door that led into the private quarters, the passageway that led to the left had been ransacked severely, the beds that the file had comfortably slept within lay upturned and the soft mattresses torn apart as the thieves searched for any wealth secreted within, the files room left in ruins and all personal belongings ransacked or destroyed, however, the recovery of their meagre belongings faded into insignificance as the safety of Eli and Y'oni sprang to Will's mind. With the file's rented rooms empty, the looters Zeke reasoned, must be within Eli's private rooms, silently the two backed tracked down the corridor to the front end of the house, with the door closed the looters within had failed to secrete their sounds as muffled voices came from behind the door. Zeke crept towards the door and placed his ear close to it, holding three fingers up Will gathered Zeke felt the occupants inside numbered at least three.

'We need to time this right' Zeke spoke as the two waited for the next noise to distract their entrance as he positioned himself by the closed door, a moment passed then clear shouts came from inside, Zeke barged the door open startling the looters busy tearing the room apart for valuables, shocked and surprised the looters numbered four, a woman looked up from a ransacked drawer with sheer horror on her haggard features, three men gathered in the far corner of the room sharply turned to see who or what had disturbed their thievery, Will stepped forward a pace and presented his loaded musket directly into the room, 'Easy now' Zeke spoke calmly 'let's not do anything foolish then shall we?' as he revealed the bayonet gripped firmly in his hand to those inside.

Will waited for Zeke's actions to determine his next move, the moment lasted an age as Zeke slowly left the doorway and entered, by the looks of things the looters had ransacked the living quarters thoroughly, the panelled walls had been jemmied from their fixings in an attempt to reveal the family wealth, Will peered over the shoulder of Zeke with his musket covering the arc of the corner, behind the three men he spied what they'd been so interested in before he and Zeke had disturbed them on barging the room.

'Y'oni?' he called towards the small figure cowering behind the men, 'Y'oni, is that you?' he repeated, puzzled by the boys presence Will lowered his musket and held his hand outstretched for the boy to seek his safety, a fatal mistake and he knew it. The upper hand over the looters was now lost, at odds of two to one the looters seeing the distraction rushed towards the door, while the woman drew a pistol from her petticoats and pointed it at Will, 'now Sir, if you please . . .' she spoke ushering Will to lower his musket. 'Best do as she says Will' Zeke answered now despondent at the control lost 'like I said, there's no need for anything foolish now is there' adding calm to the now very volatile situation. Will slowly released the lock and lowered the musket to the ground, his eyes firmly kept contact with the woman's gaze as she instructed her fellow thief to retrieve the musket from his feet 'You!' she snapped at Zeke, 'drop it, drop it I say or god help me I'll blow yer damn brains out', Zeke let go of the blade allowing it to tumble to the floor, the man moved to recover the musket, closing ever nearer he stooped to pick up the weapon from the boards where it lay. It was now or never Zeke thought to himself, he weighed up the opportunity and hoped the woman's aim was poor, as the man's eyes switched to recover the musket Zeke kicked the weapon aside him, using this distraction he lunged at the looter and delivered a sharp booted kick squarely into the man's face, the man squealed in pain as he recoiled from the blow sending him sprawling backwards across the room, in panic the other two men charged the pair but being so uncoordinated ran directly into the line of fire of the woman's pistol, the woman screamed in frustration as any chance of their escape swiftly diminished to nothing.

Will grabbed the musket and quickly drew the hammer back to fire, the unwieldy weapon was ill designed for close quarter battle in such a confined space, he snapped at the trigger and the familiar crack, fizz ignited into the pan, as the woman discharged her own firearm simultaneously into the melee.

The room filled with gun smoke adding to the confusion of the moment, at such short range the target that Will had blindly aimed for was blasted backwards as the lead bullet pounded into his chest followed by the pistol shot taking his left arm and spinning him round. the man staggered a second then tumbled through the window sending glass showering onto the street below, the second man took a blow from Zeke's fist in the jaw, he head snapped back coughing blood and spit from his mouth followed by a reign of hard punches that rendered him unconscious. The woman realising her only chance was to barge the exit threw the spent pistol at Will who ducked to avoid the blow lost his footing as he took the force of the large woman as she bolted with haste towards he exit.

The woman would not get far, Dan and Thom had heard the gunfire above and positioned themselves at the foot of the staircase expecting the flight of the escapees, with the skirmish now quashed Will rushed towards Y'oni stooping low to make eye contact with the petrified boy.

'Alright Y'oni, it's alright' he calmed the shaking boy by holding his shoulders firmly, pulling the frightened lad closer Will asked the whereabouts of Eli, his father, Y'oni choking back the tears spoke just one word in broken English 'Soldiers'. Confused Will turned towards Zeke who having secured the two unconscious looters looked up towards the pair, 'I asked him about Eli?' Will relayed the question, 'he said Sol. . ' 'I heard what he said lad' Zeke interrupted his sentence, 'we need to find the boy's father, there's little we can do here'. Will led the tearful child by the hand down the staircase 'Don't worry Y'oni, you'll be safe with us now' he spoke and offered some comfort to the boy hoping he may understand at least a few of his comforting words.

Zeke instructed the Allen brothers to scour the cellar workshop for any clues that might help the file reunite the boy with his father, 'the boy trusts you Will lad, stay here with him until I can satisfy the provost to an account of what happened'

Will placed the whimpering boy on the bottom stair and opened his knapsack, producing an apple he offered it for the boy to eat, hungrily Y'oni accepted the fruit and bit hard into its flesh, this lad had not eaten today he thought to himself before delving back into his bag for a crust of bread to satisfy his hunger. Zeke returned bringing with him the guard and leading them upstairs to the looted room occupied by the remaining thieves, Will took the boy outside forcing his painful memories to remain within their destroyed home, outside the woman had been handed over to the guard and now sat caged and dejected at her fate, seeing her captor lead the boy from the house she called after the two, 'You'll get no sense from him, the boys an idiot' she heckled after them before being silenced by the guard.

'Come now' Will assured the boy 'We'll soon find your father' as he placed his hand on the boys head, unexpectedly Y'oni answered Will's comforts looking up at him as he did so, 'Papa gone, soldiers took, papa gone' he spoke tearfully. Will thought hard to the meaning of Y'oni's words delivering them to Zeke on his return, Thom and Dan had found little other than a ransacked basement noting that everything of value had been stolen or destroyed similarly to the rest of the house. As calmness returned together the four stood opposite the looted premises, Zeke rubbed his bristled chin and thought a moment, 'We need to find the boy's father quickly' he spoke with some urgency to the matter, 'there's no telling when we'll be called back to the Regiment'. Dan dropped to his knees and looked into the eyes of the child, 'The soldiers took your father?' he asked sympathetically but frightened still, the boy shrugged his shoulders and stared quizzically at Will, Zeke interrupted the conversations bringing gravity to the situation once again, 'We've less than two hours of daylight left, the provost are closing the street until the houses are all secured from more looting, I suggest we find lodgings for the night else we find ourselves in the gutter, we can return on the morrow and pursue our enquiries then'. The four led Y'oni away from the looted home he once loved, the boy held tight onto Will's sleeve as they turned the corner away from the scene.

If finding accommodation was difficult before it became now near impossible, hundreds of the towns refugees littered the streets carrying what belongings they could, the desperate and impoverished gathered every street corner, families uncertain of their fate.

The provost's presence was firm as Howe's investigations demanded actions into the cause of the fire, it wasn't long before the four realised the whereabouts of Eli as indiscriminately the guard had arrested anyone suspected of rebellious sympathies, rivalries and old scores were settled as tip offs given to the provost became pursued regardless of guilt.

As the days sun began to set across the rooftops the file sought shelter for the night, Y'oni gripped tight onto Will's hand determined he would not lose his only protection from the chaotic streets that bustled about him and on leaving the area Zeke led the group back towards the artillery barracks now occupied by the provost guard, the streets heaved with bodies moving in all directions desperate to secure a roof for the night, but for now Will and his comrades priority was to find ward for the boy. The group made progress towards the barrack house the guards presence increased, crowds of onlookers jostled towards the building kept at bay by mounted dragoons that formed a barrier between them and the garrison, Will in fear of losing Y'oni in the crowd lifted the lad into his arms, the boy clearly frightened and tearful clung tightly around his neck and being no stranger to this kind of responsibility his siblings Joseph and Rebecca has been in his care for as long as he could remember after his father had turned to the bottle and brought neglect to their household. It was in Will's nature to protect the vulnerable, as his own family had grown and began lives themselves his new family although more than capable of fending for themselves had relied on him as much as he on them, in his heart he knew his duty to the boy much to the detriment to his own fate. Close to the garrison the cause of ruckus became clearer, dozens of men arrested on suspicion of causing the fire stood manacled together until they like cattle for the slaughter were processed systematically and herded through the heavy iron gates towards the gaol house. Shouts from the crowd contributed to the tense atmosphere as the dragoons formed line blocking the mob from getting any closer to the prisoners, some angry and bitter at the loss of the homes and livelihoods needing someone to blame, some desperate to find a loved one accused rightly or wrongly of a terrible arson.

From the creeping darkness a line of manacled suspects, devoid of any dignity came into sight through the crowd, the baying crowd kept distant by a ring of gleaming bayonets of the guard that led them through the gates, shackled with head bowed the last man shuffled through the entranceway before raising his head to view whatever fate awaited him. 'Eli!' Will shouted, in unison Zeke, Dan and Thom reacted to his cry repeating his yell in hope their combined voices might just be heard above the roaring crowd. Unheard, Will acted without thought, 'take the boy' as he handed Y'oni's clinging body to Dan Allen, the boy protested at the loss of his comfort but by now Will was surging through the crowd towards the line of prisoners anxious to intercept them before they cleared the gates, the crowd pushed and surged as Will fought through the mob taking little notice of the complaints received by those he trampled and barged. Breathless Will broke free of the mob and stumbled to the ground, scrambling to his feet he dashed through the gaps in the horsemen to reach Eli oblivious to Will's forlorn actions, with a few yards to clear before reaching the closing gates, his footing disappeared beneath him, tumbling to the ground he rolled over and over carried by the frantic pace he'd made to reach his target.

Face down Will shook his head, his felt hat long lost to the crowd, the dusty earth settled around him as he raised his head disoriented to his direction, facing him directly a long steel barrel of a primed musket met squarely between his dazed eyes, 'Steady now lad' came the voice, 'and where do you thinks you're going then?' the voice spoke gruffly. Two soldiers heaved Will to his feet lifting him with a firm hand from the earthen street, the musket still directed at him. 'You keen to join these criminals and vagabonds then?' one of the guards spoke in his broad cockney accent, 'That man' Will pointed towards the captives 'you need to free him'. 'Oh do we now' the guard answered 'on General Howe's orders I suppose?' the guards laughed amongst themselves. Ignoring the guards that blockaded Will from Eli, he barged the three aside sending them sprawling into the dusty street, racing towards the now closed gate Will cried towards the prisoners, 'Eli, Eli' he shouted with all his voice, Eli raised his head towards the sound of his name, Will had reached the closed garrison gate and yelled through the bars, seeing Will press his face to the metal Eli's heart lifted, 'my boy, my boy, where is Y'oni?' he cried 'We have him Eli, he's with the others . . . safe'.

Zeke gently swabbed the back of Will's head as he sat gingerly on the wooden stool within the crude fisherman's shack the file now occupied, 'One day lad you'll learn to think before you act' Zeke chastised him as Will ran his fingers across the base of his skull and felt the large bump that protruded from his head, 'you're lucky you only have a sore head too' Zeke added, 'the provost don't take kindly to such riotous behaviour'. Will could recall none of the events after his hurried words to Eli and Zeke relayed the episode back to him jolting his memory of the events, the guard fearing a riot had pounced on Will and with a sharp blow of a muskets butt he slumped to the hard ground, 'By the time we got to you we thought you were done for' Thom spoke with his matter of fact manner, 'It was Zeke that got you out of there in one piece' Dan added to his brother's account as Zeke continued to swab Will's cuts and bruises, he'd said his peace on the matter, though unknown to Will, Zeke had heavily bribed the guard not to arrest him, the pay off had cost the file every last penny they had. Will, still dazed and confused from the blow to his head took stock of his surroundings, 'where's Y'oni?' he spoke alarmingly, 'I promised Eli he'd be safe', 'He is safe my friend so fear not lad' Zeke replied, 'He sleeps in the back for now'.

The shack the file had commandeered linked to New York's harbour on the eastern fringe of the town, poorly secured the lock had proved a small obstacle for the likes of Zeke who soon levered it free of its mountings, abandoned within at least the file could seek a degree of shelter for the night until they had chance to figure out their plans for their ward. Y'oni slept quietly in the corner wrapped snugly in the red tunics of the file, together, Will, Zeke, Thom and Dan discussed the best options for the boys safety,

'Whatever we choose as the best plan, one thing is for certain . . .' Will clarified the situation with a pause 'we can't let the boy loose on the streets, he'll not last a day'. 'Aye, that's agreed Will, these cutthroats will skin him alive given half the chance' spoke Dan bolstering the argument, Together, Will, Dan and Thom agreed it was now their responsibility to take ward of the lad, at least until Eli could be freed but Zeke just sat back and sucked heavily on his clay pipe listening to the boisterous debate around him, 'So lads' he interrupted the headiness of the three 'what's your plan for the lad then?'. The three immediately stopped their conversation in its tracks leaving an awkward pause from their conversation, 'Listen Zeke' Will spoke up, 'the lad has no one in this world except us while Eli is detained'

'And what do you propose to do then lad?' Zeke replied with a sarcasm leaning squarely forward towards him, 'do you know of somewhere to take the boy?', 'We can surely find somewhere?' Will revealed a somewhat flimsy plan of action, 'perhaps the Regiment can care for him?'. Zeke snapped quickly at Wills stupidity, rose from his seat and began to pace the room, 'the Regiment? The Regiment you say? Perhaps a fifer or a drummer as once was I?' his voice ever stern with his contained passions he lead the conversation towards rationality as he allowed the three to speak their plans before offering a retort, 'Aye' Dan spoke up, his excited eyes following Zeke around the room, 'the Regiment would take the lad as an orphan of war', 'Perhaps you could speak with Sergeant Vaughan to take the boy as a fifer, he plays a tune fairly well does he not?' Thom reasoned on his brothers behalf. Zeke stopped in his tracks and turned to face the three 'you think a boy's life in the ranks a good one?' he snapped 'you think my years amongst the ranks have been pleasant? tis hard and bloody work I tell thee and very few live a life to reach a privates rank!' he brought the three's plan back to reality with his harsh tones, 'you fear the boy will not last on the street?' Zeke spoke rhetorically 'what makes you think the rank and file will be any kinder to him or his chances any better?'. Zeke's anger apparent in his voice brought fear into the others, fear enough not to interrupt their corporal's speech until his temper had mellowed some, 'you talk of caring for the boy's interest but you show nothing of your wisdom or sensibilities for now I tell you this,' he paused a moment calming his anger at the three, 'you chose to save the lad from the villainy of the gutter and now the conscience is yours and yours alone, turn him to the street for all I care but mark my words if you give him to the Regiment be sure he'll go the way of Walsh or White before he's a man, if he's lucky the lad might end his fate similarly to Coles but if you see my life within that boys eyes then I urge you to look hard and look hard again'. Zeke turned his back upon the three still sat wide mouthed and transfixed on his monologue, 'You think I would choose this life again given the chance? You think I would take pleasure watching friends smashed bloody and broken on the field of battle? You think I would willingly lay a dying man in my arms as his life drains away whilst comforting his soul he'll live to see the next day?'. Zeke's eyes welled as the years of trauma rushed back into his memories, 'you talk of a safe and secure life in the Regiment?' he paused, his hand lay rest on the shacks flimsy door handle, the emotion plain as his eyes glazed over as he spoke his final words, 'It would be kinder to smother the lad here and now whilst he sleeps than to deliver him to the Kings colours'.

With that, Zeke left the shack alone and into the dead of night, Will, Dan and Thom sat silently each staring hard at the floor waiting for one brave enough to break the silence, running his feet back and forth nervously Will spoke up casting a glance at Y'oni who slept obliviously throughout the disturbance, 'Perhaps Zeke is right, our obligation for the boy owes him more than a cast off on company men', 'Aye' Dan Added, 'we've been too quick to assume Zeke a good life all this time but be that as it may, the boy still needs care and it doesn't change that he cannot care for himself at least until Eli is freed', 'Assuming Eli will be freed you mean?' Thom brought the gravity of the predicament back to earth, 'for we are not so sure that Eli had no involvement in starting the fire', his words changed the tune of the conversations and slowly the three acknowledged the predicament they now found themselves within. Having expected Zeke to find a solution to their problem the three together realised this would need to be resolved and resolved quickly, throughout the night the three men bickered amongst each other as to the best option for the boys safety, one thing was agreed though throughout, to turn the boy onto the street would be a criminal act of unkindness, for all the hardships suffered the boy was innocent in this and to leave him to his fate would sit uneasy on Will's conscious, 'I promised the boy I'd care for him and I'll be damned if I don't' Will snapped with frustration leaving both Dan and Thom struck with silence at his frustrated anger. The remaining few hours of the night were spent in an uncomfortable silence as no agreement could be found as to Y'oni's future although commotion outside turned the heads of the three to the sounds of numerous soldiers running past the shack the group sheltered within.

By first light Will leant over the piled redcoats and ran his hands across the boys hair, stirring Y'oni opened his eyes and rubbed the last of the night away, 'It's alright lad' Will spoke gently 'We'll find your father today, you'll be safe soon' he added but in his own mind he had no idea on how to deliver his promise to the boy.

Zeke returned to the shack as the sun cleared the roof tops bringing life back to the quiet streets, the night patrols relieved of their duties exchanged small pleasantries with their relief before wandering off to their longing billets. Spying the child sat upright in the corner still wrapped in the oversized red tunics Zeke spoke to the collective three, 'I see you've used your time well then lads?' speaking sarcastically, Will spluttered for answers only to be interrupted by Zeke harshly, "Tis a good job one of us keeps his wits eh?' his grin broadening as he stood aside the door as it swung open revealing Eli standing in the morning sunrise, Y'oni even with his misunderstanding of the English language raced towards his dear father who offered his outstretched arms towards his son, the two embraced as a father would leaving Will, Dan and Thom puzzled to how the corporal had managed to free Eli from the custody of the provost, 'How did you free him Zeke?' Will pressed but Zeke gently tapped the side of his nose 'Let us say Will lad, every man has his price to look the other way' he chuckled, 'You paid them off?' Dan spoke 'I though we had no coin?' he asked as an afterthought but for now, how was irrelevant as Zeke toyed with the three leaving them guessing exactly how he's managed to secure Eli's freedom so quickly, 'Who said anything about paying?' he spoke wryly, 'to some it is what they stand to lose rather than what they stand to gain' he ended with a small chuckle to himself.

Will didn't pay too much attention to exactly how Zeke had reunited father and son but later discovered that Zeke's keen eye for detail, no matter how trivial often paid dividends when needed, the sergeant provost guard that had allowed the file entry into the street Eli dwelled upon had served alongside Zeke years previous and Zeke had once saved his neck from the gallows following an accusation of theft during a garrison campaign in Martinique, the provost sergeant initially denied the incident or even knowing Zeke Turner but a sharp memory soon prompted the sergeant to recall the favour owed on pain of Zeke stirring up trouble and jeopardising his comfortable position in the guard.

Having gained entry to the blockhouse that held scores of suspects, Zeke wandered alone through the corridors searching for Eli, not risking to call out his name for fear of attracting attention to himself he scanned the miserable figures cooped within the cells and spied his target, whispering, he ushered him over to the bars of the cell, Eli grinned at the sight of Zeke, 'Wait here a moment' Zeke ordered Eli sternly 'and I'll get you out'.

The other prisoners keen to see the attention the Jew had gained from the redcoat soldier scrambled to the grated opening in the cell door, 'I'd suggest you get back now' Zeke snapped his authority to the mob 'this one's for the gallows and unless you wish to accompany him you'd best stand well clear' he spoke sternly. The remaining prisoners hesitated a moment giving Zeke the time needed to release Eli from the cell, the two slammed the heavy cell door sliding the iron bolts across once again, Zeke took Eli aside and gave clear and concise instructions 'If you're to see your boy again then do exactly as I say, do you understand?', Eli nodded the affirmative and thanked Zeke over and over before silencing him with a finger to his lips, 'Remember Eli, exactly as I say'. Together the two walked through the long dark corridors of the guard house, Zeke's hand firmly gripped upon Eli's shoulder adding to their flimsy impression of guard and prisoner should they encounter anyone on the way.

Pausing outside the guard room, Zeke pressed his ear to the door before slowly opening it and peering inside, asleep and slumped in the corner a lone man seconded from another Regiment for guard duty snatched a few moments sleep while uninhibited, Zeke gestured Eli to wait in the corridor whilst he crept into the room carefully lifting his feet across the wooden boarding. Aside the guard laid the redcoat Zeke coveted, if his plan to walk Eli through the gate was to succeed Eli would need to pass himself off as just another soldier to the numerous guardsmen that patrolled the area.

Silently Zeke crouched down besides the snoozing guard with his felt hat firmly covering his eyes and clutching the red coat Zeke slid it towards him gathering it in a tight bundle before cheekily lifting the felt hat from its wearer's head as he dozed, Zeke grinned at his success and back stepped out the room removing the iron key from its heavy lock. Zeke tossed the jacket towards Eli who realised the plan quickly donned the garment and pulled the over large hat hard down on his head, in the darkness Eli at a glance might just pass off as a soldier, but anything more than that would certainly require the pairs coolness to pull off the rouse. Satisfied the guard still asleep, Zeke eased the door shut and turned the key locking the heavy door shut and removing the key he tossed it far down the corridor. With speed the two paced the corridor back to whence Zeke gained entry to the block house, both men paused on seeing figures linger outside, 'Damn' Zeke cursed 'there's too many out there, we'll need to find another way out if this plan is to work'. Zeke followed the corridors deeper into the heart of the blockhouse unsure where they might lead, turning a corner in the labyrinth the two halted sharply in the face of an oncoming guardsman, 'bluff it out Eli' Zeke whispered 'it's our only chance' urging. 'What's going on with you two then?' the guard demanded to know, 'We've been told to sound the alarm' Zeke spat the words faking a shortness of breath 'there's fire about the town'. 'Fire?!' the guard looked alarmed at the news, 'The sergeant sent us, the alarm? Where is it? Quickly man, there's no time to lose' he spoke with false urgency. The guard hesitated a moment before speaking, 'get back to your posts, I'll see to the alarm'. Racing off down the corridor the panicked guard left Zeke and Eli alone and in silence in the corridor, 'with luck' Zeke spoke, 'we can use this to our advantage'. With perfect timing the alarm sounded bringing Zeke's ad hoc plan together, the guardsman had rushed to the bell tower and pulled hard on the ropes sounding the alarm far across the town, in light of the decimation the town suffered previously all garrisoned soldiers quickly jumped into alert on hearing the alarm bell ringing once again, as Zeke and Eli made their way towards the compounds entrance panicked soldiers dashed to and fro in all directions giving the two opportunity to escape unhindered. Zeke ushered Eli towards the gates that Eli had passed through on his arrest, with just a few yards to clear a guards Officer stepped forward and challenged the two, Zeke, knowing only too well the discovery of his actions could cost him his life as well as that of Eli gripped firmly the steel shaft of his sheathed bayonet ready to commit bloody murder if needs be, 'You two men!' the officer challenged the pair 'where do you think you're going?' he spoke in a snobbish and privileged accent, Zeke's stomach tightened into knots realising what he would have to do if the rouse was discovered, his grip ever tighter on the blades handle.

With the sternest of looks the Officer again spoke at the pair, 'If you're heading towards the town, don't you think at least you should at least go prepared?'. Both Eli and Zeke looked blankly at each other, 'prepared?' Zeke enquired somewhat meekly 'With pails of water you cloth eared clot!' the Officer chastised the pair, 'there's another bloody fire in case you haven't noticed'. Zeke and Eli breathed a huge sigh of relief 'Yes sir, of course sir' Zeke kept the pretence saluting the officer in the process, 'straight to it sir'. Zeke and Eli dashed off keeping up the rouse that fooled the officer when suddenly the officer barked after them 'Hold on a minute' the officer spoke, 'You!' he snapped signalling out Eli, 'don't you salute your superiors in your Regiment?', 'err, no sir, I mean yes sir' Zeke intercepted Eli's words, knowing Eli's strong European accent might jeopardise their escape, 'This one's not the brightest sir' Zeke addressed the officer 'almost an idiot see for he lost his mind serving in the Indies he did'. Zeke raised Eli's arm in some pathetic gesture of a salute to satisfy the officer that Eli's condition of idiocy was very real, the officer shook his head in despair, 'I just don't know what this army is becoming these days' he mumbled as he turned his back on the two and hurried direction to the blockhouses and the confusion around. Zeke held his smirk long enough to allow the officer to depart before releasing a silent chuckle to himself, 'Come on Eli' he spoke 'lets get you back to the others'. The two passed through the many soldiers frantically looking for instruction having heard the call to alarm from the garrison blockhouse until they reached the small wooden fisherman shack he'd left the others within, fro, then Will recalled his own version of events as Eli overcome with emotion held his son tight in his embrace.

Thanks to Zeke's ingenuity the two reunited shook the hands of all four of the file, firmly shaking the hands over and over expressing his gratitude towards each of them with a few chosen words. 'Mister Turner'

Eli addressed Zeke with great respect grasping his hand, 'without you I would have rotted in the gaol, your ingenuity has proved valuable to me and my son, for you I am indebted for all time' he spoke in his Yiddish accent, 'I can see you are a resourceful man of many means, may you have many years ahead of you yet'. Zeke smiled knowing the value and bond of family, his own long passed but his inherited family stood beside him now, appreciating Eli's words and blessings Zeke wished Eli and Y'oni well leaving Eli to address Will alone.

The two men stood eye to eye as Will waited for Eli to speak, placing both hands on Will's shoulders Eli eventually spoke with a tear in his eye, 'Will Snow' he chuckled and paused a moment gathering his composure, 'I see greatness ahead in your life, compassion, faithfulness and loyalty most men can only ever dream to achieve, you showed me and my son faith and humanity when little was done to warrant it'. Will grew somewhat embarrassed by the emotion Eli displayed, the tears in his eyes brought a sombreness to all within the room who'd paused to listen to Eli's chosen words, 'for these reasons Will Snow' Eli spoke his name as though one word 'I give you this advice my friend, live your life close to those around you, the bond of brotherhood is a fragile one so nurse it well and cherish it for all times, for those you may lose along the journey will walk alongside you forever more and guide you on your way'.

Whilst Dan and Thom looked on puzzled, failing to understand the true meaning of Eli's chosen words although Will could interpret the words meaning perfectly, he thought a moment for Sam Coles, John White and young James Walsh, brothers indeed who had held his hand in times of painful suffering, forever they would stand beside him for all his days.

* * *

Chapter Eight

The Haerlem

The four had seen Eli and his son leave New York having quickly sold what was left of their home to a Lawyer speculating on the new demand for housing in the town, watching Eli and Y'oni gain passage on a merchantman the file bade their farewells to the pair as the ship cast its moorings and drifted across the bay towards Eli's hopes for a better life in the largely unsettled western plains.

As the vessel drifted from the harbour, Will saw Y'oni raise his hand high, tight within his grasp held the tin whistle he'd given to the boy, symbolically the cheap penny whistle would hold thoughts of humanity and kindness given to the refugees in their pursuance of a new life far far away from the trouble this rebellion brought.

The following day the file left New York to muster with the remainder of the 17th camped north of the town, Captain McPherson had been tolerant to the informal billeting of his company but now on the verge of the final stages of the summer campaign the 17th was needed for action again. The once fertile farm lands in the north of the peninsular now lay heavily crushed by excessive foot traffic of a campaigning army reducing the harvest yield to little more than a battered and withered crop. As the four trod the dusty roads towards the 17th's muster point, gathering in numbers along the way, artillery limbers drawn by hand and horse gave an indication of the scale of Howe's forthcoming assault as the campaign drew to a close in the fall season.

After a half days march the file fell in with the ranks of the Regiment counting no more than two hundred rank and file across ten companies, at this diminished strength Zeke noted the 17th had ceased to be an effective fighting Regiment but doubted little this would relieve them from the actions of the final stage of the New York campaign. The rural farm lands to the north of Manhattan Island stood heavily wooded on either side of the peninsular, glowing autumnal colours replaced the heavy green foliage of the large shady tree's that swept back and forth in the warm breeze, the rustle of the dry leaves gave a calming peace ahead of the violence that was forthcoming the closing stage of the campaign.

News filtered through to the ranks of the British army that Washington's continental army had been caught in the decreasing bottle neck terrain the geography of the peninsular offered, Washington still held on to a series of redoubts and forts dotted along the range but in order to pursue and smash the continental army Howe needed to secure these obstacles from his enemies hands. A probe towards the high ground west of the small Dutch settlement of Harlem had again bloodied the nose of the British advance, the rebel army held firm on the high ground and caused Howe again to rethink his strategy in his proposed entrapment of the nemesis, during this lull Washington redeployed his forces into the strong positions around the fortifications north of Harlem and after nearly a month of indecision Howe advanced his army in an attempt to encircle Washington once and for all.

The 17th called to arms ready to support the break through Howe's landing hoped to secure in the landings at Throgs Neck and the encirclement thereafter. To the men of the 17th the battle of White Plains meant nothing more than a distant rumble of cannon fire and a steady flow back of walking wounded, however instead of pursuing the retreating enemy as they had expected to do the Regiment found itself with others diverted towards the well defended fort towards the western side of the peninsular, the garrison at what turned out to be aptly named Fort Washington had been left to its fate, surrounded and isolated the fort faced out across the Hudson river, although the Royal Navy controlled the waterways and courses, Howe dare not risk the sinking of one of His Majesties ships from an enemy shore battery, Howe felt there was little choice but to drive hard into the forts garrison and suffer the consequences of a heavy butchers bill.

The first two weeks of November remained notably mild, although the dampness increased as Will testified with his aching joints, the harsh weather they had witnessed earlier that year remained at bay. Under strength and barely forming a fighting regiment the 17th's companies acted as composite light infantry under temporary command of Lieutenant Colonel Stirling of the 42nd Highland Regiment, removing most of their equipment less it hinder the swift movements required by skirmish troops the company formed up in loose line beneath a battery of artillery dug in facing the fort in readiness. Over three thousand men held the fort prepared to fight to the last man, loyalty such as this Zeke said was a fool's errand as Howe was determined to capture the fort whatever the cost and this cost would be heavy, for both combatants. As the men formed line facing their enemy without warning the battery just a few yards above burst its fire towards the enemy positions, with deafening noise the battle started its bloody effect, the line cowered at the thunderous din that shattered the morning's peace. 'I wish they'd give us some warning' Dan Allen shouted loudly, his and everyone else's ears still ringing the roar of the cannonade above them. 'Aye' his brother replied comically, 'I was hoping for a peaceful day and all'. 'Stand fast lads' Zeke spoke, 'we'll move out soon enough'. Sergeant Vaughan walked steadily across the line of skirmishers little fazed by the continuation of the barrage towards the enemy, 'How the hell he does not flinch I'll never know' Thom spoke to those besides him, 'Deaf as a bloody post no doubt' Will chuckled out his reply, Zeke added to the comical moment 'or something else perhaps? do you think the sergeants breeches are supposed to be brown' only those who truly knew Zeke could appreciate this dry humour.

As Zeke had predicted Sergeant Vaughan under McPherson's instruction signalled his company to move towards their target, the inexperienced bunched together seeking some comfort from their comrades but Vaughan seeing this gave a sharp warning that Light infantry operate independently to Line infantry, 'should the enemy's battery find your mark then you're all done for, spread out and spread thin he shouted arcing his arms in a broad directions. The company arced left and began a slow advance up the wooded slopes that lay beneath the forts outer ramparts, 'Steady lads' Zeke spoke reaffirming Vaughan's orders 'we'll be within rifle range soon, keep low and spread thin'. The battery behind them continued to bombard the defenders throwing debris high into the air with every impact, the receiving end of a barrage looked to be no pleasant thing as the company was soon to find out. As the company advanced the clear and formidable obstacle that was their objective came apparent, to their far right masses of assault infantry formed line ready for the signal to storm the breached ramparts once the artillery had broken through, amongst the din Will clearly heard the pipers of the 42nd Highlanders tune up their strange instruments, a sound that had always inspired him was designed to strike fear into the heart of the enemy, for many it indeed had but today the defenders had the safety of well prepared defences to bolster their resilience and courage indicating a bloody day ahead. The signal came for the skirmish companies to advance, their role in the assault was to keep down the heads of the enemy gunners until the 42nd were close enough to rush the last few yards with the bayonet, cold steel Will thought tested any mans mettle on the field as close quarter battle made death personal, the fear of an agonising death in a man's eyes as the steel plunged towards its victim, the screams as the blade struck and plunged deep leaving the prey to die in agony, stuck like a pig withering in its death throes.

The British artillery ceased as the Highlanders advanced at a walking pace towards the slopes of the redoubt, 'even our officers are loathed to slaughter their own men' Zeke commented, with Pipes blearing the Highland Regiment reached the rise of the heights of the fort, it was a slaughter in the making. Within seconds of the artillery cessation, the enemy wise to the predictable advance of the line infantry opened their own speculative barrage towards the British lines as experience of the enemy gunners told them the woodland area would hold troops as well as those advancing the gentle slopes that rose towards their batteries. Zeke had instructed his file to ground once the enemy bombardment had started knowing that round shot and trees do not mix well, those too slow to take cover soon became victims as the heavy metal smashed through the woodland canopy and splintered trunks like spears in all directions cutting down those unfortunate not to take cover quickly. The 42nd advancing across the open slopes fared little better, in line formation round shot smashed holes clean through the ranks leaving gaping holes soon merged back to one as the sergeants yelled 'close ranks' leaving their broken bodies behind. On the second barrage of round shot, the skirmish lines secreted within the woodland broke, Will could not blame any man for losing his spirit under such terrible conditions but in running free from the cover the wood offered, the enemy gunners now knew their fire had found its mark and again unleashed a heavier barrage onto the bedraggled fugitives seeking some sanctuary in the woodlands. 'A man can only take so much' Zeke cursed under his breath as still no instruction came to advance 'We are all condemned men waiting here' he added.

Zeke peered over the downed tree trunk the file had sheltered behind looking for Sergeant Vaughan to seek instruction on the company's movement, his vision found nothing more than a scattering of men cowering behind similar cover and a few smashed bodies of those unfortunates who had reacted too slow. As the enemy continued to pour fire onto them, Zeke realised their urgency of supporting the 42nd who now bore canister shot from the batteries facing them, 'Damn it!' he swore 'where the hell is Vaughan, we'll be cut to pieces staying here any longer'. Captain McPherson eventually made his way forward towards the front line of the pinned skirmishers and leapt into the hollow Zeke and the others sought sanctuary from, 'Where on earth is Sergeant Vaughan?' he demanded to know, 'Christ knows sir, but if we don't move soon we've all had it, we've lost a good number of men already' he replied to the officer, 'Very well corporal' McPherson instructed Zeke, 'until I can ascertain Sergeant Vaughan's whereabouts you will lead the company forward and support the highlanders advance'. There was no need to tell Zeke twice, '17th!' he yelled above the din, 'We're moving out, advance with haste to your enemy'.

Will grabbed his musket and pulled back the frizzen plate in readiness for discharge, the four men leapt over the trunk and sprinted forward through the wood, smashed bodies lay amongst the undergrowth, headless and limbless, twisted and contorted as the splintered trees had taken a heavy toll on the company's hesitance and lack of movement. Keeping pace with the rest Will saw Zeke momentarily stumble and falter, at first thinking he had been struck by the enemy's fire, he slowed to a halt to check Zeke's well being as he stood silently prone amongst the barrage. Sinking to his knees Zeke leant over a headless body, neatly laid out amongst the fallen leaves and branches that littered the woodland floor, 'What a bloody way to go' Zeke spoke to himself, rubbing his hand across the limbs that lay across the body, Will soon realised who Zeke grieved for, 'Oh no, not Vaughan' he cried 'not Sergeant Vaughan'. 'That is is lad' Zeke looked up into Will's eyes, 'a quick end at least, he'd have wanted this better that than slowly bleeding to death with a belly full of hot lead'. Zeke kind could only make light of the tragedy, for in such horror and carnage it often is the only way to accept the death of an old friend and comrade.

Grabbing Vaughan's musket Zeke plunged its bayoneted muzzle into the soft undergrowth leaving it as a marker to a body that would warrant a special burial, Zeke whispered under his breath to the corpse but Will clearly heard the words given to Vaughan's remains, 'Rest well now friend, your work is done, I'll be back to attend to you as soon as this bloody day is over'.

Zeke ran besides Will saying not a word until they caught up with the rest of the company on the edge of the tree line facing the enemy redoubts, ahead of the 42nd by a hundred yards Zeke with clinical and emotionless precision gave order to suppress the enemy batteries. 'Choose your targets boys and hurt em hard, let's make every shot count!' he shouted with a passion for battle Will had never seen before in him. The skirmishers shots did their job well, the enemy gunners quickly ducked for cover taking a few casualties as they did so, with the break in the heavy fire, the 42nd drove hard into the enemy lines, the famous highland charge smashing into the redoubt with great effect. Within minutes it was all over, the Highlanders had over run the batteries and the engineers attached began hastily spiking the guns rendering them useless should the enemy retake them in a counter charge, Zeke, now the senior rank amongst McPherson's company drew his skirmish line from the woods and sprinted towards and beyond the first line of defence reloading his musket whilst at a run with such skill he found himself beyond his own ranks and alone in the fray.

Will yelled to Zeke to slow down as he ran forward, but Zeke now had a score to settle. Remnants of militia that manned the ramparts fled with Zeke racing and screaming his battle cry amongst them, his bayonet stabbing any who stumbled in the haste to retreat. McPherson stood beside Will staring on at Zeke's lone advance to the enemy lines, 'What on earth is he doing?' he asked 'and I have still to find Vaughan, will someone please tell me where is Sergeant Vaughan?' he spoke formally to the ranks that formed on the captured ramparts. Will could not be bothered to reply to the officer, exhausted he struggled to catch his breath but those besides acknowledged the offices request. 'He's back in the woods sir' Thom Allen reported to the officer ramming a fresh charge down his muskets hot barrel. 'Well can someone send him to me immediately I demand to know what is going on' McPherson spoke oblivious to the fate of his Sergeant. 'Which part of him do you want sir?' Dan added his offhand comment McPherson looked on in a daze slowly realising what his men had implied, 'Dead?' he stumbled his words 'you mean to say he's dead?', 'Aye sir' Thom confirmed, 'lost his head he did, clean off by all accounts', 'Is this true?' McPherson addressed Will directly as though in disbelief, 'Yes sir, I'm afraid it's true' he nodded his head and lowered his eyes with remorse, 'For gods sake then take me to him now' McPherson demanded to see the evidence himself. Will reminded the officer that the battle still raged ahead and was not yet won, 'Of course' he shook his head bringing his senses back to the carnage ahead 'onward men, onward to glory!' McPherson drew his sword and rallied his men to follow Zeke into the battle.

Will had little time for officers, born to a privileged background, many of this class saw army life as a boyish adventure rarely witnessing the brutality the rank and file faced daily, at this moment however, Will's opinion of McPherson changed. The officer raced well ahead of the skirmish line, with sword in hand Captain James McPherson stood besides Zeke Turner, two men both years and lifestyles apart fought bravely aside each other to avenge the death of their contemporary, soon the two men grew to a dozen then to two dozen as McPherson's entire company or what was left of it drove the defenders in blind panic towards the inner defences. With the lull in fighting on the eastern side of the fort McPherson rallied the remains of his company, gathering a few stragglers to increase his numbers to twenty one able bodied men as the few walking wounded escorted the few prisoners back towards the British lines.

With the 42nd reformed to the right of the skirmish line the company took respite under the smashed ramparts and recharged their muskets, Will watched on as several Highlanders wiped the blood of their enemies from their bayonets on the skirts of their clansman's kilt, Zeke sat a few yards to his left, watching for movements through the wicker palisade that housed the captured guns.

The open ground between the outer and inner defences lay wide open save a few crumpled bodies picked off during their flight to safety, Captain McPherson liaised with the commander of the Highlanders and passed the strategy onto Zeke, now the senior man of the company. Zeke took the responsibility seriously, today's work had been bloody enough already and there was plenty more ahead before the day would be over. For Zeke to lose a man affected the corporal badly, each lost man Will had witnessed, tore a piece from Zeke's soul, he felt as though he had failed in his duty and responsibility with every casualty the company took, he knew his limits of responsibility, a hand full at most, a company was more than Zeke could handle but for this day Zeke had the lives of many under his warrant.

As drummer boys walked the line, their caps filled with cartridges for those that needed them, Zeke sprang from gathering to gathering relaying McPherson's strategy to overrun the next line of defences. 'Keep your distances wide and keep yourselves low, watch the man next to you, when he moves you lay down your fire' he instructed repeatedly to each group before returning to Will and the Allen brothers, for the men of his own file Zeke didn't need to instruct this direction, Zeke knew these men were capable of conducting themselves in battle, simply he enquired 'are you ready lads?', the three nodded simultaneously to their Corporal who turned his eyes towards McPherson awaiting his signal. The two men caught each other's gaze a moment then with a quick nod from the officer Zeke yelled the order to advance.

'Every second man, fifty yards left!', the dozen leapt over the palisade the remaining redcoats presented their muskets over the wicker work that shielded them from view from the distant enemy. The line of long muzzles cracked and spat their fire towards the enemy, looking left Will saw with textbook precision the advance party of skirmishers lay down their own fire giving those behind opportunity to advance, McPherson's company advanced wide through the long grass that offered some visible cover from the rebels doggedly entrenched on the forts summit, this would be a costly advance for Howe but one even the humblest redcoat could appreciate in its worth, symbolically and tactically, should Fort Washington to fall the British would close the summer campaign with high morale. Zeke instructed his men to lay a heavy sustained fire upon the defenders whilst the highlanders prepared for the next and final assault, the years of musket drill paid off as the few men that remained in McPherson's company poured a relentless fire onto the heads of the defenders, whether a shot ever found its target Will would never know but the company did its job and did it well as he watched the kilted highlanders trot an advance towards the defenders battered ramparts.

Fearing their own muskets would hit the Highlanders, Zeke ordered the company to cease fire on the rebels position as the advance cleared the defences and over ran any resistance offered, Will raised his head above the tall grasses that secreted them from the enemies view and watched the 42nd supported by the Hessian division go hard with the bayonet, the Hessians had suffered similarly at the hands of the forts stubborn artillery until finally silenced by the naval gunboats anchored high in the Hudson River, with at least a third of their number mauled upon the gradual slopes that gently raised towards the fort, this butchers bill would be high for both defender and attacker, any who offered resistance could expect little quarter from an enemy that had paid a high price to be the first to advance into the fort. With less than thirty yards the Highlanders upped pace and charged towards the desperate enemy, yelling their fearful highland charge the enemy knew their end was nigh. At ten yards the assault discharged its final volley towards those defenders brave enough to remain, Will peered excitedly over the inner parapet his company had secured, his blood was up and keen to see the last moments before the battle was won he observed the Scotsmen disappear in a heavy fog of gun smoke, their presence now heard only by the clash of arms as the valiant defenders where soon overrun, in a brief moment the assault was over leaving the cries of the wounded and dying to drift down the gentle slopes.

By dusk the defenders where in total disarray, over three thousand defenders had held fort Washington defiantly from the British advance, it was however, a fruitless request to expect such a gallant stand to uphold against the wave upon wave of advancing redcoats Howe had at his disposal. As the sun dipped over the horizon the iconic rebel standard lowered over Fort Washington for the last time, on this occasion however, it was the Kings colour that rose defiantly in its place.

The 17th held in reserve on the first line of defence, for the first time in his career Captain James McPherson felt more comfortable with his men than with his brethren officer, whilst the rank and file swigged what little water was left in their canteen and sought what small ration could be brought up to the line, McPherson gladly offered his hip flask to those who had rallied with him and Zeke, to a man the remainder of his company stood proudly on muster roll call and a silence befell those who had succumbed to the days battle, there was one man missing however for which every man held a moments prayer for.

Sergeant Vaughan smashed by round shot leading his men towards the enemy, Vaughan had died a soldiers wishful death, in battle facing his foe's as a true soldier always hoped to end his days, swift and painless whilst the reality for most would fall to sickness and disease or withering over a slow and agonising wound sustained by the hand of the enemy.

The darkness swept across the bay and soldiers snatched a few moments rest while others still high on adrenaline toyed with captured equipment that lay scattered amongst the destruction of the field. Thom, Dan and several others from the company amused themselves with a shared bottle of captured rum pilfered from a corpse that stood perfectly upright against the parapet, of all the carnage caused by bullet, blade or round shot this was one of the few casualties that remained perfectly unmarked, the body had a peculiar expression in death, fearful yet calm, to those who's stomachs not yet sickened by death, the lifeless body provided some bizarre amusement to its macabre posture, like overexcited schoolboys these few men callous to deaths dignity soon tired of their japes and tossed the body without ceremony over the palisade, laughing as it tumbled down the bloody slopes that claimed so many lives in securing. Shortly after the company muster Will became aware of Zeke's absence from the ranks, knowing from familiarity exactly where to find his friend Will wandered down the slopes towards the thin wood he easily sought out Zeke despite the poor and fading light. Zeke had returned to his Sergeants body soon after the fort had been secured and the defenders surrender taken, wasting little time he dug in the soft earth what would be Vaughan's final resting place and wrapped the smashed body in a blanket taken from the defenders loot. Will paused as he walked towards the burial site, fearing his presence infringed Zeke's final moments with a fellow lifelong soldier, he felt an awkwardness in his approach as if he had no right of entitlement at such a sombre moment, moments such as these should be reserved for those who earned the right to a dignified ceremony, far different from the mass graves the dead might usually find themselves within but an old soldier like Zeke Turner needed not direct vision to detect a human presence and somehow he knew the presence belonged to Will, without looking up from the grave side he spoke, 'Come lad, I fear our old Sergeant would be happy to see you again'. Will smiled uneasily at Zeke's gallows humour and stepped towards the shallow graveside, stooping besides it he crossed himself paying a moments respect to the man who had made McPherson's company the pride of the 17th that it was. 'Will lad' Zeke spoke 'I fear that after this day we shall ne'er be the same again our numbers are fewer with each encounter with our enemy and this will prove to be a dark day for us all'. The shrouded body lay silently in its grave as Zeke shovelled the dug earth sealing it for eternity, using his bayonet Will hacked a sapling for a makeshift cross, the two sat beside the grave in the evenings darkness while Zeke carved as best he could, a short marker to one of the few men he had truly respected as a soldier. Zeke's silence unnerved Will, clearly he had had taken the Sergeants death badly, in all these years Will had known him Zeke had taken each day as it had come, the losses had been inevitable and all part of a soldiering life, Will himself had seen his Regimental men come and go, some he knew well some he never had the chance barely lasting beyond their first engagements.

In the darkness Zeke placed the wooden cross at the head of Vaughan's grave bowed his head with his final words of respect 'farewell my friend, you served us all well' superstitious as only old soldiers can be he pushed a single penny into the soft earth, 'it pays the ferryman for a safe journey to Valhalla' he winked at Will who looked on perplexed at such an archaic custom in this now enlightened age, puzzled in his infinite naivety Will had no idea to who or what Valhalla may be.

The two walked back to the palisade that sheltered the company for the night, 'You'll take Vaughan's role as company Sergeant now then Zeke?' Will enquired, 'That'll be decided by the Regiment lad, McPherson can suggest whoever he likes but the position will go to the most senior man in the battalion, I fear old Skinner might show an interest'. Will stopped dead in his tracks, 'Skinner? Never?' he snapped in disbelief, 'I would not be surprised to see it Will lad, you know only too well his hatred to us, this would be a good opportunity for him to finally have his revenge upon us all', 'But you'll offer yourself though wont you?' Will pressed his words, 'Aye that I will lad, but remember this, Skinner outranks me already and if he's smart enough and we both know he is, then he'll have considered his plan from the moment he learned of Vaughan death, keep your guard up and eyes wide open for his next trick and it may just save us. all of us.

The two entered the makeshift camp and sheltered from the night chills around the small fire beneath the smashed ramparts, the Allen brothers already consumed by alcohol slumbered as the damp chill bit into the bones of those exposed to the chilling night air.

Surprisingly, Captain McPherson kept company with his ranks that night, whilst his brethren officer dined in luxury and basked in the glory of the days victory, McPherson on this occasion preferred to share the camaraderie with his rank and file, as pockets of men sat idly round smouldering fires, McPherson moved amongst them sharing a few words with each, Zeke kicked the boots of Dan and Thom Allen as McPherson approached the file, 'Jump too lads, Officer present.'. McPherson despite his privileged youth recognised with reverence the bravery of the few that stood in the ranks of his company and addressed the file with humility, 'Rest yourselves gentlemen, the honour is all mine to serve alongside such brave and stout fellows as you'. With McPherson's permission Will, Zeke, Thom and Dan, slouched lazily about their fire, secured by its warmth as the officer eased himself between the group and warmed his hands against the glowing embers but out of sight Sergeant Skinner unsettled by

McPherson's familiarity with the ranks waited in the wings of the remains of the company, biding his time to press his influences on the excitable officer who relayed the thanks given by Mawhood's staff officers.

The hot charcoals illuminated the faces of those fixated by its glow as the officer passed through the pockets of exhausted men, 'Sergeant Skinner will be amongst you shortly with a token of my gratitude for today's heroics' the officer parted the file in pursuance of further euphoria. Will fumbled his words, 'Skinner?' he paused a moment in confusion, 'What has Skinner to do with this?' he asked angrily, 'It would seem our 'friend' has infiltrated our ranks already, my guess is that he's offered himself for Sergeant already' Zeke replied. Will stood to his feet in an instant, 'this can't be' he yelled in his temper, 'That bastard has no right to command this company, you know that Zeke, we all know that'. Desperately wanting to suggest Zeke fill the sergeants rank left vacant by Vaughan's death, Will motioned to call after McPherson in some last ditch attempt to make sense of the situation. As Will drew breath to yell after the officer Zeke interrupted him sternly, 'Hush your words lad for the die has been cast and we all have to live with it now'.

The silence was abruptly broken from the darkness by a voice that filled Will with dread, 'You'd do well to listen to your corporal boy', Will winced upon realisation that Skinner had heard his ranting, 'Now is that a way to welcome your new Sergeant to the bosom of your company?' Skinner spoke as he strutted his way into the files camp. Anger began to consume Will as Skinner staggered drunkenly towards the files campfire, 'You've no place in this company Skinner, what trickery did you to gain Vaughan's rank?', ''Twas no trickery boy' Skinner slurred 'the officer recognised good soldierin when he see's it'. Will postured himself aggressively towards the Sergeant, 'you're a thief, a murderer and a coward Skinner and I'll be damned if this file serves under you'.

Skinner squared up to Will and calmly reminded him of his place as a private soldier, 'Listen boy, you belong to me now, you can forget your sentiments to Vaughan, he's dead and gone now, you'd do best to leave his memory in the ground you buried him in' he sniggered with contempt for the dead Sergeant's memory.

Zeke defused the tension between Skinner and Will, 'Calm yourself Will' he eased his words towards the two that squared each other aggressively, 'there's no sense in this hostility between us any longer, the Regiment has seen fit to appoint Sergeant Skinner to our company in light of our losses, we can put our past indifferences behind us and confirm the company to its past honours' as he pulled a bottle from his knapsack and offered it as a token towards the newly appointed company Sergeant. Skinner having consumed Captain McPherson's gratitude himself slowly drew his hand towards Zeke's offering, sensing no trickery Skinner uncorked the bottle and placed it to his lips, swigging generously from the full bottle.

Pausing a moment to wipe his wet lips Skinner grinned a black toothed smile with contempt, ''Tis a fine spirit Corporal Turner' he exclaimed, 'too fine for the likes of you's though' with that Skinner upturned the bottle onto the fire, the embers sizzled as the liquid doused the warmth generated from its glow, 'now return back to the stone from which ye crept'.

Will's subconscious had prepared himself for this moment, desperately looking around at the expressions of his fellow file members his anger consumed him like never before, lunging forward towards the Sergeant with fist clenched Will struck his blow hard upon Skinners unshaven pock marked jaw, the Sergeant recoiled at the strike, falling hard back onto the hard earth. Shaking his head in shock Skinner rested himself on his elbows, Will towered over the fallen sergeant, 'get up you coward and fight me' he yelled when he felt himself pulled back and thrown to the ground with a hard jolt, Zeke straddled his bewildered body, 'you never know when to shut up do you lad?' he spoke with a chastising tone. The last thing Will saw was Zeke's fist coming towards his shocked face.

Will woke with a sharp pain throbbing from his jaw, clutching his chin his vision cleared to the sight of Dan raking the embers from the stone cold fire, 'What happened to me?' he enquired, 'Oh, you're awake' he replied without turning to acknowledge, the contempt clear in his voice, Will again asked the question his friend had failed answer, 'What happened Dan? answer me will you!'.

Dan stood from the ashes and stooped down to Will's level and spoke firmly, 'Zeke saved yer damn neck from the noose Will, that's what happened' examining his bruised jaw roughly, 'Damn it' Will uttered as his last moments of the night caught up to him, 'Where is Zeke now?' asking as he scrambled to his feet, Dan answered without emotion 'Skinners called the company to parade and Zeke's reported you sick save you commit yourself to the gallows with another outburst'.

For the first time in his life Will swore hard, 'fuck' he muttered to himself realising the embarrassment caused to himself and his file and the severity his actions would have caused, 'where's our company now Dan?' he pursued Dan for conversation who still cared not to make eye contact with him, 'Out of harms way you damned fool' Dan answered and seeing Will gather his belongings together stopped his chores walking towards him, 'Listen friend, I'm under Zeke's direct order to keep you here, I'll put you down myself if I have to, don't make me do it now.'

The embarrassment and frustration overwhelmed Will as he threw his equipment down to the hard ground, for a brief moment he contemplated finishing Skinner now, once and for all but despite his emotions still running high realised the repercussions his friends would face and the dishonour to the Regiment of a drum head courts martial.

By midday, Zeke and Thom returned to their makeshift camp, Will stood upright as the company fell out of file and moved towards him, ready with his apology for his outburst Zeke pre-empted the situation, 'Leave well alone Will' he spoke as he lay his musket against the barricade, 'you said what we all felt, you did what we all wanted to do, there's no harm done except to your jaw and your pride and for now at least Skinner has agreed for me to place you under my personal watch, the last thing he wants is an courts martial incident this early in his appointment, consider yourself lucky this time you've fate on your side, next time you may not be so lucky', 'but Zeke' Will wanted so desperately to speak his apology but his words were interrupted yet again, 'Listen lad, Skinner now has the senior rank in McPherson's company and we need to recognise the fact, the Regiments ranks are so thinned that ours and Captain Leslie's companies are to merge until the spring and with no replacements this side of Christmas we're to quarter across the bay on the mainland, we move out tonight and three days march is all we'll have to bear with Skinner, then we over winter north of the Delaware river, this campaign is nigh over now so you'd best put any hot headedness away at least until we face the enemy again'.

That night the harsh North American winter arrived, biting cold winds bit hard into those left exposed on the slopes of the Manhattan Peninsular, despite an unseasonably mild Autumn, Lord Howe's chain of supply logistics had failed to provide adequate blankets for those camped outside and several helpless wounded frozen to death overnight, Will heard a junior supply officer speak of the tragic oversight, whilst he himself had dined well on roast beef and fresh vegetables hastily brought forward so the officer classes could celebrate the end to a successful campaign season, successful? He thought to himself, tell it to the infantry, tell it to the dead.

*   *   *

Chapter Nine

The Delaware

Sergeant Skinner formed the composite companies at dawn, the sun yet to offer any warmth to the dawn chill. Forced to stand idly, the company chilled to the bone until Skinner saw fit to move his command from the exposed ground that faced the winter snow, ever keen to impress his new officers. 'If this is Skinners idea of competent command with our company' Thom Allen quipped 'he'll not last too long', 'If he stands us here much longer none of us will last long, we'll all bloody freeze to death' Dan added with a raised eyebrow. Captains McPherson and Leslie greeted the company in full regalia before summoning all non commissioned ranks for a briefing, Zeke fell out of line and trotted towards the small group that gathered around the officers to receive their orders as Will watched with anticipation eager to gain comprehension of his Regiments forthcoming movements on the mainland.

With a sharp formal salute Zeke left the officers presence and fell back in with the thinned ranks of the Regiment, Will pressed for news of their deployment over the winter, 'hopefully' he said 'we'll dwell in comfort over these coming harsh months', 'Aye' both the Allen brothers replied simultaneously, 'may a warm billet be obtained for us all', Zeke whispered under his breath the details of the Regiments orders, 'we're to march on some town named Princeton over on the mainland, we'll over winter there, advance reports are claiming it a town loyal to the crown so unless Washington's armies try some trickery we can expect to see a safe period until the campaign season starts again come spring time', 'Us alone?' Will enquired 'or are we part of the brigade?' hoping for a change from the crowded billets they'd inhabited previously. 'The Hessian brigade will occupy the town that straddles the Delaware River so we're to billet alongside the 40th and 55th Regiments, although our precedence in line should give us priority for the more comfortable billets', 'Hmm' Will rubbed his fingers across his scalp, 'haven't we heard that before?' stating rhetorically, 'Ah though, this time lads we're all poor bloody infantry lad, no cavalry to lord it over us today' Zeke reassured them.

The company crossed the Hudson River courtesy of the naval barges that brought supplies ashore from the merchant ships harboured along the coast line, the relentless snows drove hard into the faces of the exposed men as they jumped clear of the hulks as they crashed into the surf of the mainland pebbled beaches, the tree line stood bare along the edge of the beach gave little shelter from the biting winds that cut hard into those that idled about awaiting their orders, sensibly the file through experience of years campaigning shrouded themselves in the single blanket the army had the thought sensible to issue them. The scene looked almost comical, like a herd of fish wives huddled around to gossip the business of others but the slightest warmth gained over ruled any smartness the British army redcoat might have displayed in there usual regalia. As the last of the Regiment disembarked from the barges the men formed into column ready to move out, the Regiments baggage loaded onto wagons ready for the three days march onto Princeton. The lame, frostbitten for the lack of decent footwear hobbled behind whilst a few managed to hitch a ride on the train of wagons that dictated the pace the column travelled. The file had the sense to follow Zeke's lead and bind their feet with strips of rag salvaged from the spoils of Fort Washington, the snow, slush and mud seeped in through the stitching of their shoes already straining under the wear of a long campaign rotting the feet of those unfortunate enough not to be issued with a better a quality of footwear. The Regimental cobblers would see themselves work tirelessly repairing footwear until there became little left to stitch, at that point, with a few coins to persuade the Regiments quartermasters a new pair of shoes was in order and the wearer would suffer unbearably until the stiff leather eased to the shape of the foot.

Seeing the burliest of men cry with agony, the snow trailed scarlet behind the bleeding feet of those that none envied. Every hour the Regiment fell out for a few minutes rest, collapsing under the strain of exhaustion Will attempted to ease his shoes from his swollen feet, 'Leave em on lad' Zeke ordered whilst stuffing his pipe with fresh tobacco, 'you'll be hard pushed to get em back on if your feet swell' he added holding his clay pipe firmly between his teeth, knowing Zeke's words and advice had yet to let him or any other down, his campaign experience was well considered by all that knew him. With the wagons horses fed and watered, the column rose to its feet and began its march onward to their objective for that day, some battered old craggy sign gave indication to the Regiments destination for the night, Newarke said the sign pointing along the twisting road that led towards the gloomy winter's sunset, eight miles.

The setting sun dipped below the horizon and the occasional biting sleet resumed once again to thick snow and quickly settled on the ground, freezing hard without the dulling sun to keep above melting point. The column now stretched over several miles, longed to reached a welcoming billet for the night, a hot brew and hopefully hot food awaiting their arrival. A well disciplined European army would under good circumstances cover an average of thirty miles in a day, these however were far from good circumstances, the close column fractured and separated on the uneven road towards its destination, trailing far in the distance a good commander would keep the columns pace to its slowest speed less the stragglers fall behind and become victims to the bitter cold winters night.

Occasionally a group of horsemen would trot by passing encouragement to those flagging under the strain of pace, with horse a man could reach his goal well inside a half day and long before these weary infantrymen would arrive at their destination this squadron of light Dragoons would be comfortable in the choicest of billets leaving those on foot to scramble for whatever was left. 'Typical aint it' Zeke muttered, 'I always knew I should have been a cavalryman' amusing the file with his sarcastic wit, 'Aye Zeke' Dan spoke 'nothing to do but shovel shit for two hours a day', 'a horseman's life for me' Will joined the banter whistling some half remembered soldiers ditty.

The company fell out with just a mile to go before reaching the town of Newark, giving the straggling column ample time to catch up, McPherson riding alongside Captain Leslie stopped beside Zeke as he fell the company out of line, 'Sergeant Skinner is too far behind Zeke' pointing back along the distant trail the column had travelled, 'Claims his old campaign wounds are playing him up wouldn't you know' adding with his upper class accent 'you sir, will have to honour to lead the Regiments first company into the town', 'and of Skinner?' Zeke enquired, 'Claims he can't walk on account of his invalidity old boy' the officer replied as he looked on towards his destination standing high in his mounts stirrups he spoke without eye contact to his company Corporal, 'I've placed him in a wagon with the baggage' he spoke and ended the conversation with a crack of his whip and a sharp dig of his heels into his rides belly.

As the officer cantered onwards Will remarked 'Invalidity?' he exclaimed 'what damn trickery is his feeble mind playing now?'

'And what campaign wounds too?' Thom Allen added with puzzled expression 'He never left the shores of Britain till we departed Edinburgh', 'Aye' his brother joined in 'I remember his sickness on finding his sea legs, as soon as we lost sight of land he clung to the deck like a baby'. The group laughed in remembering Skinners image, the vision amused Will as the column walked the last length of their long days march. Zeke presently fell the company in as the remnant of the stragglers joined up the ranks and addressed the files. '17th, close up and form ranks' he barked a true soldiers orders, 'Tenshunnn' and collectively the company stood firm on his command, seeking no authority he addressed the proud men of the Regiment 'Let us do the 17th proud eh lads and unfurl those colours and all their glory shall we?'. The Regiment's silken colours laced with fine gold thread and complex embroidery flew fully in the firm winter breeze, The Kings Union flag with its numerals denoting seniority in the line, 17th, Will gazed upwards, XVII, a proud Regiment, his Regiment and with Zeke given the honour to lead them forwards the company marched firmly towards its welcoming winter quarters. As the column reached the outskirts of Newark town, lights flickered from the small glass windows giving a longing sense of warmth and hospitality to the weary soldiers, tavern keepers keen to improve their profits held wide open their doors revealing a roaring fireside for which to tempt those chilled to the bone, it was a luring sight indeed, a full days march and half into the night the company finally reached the towns centre, Zeke stood the ranks firm until McPherson's with acknowledgment permitted his Corporal to fall out the men.

Zeke firmed his posture ready to deliver McPherson's wishes, 'Company, company, Shun . . .' he yelled and in unison the ranks jolted firm, 'Company with permission of the gentleman officer will fall out'. Damn this formality Zeke' Will thought to himself, 'just get on with it, we've stood here freezing to death for long enough'. All eyes faced front waiting for Zeke's order who snapped his head up towards the two mounted officers anticipating the given word, 'If you please Corporal' McPherson instructed with a gentlemanly nod. Zeke fell the company out with a sharp bark, 'Company . . . 'he paused a moment 'Company fall out!'.

Will loosened the heavy pack from his back, the leather straps dug in hard into his flesh, cutting almost permanent grooves into his bones, dropping his load to the frozen earth he glanced around to find his bearings about this unfamiliar town. Despite the late hour the town bustled as busily as ever, peddlers fell upon the soldiers as soon as they were dismissed from formation, pushing cheap watery wine these rogues could make a huge profit from the exhausted troops eager to find a warmth in their belly's whilst whores yelled suggestively from the open upper floor windows beckoning the soldiers beneath, with his men dismissed Zeke rejoined his file announcing the urgency to quickly find decent billets for the night before the town got over run with the incoming companies. Straining with ever stiffening bones, Will hoisted his equipment back to his shoulders and followed Zeke towards the open doors keen to offer host to the incoming soldiers, Dan and Thom eager to make the most of the women calling down from above laughed between each other whilst cheekily coaxing a cheap view of their fruitful wares on offer. Will shook his head as whores eager to extract as much coin from the soldiers bared naked breasts without shame from the houses that accommodated them, 'Come Will' Thom yanked his tunic 'Ye complains too readily of aches, surely a tender caress will soon sooth your bones', 'Or break em even further' his brother added laughing as the two walked towards their selected hospitality, Will declined the offer, choosing instead the company of Zeke and a select few others in quiet peace.

A campaigning army attracted scores of camp followers eager to capitalise on the opportunity for quick profits, prices soared quickly as the demand outstripped the supply for luxury goods, peddlers, thieves and beggars converged on the town that under normal circumstances scarcely populated a thousand souls. The Taverns and Inns heaved as hundreds of redcoats bartered for lodgings and rents increased on each transaction the innkeepers made. The army's war chest paid a high price to billet its soldiers and the harsh winter months guaranteed a good stable income for those offering goods and services in high demand. Watching the continuing column of troops rapidly fill the town and seeking only a quiet end to their weary day, Zeke and Will headed towards the quieter side of the town. Zeke's logic was simple, although the billets would be less comfortable than the elaborate and well furnished hostelries in the centre of Newark the further from the centre would be more readily available to those prepared to walk a little further, besides Zeke argued, with such demand you could queue all night and still find yourself without a bunk. The two traipsed through the crisp frozen snows towards the southern side of town, the lines became thinner and the prices for a billet fell dramatically, 'Here seems a fitting place to stay the night' Zeke stopped and spoke. Looking upwards to the taverns swinging sign, Will read its words aloud, 'The Kings Arms' he rolled his eyes far too tired to see the comedy in his friends statement, Zeke spoke further 'Tonight Will lad, we'll sleep safely in the kings arms'. The two entered the shabby Inn, although far from as empty as Zeke would have liked the chances of a quiet warm place to sleep tonight looked favourable, 'The roofs tuppence each for the night and I's got no bunks but you're welcome to my fireside' the inn keeper issued the same statement to everyone who entered through the door while a negro serving boy moved through the crowd extracting coin from those that stayed long enough to assume the hospitality. Zeke, familiar with these practices tossed the coins towards the boy, 'Two jugs of ale if you please too young sir', the youngster bowed his head and scurried off towards the tapped oaken barrels to pour their frothy beverages. The two settled themselves into a quiet corner of the tavern and thawed their chilled bones, Struggling to keep awake Will heard the church bells strike midnight, after more than sixteen hours on the road he could finally rest. Despite the noise generating from the busy tavern he snatched a few moments inner peace when Zeke suddenly poked hard into his ribs startling him back to his senses, 'Wake up lad, look who's here'. Sergeant Skinner casually walked into the Inn, shamelessly barging his way towards the taverns crude bar demanding his immediate service, 'Keep your eyes down Will, maybe he'll not notice us' Zeke muttered holding his tankard to his lips 'his company tonight will surely ruin us both'. Will held his hand over his forehead desperately hoping Skinner would not recognise him or any other from his company, Despite the house being busy with similar red coated soldiers somehow the Sergeant sniffed out the two, Skinner grinned as he eyed Will and Zeke, despite desperate attempts to remain incognito Will looked directly into his sergeants gaze, 'Fuck!' Will muttered 'He's seen us', 'Damn it' Zeke responded, 'too good to be true that he'd leave us in peace I guess?' he spoke quietly. Sergeant Skinner waded through the crowd that occupied the tavern, 'Corporal' he addressed Zeke, 'mind if I share your evening?'. Ignoring Will's presence

Skinner barged him aside making room on the narrow bench for his gangly frame, 'I see your wounds have healed well?' Will asked sarcastically noticing his miraculous recovery after being invalided from the columns march earlier that day, 'Shut it boy' Skinner snarled 'You should learn to speak when you're spoken to and not before', 'Leave the lad alone Mathias eh? He means no harm' Zeke attempted to calm the tension between the two, 'No harm you say?' Skinner stared into Zeke's eyes with a hatred they'd both seen before 'This boy is owed a beating and I swear by god he'll get it if he opens his mouth again'. Will kept his head bowed subserviently in the presence of Skinner who sat grinning smugly between the two, provoking him Skinner reached for Will's ale and emptied the vessel before gasping his satisfaction in humiliating him, 'Piss water!' he directed his contempt to Will directly, the remnants of froth and spittle dribbled from his lips down his chin. His provocation this time gave no yield but Skinner felt his sure chance would come again if he kept with his antagonising methods. For now though, Zeke would have the last word, leaning casually towards his sergeant he dropped all protocols of rank and whispered quietly and calmly into Skinners ear, 'You instigate a brawl in here Skinner and I'll be sure you're the first to go down'. Sergeant Skinners expression dropped as he heard Zeke's very real threat, 'Now clear out before I stick you myself'.

Mathias Skinner knew this time he'd been outmatched, rising sharply from his seat he barged through the crowded room oblivious to the altercation that had occurred. Zeke cleared the silence with a sensible monologue, 'Listen Will' he spoke 'I know your fears and I know your desires to avenge his wrongs but this game is for the long, I've told you already that the campaign is over now, we'll quarter in warm billets all nice and peaceful likes then we'll reequip come the thaw and find ourselves a new sergeant just like old Vaughan, happy days eh lad? But for now we keep our friends close and our enemies even closer right?' but Will heard none of Zeke's reasoning, exhausted he slipped into a long slumber, Zeke pulled his tunic over his shoulders and left his friend in peace. The long day had taken a toll on him, whilst the town filled with arriving troops at least the file would be protected from the cold as the snow began to fall heavily outside.

The following morning Will woke to find Zeke has drawn his ration from the Regiments store, slices of salt pork for breakfast made a refreshing change from weevil infested oatmeal the ranks had fed upon the last few days, Zeke on seeing Will awake placed a jug of small beer on the tavern table, 'I don't trust the water here, drink this instead' thrusting the vessel towards him. Cholera often claimed more victims than the enemy's muskets, a spoiled water source could and would easily decimate a company, in these unfamiliar lands loyalty to the crown could not be assumed by local reports alone, rebellious sabotage could easily ruin the effectiveness of a company.

As the winters sun began its late rise Zeke called men from McPherson's company to account, '17th!' he yelled 'gather your kit, a quarter hour and we fall in' he added. Will gathered his belongings and moved outside into the crisp early December morning, moving amongst scores of men from other Regiments Will distinguished those of his own Regiment via small differences on their red coats, a cuff pearl white signified a man from the 17th, yellow for the 55th proved an indication of the size of the brigade billeted within this small town. Spying a group from his own Regiment, Will fell in and gathered a trot to the rally point marked by wooden stakes a mile from the town centre. Unfamiliar with his peers, he kept quiet as those from other companies fell in besides them similarly recognising the distinguishing marks of his Regiment.

The open fields that surrounded Newarke town lay covered in fresh and crisp snow, the sound of the frozen fields crunched under foot as scores of men waded across towards their rally point as the faint winter sun barely rose above the twisted lifeless tree tops that surrounded the perimeter of the open grazing meadows. Sighting Dan and Thom Allen clearly the worse for a nights 'entertainment', Will left his party and fell in besides the two and his fellows from his company, The chill form a northerly wind cut into exposed flesh as the men waited for instruction,

Sergeant Skinner hovered on the fringes of his company idling his time until his superiors gave order for company movements. Zeke arrived after gathering the last of the company from the town, standing in his Corporals position Will risked a whisper towards the corporal, 'What news Zeke?' he uttered almost silently, 'We move out at mid morning, get yourselves back to Newark and settle your affairs and accounts quickly, the road east leads to a small town named Brunswick and by the sounds of it billets will be short, if we can get ahead of the main column we'll have a sporting chance of a good billet tonight'. Skinner dismissed the company and collectively the four raced back to Newark to gain some ground upon the column that en masse would travel the road east.

The town still busied itself with scores of troops idling around waiting for their day's orders, the baggage train readied itself for the column to form up ahead, mules tethered to heavy carts snorted their breath into the cold winter's air, restless after the cold night past. 'Gather your belongings as quickly as you can' Zeke spoke as he hurriedly pushed the brothers towards the whore house that had accommodated them overnight. The Allen brothers dashed off to collect their equipment sharing a quiet joke as they made way through the scores of red coats gathered around.

'Well lad' Zeke spoke to Will, 'If our lucks in we'll gain good ground on the column and have a choice of good billets', Will nodded in agreement while keeping an eye on his surroundings, shortly Dan and Thom returned pursued by the cat calls of the whores who'd entertained them previously, 'Trouble?' Will enquired as the two arrived back, 'Ah, just some old trick being played upon us' Dan answered, 'We've had familiarity with these types before' his brother added 'claims we didn't errr' he paused a moment thinking his next words carefully 'let's say settle our bills'. Will looked on with naïve puzzlement as the two slapped him on the back, 'One day Will lad . . . one day' the two spoke with a wink.

The remains of McPherson's company arrived back at the town and disappeared into the dwellings returning to form column ready to begin the march east leaving Zeke to fall the disorganised company on Skinners absence, the ranks thickened until the Regiment or what was left of it was ready to embark towards their next destination. Flurries of snow fluttered through the air as more snow clouds formed above indicating this would be a long laborious trek for those on foot, those fortunate enough to secure transport in the baggage train had best sense to wrap themselves warm, as soon as the sun dipped the temperature would plummet to several degrees below freezing, the sick should be wise to recall all their favours else succumb to the peril of the night. The column, lead by a cortege of mounted officers slowly moved forwards leaving the security of Newarke town behind them as the entered the open terrain that lay before their next destination. It took little time before a disciplined column broke into a fragmented thin line of straggling troops, those close to frost bite begged passage on the ox drawn wagons that dictated the columns pace, if you were lucky a comrade might carry one's equipment to ease the strains of the march, though these favours came at a high price, men promised what little wealth they'd accumulated in return for a few miles march unloaded with an infantryman's lot.

The road that led towards Brunswick Town lay fallen with fresh snow, a party of engineers had marked the trail the previous night with a series of markers but the hard frozen earth had prevented them securing the stakes deep enough, mostly the markers had tumbled overnight as the winds and snows had blown across the lands, every mile or less the officers halted the column whilst they studied local maps borrowed from loyal notorieties, neither accurate or legible the column fell badly behind schedule.

With no clear signs or indications the column was travelling in the proper direction things looked desperate for hundreds of men already fighting against bleak conditions, should the column be caught in a sudden blizzard the death toll would be high.

The file fell out of line on Skinners reluctant orders, men stretched their necks forward hoping to get some idea of what was going on, Zeke muttered to himself 'at this rate we will lose more of our own than any damned rebellious militia could ever manage' his frustration at this poor command clear in his tone. The column stalled on the stony snow covered trail grew restless as time drew on and provost riders paced the line showing authority in a potential mutinous situation, 'Corporals and Sergeants rally forward' a rider cried as he galloped along the disorganised line of men, 'Finally' Will expressed, 'something's happening' he straightened his stiff back rising to his feet, Zeke shouldered his musket on which he'd rested his weary arms and straightened his attire for the benefit of his audience with the officers. Dan drew a half bottle of brandy from his pack, swigged, rinsed and swigged again before passing about those in his presence, hands appeared from nowhere eager to gain some warmth in their belly, soon the bottle ran empty and Dan who sucked the last remnants from its neck tossed it far into the snowy fields that surrounded them, the bottle lay abandoned half buried in the deep snow as the column look onward in anticipation of its movements.

The column stalled for almost an hour whilst a decision was made to either turn back or press on despite day light fading fast, snow clouds formed above threateningly causing concern to all and eventually Zeke returned to the company and fell the ranks back into formation in anticipation to move onward. 'What news Zeke?' came to calls from the company's men eager to press forward rather than face a laborious march back from whence they came. 'We march on' Zeke announced much to the relief of the line 'But we're to keep a quota in reserve to assist the wagons, with heavy snow likely there's no chance of them making the town before midnight unaided' he spoke with reason although not entirely convinced of the logic himself. 'Which company remains Zeke?' Will enquired but Zeke needed not to answer, 'Ours, and before you complain twas not my doing lad, the fool that leads us has again undone us . . .' Zeke handed his musket to Dan fumbling into his pocket for his tobacco pouch, his gnarled clay pipe grasped between his teeth stuffing the last of his tobacco generously into the pipe bowl Zeke explained the company's predicament, 'Sergeant Skinner' Zeke said in dulcet tones 'complained to McPherson that his wounds could no longer manage such a lengthy trek in such cold climes and begged to be placed on the baggage train again to relieve his sufferings' pausing a moment to strike the tinder in his pipe bowl Zeke continued 'But McPherson is getting wise to Skinners tricks, he'll allow Skinner the privilege but only if his ranks accompany him so we're to stay in reserve and escort the wagons', 'Then damn him to hell says I' Thom cursed 'it's time McPherson learned the truth', 'You hold your tongue Thom lad' Zeke snapped 'I've enough to contend with Will's irrationalities let be confounded by yours too' he added with a growl 'now pray do as we're ordered and we'll be shot of him soon'.

The companies set to move immediately fell back into formation and departed the heavier baggage that would be guarded on its slow journey, the long thin line of red marched into the distance as the sun arched over head towards the distant town. McPherson's men fell to the trails sidings as the column slowly moved out, the lighter, faster wagons that could keep up the columns pace soon over took the much slower heavy wagons pulled by oxen or dray horse and soon enough the line faded into the distance leaving a ghostly essence of itself alone on the snow covered trail. Sergeant Skinner hobbled pathetically back to his company and selected a heavy wagon with canvas coverings to house him the journey ahead, contempt ran deep in the ranks of those under his command as eyes burned hatred into his back as he passed, consolation, Will thought to himself was if this fool continues like this he'll be done for by new year, Skinner had broken his old companies spirit early on but Vaughan's would not suffer fools so gladly, Zeke as he recalled had said Skinners undoing would be his own, perhaps this was the start, Will could only hope.

Progress was slow as dusk fell upon the open trail, thick snow dragged along the heavy axles adding increased weight to the already straining beasts that struggled through the treacherous weather, often drivers would call to troops to heave the wagons free from drifts invisible until it was too late to avoid them, Oxen stuck fast had to be unhitched from the carts while it was dragged and manhandled back onto the invisible trail, a frustrated beast had tendencies to dictate where and when it wished to move despite the whips and rods of the drivers that commanded them. Zeke had predicted that travelling at a steady pace the baggage train would arrive at Brunswick town an hour past midnight, at this rate they would struggle to arrive before dawn, 'so much for a decent billet he quipped', the irony was far from lost.

The wagon trains progress was slow, hampered even more so by the increasing snow that fell heavily from the skies and soon the wide wheeled wagons ground to a halt as the snow settled thick upon the ground, the exhausted beasts that hauled the columns baggage could move no further until the snow that held them fast was cleared from the trail ahead. The columns baggage train carried all manners of equipment, everything a campaigning Regiment would need to survive off the land that supported their movements, with shovels distributed amongst the able bodied troops the remainder unloaded the weight from the wagons allowing the brute force of the men to heave the stuck carts from the drifts.

A quick inspection of each wagon gave Zeke Turner a rough idea on the best way to even the weight throughout the wagons load, it also gave him a method to settle the scores with Sergeant Skinner, looking upwards from the wagon Zeke called after the company drummer boy, 'Take these blankets to the Sergeant' he ordered the lad, 'and under no circumstances tell him they came from me, should he ask you're to tell him you feared for his health in these cold climes, then you're to return straight back to me you understand' he added to his instruction. Zeke and Will watched as the boy gathered several blankets and trot towards the covered wagon Skinner sheltered within, Zeke smiled as Sergeant Skinner leant over the side of the wagon and took receipt of the blankets the boy provided 'Typical' he smirked to himself 'no gratitude whatsoever' as he watched Skinner cuff the lad about the head yelling harshly at the youth for not thinking of his comforts sooner. The drummer boy scurried back to Zeke 'all done Corporal, just as you asked' his boyish voice spoke, 'Well done lad, now as soon as we start moving again your to keep our beloved sergeant lubricated with as much of the rum ration as he requires' Zeke spoke softly in the boys ear. Smarting from Skinners fists the drummer boy rubbed the side of his head looking puzzled at Zeke's request, 'Begging your pardon sir' the boy pleaded 'but that's company rum and its theft is a flogging offence', 'Don't you fret yourself lad, now should the blessed sergeant call for more you makes sure that you have plenty to witness his demands' Zeke assured the boy. The moment dawned upon Will to Zeke's game, Skinner would be drunk as a lord as the wagons arrived back with the column and all seemingly his own doing. Zeke leant on the shovel he used to dig the wagons wheels from the snow, 'See lad, revenge is a dish best served cold' he spoke with a wink in his eye 'now ease back and watch our sergeant undoes himself', 'Clever Zeke, very clever' Will said as the company pushed the last of the wagons back onto the roadway.

The convoy slowly moved through the snow covered trails that lead towards the distant township, sensibly those on foot walked ahead and pounded the path smoothing the strain on the wagons that followed, candle burning carriage lamps held high illuminated the way as the snow eased to a flutter in the nights breeze. The silence occasionally broken by Skinners call for more rum, 'Bring the damn barrel boy!' he yelled at the drummer who accommodated his demands, over the course of the night Sergeant Skinners shouts moved through every emotion, from 'his beloved men to I'll flog the lot of you', Will smirked to himself as Skinners rants got louder and louder.

The last leg of the journey made good time, arriving as Zeke had anticipated just before dawn, the town's sentry guard called 'stand too' as the baggage train came into view just a short distance from the towns limits. 'Perfect . . . now we'll get see some fun' Zeke said as the company marched through the darkness towards the picket fences guarded by the night watch, '17th coming in' Zeke shouted to the calls of the guard. The wagons drew up in the towns square not dissimilar to that of Newarke, coming to a halt Zeke played the last part of his act, Skinners wagon lay silent, the sergeant within long succumbed to the effects of the companies rum ration. Quickly, Zeke fell the men into line ready for Captains

McPherson and Leslie to take receipt of the baggage train, the twenty men formed ranks as Zeke directed a few yards in front of Skinners wagon, waiting his moment Zeke spied the two officers emerge from their quarters, with timing perfect Zeke banged his fist on the side of the wagon rousing its occupant, 'Sergeant' he cried out in a panicked voice, 'the enemy is fast upon us, surrounded we be, all hope is lost'. Even for Zeke, this prank went better than anyone could have possibly imagined, the wagon shook as Skinner fumbled around under the cover of the heavy canvas that shrouded it. His timing impeccable, Zeke Zeke fell innocently back in line with the company just as the two officers arrived, the wagon shook comically leaving both McPherson and Leslie with a puzzled concern.

The Company struggled to contain its laughter as Skinner threw back the canvas sheeting, dishevelled and half dressed without his breeches Skinner held his palms towards his imaginary enemy, with bleary eyes his vision saw only vague figures about him, babbling his words incoherently 'pray to give sanctuary for old Mathias, he's never meant anyone any harm'. The moment was perfect, the whole company continued to hold its composure as their sergeant screamed incoherently in his drunken condition, 'Sergeant Skinner!' McPherson yelled in disbelief 'What is the meaning of this outrage?'. The look of horror on Skinners face was priceless, confused yet still silly drunk Skinner attempted to gain stock of his embarrassments on realising how the situation looked, pausing a moment Skinner looked down and recoiled in embarrassment on discovering his modesty, 'It must be colder than I thought' Dan joked to the amusement of those within ear shot.

Sergeant Skinner swayed back and forth under the influences of alcohol he'd consumed before finally collapsing backwards into the wagon, 'Corporal' Captain McPherson addressed Zeke 'may I suggest Mister Skinner be handed over to the guard until he be found fit for duty', 'Yes sir' Zeke replied with a smile 'right away sir'. Will climbed into the wagon as several men formed around to carry the sergeant towards the guard house, it was a pitiful yet amusing sight, slumped helplessly and barely conscious

Skinner mumbled incoherently as Will without care pulled his limp frame and tossed him over the side onto the snow covered ground below, Skinner groaned upon landing before being hoisted unceremoniously onto the shoulders of two company men acting temporarily as his guard until Zeke formally handed him over to the provost, the charge, drunk whilst on duty, negligence of the King's regulations and insubordination in the presence of an officer. Zeke signalled Will, Dan and Thom to accompany him to the guardhouse, 'Let us savour this moment gentlemen and enjoy it for what it's worth'. The four men all grinned from ear to ear as Skinner on realising his trouble was only just beginning pleaded for reason 'Must've been some bad rum' he stuttered 'I's only had me rations worth I swears I did'.

The provost guard took receipt of the prisoner shackling leg irons around his ankles and binding his wrists the same, stripped of footwear Skinner stood shakily on his feet, shivering in the winters cold, 'You'll be needing these Sergeant' Will called out throwing Skinners piss stained breeches towards him, the amusing part would be how Skinner would dress himself whilst clamped in leg irons, Skinners final words would keep the file chuckling for the rest of the night. Simply 'fuck it' as the guard led him into the dark cold cells.

The file found themselves a small but comfortable private billet, the wife of the family that housed them cooked a warming broth as the four men warmed themselves around the open hearth of their modest home, combining their meagre ration, the wife put the ingredients to good use and for once the file dined a healthy well cooked meal. The family, loyal to the crown obliged the soldiers with a bottle of port to share with their supper, 'We dines like Kings eh lads?' Zeke toasted the future good fortunes of those he'd served with all these years. The following morning Zeke fell the company in around the town square, the wagons un-tethered from the beast that pulled them lay covered in a fresh sprinkling of powdery snow, by day light the town bustled full of its usual daily business as the rebellion had yet to affect these provincial towns, the townsfolk went about their day unhindered by the politics of government, to these people life carried on regardless. Will commented to Zeke regarding the inhabitants of these colonies 'Of all the troubles we've seen here Zeke' he asked 'I fail to see anything but smiles and sympathies to our likes', 'In our presence you do lad, you'd wonder why we are here at all' he replied in rhetoric, 'Do you remember when we arrived at New York those months ago and witnessed the flag of rebellion torn down, well who do you think placed it there? None other than the very same that shredded it before your very eyes' he paused a moment whilst Will contemplated his words, Zeke continued as the file waited to move towards its final destination of the journey, 'See lad, to most folk it matters not who's governs them, for them nothing will change no matter who wins this turbulent fight, the rich will get richer, the poor will get poorer, and eventually our dry old bones will be quickly forgotten if this rebellion is ever put down' he finished his words by tapping his pipe against his heel and stuffing fresh tobacco into the bowl, 'So who do we fight then Zeke?' Will enquired further, 'Lad' Zeke took a deep breath and paused a moment, 'We fight the same kind of men as ourselves, the common man tricked into service either through a promise to relieve his debts or a small scrap of land, for don't all men wish to better themselves?' he continued 'and take my word on it my friend, when this bloody war is over for most of these me, nothing will change'.

The following morning, Regimental drummers beat their drums and fifers tuned their pipes signalling the column ready to embark,

'Ten'shun' Zeke balked, bringing a sharp stiffness to the line of men. Captain McPherson mounted his steed and kicked his heels into its firm belly causing it to jolt, Zeke stood a pace to the side of the column and yelled his firm commands, 'McPherson's company' he paused, choosing his moment he continued his orders firmly 'Will advance by the left foot . . . forward'. Instinctively the company marched on the left foot, Regimental drummers beat time dictating a steady pace that would govern the journey to Princeton.

Far ahead of the column, the officers of the brigade Regiments rode on, the roads south from Brunswick fared much better than those to it from Newarke, with temperatures below freezing the fallen snow packed hard onto the wide tracks that scattered from the town, although those on foot might slip and tumble on the icy paths the baggage train that had previously slowed the columns pace moved at good speed. General Howe's army now controlled New Jersey with a firm and hefty presence thus allowing his army's support troops and slower baggage trains to move unhindered through the colony, flocks of sheep and herds of cattle the army required to feed the thousands of troops on campaign moved south towards the winter quarters of the army.

The 17th arrived into Princeton in good order, an hour before sundown gave the company good time to arrange itself into their allocated billets, as Princeton would be the Regiments home at least until the thaw, the brigades general staff had wisely arranged for permanent private billets alongside the loyalist militia barracks for the thousand men that composed Colonel Mawhood's brigade.

Assigned to private billets, Zeke, Will, Dan and Thom settled into the vacated house that had been previously occupied by a cooper and his family, little evidence of their inhabitancy existed as anyone with half an ounce of sense had either sold off or taken with them anything of value else it be looted or destroyed by troops idling away the winter months.

Princeton town stood 10 miles north of the Delaware River far more prosperous than most towns within New Jersey due to the dominance of the college that dominated, Princeton flaunted its wealth within its structures, elaborate architecture and fine craftsmanship bloomed within its buildings that formed this college town. Unlike the other towns Will had passed through whilst in the Americas, Princeton had an aura of grandeur about itself, as its inhabitants went about there business sporting their latest fashions, until now the rebellion had left Princeton in peace, he smiled to himself as he and the others explored the town that would home then over the winter months, goods plentiful and services cheap as the towns merchants had stocked well their provisions in expectancy of the brigades arrival, for this day saw the end of the campaign that cost the men that fought it dearly and those left within the ranks rested their tired bodies in peaceful and comfortable surroundings the town offered.

With the practically campaign over, all but the picket guard were required to submit arms to the brigade quartermasters, hundreds of troops formed line ready to surrender their muskets to the Sergeant Major. The army had learned long ago that idle troops and temptation do not mix well, Howe thought best to remove from his troops the method to aid in such criminal activities. The lines of troops queuing to submit their arms trailed far across the town square the buildings focused around, each company was briefed repeatedly by the respective Sergeants on the penalty for looting, drunkenness, desertion and theft. Will glanced across to the centre of the square noting engineers constructing sturdy permanent gallows, either as a warning or ready for its first victim he cared not to know, a loyal town such as Princeton would be severe in upholding the law to protect its citizens and bolster its faith in the occupying army's presence. Zeke noticed Will's fascination with the gallows and remarked with some jest, 'Pray you do not find yourself better acquainted lad, for Howe will not now tolerate even the smallest of crimes', 'What do you mean?' Will replied only half listening to his friend's words, Zeke sighed 'Our beloved generals value the properties of these towns higher than the lives of his men that fight to protect them and should a crime be committed, the accused will have little chance of offering any defence as such. Howe would rather show example than justice'. Those that heard Zeke's wisdom seldom thought it any but the best of advice, Will felt a dryness in his throat as the words rested uneasily on his mind, 'Come Will, I does not wish to scare you witless, tis good advice to us all' Zeke added 'let us unload our arms of these tools of war and secure ourselves for the eve', 'Aye' spoke Dan, 'We've a full purse that Thom and I are eager to put to use tonight'.

The line pushed closer to the guard house, stacks of muskets lay gathered in the commandeered storeroom behind as each man gave his name and that of his company to the clerk who entered the details in the

Regimental ledgers. Will reached the head of the line, 'Name?' the clerk asked abruptly without looking to see his subject 'and of who's company?' he added with a drawn out tone, 'William James Snow' Will replied 'of McPherson's company' he handed his musket to the corporal instructed to briefly examine each weapon. The Corporal cocked the weapon and checked its action, half drawing the ram rod he satisfied its presence 'In good order' he methodically delivered his verdict to the clerk as he noted its condition into the ledger, 'move along, next man forward' the clerk spoke looking over Will's shoulder to the man behind, Will saw this as his permission to take leave and stepped left from the line to rejoin his file as they made their way to their billets.

Thom Allen cursed as he merged with his friends 'That bastard clerk' he slammed, his profanity, 'he's done fined me six shilling for a busted musket' he spoke with his rural accent drawing put his words, 'It worked fine this morning' he continued to object somewhat puzzled to how his weapon could become damaged without his knowing. Will kept quiet as Thom and his brother Dan complained at the loss of funds assigned to the nights drinking. Zeke caught Will's eye and teased a sly wink, 'you?' Will whispered in Zeke's ear 'How did you manage that?' he asked curiously as Zeke grinned, 'whilst you all gazed on towards the gallows, it was easy to jam the pan cover closed with a sharp kick downwards, as luck would have it the line jostled forwards as I struck giving none of you any clue to my deceit, but Will my friend, it has probably saved at least one of us from a run in with the provost' he gestured to the two brothers still bickering amongst each other, 'tonight, I's controls the purse strings and thus I controls their actions'.

Will smiled as Zeke's story unfolded, 'Your cunning never ceases to amaze me Zeke, nor ever will it', 'You see Will lad, I was once like the three of you, worse even, foolish, naïve and senseless, I'd have found myself on the gallows too if I hadn't been taught a trick or two', 'So you learnt these tricks from someone you served with then?' Will asked eager to learn some of Zeke's past life,

'Of course lad, the art of good soljerin' Zeke spoke softly 'is inherited from those around you and come one day you may well pass on the tricks you see yourself to those around your future company' Zeke ended the conversation as he always did, fumbling around his pockets for his pipe, this was always Zeke's way to end the talk he felt warranted no further pursuits.

The files secured themselves in their allocated billets and settled for the evening, a rise in temperature and heavy downpour of seasonal rains thawed the snows and ice that settled around the countryside, by morning the deep snow drifts had melted away to nothing but isolated pockets of packed snow cleared from store fronts and walkways. Zeke reported the file fit for duty early each day to the Regimental headquarters, lots being drawn amongst the Regiment for picket and guard duties, these lazy days were good for Will although the Allen brothers complained bitterly at the lack of interest for those without coin to idle away their time so Zeke set the file to work in repairing their equipment, better keep an idle man busy than let him stray to temptation he would speak often when either of the brothers complained of the monotony of winter quartering.

Satisfied the enemy had withdrawn from New Jersey Howe stood his army down over the festive season, with the picket guards reduced and ammunition resealed into wax lined boxes, the guards that manned the perimeter of the picket line did so with a handful of cartridge and the bayonet, Will pondered what chance they stood should Washington's army elect to strike over the relaxed period. Eventually, the file drew a period of guard duty, picketed three miles south of Princeton on the old road that led towards the Delaware River, a small woodsman's cabin housed the file as it acted as a sentry post with authority to question those that travelled these roads, Mathias Skinner now reaffirmed into his position of Sergeant had assured Zeke that the roads south had little activity due to the presence of the Hessian brigade garrisoned further south on the river town of Trenton.

In relieving the previous guard, Zeke too receipt of twenty rounds of ammunition allocated to the guard, the dampness and depressing rains has spoiled at least half of them beyond use, knowing these rounds would need to be accounted for Zeke placed them on the inside of the hut that offered small protection from the elements and little warmth from the rusted stove that dominated within it, 'damn book keepers' Zeke exclaimed 'be the ruin of this army yet, twenty pitiful rounds between us and whatever Washington might throw at us' he shook his head disappointingly as he separated the good from the bad.

An hour passed before the first travellers came into vision the daylight fast fading, Thom called Zeke from the hut to investigate who might be travelling in such treacherous weather, the dim lantern that hung from the rafters that supported the shingled roof was removed and waved by Zeke signalling to the travellers the guard post would require them to divulge their intensions and destination.

Will peered into the darkness making out the figures of three horsemen now halted a distance down the road, silently Zeke rubbed his bristled chin pondering the movements of the mysterious travellers. Zeke's instinct kicked in with no warning, 'fix bayonets' he yelled aloud 'now!' he barked his orders as the three jumped into action, Will, Thom and Dan jumped to life and snapped the sharp steel onto the socket of their muskets with a click, 'What is it Zeke? Tell me what you see?' Will looked towards Zeke, 'I see's nothing yet Will, that's the trouble lad' he continued to fix his gaze down the track, Puzzled, Will followed Zeke's lead and sought refuge behind a large wood pile opposite the hut, 'Something's not right here' Zeke mumbled to himself, 'Thom' he added still maintaining his vision forwards, 'take half the ammunition we have and secrete yourself a hundred yards into the woods behind us, keep yourself out of sight you understand?'. Silently Thom nodded, snatched his musket and the few rounds of shot and dashed into the gloom of the damp woods, within a few yards merging into the undergrowth and invisibility of its embrace.

'Keep your wits about you Will lad' Zeke spoke, 'you may yet be running back to Princeton', 'To raise the alarm you mean' he whispered quietly, Zeke laughed at Will's words, 'Why do ye whisper lad? Whoever they are, they know we're here anyways' he continued, 'what troubles me is their need to halt' he spoke rhetorically to himself, 'a hesitant man often has something to hide'.

The standoff continued for a few minutes, from the distance the three horsemen conversed amongst each other then swiftly kick their spurs into the bellies of their rides and turn off the road into the woods besides them, 'Damn it! I feared this would happen' Zeke cursed, 'pray Thom holds his ground and heeds my words'. Will stretched his neck into the misery of the nights rain and in losing sight of the mystery horsemen he turned to Zeke for what to do next, Zeke kept his eyes fixed into the distance 'who ever they are' he said 'they can be of no good to find the need to avoid our presence', 'What's to do now then Zeke?' Will enquired as Zeke thought a moment, 'Go find Thom, quickly now but keep your wits about yourself my friend, keep yourself low and silent and you'll find Thom about a hundred yards into the woods'. Will nodded, snatched his musket and ran into the gloom of the woods that secreted Thom Allen, heeding Zeke's words he stooped low as he paced the damp floor of the thin woods, true to Zeke's instruction he ran into Thom sheltering behind a long fallen tree, his own musket primed he passed a cartridge, 'Charge your weapon friend' Thom spoke softly 'I fear things could get ugly' he added as he gestured towards the now dismounted horsemen leading their mounts carefully through the trees, Thom placed his finger on his lips, 'Shush . . .' he whispered 'Zeke was right, look ahead'.

Will teased a view through the branches of the fallen tree that hid them from obvious sight, one of the horse men raised his hand and signalled into the distance beyond, a party of riflemen skulked through the thickets towards the horsemen, 'this looks like a rendezvous of some sorts to me' Thom spoke as he rested his charged musket against the cover they shared, 'wait here a moment, I'll try and get a better view of things'.

They say a true soldier instinctively knows his comrades thoughts and on this occasion it proved the case, thus for Thom to wield his cumbersome musket through the thickets and undergrowth his movements and stealth would be hindered, this county lad had spent many a day poaching on his lordships land, for Thom this challenge was child's play.

Thom dropped to his belly and crawled stealthily through the dank floor of the woods, the darkness soon consumed his form like a shadow might disappear on a cloudy day and in the darkness Will pulled back the hammer of both muskets, pulled his leather breach cover from his tunic pocket and placed it over the spare musket, the dampness consumed everything in these woods and damp powder could mean the difference between life and death for poor Thom as he ventured nearer the horsemen as they rendezvoused with the other men. Time passed and Thom had yet to make a reappearance, there's nothing to worry about Will thought to himself, Thom knows what he's doing, I know he does he said to himself over and over again for reassurance. The obscurity distorted much as Will rubbed his eyes trying to accustom them to the dark, with no moon that night and the heavy canopy above he could rely on his ear alone, a fox might bark, an owl may hoot but these sounds play tricks on a man's mind as Will clutched his musket and slowly presented it over the trunk of the tree he sheltered behind, better be prepared he thought and ran his vision down the length of the steel barrel when suddenly and without warning the barrel lifted sharply catching Will hard in the face, bewildered he shook his head and immediately recognised a familiar voice, 'Careful where you put that friend, could do some serious damage in the right hands' Thom joked as he scrambled back to the cover of the fallen trunk, 'Thom!' Will hushed the sound of his voice 'damn near scared me witless' cursing the brother as Thom giggled fits of laughter. The two gathered their equipment and raced back to the outpost, Zeke and Dan heard the two as they broke through the undergrowth and onto the track that ran parallel to it and cautiously stood firm with sharp steel bayonets threatening the figures as they appeared

'Well?' Zeke asked 'Did you see anything?' as the two arrived back at the shack that sheltered the makeshift guard house, 'Aye that we did Zeke' Thom spoke struggling to catch his breath as Dan offered his canteen to the two who spluttered out their sightings, 'the horsemen led their beast past us and for good reason too' he added, 'it seems a meeting along this road was due, whether they thought they'd out witted us by leaving the road I know not but I saw the rendezvous with my own eyes and saw documents passed between the two parties', 'Hmm, documents you say, did you hear their voices?' Zeke urged, 'Aye Zeke, that I did, they knew each other of that I could tell for they spoke with familiarity, they talked of billets full of redcoats and the few Dragoons that patrol these roads, another of them asked after the heavy guns positioned around Princeton town but of that I could tell you no more'. Zeke rubbed his chin deep in thought 'we'd best keep alert tonight and Will, I need you to travel swiftly back to Princeton with this information, seek out the first officer you find and relay this information concisely but discretely, it seems our enemies have not yet heard this campaign is over'.

Will leant against the shack that sheltered them from the elements as Zeke, Dan and Thom distributed what little cartridge they had amongst themselves, 'Drop your equipment Will' Zeke instructed, 'you'll need speed with you if you're to reach the town unhindered, remember lad, the enemy may well be out there so stay clear off the road'. Will nodded and laid his equipment on the floor of the hut, his canteen would be his only possession as he raced through the night on his mission to deliver Thom's intelligence he began his journey alongside the winding lane that led to his destination, the mud, slush and ice hindered his speed as he remembered Zeke's advice to stay clear off the tracks, the wet long grasses soon soaked the winter leggings that protected his breeches from the muck and grime, with the moonless night offering no visibility Will relied heavily on his instincts to direct him, three short miles by road but with no markers or pathway to direct him disorientation soon settled in his mind, short on breath and beginning to panic Will stopped a moment to gather his senses, his panting breath showed far and wide into the cold night air and nights like this spooked the best of men, his nerves got the better of him, turning left then right his direction now completely lost

Will slumped to the ground in despair. Taking deep breath to avoid blind panic he composed himself, his file relied on him to deliver this message, his company relied on him, for all he knew the future of the Kings army relied on him and visions of disaster befell about his mind, his comrades slaughtered for the lack of a sense of direction, his mind ran away with him as he rose to his feet. Keep calm and think he continued to mumble to himself, it's one way or another then as he made his final decision on his direction he heard it, a strike of a bell, thank god he spoke aloud to himself and listened again, gaining a bearing on the noise Will ran towards the sound, Princeton, it's faint lights glowed in the distance giving hope to his heart.

'Hold yourself right there' the picket watch yelled as Will came into their line of sight, a dozen or more muskets appeared over the barricade that defined the towns limits, 'Quickly' Will replied, 'come quickly' he blurted out his final words before stumbling exhausted towards the ground.

A lone dragoon, pistol drawn cantered his horse towards Will as he mustered enough strength to barely keep his footing, the dragoon circled around Will uncertain of the situation, 'For God's sake man take me to your commanding officer' Will cried as the Dragoon continued to circle around Will, 'From which Regiment do you hail?', '17th!' Will struggled to answer still short of breath

'Who's 17th?' the rider demanded to know unsure of Wills plight as he looked down with a doubtful stare, exhausted after the arduous race back to the town, 'Mawhood's 17th you cretinous fool, who else?'. The Dragoon continued to circle around, his pistol aimed at Will's head 'Right lad, on your feet and get walking' the rider ordered positioning his horse a few yards behind Will. Howe's end to the campaign had given a sense of security to the brigade stationed at Princeton, such a hue and cry from a fugitive appearing alone at the perimeter of the town, especially without his tunic to identify his Regiment gave concern to the perimeter guards that manned the post. With pistol still drawn the rider paced his mount steadily behind Will as he struggled to lift his feet the few yards distance to the guardhouse 'any trickery and I'll blow your god damn brains out' the Dragoon shouted aggressively.

On arrival at the guard post, the Dragoon spoke to his trooper sergeant, a middle aged man not dissimilar to Zeke with long wide side whiskers the rider dismounted and pushed Will towards the collective of men that formed the perimeter guard, 'claims he's from Mawhood's Regiment' the Dragoon announced 'but with no tunic or insignia I reckons he's a deserter myself'

Will protested 'A deserter? No you fool! take me to McPherson or Leslie' he struggled to free himself from the men that held him fast, 'Seems we've caught a feisty one eh?' the sergeant laughed 'put him in the lock up until we can vouch for his identity'

Will jerked his arms free of the two men aside him 'you don't understand' he snapped 'my friends are out there and the enemy is moving across these lands', 'The enemy you say? really now?' the Sergeant said patronisingly 'lad, the enemy has no presence in these parts and as long as we're here they never will, you've fled to the wrong side boy, the enemy has had its ass kicked firmly this time, they'll be no more damned rebellion here' the Sergeant continued and refused to listen to Will's pleas, 'You've got to let me go, I must reach McPherson' Will shouted, 'Let you go so you can abscond again you mean? I reckon there'll be a hanging for your desertion'. Will lost all reason to continue his pleas, a sharp kick in the groin left the Sergeant reeling, doubled up the man groaned and slumped to the floor, Will shook his arms free of the grasp of his captives and struck firmly the man to his left who tumbled backwards into the stacked boxes that formed the pickets barricade, turning sharply to make his escape Will felt a sharp blow to the back of his head and slumped to the hard floor.

Will woke with a start, an icy pail of water thrown over his head shocked him to his senses, shackled and bound to the cold heavy stone walls, the jailer towered over him, a huge collection of keys hung loosely from his wide leather belt, Will squinted, uncertain of the time of day he could only be sure that the night past was long over, how long had he been there he wondered in confusion

'Where am I?' Will asked answered by only a spiteful sneer from his captor as he turned to reveal an unwelcome sight obscuring the door way, 'Sergeant Skinner!' Will recognised the figure 'thank god it's you, I need to speak with urgency with Captain McPherson'. Skinner stooped down and held Wills jaw firmly in a tight grip preventing any speech from spoiling his game, 'My my boy' he sneered 'a charge of desertion eh? you have got yourself into a scrape haven't you now let's see how you takes to a night clamped in irons', Skinner pushed Wills face hard back against the thick stone and stood upright 'Sorry' he addressed the jailer 'I's may be wrong but he don't look like one of mine'. 'What?' Will objected aloud 'fetch Zeke, fetch Zeke Turner and he'll vouch for me' but the jailer only ignored his pleas slamming the door shut, the heavy lock turned shut sealing him inside, he attempted to stand but the short rusting chain restricted his movements 'Skinner!' he yelled 'Sergeant Skinner' but Skinner was gone, left alone he struggled with the chains that bound his limbs, shoeless the binding irons cut into his flesh causing him to wince in pain, the jailer reappeared at the small opening at the cell door, 'button it lad, else I'll thrash you myself', 'Do your worst' Will goaded back at him, 'do your fucking worst', the jailer jeered through the door bearing his rotten teeth in a crooked grin, 'You carry on lad, at this rate they'll be a hangin come noon'.

Within an hour the cell door creaked open once again, this time a more friendlier face Will could not have wished to see, Zeke entered the dark room accompanied by both Captains McPherson and Leslie, 'Jailer' McPherson spoke with authority 'release this man immediately'. The jailer removed his keys from his belt and fumbled through them to find the correct one to undo Will's leg irons, the cold iron lock snapped open and Will ran his cold palms over his grazed ankles, 'That bastard Skinner' Will cursed 'told the jailer he'd never seen me before so he did'. Zeke stooped besides his friend and ruffled his dirty lank hair, 'you need not worry friend' Zeke comforted him 'McPherson knows the truth now, Skinners been brought to task over this infringement of his authority, he's pleaded to McPherson that your dishevelled state hindered his judgement', 'Barefaced liar more like' Will replied 'he knew damn well who I was and said as much'. Zeke offered his hand to Will, helping back to his feet 'If anything has come to light from this it's Skinners bravado, McPherson knows his agenda now, one foot wrong and he'll lose his stripes for good'.

With a freezing dense fog enveloping the area Will was taken back to his billet and given some warming broth prepared by Dan Allen, having not taken food for well over a day Will slurped it down and tore a hunk of crust from a loaf that accompanied his meal mopping the lining of his bowl with it, 'Easy yourself lad' Zeke spoke 'and take your time, we don't need you sick for Captain McPherson requests your report on your encounter with the enemy', 'My report?' Will spoke slurping greedily the last drops of his meal from the wooden bowl it served in 'It was Thom that saw it not I'. Zeke calmed Will's concerns 'Don't worry yourself lad, the brigades staff officers will want to gather as much information as possible before making a judgement on what you both saw'. The stove that served the billet warmed a large pot of water of which Will used to wash the grime from his body, the filthy rag rinsed into the steaming water soothed his bones and brought life back into his shattered and exhausted body. Dressed and presentable the file presented itself at the towns courthouse and was led to a room that housed the general staff that were to interview the men for their personal accounts of what they'd seen, Zeke was the first to be called followed by Dan then Thom then finally Will, a staff Sergeant Major escorted him into the comfortably furnished room within the courthouse, 'hat off lad' he spoke and gave a friendly wink as Will stood firm in the presence of the high ranking officers, 'Name and rank?' the adjutant asked formally and noted it down in the ledger that documented every event the Regiment had faced, 'and in your own words' the adjutant continued 'your recollection of the events you witnessed'. Nervously Will spoke 'My name is William James Snow, a private in His Majesties 17th

Regiment and I have served to the best of my abilities these six years past' he continued clutching his felt hat tightly to his chest 'I was given to patrol the roads south of here on the night just past, we saw none travel in either direction until the sun dipped some below the horizon' when his account was interrupted by an unfamiliar officer marked by his facings from the 55th Regiment 'Yes, yes' he objected 'we've heard all this from your corporal now cut to the damn chase man'. Whoever this officer was his presence unnerved Will, several years younger than him, this man had been born to gentry, a swagger and arrogance of a type that soldiered for fun and japes and often belittled those he felt inferior of him.

Will cleared his throat and continued 'Once the horsemen had spied us they briefly conversed and pulled aside the lane moving into the woods adjacent to our outpost', he delivered his words when the officer interrupted once again 'for God's sake man, just tell us what you saw and heard else you bore us all to death damn you', 'Then I heard nothing Sir' Will replied, 'You see' the officer butted in, 'the mans a fool, I say still Washington's army is driven from these lands and his piffling rebellion crushed, with the Hessian brigade stationed at Trenton he dared not show himself else we whip him once and for all'. McPherson had sat silently during the investigation suddenly spoke up directing himself towards the officer of the 55th, 'I have served with honour with these men and I doubt they scaremonger as easily as you claim sir, now Private please continue' he added, Will spoke again 'Not much else to say really Sir, twas Thom Allen that closed upon the parties, I was too far away to see clearly enough to comment with any accuracy'. The arrogant young officer again butted in to Will's speech and huffed his frustrations in his opinion to a pointless exercise 'and yet again we have nothing substantial, If Washington has men of any number in this province I'll eat my damned hat, these spies you speak of are doubtless nothing more than common vagabonds and rogues'. Captain McPherson realised his efforts where in vain and drew the enquiry to a close 'we thank you Private for your help in this matter, you are dismissed from this enquiry pending light of further evidence'.

The Sergeant Major formally dismissed Will from the presence of the officers who gestured the formality of a salute back to him, escorted to the main doors the Sergeant Major consoled him with a few words "don't fret yourself lad, these aloof types are the ruin of us lately".

Will left the courthouse and merged with Zeke, Dan and Thom as they waited outside for him, 'Pointless eh then lad?' Zeke spoke having heard the same tale from both Allen brothers on their return, 'come now, let us rest ourselves of such incompetent leadership'. The four men made their way to the nearest tavern and spent a few hours quaffing ales and talking with fond memories of times past, with Christmas day almost upon then the army relaxed its curfews allowing merriment till the late hours, with experience of campaign soldering behind them the file knew when the time to leave a tavern had come, cheap ale and an abundance of soldiers often brought conflict between rivalries of Companies and Regiments alike, as candle light replaced the fading daylight Zeke announced the file should return to their billets for a quieter evening of entertainments in their own presence, the four settled their bills with the tavern keeper and slowly paced the streets back towards the house that billeted them.

Candles flickered in the window ledges of the few houses still in private occupancy and a few local businesses kept their doors open for some occasional passing trade but at after dusk most soldiers sought the business of taverns and alehouses only.

The file passed a tanners shop trading under contract to supply the army garrisoned within the town, the tanner stretched a hide tight against the frame he worked upon and the furnace glowed bright in the darkness illuminating the interior to those that chanced a curious glance inside, 'Wait' Thom spoke starkly stopping the file as it passed, 'that man in there' he pointed directing the file to his attentions 'I saw him in the woods, he met with the riders we saw', 'Are you sure?' Zeke asked, 'I'm so certain of it that I'd wage my life upon the fact' he answered. The four men stopped opposite the tannery whilst Thom raked his memory of the rendezvous he'd witnessed and studied the figure inside, aware of being watched the tanner glanced up giving Thom a clearer view of the man's face, 'He's definitely one of them and I recognise the stench of piss' he spoke with a wry smile

The tanner detected he was being watched and placed his tools on his workbench squaring up to the four, a man wearing a broad leather apron yelled across the street abruptly 'I'm closing, come back tomorrow if you want anything' and violently slammed the shutter doors closed, 'There's someone in there with him' Will announced 'and looks like a soldier'. Zeke dashed across the wide street 'Thom, Will get around the back quickly else he get a chance to escape us'. Thom and Will together ran the length of the long row looking for some alleyway that might lead to the rear of the tannery yard, a hundred yards passed before Thom found one 'In here' Thom yelled a few yards ahead of him, the two dashed down the brick lined alleyway and turned right on its junction, Thom made good progress through the narrow corridors that supplied the rear of the street businesses, at intervals the passageways broke for a doorway obscured in the darkness and after a distance doubling back equal to what they'd ran the two reached the proximity of the tannery, a door to a rear yard barred their entry so Thom quickly clambered up over the frame and dropped into the yard, with the bolted door unlocked Will accessed the yard which lay silent of occupancy, the tannery door stood firmly closed ahead of them both and Thom and Will stepped closer the workshop interior and banged hard on the door, 'Fuck off!' came the tanners voice from within 'we're closed'. 'Open up in the name of the King' Will chanced his arm at some authority, 'Else we'll smash the door in' adding a firmness to his voice. A moments silence befell the tannery then 'Wait there a moment' the tanner replied gruffly 'I'm coming, I'm coming' with a nervous hesitance in his voice. The bolt slid back from the premises door that kept the two out, 'I trust you have grounds for such fierce intrusion?' the tanner demanded to know, Thom drew his bayonet 'this is all the authority I'll be needing mate' and held the blade against the tanner's neck 'now where is he?'. The tanner recoiled with the blade pressed firmly against his throat 'I don't know what you're talking about' he protested 'there's no one else here but me', 'You lie' Will spoke 'We saw another in here now tell us and you'll live'. The Tanners eyes widened as Thom pressed the blade harder against his neck, 'I tell ye' the tanner insisted 'there's no other here now so clear out before I call for the guard'. Thom relaxed his blade against the man's throat and snarled, a false accusation against the file might cause them trouble none could afford as Howe's insistence of keeping the population on a favourable side limited a soldiers powers of search and an accusation of brutality would mean an official enquiry and potential courts martial, if he was lucky the accused might just face the lash, the unlucky ones faced the gallows. Without proof Will turned dejected back to the yard the two had entered but the yard door was closed not as he remembered it, a quick dash across the cobbled yard he yanked open the gate and peered along the length of the alleyway, a figure ran away in the distance, the figure he's seen a moment ago inside the tanners workshop, 'Here' he shouted back to Thom 'over here!'. Thom smiled sweetly at the tanner and paused a moment, the tanner knowing his rouse was over smiled back knowing imminently what was to come. Thom, and his brother Dan had both grown up without ceremony, with no education or refinement life for the Allen brothers was hard and matters often settled quickly and the only way they knew, Thom clenched his fist and dealt a harsh blow to the tanners ribs, doubled in pain the tanner slumped to the floor knocking over a pail of piss used to cure the hides, 'I never could stand a liar' he quipped as he stepped over the crumpled man and raced after Will. Thom ran towards the distant end of the alleyway, the darkness and heavy fog obscured much of the visibility in an otherwise unlit narrow alleyway, 'Will!' Thom cried out 'Where the hell are you?'. Will emerged from the far end of the alley clutching his jaw, 'bastard laid me flat out' he spoke his head bowed in regret at losing his catch, 'Where is he now?' Thom spoke keen to pursue the absconder, 'over the damn wall' Will replied 'and I took kick in the face for it too'. Thom laid his hand on Will's shoulder 'don't worry mate, I think we've enough evidence to call the guard on our tanner fellow'.

The two walked slowly the path back the front of the tanners yard, Zeke in his wisdom had alerted the guard on hearing the commotion inside, on the broad street that ran the length of the town soldiers gathered outside the tannery eager to glimpse the attention inside. The scuffle was soon over, with a swift boot to the barred door and a rush inside, with the tanner bound hands and feet the guard dragged him unceremoniously outside, standing domineeringly over his agonised body still twisted in pain from Thom Allen's blow. One of the guards rifled through the pockets of the heavy winter coat that hung from the splintered door, pulling a pistol and small ledger of documents from deep within and being illiterate as most were, the soldier handed the documents to his Sergeant who quickly thumbed through the pages, grinning, the sergeant nodded towards the file, 'you've done well lads' he smirked 'looks like this one has some answerin to do'. Not for the want of trying this man offered no resistance as the guard led him away to be questioned on his happenstance of such documents, whatever they contained the file would never know for the tannery remained secured and under an armed guard over the next few days.

The days up to Christmas were idled away as light sprinklings of snow dusted the hard frozen ground, other than the occasional town patrol the file was not required for duty giving ample time for the men to spend their time as they wished, insisting on his file keep their equipment in good order encouraged them to keep from temptations that easily led many a good soldier astray. As this turbulent year drew to a close Will reflected on his times in the colonies, a little older and a fair bit wiser certainly wiser than when the company first landed at Boston a year past. Zeke often complained at the incompetence of the army's leadership abilities, Howe had replaced Gage, now rumours circulated of Cornwallis being in line to replace him, would this coming year crush this rebellion finally Will asked to himself, Zeke seemed to think not, our army is too concentrated he claimed, Washington and his Generals knew a direct confrontation against the Kings army would end in disaster, the past summers campaign proved that certainly despite being of pyrrhic victories.

This massed presence of soldiers secured the immediate area but south of the townships and across the Delaware River the enemy roamed free, free to recruit, reequip and harass citizens loyal to the crown and in Zeke's opinion the Hessian presence should be used firmly to end this rebellion, the crown chooses to empty its coffers on a mercenary army then it should use it to its full capability instead of pussy footing about. Hessians or mercenaries as Zeke referred to them, a different language, culture and breed, with their tall appearance exaggerated by high bear skin caps, their long moustaches groomed to amplify their proportions struck a chord of inhumanity to those that faced them in battle, a uniform made a man the same as his peers Zeke said but these men looked total and absolute clones of each other and most importantly they favoured the bayonet, the stark fear of any they faced, a bullet often lead to a quickened end to a battle field wound, sharp steel however brought an twisting and agonising death to those that suffered it.

For now though as Christmas approached, the garrisoned army rested at Princeton in peace, twelve hundred men, well armed and well trained protected this town and three hundred more garrisoned with the Hessians at Trenton, for now it seemed Colonel Mawhood and his headquarters at Princeton had good reason to stand his men down. The file settled into the tavern opposite their billet, candle lit and enhanced by the roaring fire that occupied the centre of the large room that served host to dozens of redcoated soldiers keen to share time off duty with their comrades. The empty tavern soon filled as company after company was dismissed from duty after a brief inspection by their respective commanding officers, Captains Leslie and McPherson invited the men that filled the ranks to raise good cheer on their accounts and obliged each man with a shilling extra in their pay.

However, the clear starry night above Princeton gave no clue to the events unfolding a few miles south across the Delaware River.

Washington's army had massed on the far shores opposite Trenton town, unbeknown to the few Hessian sentry's that kept a half eye on the approaches to the town two and a half thousand men, armed and matched for combat waited patiently for the moment to cross the Delaware that divided the lands controlled by the crown and those occupied by this secreted army, despite a handful of minor skirmishes with rebel militia the commanders of the Kings army gave no concern to any enemy presence deemed real or not, but Washington's spies had done their work well, those unlucky sentries stuck to their posts after drawing their lots poorly had little knowledge of the massed gatherings less than a mile away. The freezing Delaware River, in places no wider than a hundred yards, would give the rebel army a swift advantage to launch a surprise attack on the garrison that made merry in Trenton town on Christmas night. In the small hours of the 26[th,] General Washington authorised the crossing of his army a mile north at McConkey's ferry, the shortest point of crossing, inside half an hour the army massed ready to strike a critical blow into the heart of the Colonel Johann Rall's Hessian brigade.

At Princeton, these events passed as much unknown as they did to the Hessians who were about to face the dogged determination of the continental army desperate to secure a victory in an otherwise lost war. Back at the tavern, the file consumed jug after jug of frothed heavy ale and similarly did every red coated soldier that took leave in the licensed inns and taverns that operated in this prosperous township, settled for the night the atmosphere raised the good spirits of those lucky enough to enjoy the hospitality of their hosts. With midnight passed the men wished a healthy and fortunate year ahead as the final days of the year approached, McPherson and Leslie entered and placed a guinea in the hands of the landlord providing for the remainder of the night ale that flowed freely thanks to the kind goodness of the gentlemen officers that stood good for the taverns bills. On hearing two bells Zeke stood to his feet and finished the last of his tankard and announced his retirement back to the billets that homed them, 'Wait a moment' Will spoke as he struggled to pull his tunic through his arms, the drink had affected him worse than he'd thought, 'Stay a while my friend' Zeke spoke 'there's no need to end your enjoyment on my account'. The Allen brothers bolstered Zeke's words insisting on another jug of ale, 'Aye Will' Thom spoke 'the night is yet young and we have no duties on the morrow, at least allow yourself one more drink before you retire?', with Zeke's approval Will resumed his seat and poured generously into the empty vessels that littered the tavern table, Zeke offered a coin and slid it across towards the three, 'With my pleasure lads but not too late mind, this Washington fellow has a strange behaviour that may catch us unawares yet'. Zeke's final words drowned under the noise of the tavern, with a gentle smile he bid farewell to his comrades and made for the tavern door leaving Dan yelling above the din to attract the attentions of the serving girls.

Over the next few hours the taverns of Princeton town quietened as copious volumes of drink ran its effect on the men that consumed much over the past eight hours, citizen and soldier alike slumped and slumbered where they fell leaving fewer and fewer to spend the last of their coin until in likeness to their purses the barrels ran dry. The last of the red coats turned out by the landlord stumbled onto the cold streets, a few pockets of soldiers roamed the streets unhindered desperately looking for a tavern that lay its doors open, for Will, Thom and Dan enough was enough and they slowly wandered the streets and back alleys towards their billets, If their luck was in Zeke might have lit the fire warming the room they dwelled within but being this drunk the nights chill would go unnoticed. The three men found their way to the billets, Zeke sat besides the fireside, lit as the three had hoped and the glow of the flames illuminated his weathered features as he typically sat with his pipe grasped between his teeth, his long hair dangled loosely around his shoulders, like a paternal figure Zeke had prepared the room in readiness for their return, hot water boiled steadily by the fireside grate, 'Tea?' he asked 'It'll sober you's up some for the morning' he added already pouring the pot into four cups warming from the heat of the fireside. Swigging the warm drink sweetened with molasses Will removed his felt hat and tunic and lay upon the mattress that served as his bed, inside minutes slumber had consumed him, Zeke leant over to cover him with the issued woollen blanket and grinned, 'sleep well lads, you've earned it . . .'

The commotion outside woke Will from his late morning slumber with a start, dizzy from the effects of alcohol he stood to his feet as Zeke peered through the dirty window and wiped the grime from the glass panes. Three frantic riders galloped down the street steering towards Mawhood's headquarters waving their hats with a hue and cry 'Call out, call out!' they shouted as they rode past 'Trenton is lost! Call out, call out!' as they galloped along the street. Zeke snatched his tunic and opened the door stretching his neck far down the street as dozens of inquisitive troops poured onto the street seeking a better vantage point to the incident as Will slipped his boots on and followed Zeke onto the street, outside the headquarters the riders dismounted and hurried towards the court house, Dan Allen peered over the shoulders of the two as they waited for confirmation of the riders news, 'What's the commotion?' he asked rubbing his bleary eyes, 'They say Trenton is lost' Will answered 'but it can't be can it? An entire brigade?' he spoke turning to Zeke looking for the answer. Zeke kept his eyes on the courthouse looking for clues to the events that shook those that heard it as the riders raced into the town, 'Get yourselves presentable' he instructed 'we'll be on high alert now until this news can be verified'.

Will scraped the remnants of last night's fire from the basket grate and prepared the fire afresh, striking his flints against fresh tinder and kindling the fire leapt to life once again, warming his hands against the licking flames he looked down to his scared palm of his opened hand, having never properly healed to regain full use a thick scar ran the length of his index finger to his wrist, lost in the moment Will gave a thought to the events in Ireland and Keira, the girl who had with all her beauty and charm captured his heart, deep in thought he closed his eyes and smiled to himself. Consumed in memories he winced in pain as the rising flames leapt through his fingers, Will clenched his fist in pain drawing his hand from the fire bringing him sharply to the moment at hand, 'Get to it Will lad' Zeke snapped 'there's no time for daydreaming, there's work to be done'.

The file loaded their equipment and formed on the street outside, Sergeant Skinner formed the company along the hard packed earth that served as the road, 'Corporal Turner' he barked 'present yourself to me immediately'. Skinner had a habit of exhibiting his authority for the benefit of others and in doing so demeaned those he addressed but for those familiar with him it only served to draw further contempt towards his leadership abilities, Mathias Skinner was rapidly running out of allies. The Sergeant and his Corporal made towards the brigades headquarters and took receipt of the Regiments orders, on return Zeke informed his file the company was to form a holding line half a mile outside Princeton, squadrons of light dragoons would probe deep into the countryside to seek verification of the earlier reports.

The armoury doors unlocked and swung wide open, the provost guard formed the companies ready to take receipt of the muskets that previously had been locked away under Howe's direct orders, the issuance seemed to take forever as the crowns clerks insisted every man would need to sign for the weapon assigned to him yet after an hour only a handful of muskets had been reissued and none yet took receipt of powder or shot. For McPherson, these delays proved too much, mounting his horse both he and Captain Leslie rode to the head of the queue yelling at the clerks to hurry the issuance of arms, the clerks pleaded the logistics of accountability but McPherson demanded away with this stupid bureaucracy in an urgency such as this. 'Damn your ledgers sir' he snapped 'there's a war to be fought and god help me if I turn my men out ill prepared and we lose this town'. The clerk submitted to McPherson's authority and reluctantly closed his ledgers mumbling to himself in doing so, the armoury soon emptied as soldiers clambered for their firearms eager to face the enemies and the sealed cases of ammunition smashed open with axe and bayonet distributed freely amongst the men. Filling his cartridge box Will placed a hand full of extra shot into his deep tunic pockets and fell back in line as Captain

McPherson paced along his company his officers sword unsheathed and ready. Zeke was in his element, ready to face the enemy directly, man to man, musket to musket, he oozed confidence in the presence of fear from those newer recruits yet to face the enemy directly. The majority of the brigade marched proudly along the road that led to Trenton leaving a small detachment to guard the town, guided into position the companies formed line and waited . . . and waited but no enemy was to come.

Soon, some began to question the accuracy of the riders that first raised the alarm earlier that day and by noon the dampness had began to affect the powder issued to the infantry, 'We'll be relying on the bayonet alone at this rate, this dampness will ruin our musket volleys' Dan commented but Zeke wasn't to complain, the bayonet brought a quick and decisive conclusion to a battle, it relied on a man's skill at arms rather than slog it out waiting for a bullet with one's name on to strike its mark. Standing idle in the winter elements took its toll on the lines of men, in the urgency to field his army Mawhood had neglected to distribute the mornings ration, those with sense consumed what little they'd saved from the previous night but in these conditions the sustenance gained didn't last long, those freezing and hungry, fell faint onto the hard frozen ground only to be man handled back into line, exposure to the driving icy winds reduced the effectiveness of the ranks to almost nil and after several hours waiting it now seemed obvious the enemy was not to come, the light dragoons that probed deep into the countryside finally returned with grave news, the town of Trenton had indeed been lost to General Washington's continental army and all but a handful of defenders captured. This news unsettled the troops that waited nervously for their enemy to appear, rumours passed amongst the ranks of an enemy numbering some ten thousand strong but Zeke quickly dismissed these as wild exaggerations, 'an enemy of that magnitude would be upon us by now and we'd all be in flight back to New York if this were true' he assured those fretting on this unfounded gossip, Will trusted Zeke with his life as he seemed to know by instinct his enemies movements even before his they had made them 'whether it be a Frencher or a Spaniard, a Rebel or an Indian, all men behave the same on the field of battle, the trick is' Zeke commented 'is to do it to him, before he does it to you'. In serving more than twenty years under the Kings colours, the skills required at outwitting one's enemy were now finely tuned, a few more men like Zeke Turner and this war would've been won months ago.

The brigade drew back to Princeton under cover of the mounted dragoons and heavy artillery drawn up to protect the flank should any attack arise, eerily the sloping ground that lay afore Princeton town stood silent in a ghostly quiet, perhaps Will wondered as he glanced back across the fields, they'd been cheated of claiming the mortality of those that massed upon them that day.

On return to Princeton the company drew hot rations prepared by auxiliary troops, salt pork and beans supplemented with half a loaf of sour bread each, the ration scheduled to reinforce Trenton would not now be needed much to the welcome benefit of the garrison at Princeton. On standing orders, the Regiments that constituted the defending brigade waited anxiously for news, that night hardly a soul slept for all night riders came and went with intelligence gathered from the surrounding area or fresh orders from Cornwallis and Howe's headquarters.

Over the next few days hundreds of troops poured into Princeton supporting Mawhood's brigade in anticipation for retaking Trenton from the continental army, the humiliation struck home to the senior commanders of the Kings army, caught with their pants down as Zeke called it, this term amused Will greatly who sniggered at Zeke's bold comedic statements. New Years eve came and passed without incident, devoid of any celebrations all available troops stood on high alert speculating their enemies whereabouts, this uneasy standoff unnerved the rank and file, Zeke spoke at length to a dragoon who'd daily patrolled the roads towards the small towns of Maidenhead and Allenstown and relayed the information weeding out the gossip from the truth as best he could.

Eight hundred Hessians had been lost to the enemy on Christmas night, the handful of fugitives that had escaped scattered wildly, panicking any of their kind they came across and Zeke had predicted correctly that General Washington had yet to end his campaign as Howe had done much to the cost of the garrison at Trenton and Earl Cornwallis had been hastily recalled to the line cancelling his plans to return to England as Zeke explained the significance of the losses at Trenton to the wider picture.

This once ragged and rebellious militia, with its antiquated weaponry had developed and developed well into a now highly disciplined force capable of delivering a few shrewd knocks towards what was considered the most formidable army of its age, in this environment well disciplined troops counted for little if their leadership failed to properly estimate their enemies potential and although the Kings army had ended the summer campaign in full control of New York and the Manhatten peninsular it had come at a cost, a cost Will appreciated only too well for he'd seen the dead, and yet more disturbing he'd seen those maimed and invalided from useful service, sent to spend their days begging in the filthy streets of the garrison towns they had enlisted in, the lucky ones might gain some charity in the garrison hospitals in London but most stood to face poverty beyond comprehension, these colonials had more to fight for and fight they did, a penny a day was a redcoats only reward but for those men who fought for their freedoms and liberties the rewards were much, much higher. The Continental army gains at Trenton, lifted the moral of Washington's ranks to new heights, after losing New York and control of the Jerseys and on the verge of collapse this surprise victory inspired any doubters that Washington's army could fight the crown, and win.

These recent events had worried Zeke, he relayed his fears to the file, the hesitance of the crown army to deploy into the field and regain Trenton would give further confidence towards the rebel army who now bolstered their numbers to almost unprecedented figures and Howe's general staff only dallied and stalled unsure on the enemies dispositions, finally on the first day of the new year the brigade received detailed instructions of the plans to retake Trenton from the enemy, the sooner the better Zeke argued and although the severity of the blow to the Hessian garrison had been slight, the impact was with the benefit to Washington's success at leadership and command, his troops, bloodied and battered after being driven from Manhattan fought ragged and bare foot with broken and antiquated arms as seen in the plight of those that had given their surrender at Fort Washington, 'this is not a game of sport' Zeke continued to state his opinion, 'the army should smash em, like we smashed the Frenchies, once and for all'.

On the first day of the new year Colonel Mawhood gave his orders to his junior commanders, all companies of the 17th still fit for deployment would remain as a rear guard in the town, 'fit for deployment?' Will thought to himself, the grenadier company under Brereton could barely field a dozen men and the light company had draw the last of the replacements that arrived from England, disease, sickness and the occasional desertion had reduced the line companies to half standing at best, already a composite company, McPherson's ranks had been under strength since Staten Island and even now it held less than twenty men and none of the other companies feared any better. Captain Leslie and McPherson however, keen for adventure would accompany the advance column as it moved towards Trenton, both high in their horses saddle they showed dogged excitement as the lines began to move slowly towards its destination.

Desperate for reinforcements Colonel Mawhood's 17th, 30th and 55th Regiments would remain at Princeton acting as its rear guard over the brigades baggage and pay chests whilst Cornwallis would drive his forces along with General Grant's division into Trenton and push the enemy south into the Delaware River, the file watched from their billets as the endless lines of infantrymen passed through the town, theirs has been a forced march over night from Brunswick and over five thousand men passed through the town to finally merge with Grant's force before advancing onwards to Trenton.

The weather had turned unseasonably warm over night and hours of torrential rain soaked into the already water logged ground and the eleven miles distance between Princeton and Trenton would take longer than expected to travel after the night heavy rains had churned the tracks and turnpikes into a sea of mud and barely a half mile outside the town the heavy cannon and artillery limbers sank up to their axles in a thick rain sodden clay. Men heaved and pushed in an attempt to loosen the guns from a terrain that refused to give them up, in observing the slow moving advance column the abandoned Princeton the streets seemed empty by comparison now no longer inhabited by the sea of red, finally a degree of normality returned to the citizens of Princeton. The dark winter clouds failed to lift on that early January day and later what might be mistaken for a storms thunder gave an indication of the events south at Trenton, both citizen and soldier alike stopped in their tracks as the distant rumble of cannon broke the silence across the fields between the two armies. 'Give em bloody hell' someone cried as the dampened spirits of the troops was suddenly lifted on knowing the assault to retake Trenton had finally begun, over the next few hours a few wounded arrived back at Princeton and eager for reports, the garrisoned soldiers pressed them excitedly for news of the attack, Zeke, Will, Thom and Dan however had seen too much bloodshed already to revel in accounts of such butchery occurring to the south. Amongst the trail of wounded rode a frantic Captain McPherson, his ride exhausted after tearing along the road back to Princeton, beside him slumped in his saddle was Leslie, his youthful face splattered now with congealed blood, company men raced towards the two as McPherson babbled his words incoherently as Will tried to make sense of the confusion.

Cornwallis has sent he two officers back to Princeton with orders for Mawhood to move south early on the morrow, just a mile south of safety the two officers had joked amongst each other of the route Washington's army was now in when with no warning a rifled bullet found its target in Captain Leslies belly and tumbled him from his horse, McPherson alone bar a few wounded that trailed the road hastily placed Leslie back into his saddle and made as fast as they could for Princeton and help as Leslie spilled his blood from his awful wound. Orderlies delicately lowered the officer from his sweating horse and carried his unconscious body hastily towards the officer's quarters, the file stood silenced with the sight, this young officer of wealthy and aristocratic stock now twisted and contorted as the orderlies rushed him to a surgeon, death it seemed had no preference. Will turned to the few soldiers that had returned with the riders, his expression gave away any question he might have asked, the soldier, his elbow shattered by a bullet told his rendition of events, the enemy was proficient with rifles, although slower to load than the more common muskets had an accuracy and range to give a serious edge over the British who still preferred massed volley fire over disciplined aimed shooting, the thin woods south and west of Princeton has provided an opportune chance to pick off a chosen target, 'wrong place and wrong time I guess' the wounded soldier spoke flippantly before he shuffled off seeking assistance for his wounds.

Later, the ranks enquired after Captain Leslie's condition at all available opportunities and tempers rose in response to this ungentlemanly conduct acted upon a well loved and well respected officer, with his memory jogged, Will recalled the times at Boston under Leslie's temporary command and remembered them fondly, despite being born worlds apart Captain Leslie bonded well with the men under his ward and few had an ill word to say of him. That night Zeke caught a chance to speak with McPherson and relayed the demise of his brethren officer infuriating all that heard it, their blood was up and raring to face the enemy for retribution. Cornwallis' column had encountered the enemy initially a few miles south, with a delaying action the continentals army harassed the advance enough to slow the drive into Trenton, with the British guns brought forward any resistance from the enemy was soon swept away and by sun down Washington's generals withdrew their troops through the streets of the town they had taken the previous week, the General gave orders to postpone the drive into Trenton with the days light fading fast, a reprieve perhaps for the enemy but for now the mood amongst the redcoats facing the rebels was optimistic, with a dogged determination this days work could be complete tomorrow.

The few heavy guns operated by the rebels on the far banks of the Delaware boomed long into the evening harassing the British advance as they began to occupy Trenton, advance scouts and Hessian Jaegers suggested Washington's force unable to cross the river and now lay trapped by Cornwallis. The enemy began their hasty fortifications of the trenches east of Trenton. And Cornwallis waited and watched.

January 3rd 1776, the dawn broke bright and cloudless, the previous night brought a heavy frost to the fields between these two towns contested by rebel and loyalist, whilst Will's file slept safely in their billets orders arrived from Cornwallis for Mawhood's remaining troops to advance towards Trenton and press home their final assault to end Washington's ambitions on the Jerseys. Colonel Mawhood followed his instruction to the letter and fell in the 17th and 55th Regiments leaving the 40th to guard the brigade's wagons and baggage, this would be a day of glory and the 17th was given the honour to lead the advance to face the enemy. The companies formed up outside Nassau Hall which formed part of the college buildings, an impressive structure of immense magnitude Princeton College until now had been strictly off limits to the enlisted men. Like most in the colonies, Princeton's buildings featured large modern renaissance styling, nothing like the cramped poverty of his hometown where everything was reused and reclaimed for use again once a building fell into ruin, the halls architecture dominated the township, spacious, modern and clean, a symbolic icon perhaps to this new world's ideals. Junior ranks scurried between the companies as they formed position ready to advance from the town towards the enemy, Zeke fell the file in line, 'Today's the day lads, we'll give it to em' he spoke buoyantly, anticipation clear in his voice. Zeke's announcement brought dryness to Wills throat, fumbling for his canteen he swigged the cool water and rinsed it about his mouth, 'On a day like this lads' Zeke commented 'they'll be issuing extra rum and it won't be to take the chill from your bones either'. Opposite the hall, several soldiers stripped off their Regimental red tunics and unloaded small barrels from the back of a hand cart working through the lines of soldiers, a long iron ladle plunged deep into the barrel and drew a generous volume of grog for each man as he stood patiently in line, Will held the ladle to his dry lips and slurped the contents down thirstily, he coughed, tavern rum this wasn't, this was rough army rum known more commonly as grog and it burned the throat all the way down to the stomach. Along with the rum the company took its days food ration early, tucking a pound of bread and some strips of greasy pork inside his knap sack Will pulled his musket onto his shoulder and stood back into the company lines, 'Looks like we'll be in the field tonight' Zeke spoke 'best make your snap last lads for who knows when we'll be fed again'.

The head of the column uncased the Kings colours and the drummers began to beat time as Sergeants yelled bringing the column to attention, Captain McPherson exhausted from a sleepless night at Leslie's bedside led the company from the front, his sword drawn and ready to face the enemy, to some his preference today to march on foot with his troops was born from his trauma the day previous but to those that knew him, McPherson wanted vengeance, today he would fight as a soldier side by side with his men as he had done gallantly at Fort Washington. Will counted the church bells, five strikes as the column fixed its bayonets, shouldered arms and moved towards the main army south unknowing to the events outside Trenton that took an unpredictable turn against the British.

Over night General Washington had stealthily withdrawn his army from the fortifications and trenches right under the noses of the British, whilst a handful of volunteers instructed by Washington to fool the British into thinking the defenders were hard fortifying their position, his main force stole away and pressed north toward Princeton hoping to catch its few defenders unawares. The road south forked roughly a mile from Princeton town, the main leading towards Maidenhead and Trenton, the left splinter sunken largely from view led a long and winding lane towards a small collection of dwellings at Sandtown, It was Washington's plan to catch the British unawares, take Princeton and more importantly the pay chests housed there in. However, unaware to Washington's own intelligence Mawhood now advanced his two Regiments and several wagons containing provisions along the road, the two armies destined to collide. The thin tree's obscured the column of the danger that progressed towards them and with high spirits keen to avenge Captain Leslie's demise soldiers joked amongst each other on whether the bayonet or a bullet brought the most agony to its recipient, 'Sergeant Skinner' Zeke called out 'perhaps you'd like to remind us of your heroics in the battlefield and enlighten us all to how to deal best with our enemies' he joked, those close chuckled as Skinner shuffled on pretending not to have heard Zeke's sarcasm.

Washington's Continental army that advanced towards Princeton outmatched Mawhood's 17th and 55th Regiments at odds over four to one, led by General Hugh Mercer, highland born and a highly competent officer having served well in the seven years war against the French and General John Sullivan, the third son of an Irish immigrant and a former loyalist together led five thousand men towards Princeton with designs on its prize. Between them stood Mawhood's brigade accompanied by a squadron of mounted Dragoons, the column steadied its pace along the turnpikes with the churned mud now frozen solid from the night's previous hard frost, three hours into the march the sun reluctantly rose above the horizon bringing a little warmth to those exposed to the cold night air.

The Dragoon troopers in needing to keep their mounts warm galloped back and forth along the slowly advancing column and as the dawn exposed the terrain enough to outline the rise of the landscape to the east, for sports a few Dragoons galloped their steeds towards its rising summit. Will watched the riders race each other playfully then suddenly and without warning the riders pulled up their steeds and dismount, pointing towards the Dragoons Will spoke up observing the commotion on the brow of the hill, 'Over there, there's something wrong' he spoke as heads turned and looked for a better sight into the low light. The panicked Dragoons remounted their rides and galloped back towards the column, the heavy hooves thundered on the hard solid earth as they reached

Colonel Mawhood and his staff, all eyes watched as a Trooper Sergeant relayed his findings frantically gesturing with outstretched arms. Several riders peeled away from the column and sped back towards Princeton for the handful of Dragoons could well make the difference between saving and losing Princeton to the enemy. Zeke stepped from the column and conversed with Skinner and McPherson, unsure of numbers the enemy had been sighted over the rise and through the thin woods, If Mawhood could alert the garrison at Princeton quickly they might have enough time to prepare a reasonable defence with the few guns left behind and hold off the enemy until reinforcements could be mustered from Cornwallis' army still camped at Trenton, for now though the essence was with the 17th to delay the enemies advance, this would be a hard fought action and one where heroes would be made.

McPherson gave his orders for the company to wheel left to face the enemy, at this stage there was a good chance the Continental army had not yet discovered the columns movements so the ranks needed to act fast. Most soldiers hated drill manoeuvres, left turn, right turn, about turn, the drill sergeants would yell repeatedly, it was however times like this when a disciplined soldier would gladly have shook the hand of the very man who taught the disciplined manoeuvres during his initial training period.

With pinpoint accuracy the remainder of the column turned in formation and began its double back towards his enemies target of Princeton town, it had taken three hours for the column to travel this far, with the Regiments drummers beating double time the ranks could reach its destination inside one, giving the ranks of the 17th precisely that amount of time to delay the enemy enough to defend the town.

The Dragoons that sighted the enemy had given a sketchy account of the enemy strength and numbers, assuming it only a probe the 17th turned to face an enemy if though of equal strength, the fiery red coated soldiers felt this day they could match the very best Washington had to offer. Preoccupied with the sighting east Colonel Mawhood blundered his regiment towards Mercers secreted brigade, as the red coats poured across the stone bridge that marked the limits of the town proper, Mercer brought up his skirmishers ready to engage the British to hit them hard before they could reinforce the garrison at Princeton. Mercer raced his troops parallel with the red coats using the low ground as cover from Mawhood's view and snapped their rifles towards the British line but Charles Mawhood was a clever soldier, utilising his command he gave orders for the companies of the 17th Regiment to engage the enemy guns unlimbering on the hillock east, knowing if the artillery had opportunity to unleash its canister shot against unprotected troops the ranks would be decimated on the open road. To the left of the turnpike lay a small orchard surrounded by a stone wall, McPherson signalled his company to quickly muster in its cover whilst the remainder of the Regiment caught up and reinforced it ready to engage the enemy head on. The heavy breaths of sweating soldiers mixed with the cold January air as troops dropped their packs ready to engage the guns trained on the departing column, the company merged through the orchard just as General Mercers troops arrived on the opposite side and laid down a barrage towards the advancing sea of steel, branches splintered and bullets thumped into flesh as Mercers riflemen found their mark on the advancing opportune targets, the British line stalled as both lines exchanged volleys into each other and although extremely effective at long range the rifles used by the continental army were slow to load and had no fixings for bayonets, being now this close, the odds where in favour of the redcoats as they rose from their cover and charged the low stone wall sheltering Mercers men. Zeke gave the order to charge forward as McPherson stood by his side, 'For Leslie!' someone cried 'Aye! for Leslie' yelled another as the company charged across the orchard and hit hard Mercers defenders that bravely but unwisely remained for hand to hand fighting, a splash of red and Mercer's defenders lay slumped against the wall they sought protection from, now in full flight the rebels fled in disarray towards the summit of the slopes that overlooked the orchard, like wild devils the redcoats pursued their foes yelling and screaming their own battle cries hot on the heels of their prey, any man that stumbled stood little chance of evading the most gruesome of deaths, skewered like pigs they pleaded for their lives, overrun they twitched in agony as the fierce red coats plunged their blades into them again and again, although a terrible sight to see Will ran with the pack plunging his steel into any who fell, theirs this day was a dirty work.

McPherson slowed the advance as it staggered up towards the summit of the hill, this next assault would need a discipline, everyman was needed to hit the enemy in coordination to drive them from the field, glancing left and right Will saw the ferocity of those amongst him, bayonets dripping with fresh blood, indeed a sickening sight. He caught his breath as the line formed ready for the next push, 'Charge' McPherson yelled and in unison the men of the company gave again their battle cries, 'For Leslie' over and over again as the line of steel pressed hard towards the enemy as it fled from the field. General Mercer mounted high on his steed desperately attempted to rally his troops but all in vain, in full flight the situation was hopeless as fleeing soldiers cast away their arms and anything that might hinder their escape, Mercer circled his mount yelling his men to stand and face their enemies 'Stand fellow Americans! Stand for the sake of freedom and liberty?' he called aloud as the advancing redcoats discharged a volley towards him, his horse stumbled taking Mercer tumbling to the frozen ground and in seconds the red coats were upon him.

In moments this brave generals life would end, stumbling and disoriented from his fall, Mercer flung his broken sword towards the charging British, a noble gesture Will thought but one that would see no quarter for him now, stabbed and clubbed by a mass of blood thirsty men circling him Hugh Mercer lay dying from a dozen mortal wounds. With Mercers demise the last of his men broke and fled, the tide of red that washed across the orchard slaughtered without mercy any who pleaded for quarter on this day, as junior officers desperately tried to muster some resistance to the onslaught but this tide was unstoppable as in turn they were overrun on the point of the bayonet. Beyond the last few riflemen offering resistance stood the enemies guns, positioned high upon the summit, their capture would be considered a trophy of war and McPherson advanced his company keenly upon them with a renewed vigour and ferocity whilst scattered across the field the panicked remnants of resistance ran in all directions as the 17th poured volley after volley into their dissipating lines.

Ahead now, lay the undefended limbers of the enemy, McPherson advanced his company towards them with designs to turn them on the fugitives as they fled the field, heaving the limbers around the cannon belched its fire over the heads of the fleeing rebels racing towards the woods for shelter, 'Load it with canister' Zeke shouted to the gunners 'and mash em up'. Behind the British advance lay a wake of death, the frosty ground etched with crimson leeching from the bodies of the dead and dying, Will leant against his musket exhausted from the heroic action the few had achieved against the overwhelming odds they'd faced. Ahead, the enemy now in total disarray melted into the woods for shelter and Mawhood had finally caught the advance and instructed the fractured line back into formation ready for the next push. In a macabre gesture the returning redcoats wandered through the carnage they'd created, ignoring the dying, jokes and rum were shared as they trod over the twisted bloody mess beneath their feet and regrouped in the orchard, the 17th mustered all but four men, the enemy however had lost well over thirty and more significantly several high ranking figures of the revolution. Captain McPherson briefly met with Mawhood who personally congratulated him on this epic action, Mercers force had been decimated to practical ruin but this day was far from over yet as Washington poured thousands of men into the area.

McPherson returned to his company in high spirits, his orders were to merge with Captain Clayton's company and engage the enemy wherever they found them after a fresh body of rebels had been sighted moving towards them from the direction of Princeton and now with fire in their hearts the two companies chased after the remnants of Mercers force who's flight had caused disarray in the advancing rebel reinforcements.

The confusion of battle fogs the mind of clarity as a vision of chaos littered the land, in circumstances like these a man's behaviour becomes erratic, screams and cries haunted the air, the dying called for their loved ones and those already embraced by death lay in peaceful silence, Will observed in the distance a man who's entrails littered behind him stumble forwards, fall then rise, only to fall again. 'We shoot horse for less' Zeke commented.

Gun smoke drifted across the landscape, like a heavy fog but pungent in the air, the stench of death filled the nostrils, 'Upsee lads' Zeke spoke noting McPherson and Clayton draw their swords, 'Looks like we've for more'. Will clutched his musket and levelled it at his shoulder, the line of steel now faced a new enemy as they appeared in range, 'Fire' Zeke shouted as the company gained momentum towards the enemy, the field enveloped in smoke and fire as forty muskets spat hot lead towards the enemy lines. Facing a bayonet charge, the rebel lines already unnerved by Mercers route threw down their arms and fled barely offering any return of fire. As the advance closed the distance towards the enemy lines Sullivan's artillery opened up with a tirade of heavy fire, the advance stalled as men slumped to the earth with a dull thud and now desperate Washington threw everything towards the 17th in an attempt to stem his army's route. Under Mawhood's orders the 55th Regiment now relived of its commitment to battle hastily returned to Princeton to assist the 40th Regiment in their defence of the town leaving the few men of the 17th to harass the enemy as long as they could. Seeking a temporary refuge from the artillery barrage the companies sheltered beneath the slope, McPherson consulted with Clayton on the best opportunity of escape for Washington now drew his troops closer to the orchard and the 17th's wagons. Will fumbled his ammunition pouch and felt inside, just eight rounds, the company would retire in sections each laying a volley to cover the retreat of the next, 'Prime your muskets' McPherson ordered his men back into action as the two companies formed line and presented their muskets towards the enemy now rallying in the distance, 'Right lads'

Zeke spoke 'you know the drill gawd knows we've practiced it enough, retire in sections at hundred yards'. The enemy lingered on the fringe of musket range and took pot shots with their rifles towards the retreating British lines, a redcoat on the left flank groaned and slumped forward as a rifle found its mark, 'Clayton's company will retire fifty yards' Clayton's sergeant yelled the command. 'McPherson's company' Zeke shouted 'Present . . . fire!'. Will squeezed his muskets trigger and the hammer slammed down onto the weapon igniting the powder, at a range of more than eighty yards the effectiveness of the brown bess was questionable but in such an emergency it might stall the enemy as they moved towards them, if nothing else he thought, the smoke would at least obscure their withdrawal. As soon as the volley's departed the long barrels Zeke ordered the retire, in unison the company fell back to the proximity of Claytons company and merged through the lines as his men presented their arms towards the enemy, Will quickly recharged his musket as Clayton's men fired their volley towards the now closing rebels, still short of their targets Zeke took note and shouted for his men to aim higher, 'drop yer shots on their bloody heads' he yelled as the battle raged.

Within the count of six the company had loaded and stood firm to face the enemy, checking the lines musket elevation he gave the fire command, this time a few advance rebels succumbed to the hot lead that flew through the air but with overwhelming numbers the rebel advance closed ever the gap between the two lines, how quickly the tables of fortune are turned, less than ten minutes ago Washington's army looked in full flight, now the redcoat line was on the verge of collapse and facing encirclement by a much larger force.

The enemy riflemen fired without respite into the British line, Sergeant Skinner who until now had remained silent in this action pleaded with McPherson to allow a full scale retreat, McPherson stared hard into Skinners eyes before speaking, 'You sir, are a gutless coward' striking him across his face with his gloved hand, Skinner recoiled and tumbled backwards into the muddy mire knowing better than to return a blow at an officer at least in the presence of others, Skinner snarled 'then damn you I say, damn you all to hell' scurrying backwards from the volume of peering eyes that befell his cowardly actions. Dan raised his musket as Skinner fled from the diminishing lines and took his aim but Zeke pushed the long barrel away before he could take his shot, 'Best save it for someone worth your time Dan' he spoke 'he's done for either way now and we need to preserve every round for a more pressing enemy'.

'Fire' Clayton's Sergeant barked and his company ploughed more lead into the advancing rebels, the distance between volleys grew shorter as the companies reached the orchard wall, as the last of McPherson's men reached the sanctuary of the wall Clayton's company fired their final volley, with barely a handful of ammunition the remnants of the company was advised to make their way as best they could towards Princeton, from now it was each and every man for himself as the rebels appeared atop the rise of the slope and poured their rifles onto the heads of those below. Captain McPherson made his way towards Zeke and addressed his fellow soldier warmly, 'It's time to save the colours Zeke', 'That it is sir' Zeke replied, the noise of battle seemed insignificant at that moment, 'I trust you'll do them well' he added. Captain McPherson bowed gentlemanly had wished those remaining behind God's blessing as the officer led the remains of the colour party through the orchard, with luck Zeke and the handful that chose to remain would buy enough time for the remainder of the Regiment and the colours to escape back to safety. The wounded sought shelter beneath the stone wall and given muskets to load whilst those fit enough fired a constant barrage at the enemy, with an eye towards the rear Will observed the last of the company evacuate the perimeter, McPherson being the last man to leave, turned and stood firm, raising a salute back towards the brave souls that elected to stem the enemy advance, Zeke nodded his approval before presenting his musket over the wall towards his enemy.

The enemy riflemen probed towards the defenders as the kept a constant fire towards them, but the riflemen began to find their mark reducing the gallant defenders number to even fewer. The Allen brothers remained ever vigilant in their upkeep of harassment of the enemy and Dan discharged his final round into the enemy ranks as they circled the remaining defenders, yelling his need for ammunition, Will fumbled through his case 'only one left friend' as others similarly replied and in laying his musket against the wall his brother Thom dashed backwards to retrieve an abandoned cartridge case a few yards behind, as quick as he could he snatched the prize and scurried back to safety, 'You damn fool' Dan chastised his brother 'you'll get your damn head blown off' as Thom grinned devilishly and folded back the flap that secured it 'don't say I never look after you brother' Thom grinned when suddenly the air was broken by a dull thud.

Thom's expression changed to puzzlement as the spread of crimson ran down his white cotton shirt, 'Thom? Thom!' Dan cried in disbelief to what had happened, Thom Allen stumbled forward and sank to his knees as blood tricked from his mouth he tried to speak, being shot through the lungs he slowly began to drown in his own blood, 'Get him against the wall' Zeke shouted as his own musket spat its final round towards the enemy, Dan and Will carried his limp body towards the cover of the wall and lay him down as he struggled to speak a few words, 'Calm yourself brother, don't try to speak' Dan uttered as tears welled in his eyes, Thom's eyes fluttered with fear and panic as his life slowly ebbed away, 'Stay with us Thom' Will spoke urging his friend to cling on to his life but all in vain, his eyes glazed over as he gulped desperately for air, then silence befell.

Thom Allen, the older of the twins had entered this world minutes before his brother Dan, in life they'd known only each other, they'd entered it together and in grief Dan would make sure they left it together. The surviving twin clenched his teeth and ran his hands through his siblings blood splattered hair, 'I'll see you in the next life brother' speaking his final words he grabbed his musket and leapt the stone wall that sheltered them, Will could only watch as Dan stricken with sorrow screamed his final cry towards the enemy, a plume of smoke enveloped him as he closed towards the enemy lines at almost point blank range, by the time the gun smoke had drifted it was all over. At least it was quick Will thought to himself as Zeke lowered his head in a moments silent prayer and lay his empty musket against the wall.

With ammunition spent Zeke pulled the defenders closer together and tallied each mans condition, between them their position had become hopeless, the wounded where propped against the wall and the muskets smashed against trees rendering them useless to the enemy, despite the butchery of the day it was still hoped some mercy would be found for those taken prisoner.

The defenders numbered just able bodied five men, Zeke and Will accompanied by two from Claytons Company and a single Dragoon separated from his squadron, this ragged outfit had decimated Mercer and delayed Sullivan's advance giving the remainder of the Regiment valuable time to escape the encirclement they now themselves faced. To fight on would only mean more deaths, the defenders had accomplished more than any could've wished for, McPherson had saved the colours and with them the Regiment's honour but at a cost of heavy losses, whilst Howe's official return would list eighteen killed, fifty eight wounded and over two hundred missing, the reality however was far higher as the dead lay far and wide across the fields that surrounded Princeton town.

The enemy entered the orchard as the remaining defenders lay down their arms, despite the carnage and butchery Washington had ordered all British prisoners to be treated well whatever the action and such treatment like this had a positive effect on the morale of any tempted to surrender the fight against these Americans. The wounded were tended by orderlies and made as comfortable as the situation allowed whilst those fit to walk were herded under armed guard along the roads to Morristown further to the north, stripped of his familiar red coat Will recognised a few from McPherson's company but the majority he failed to acknowledge with the exception of one. Skinner had fled the British lines and fallen into the path of the advancing rebels, he'd offered no resistance to his capture and welcomed his escape from the battle field and harms way and now herded along with the long trail of prisoners Skinner shuffled towards the stockade at Morristown that garrisoned Washington's army. By midnight the fugitives arrived and where ushered into the pens hastily constructed to house them, too late in the day to take a tally the prisoners were each given a crust of bread and hot broth to warm their bodies, most stood more than satisfied at their treatment by their captives. Skinner made his way through the prisoners looking for some sympathy amongst his fellow soldiers, ignored by Zeke, Skinner pleaded his case to Will on account of his actions in the field, Will stared hard into Skinners eyes with contempt as his former sergeant attempted to convince him of the events earlier. Zeke interrupted having heard enough to turn his stomach, 'keep away from us you damn coward' he snapped holding the man firmly by the throat 'I'd kill you myself given the opportunity'. The guards sensing tension between the prisoners yelled across the stockade 'Enough!' and Skinner knew his pleas were now worthless, alienated by all he'd ever harmed he stood alone shivering in the winter night as the starry sky chilled the air to below freezing.

Will and Zeke wrapped themselves in the moth eaten blankets issued once the temperatures began to freeze and watched the guards pace back and forth across the fencing, exhausted from the day, the prisoners one by once slipped into an exhausted slumber until silence befell them all.

Will was woken by a firm shake to his shoulder 'Will, Will' came the whisper, blearily he opened his eyes and squinted into the darkness, 'Sam?' he questioned his own eyes in disbelief 'What are you doing here?' he asked in confusion, 'Shush' the voice replied pressing his hand over Will's mouth, 'I'm going to get you out of here, wake Zeke and the two of you can go now before they count your numbers in the morning, with luck the guards will not notice you've gone', Will nodded and acknowledged the plan of escape and the three trod carefully amongst the sleeping men until they reached the fencing, Sam Coles carefully removed a section of timbers that held the prisoners and led Zeke and Will to freedom, as

Coles began to replace the fencing a voice from the prisoners threatened to jeopardise the whole escape.

'So Sam Coles turned coat eh?' Skinner approached the fence, 'you'd better let me go too lad else I'll wake this whole bloody camp and with the position you're in I'd wager you'd have some explaining to do to your new friends'. Coles looked on and paused a moment relishing his next action

'Come here you old scallywag and I'll see to you all right' Coles beckoned his former Sergeant towards him. Skinner widened his grin assuming his freedom imminent when Coles raised his musket plunged the bayonet through Skinners chest 'now rot in hell you dog'. Skinner sank to his knees and sobbed in his death throes, both Will and Zeke looked wide mouthed towards Coles as he twisted the blade free of Skinners twitching corpse before it tumbled sideways, 'Now go before the guard arrives' he spoke and gestured the two towards the safety of the British lines, 'Come with us Sam' Will pleaded, 'We all know I cannot do that Will, I've done what should've been done years ago, my only regret is that many have suffered at this dogs hands before I found the courage in myself to end his miseries, now leave this place quickly, you'll find safe passage to the south for I hear Princeton is back in British hands'.

Zeke tugged Will's shirt away from the scene, 'The lad speaks sense Will' he spoke 'if we hurry by dawn we should be nearing our lines and Sam, I thank you with fondest respect' he added with a familiar wink 'may we never meet again'.

Coles grinned as the two dashed off into the dark night and muttered to his self 'Yes Zeke, may we never meet again'.

Will gazed out onto the familiar streets of the town he was born within and spoke to the smitten crowd that now surrounded his presence, 'And what of Coles you may well ask?' he teased the words towards his audience 'Sam Coles made back to Boston to seek out his beloved bride but on arrival found her to have succumbed to fever, the very fever he too had suffered and so consumed by anger and grief enlisted in Washington's army to seek revenge upon those that he believed the cause of her death, but for Coles . . .' he paused a moment as a familiar scent of tobacco vented his nostrils, 'Coles never did lose his sense of comradeship to his brethren soldiers and this says I, a soldiers bond is stronger than any blood tie, for a soldiers bond is a bond for life my friends'. A cheer went up amongst the taverns patrons as he continued his speech, 'So lads, you now see the very adventures to be had in His Majesties service, now come with me those that are brave and raise a cheer to the men of the glorious 17th', he raised his tankard and looked with pride into the eyes of the recruiting Sergeant for approval, 'Aye' Zeke replied with a wink of the eye 'three cheers to the 17th Regiment and the Heroes of Princeton'.

The End.

*　　*　　*